Diversion Books
A Division of Diversion Publishing Corp.
443 Park Avenue South, Suite 1008
New York, New York 10016
www.DiversionBooks.com

For more information, email info@diversionbooks.com

First Diversion Books edition September 2015.
Print ISBN: 978-1-62681-717-3
eBook ISBN: 978-1-62681-716-6

A SAM PERRY
MYSTERY

K. A. TRACY

DIVERSIONBOOKS

PROLOGUE

It was an unseasonably hot night, even for the desert. A storm front passing through the mountains saturated the air with humidity, turning the foothills into a steaming swamp. The man shuffled across the sand as if he were wading through mud, his shirt soaked from exertion and fear.

The moon hung directly overhead, casting sharp shadows off the rocky cliffs that tricked the eyes, causing the man to slip and stumble. He heard the *whoosh* of a car passing in the distance. He needed to get to the road and flag someone down. But that would mean leaving the safety of the rocks and risking the long, open expanse of desert that lay between him and Highway 111. He backed up against a large boulder, needing to rest. His legs were rubbery from exhaustion and his battered body throbbed. He cradled his shattered right hand gingerly against his stomach and listened so hard for any sounds that his head ached. But except for his pounding heart and wheezing lungs, the desert night was eerily silent.

Sliding to his knees, he angled his body toward the rock. The stone felt cool and comforting against his cheek. Above him, a triangular shelf of stone jutted out, casting a protective shadow and for a moment he considered staying there, curled against the boulder. He closed his eyes…

The man jerked his head back, shocked to realize he had dozed off. His heart was racing and he tried to push down the panic. He knelt motionless a few minutes then reached into his back pocket and pulled out an envelope, damp from his sweat. It was folded in half, and he ran his thumb along the frayed crease, aware he risked much worse than a beating by keeping this.

Using the envelope as a makeshift scoop, he dug a shallow hole in the sand. He smoothed the envelope flat and buried it, patting the loose sand down into a nondescript mound. The jutting rock overhead would be an easy marker to find it later. He stood slowly, leaning against the rock until the dizziness passed.

He closed his eyes again, visualizing the map he'd bought his first day in town. On the other side of the next ridge should be a small trailer park beside a rental shop. He prayed someone would answer their door to a stranger in the middle of the night.

He sidestepped slowly along the rocks, careful to move silently. Clouds had gathered over the mountains casting the night into shadowy darkness. He squinted and listened for any sign of movement.

A few yards beyond him a deep crevice snaked up the mountainside, eroded rocks forming a natural, if precarious, ladder. Going straight up and over would be harder and longer but safer than trying for the road. He sucked in several deep breaths to steel himself for the long climb, wishing he'd never come to this hellish place.

The sound of cascading sand sent a shard of fear through his gut and he struggled not to vomit. It was impossible to say for sure what direction it came from. He stood clinging to the rock face, immobilized. The full moon glided through a break in the clouds, and out of the corner of his eye he saw a familiar face striding toward him. A rush of adrenaline gave him a second wind, and he turned to scramble up the crevice. Instinctively, he reached out with both hands, but his mangled right fingers lost their grip, and he fell backward onto the sand. The man rolled onto his knees, shivering uncontrollably in the hot, humid night. "Please…"

His last thought before the pain turned to nothingness was of rolling green hills he'd never see again.

CHAPTER ONE

"Dry heat, my ass."

Samantha Perry wiped the sweat off her face with the sleeve of her damp T-shirt. At just a little past 7:00 a.m. it was already ninety-five degrees, the air thick and sticky. The most humid summer in local memory was making a mockery of Palm Springs' touted year-round arid climate. But not even the swelling heat index dampened Sam's spirits after an invigorating five-mile Sunday morning walk. She loved the desert, especially the sight of the nearby mountains suspended against a crystal blue sky, every rock and crevice etched in sharp detail. It looked like the backdrop of a Hollywood Western, too perfect to be real.

Sam jogged up the back stairs of her condo building to the third floor. Hers was the corner unit at the end of the hallway. She walked in, turned up the central air and shut the door in one continuous motion, and headed directly to the kitchen, followed by two small, prancing balls of white fluff. She was finishing a second glass of iced tea when her cell phone's message alert sounded, playing *Dragnet's* theme song.

"Ok, girls, hopefully duty calls."

Sidestepping the dogs crowding her ankles, Sam grabbed the phone off her desk and went onto the balcony, flipping the switch for the overhead fan. She dropped into one of the swivel rockers and put the cell on speakerphone while Alpha and Omega jostled for position on her lap, cotton candy fur blowing in the swirling breeze.

Sam, it's Marlene. Sorry to bother you, but we got a tip I need checked out and I think you're the best person to look into it—

"That's it, play to my ego." Sam held Alpha up by her front legs and made her do a little dance.

...Call me as soon as you get in, and I'll give you the details.

"Great. Probably another bingo bilking ring."

At home, Sam routinely talked to her pets. The African Grey, named Dorian, occasionally talked back.

Sam decided to take a quick shower before checking in with her editor. Not feeling compelled to jump every time a story loomed was just one of the ways her life had changed since moving to Palm Springs a few months earlier from Los Angeles.

After drying her hair and pouring another glass of iced tea, Sam sat down at her desk and called Marlene, who picked up after the first ring.

"Hi, it's me. You called?"

"There you are," editor-speak for *It's about goddam time.* "I got a tip from a cop friend of mine. They found a body off Highway 111. Apparently some guy got himself murdered."

Sam automatically grabbed her notebook then caught herself and carefully set it down, "And?"

"*And* I was hoping you'd go check it out."

Sam moved to Palm Springs adamant she was finished with dead bodies and the tragic stories behind their untimely deaths. She made it unequivocally clear she didn't want any more blood on her shoes or in her dreams and resolutely insisted that murder no longer held any fascination or interest for her. Apparently her editor remained unconvinced.

"Marlene, I'm officially retired from the murder beat, remember?"

"I'm asking as a favor. You don't have to inspect the corpse," she reasoned. "You *can* keep your distance, you know."

Sam's mind stirred. The reality was, covering civic stories and "clean" white-collar mischief was more than a bit dull. It was, in a word, numbing. Even so...

"I just don't know."

"Sam, I wouldn't ask if there was anyone else with your experience reading a scene. You know what to look for and what to ask. Just get me the basic facts and I'll assign it to someone else tomorrow. No pressure."

Sam hated to admit it, but the familiar rush of adrenaline easily eclipsed any lingering anxiety. For the first time in months, the old hunger warmed her gut, and Sam realized she had missed it. A lot. Feeling like a junkie about to lose their sobriety, she reached for her notebook. "All right, how long ago did they find the body?"

"Maybe an hour. I don't know for sure."

"I better get out there before they take it away. I'll call you later."

Sam hung up and stepped outside to turn off the balcony fan. She leaned against the patio table, staring out at the mountains for several minutes. The fable about the scorpion and the frog ran through her mind and she saw herself in both roles. Had it been misguided self-indulgence or simple ignorance to think she could change her nature? She hugged the dogs goodbye, grabbed her backpack, and was out the door aware she was walking into a past life.

* * *

Palm Springs was Sunday morning quiet as Sam drove through on Indian Drive, the four-lane northbound thoroughfare through downtown. Located in the Coachella Valley at the foot of the San Jacinto Mountains, Palm Springs first attracted people because of its mineral springs. It later developed into a winter refuge for those wealthy enough to flee the East Coast's cold and snow. Now the resort was a year-round haven for athletes looking for a golf fix, Hollywood types seeking a weekend getaway, and Fortune 500 executives attracted by the climate and relatively cheap real estate. Despite its sophistication, Palm Springs retained a small town pace and attitude that she found therapeutic.

Sam had been a crime reporter at the *Los Angeles Times* for ten years. Her first job out of UCLA was at a glossy magazine called *SoCal*, which broke up the relentless pages of advertising with an occasional story. Her specialty there was local crime features. On a whim, she applied at the *Times* and to her surprise was hired. Armed with a natural instinct regarding criminal behavior and a blue-collar mentality that took sixty-hour workweeks in stride, Sam soon became one of the city's top investigative journalists. In her spare time, she'd churn out books on some of the more unique cases she covered.

The turning point came when Sam covered a particularly savage slaughter of a family by some drug lieutenants. So when a film studio paid a staggering amount of money for the rights to her latest book about a local serial killer, Sam took it and ran—but not *too* far. She decided to live full-time in her Palm Springs condo, bought with the advance from her first book years earlier, and see if the change of scenery would improve her outlook on life. Over the last few months she realized the move had been less about running away from her past than it was running toward the hope of a new beginning.

At Alejo Road she swung over to Palm Canyon Drive, which morphed into Highway 111 by the Aerial Tramway turnoff. The Tram, which ferried people to the top of Mt. San Jacinto, was touted to have the steepest vertical cable rise in the United States; second in the world. Sam remembered reading that during the summer it was up to forty degrees cooler at the top of the mountain that loomed 8,500 feet above the valley floor.

"And yet, here I am headed deeper into the desert."

It occurred to Sam this was the first time she'd worked on a weekend since leaving LA and she welcomed the change of pace. Her old *SoCal* editor, Marlene Ryan, now ran the *Weekender*, Palm Springs' alternative paper that only published a coupon- and advertising-laden paper version Friday through Sunday. Unlike major newspapers that bled both readers and revenue as the Internet exploded, the *Weekender's* spare print model served it well as papers entered into the digital age, and the publication's readership actually expanded once it started providing daily digital editions that concentrated on local news. When other papers were slashing editorial staffs, the *Weekender* found itself shorthanded.

Marlene offered Sam a job with a promise to respect her request for assignments that only covered the living. That was four months ago and while not exactly wishing for carnage, Sam itched for a story with some meat on it. Her biggest investigative report to date was an exposé about weighted bingo balls, with her thoughtful human interest piece on the sudden rise of fleas a close second. She suspected Marlene intentionally fed her bland assignments to make a journalistic point. If so, it was working beautifully.

With Palm Springs shrinking in the rearview mirror, Sam passed a group of kids riding their all-terrain vehicles in the sand dunes. Just over the next rise were two patrol cars, an unmarked detective's sedan, and the coroner's van parked on the shoulder of the incoming southbound lanes. A natural median of scrub brush separated the north and south lanes of the highway and Sam drove another half-mile before finding a turnaround. She parked ten yards behind one of the black-and-whites under the sparse shade offered by a few windblown trees.

Far off to her right, in the womb of Mojave desolation, she spotted a group of people hovering near some large boulders. Although the shelf of rocks looked fairly close, the lack of a reference point made it hard to estimate the distance.

"Ten minutes tops," she decided with optimism.

It took twenty-five. The ground was a mixture of gravel and soft packed sand with occasional patches of dehydrated underbrush. Sam walked at a steady pace. By the time she got to within hearing distance of the cops even her elbows were sweating.

One of the uniformed officers walked over and held out his hand like a traffic cop, directing her to stop. He looked barely out of high school. Sam handed him her Riverside County police press badge. Before moving to the desert, she called in a few favors to get the credential, which allowed special access at crime scenes. Normally, only selected reporters and photographers from dailies or wire services were granted the coveted passes, but she couldn't imagine leaving home without one.

The young cop studied the badge as if examining a potentially counterfeit bill. After making sure she was the brown-haired, brown-eyed, 135 lb., 5'9" unsmiling individual depicted in the photo, he gave the ID back without a word and moved to let her pass. Instead she opened her notebook, the pages damp and stuck together.

So professional, she sighed. "Officer Powell, do you know who found the body?"

He hesitated. "Do I know you?"

She pointed her pen at his name badge.

"Sorry." His smooth cheeks turned crimson. "You really need to ask Detective Larson." He gestured in the direction of a slender man wearing a white short-sleeve shirt, blue slacks, and clunky black shoes.

Sam trudged over to Larson, thinking his feet had to be steaming. Up close he looked more like an accountant than a detective with his wire rim glasses and slight frame. But his body language and darting eyes screamed cop. He watched Sam approach, his confrontational arms akimbo stance making it clear she wasn't a welcome sight.

"Detective Larson, can I ask you a few questions?"

"Who are you?"

"My name is Samantha Perry. I'm a reporter—"

"You're not from the *Tribune*."

"Correct. I'm from the *Weekender*. I've been recruited to be their crime reporter."

"You've got to be kidding."

"You mean you missed my exposé on the weighted bingo balls?" Sam asked. "It was the talk of the desert."

She couldn't tell whether he actually smiled or just suffered from a twitch. "What's your name again?"

"Samantha Perry."

"Frank Larson." They shook hands. "Why does your name sound familiar?"

"I used to write for the *Times* in LA—"

"You did a series on the Surfside Killer," he interrupted again, remembering. "We had a copycat down here, so I read up on him and saw your stuff."

"You had a copycat to the Surfside serial killer down here," Sam repeated skeptically. "I find that odd since you don't *have* a surf."

"The guy improvised. He tried to drown two women in their pools, but both times they escaped. Anyway, we finally caught him." Larson took off his glasses and wiped under his eyes. "I heard you helped catch the guy. That true?"

Sam shrugged. "A lot of people aren't comfortable talking to the police so sometimes I'm in a better position to find things out. If I came across information material to the Surfside investigation, I passed it on, as long as it didn't compromise a source. I learned fairly early it's not good business to scoop cops in print—gets them cranky. And cranky cops are not helpful cops."

Larson nodded and put his glasses back on. "So what do you want to know from this cranky cop?"

"Do you know who the victim is?"

The body was partially covered with a yellow tarp. The medical examiner knelt in the sand taking notes while a crime lab technician scoured the area for physical evidence.

"No, we haven't made a positive ID yet."

"Was there anything found on the body to indicate whether he's local or a visitor?"

Larson hesitated. "Based on some receipts in his wallet, it appears he's either from town or was spending some extended time here."

"So robbery doesn't appear to be the motive."

"Why would you assume that?"

"Because he still had his wallet."

Larson looked at the body. "No, we don't think it was robbery. He still had twenty bucks on him. But that was the only thing in his wallet. No driver's license, no pictures, no credit cards."

"What happened to him?"

"A lot."

"Can you please be more specific?" she asked politely, hiding her impatience.

Larson drummed his fingers on his thigh, debating. They both knew the autopsy report would eventually be made public; death was not a private matter.

"Off the record, Ham—Hamilton Newman, our deputy coroner—says the victim had a couple broken fingers, burns, a busted nose, split lip, and at least a dozen knife wounds but none fatal on their own. Cause of death was the head wound. Looks like somebody dropped a bowling ball on his forehead."

Sam recalled another crime scene where a man had beaten his four-year-old stepson to death in a drunken rage because the boy ate a sandwich left on the kitchen counter. He used a pipe, and the kid's head looked like a rotten pumpkin that had caved in on itself. She pushed the memory aside and focused on what Larson was saying. "...so officially we have no leads as to motive."

"You don't really mean that, though."

Larson looked at her impassively. "Why wouldn't I?"

"The shallow knife wounds. Maybe somebody wanted the victim to tell them something he wouldn't...or couldn't. Either one of those are potential motives."

The detective's eyes narrowed behind his glasses. "Yeah, I considered both scenarios. But I don't like thinking out loud in the press. If someone was torturing him for information, he either didn't know what they wanted, or he was one stubborn son of a bitch to take that many cuts."

"Any indication of how many perpetrators there might have been?"

"Can't say."

"Any signs of a struggle?"

"None apparent."

"Who found him?"

"A couple of kids riding their off-road vehicles. Their dad called 911 from his cell phone. And before you ask, Ham figures he was killed sometime after midnight."

"Care if I look around a little?"

"Don't go inside the tapes—forensics still hasn't finished—but I can't stop you from the rest of the desert."

Sam headed toward Dr. Newman, now leaning against a rock several yards away from the cordoned off crime scene, watching the body being photographed. She caught a glimpse of the victim. The top of his head was missing but the youthful face was intact, a death mask of incredulity. His eyes were open and clouded over. Back at the dawn of forensics, criminalists believed the last image a person saw before death was permanently imprinted in the eye. If you could see deeply enough into the pupil, the face of the killer would be revealed.

The photographer finished and Sam introduced herself to the deputy coroner. "Doctor Newman, can I ask you a quick question?"

"I don't know why not." He jabbed a thumb in the direction of the body, "That guy's not being much company."

"Was he killed here?"

"I'd say yes. There were no tracks in the sand indicating he was dragged to this spot and there's plenty of blood underneath his head. Those knife wounds were a nasty bit of work. Forensics will have the final word on that, but that's how I see it."

Sam thanked him and wandered over to where a trio of boulders jutted out, forming an overhang. The base sloped sharply back, forming a convenient natural cove. Unless you were headed here from straight ahead, this area would be hidden from view. Out of habit, Sam pulled a small Nikon digital out of her bag and began snapping pictures of the crime scene. Most reporters had switched to their cell phones for photos, but the Nikon was more likely to pick up some detail her eyes missed.

Off to her right Larson and some other cops stood in a loose circle talking. So she headed the other direction. Over the years, she'd found all sorts of interesting things by walking *away* from crime scenes. The location of the victim was often the end of the story; the beginning may have started somewhere else, and backtracking was one of the best ways Sam knew to find leads.

The sun reflected harshly off the nearby rocks, and she squinted behind her sunglasses, studying the stark surroundings where the victim spent his final moments. At night, deceptive shadows full of footfalls would make navigating difficult. And the isolation would be total—you couldn't even see the highway, which was blocked by a row of trees planted along the shoulder of the road.

A natural assumption would be that the killer, or killers, had taken the victim to that remote location. If not for the kids on the ATVs, who knows how long it would have been before the body was found. Sam tapped her pencil against the pad. She couldn't explain why anyone would be out here in the first place, especially in the middle of the night. The boulders offered ground cover and plenty of hiding spots. What if the victim led the killer or killers to that spot?

Sam walked another fifteen minutes, stopping when the laces of her right shoe came loose. She squatted to retie them, heat billowing off the ground like a steam vent. The theme song to the *Death Valley Days* TV series popped into her head, accompanied by visions of her sun-bleached bones.

"This is seriously insane." Fatigued and uncomfortably thirsty, she decided to head back to the car.

It wasn't until Sam braced to stand that she saw it. Twenty feet away, beneath a relatively healthy bush, something yellow was half-buried in the sand. She trotted over for a closer look. It appeared to be clothing. When covering crime full time, Sam always carried latex gloves for situations like this. Now she had to improvise. Unable to find a stick she used her pen to carefully tug the cloth out of its shallow grave. It was a lightweight windbreaker and the white racing stripes down the left sleeve were spotted with rust-colored dots that could be dried blood.

Pinned to the vest pocket flap was an *Elect Konrad* campaign button, black letters against a green background. Posters of the same logo were plastered over every bus bench in the city. Ellen Konrad was an Oscar- and Emmy-winning film and TV star turned local political dynamo running for mayor.

Thinking she was going to die of exposure any second, Sam lifted the flap and peered inside the pocket. On top was a pack of matches with *Crazy Girl Lounge* stamped on the front, the G in the shape of a girl kicking her leg in the air. She nudged the matches aside and underneath was a $10 bill and a driver's license. The face in the picture gazed at the camera with a self-conscious smirk, unkempt hair falling to his eyes. Sam recognized the face and maneuvered the license until she could read the name and address. She wrote the information in her notebook then closed the flap.

Sam took pictures of the jacket then surveyed the craggy terrain. The windbreaker's bright color and racing sleeves would be an unwelcome beacon for someone trying to disappear into the mountainside.

"So, Jeff Rydell, why were you out here in the middle of nowhere in the first place? And who were you running from?"

* * *

Two morgue attendants were maneuvering Rydell into a body bag when Sam got back to the crime scene. She took Larson aside and told him what she'd found. "I recognized his face from when they were photographing the body."

"You touched the jacket?"

"Not with my hands, no."

"But you still moved it."

"It was a mile away from here," Sam replied calmly. "Once I realized it was related to the case, I left it and came straight here to tell you."

"I'm sure you did," he sounded annoyed. "Okay, where is it?"

She pointed off to her left, "Beneath a bush that way."

"Okay," Larson took off his glasses and pinched the bridge of his nose. "You need to withhold the name until we notify relatives."

"We don't go to press for the print edition again until Thursday night," Sam hedged, unwilling to commit. If Rydell was a transient, finding relatives might prove difficult.

Larson nodded and strode unhappily away.

Twenty-five minutes and a half-quart of sweat later, Sam called Marlene from the car.

"Where are you? I can barely hear you," her editor yelled into the phone.

"Sorry." She turned down the air conditioning. "That better?"

"Yeah. So tell me."

"The short version is the victim was named Jeff Rydell. He was tortured then had his head bashed in to resemble Hannibal Lector's last meal."

"Descriptive literary allusion."

"Thanks."

"So, do you want me to assign the story to someone else...or did you want to work it?"

Sam fiddled with the air vent. As emotionally and spiritually draining it was to witness the brutality of murder, the intellectual challenge and life-and-death drama inherent in reporting crime was addictive as an opiate. If only human beings weren't involved it would be a perfect profession. "Let me see how it goes today," she finally said.

"Fine. I'll leave it in your hands." Her editor was gracious enough to say it without a hint of *I told you so.*

* * *

Between Alejo and Ramon, Palm Canyon turned into a one-way street through downtown, becoming Indian Drive's southbound counterpart. The patios of every restaurant Sam drove past were shrouded in moist fog from water misters cooling the hardy souls eating outside. She spotted Ellen Konrad's green and black draped campaign headquarters on Arenas Road. Sam reasoned that if Jeff Rydell supported the candidate enough to wear a campaign button on his clothing, he might have been inspired enough to volunteer.

Based on the mission-inspired shape of the doorway arch, the headquarters used to be a Mexican restaurant. Sam parked across the street and peered through the sparkling clean windows. Despite being a sultry Sunday morning, the office was abuzz with activity as busy worker bees manned the phones and scurried around with clipboards and computer printouts. Even if they weren't accomplishing much, they certainly looked dedicated.

Nobody noticed Sam walk in. After waiting politely and being completely ignored for a few minutes, she grabbed one of the earnest workers rushing by.

"Excuse me; can you tell me who's in charge?"

"Are you looking to get some literature or to sign up as a volunteer?" the young woman asked hopefully. She wore tinted glasses and her hair hung loose, covering much of her face. The delicate features reminded Sam of Daphne on *Scooby Doo.*

"Neither. I'm looking for someone who might help out here. His name is Jeff Rydell." A flash of anger briefly animated the girl's eyes then was gone just as quickly. "So you do know him?" Sam asked, intrigued by the reaction.

"Yeah, but I don't think he's here," she said, her demeanor now decidedly less friendly. "Are you a friend of his?"

"No. I'm a reporter."

The girl she took a wary step back. "You should probably talk to Luke. Lucas Konrad."

"Any relation to the candidate?"

"He's her son. But he's in a meeting right now."

"With his mother?"

"No, with Phil. Atkins."

"And who is that?"

"He's our campaign manager." She moved away, avoiding eye contact, "I'm sorry, I have to go," and retreated into one of several small cubicles lining the left-hand wall. Next to the girl's work space was a well-used mountain bike with a gray and black messenger bag hanging on the handle bars. Sam half expected the girl to jump on and take off.

At the far end of the room was an office with glass panels on either side of the door, through which she could see two men hunched over engaged in an intense—bordering on heated—discussion. Sam strolled to the door and knocked, amused to see them both jump. Luke was tall and lanky with dark hair and anxious eyes.

And this would be Shaggy, she smiled to herself.

Phil Atkins looked straight out of Central Casting: middle-aged, balding, a cigar clenched between his teeth, shirt sleeves rolled up to the elbow…every bit the stereotypical politico—or the living embodiment of Mr. Spacely on *The Jetsons*.

I've been watching way too much Cartoon Network.

Atkins opened the door. "May we help you?"

Phil's smile stopped at his lips and Sam distrusted him on sight. "I hope so. I was wondering if either of you knows a young man named Jeff Rydell?"

The smile faded. "Should we?" Atkins asked.

"Shouldn't you?"

"Who are you?"

"My name is Samantha Perry. I'm a reporter for the *Weekender*."

"I didn't know the *Weekender* was starting to take such an interest in politics."

"Oh, we know we're number two, so we're trying harder these days. But this isn't really about politics."

"Whatever it's about, I'm afraid we can't help you," Atkins said impatiently. "Nobody by that name is here."

"I didn't say I wanted to *see* him, I just wondered if either of you *knew* him."

"Why?"

"Jeff Rydell was found murdered this morning."

The silence in the room was so sharp she could hear the ticking of Atkins' wristwatch. Neither man moved for several seconds. Sam waited, feeling suspended in a still life.

Luke finally spoke. "I know Jeff," he acknowledged, ignoring Atkins' glare. "I'm more involved with our personnel than Phil is. Are you sure it's him?"

"Completely."

"What happened?"

"He was basically beaten to death."

"Oh, God," Luke went pale and Sam moved to the side—vomiting was a common reaction to murder.

"What can you tell me about him?"

He ran his fingers through his hair. "Jeff was very…dedicated."

"I meant, can you tell me anything about his background, like where he was from, or if he ever mentioned family?"

"No, it never came up. Our relationship was all about the campaign so we didn't really get into personal stuff. Around here we mostly just talk politics."

"You don't ask your volunteers for any kind of personal information?"

"They're not being paid, you know, by the campaign," Konrad said.

"Any idea where he worked or hung out?"

Luke shook his head and looked away. Sam noticed sweat stains forming on his shirt.

"I don't suppose you know of any reason why someone would kill him? Could he have been involved with drugs or some other illegal activities?"

Atkins bristled at the suggestion. "As far as we know, none of our workers are involved in drugs. We run a clean ship. We have to," he added with a conviction that bordered on menacing.

Sam doubted Atkins would stand for somebody's unsavory habits getting in the way of an election, and he was clearly a man with a tempter. But there were easier ways of bouncing a volunteer than killing them. Still, it was obvious both Atkins and Konrad knew more than they were letting on. She fished two business cards out of her pocket and put them on the desk.

"If you think of someone who might know anything about Rydell's background, I'd appreciate you giving me a call. We'll be running a story in Friday's edition."

Sam closed the door behind her and resisted the impulse to turn around. But she was sure Atkins and Konrad watched her until she walked out the front door and into the blinding sunlight.

* * *

A trail of discarded, damp clothes littered the floor from the front door to the master bathroom. Sam stood under the spray of water, her second shower before noon.

"Do you suppose Lady Macbeth started this way?" she asked Alpha and Omega while drying off.

Sam dressed quickly and finger brushed her wet hair. She sat at her desk and scanned the Palm Springs phone book. There was no listing for any Rydell. But then again, there wouldn't be if he was a new resident. Sam called directory assistance and was connected to an automated operator.

"Are you looking for a business or —"

"A residence," Sam impatiently spoke over the recording; voice recognition systems annoyed the hell out of her.

"I'm sorry…I didn't understand you. Are you looking for a business or a residence?"

"A residence."

"What city?"

"Palm Springs."

"That's Palmdale, correct?"

"No, that's not God damn correct—"

"I'm sorry. I didn't understand you. What city?"

Sam angrily punched buttons until she got a live operator. "In Palm Springs or anywhere nearby, is there a listing for a Jeff or J. Rydell? It's probably a relatively new listing."

When trying to find someone, the obvious approach was the one most frequently overlooked. Although celebrities and bigwigs of all types have unlisted numbers, the majority of people who had land lines were still listed in the local white pages.

"There's a Jeffery Rydell in Palm Springs."

"Is there an address listed, too?"

"3101 Desert Wash Road. Please hold for the number."

The address matched the one on the license so this was the right Jeffrey Rydell. Sam dialed the number hoping to reach a roommate, but the phone rang in apparent solitude.

Sam leaned back in her chair to mentally organize her day. The clock on the microwave read 11:27. Should she go to Rydell's address right now before the cops had a chance to or grab a bite at Elmer's first? As she debated, her eyes drifted to the wall calendar…

Sam slammed her hand on the desk. "*Godammit!*"

The dogs scattered, and Dorian flapped his wings in alarm,

blowing a blizzard of seed onto the hardwood floor. "Oh *shit*, Joe…I forgot about Joe."

Joe Sapone, her best friend since high school, was flying in today from Chicago for a visit, and she was supposed to pick him up at LAX. His flight was due in at 1:00. It was usually a two-hour drive.

"Dammit, dammit, dammit."

Sam raced through the condo, grabbing her keys and wallet. Now confident they were not the objects of her upset, Alpha and Omega trotted behind her expectantly. Sam gently pushed them back with the side of her foot. "No, you guys stay." But when she opened the door to leave, the girls stood at the threshold with tails wagging and heads tilted in unison. An easy touch for canine manipulation, she gave in. "Oh, all right, come on. But hurry up, we're late."

Sam didn't relax until she was speeding down Highway 111 significantly over the posted limit. She had a convertible but kept the top up, always half-worried the dogs could blow out of the car. Sam glimpsed herself in the rearview mirror and felt a shot of despair—she never blow-dried her hair. She'd see Joe for the first time in two years looking like Edward Scissorhands.

"Just great," she muttered. Alpha, the runt of her litter, yawned and shamelessly pushed onto Sam's lap, curling into a comfortable ball while Omega sprawled out on the passenger seat. "And look at you two…you're beginning to look like sheep."

Her mental note to call the groomer first thing in the morning was interrupted by the half dozen police cruisers parked on the opposite side of the highway. Sam slowed down and counted ten cops walking methodically over the ground she'd covered this morning. Larson wasn't going to risk missing any other evidence. Sam appreciated the detective's thoroughness but suspected Larson's troops must be cursing him under their charbroiled breaths.

Sam pressed down the accelerator and was cruising along at 80 mph so she paid no attention to the old, blue car parked on the side of the road with two distinctive green and black *Elect Konrad* stickers adorning the back bumper or the man behind the wheel watching the police grid search.

CHAPTER TWO

It was 1:25 when Sam's car screeched to a stop in the loading zone. The sidewalk was deserted except for Joe. He sat on one of two large suitcases, leafing through a *Vogue.* Sam released the trunk on her Eclipse Spyder and hopped out of the car. Joe smiled and looked at his watch.

"I'm so sorry I'm late. I would've been here on time except there was a traffic jam in Claremont because of a fender-bender." *Not to mention I'd completely forgotten about you until the plane practically landed.* "And I forgot my cell phone at home so I couldn't call. Have you been waiting long?"

"Just long enough to have two people ask if I'd like to take a personality test, a scab cabbie offer to drive me anywhere for forty bucks, and several men in business suits and turbans—a very nice touch, I must say—try to recruit me for a retreat."

Joe stood and held his arms out. Sam stepped forward, and he gave her a bear hug. "And that was only in the first fifteen minutes."

"I'm really sorry," Sam said again, pulling away to look up at him—still blonde, still youthful, still tanned, still tall. "How is it possible you've looked the same for twenty years except for the haircut? You supporting some plastic surgeon?"

"And you look..." Joe gave a low chuckle and gingerly touched her unruly hair, which had dried into windswept crests on top and wingtips on the side. "Been wearing your hair like this long?"

Sam finger combed her hair into submission. "I'm usually much better coifed. I just didn't have time to dry my hair before leaving."

"Because you suddenly remembered you had to pick me up?" Joe teased, trying to stuff his second bag into the small trunk. An airport policeman headed toward them, motioning for Sam to move along.

Alpha and Omega gang-jumped Joe's lap when he got in, staking out fresh nap territory. "Poodles? You said they were mutts."

"They're *not* poodles," Sam corrected him, putting on her seatbelt. "They're a toy poodle-bichon mix, which to me *is* a mutt."

"They're poodles...and I see you take them to your stylist."

She shifted into first, "Funny guy," and accelerated fast enough to whip Joe's head back and knock his sunglasses off.

"I missed you, too," he said through gritted teeth.

They spent the drive home catching up on the details of each other's lives. Joe had been uncharacteristically MIA since Sam's last visit to Chicago a couple years earlier so she had been pleasantly surprised when he called the previous week asking if she wanted company.

Joe was the last strong tie to her hometown. Sam's dad and her sister's family still lived in the area but there wasn't a close connection anymore and communication with them was sporadic at best. Sam hadn't spoken to her mother since moving to California almost fifteen years earlier to attend UCLA.

Joe read her sudden mood shift. "Ever hear from your mother?"

"No reason to. I get to see enough cruelty and violence at work."

He knew to leave it alone. "Do you like your new job?"

"It's okay. It's sure a lot quieter down here."

"Isn't that what you said you wanted?"

"Yeah, well, be careful what you wish for, right?" Sam took a deep breath. "My editor asked me to check out a homicide this morning. I think I'm going back on the beat."

What surprised Joe was that she actually seemed conflicted over it. "You *think*?"

"I'm not absolutely sure I should." She glanced over. "I'm afraid of crashing again."

"Samantha," Joe angled his body to face her, "I can't begin to imagine what it was like seeing the aftermath of a family tortured and slaughtered. But you can't let it dictate your life forever."

"One of the first cops on the scene who found the bodies ended up on medical leave. They don't think he's ever coming back," she said quietly.

"You'd have to be superhuman not to be affected. And with everything else that was going on in your life with what's his name and your grandmother dying...you just needed to regroup and take a step back for a while. But *not* forever." Joe shifted to face forward. "Sam, being a crime reporter is who you are. It's also what you do better than almost anyone. Besides, aren't you bored out of your mind yet doing fluff?"

The work she'd been doing at the *Weekender* was emotionally user-friendly but her brain felt as if it were atrophying. Was it really just a matter of time healing her emotional wounds, or did she simply have a genetic affinity to violence? Either way, Joe was right—she was bored with being bored.

"Well, shit," she finally said, "since when did you become so perceptive?"

"Since you became so transparent." Joe checked his hair in the vanity mirror. "So what's the story you're working on?"

"The police found a body out along Highway 111; a young guy named Jeff Rydell who'd been tortured and murdered."

"Rydell?" He flipped the mirror shut.

Sam glanced over. "You know him?"

"No, why would I? So tell me about it—and don't leave out any of the gory details."

By the time Sam recounted the morning's events they were already sailing through Cabazon and were less than a half hour from Palm Springs.

"Whatever Rydell was doing out there, it had to be awfully scary. It's not like you can go pound on anyone's front door for help."

Joe stayed quiet a few moments. "What will you do next?"

Sam considered her options. "I'll probably stop by Konrad's campaign headquarters again tomorrow. Somebody has to know something about this guy. And I'll talk to some of Rydell's neighbors to see if they know anything."

"Why not go today?"

"It's Sunday. I thought we'd have a swim, go out for dinner, walk around, or whatever."

"We can still do that later. Why don't we go talk to Rydell's neighbors today?"

"*We?*" she glanced at him in surprise. "You want to come?"

"Why not? It'll be fun watching you work, Ms. Investigative Reporter. Sure beats being a shoe salesman."

"Shoe salesman, my ass."

Joe was a buyer for an exclusive Chicago design house—so exclusive Sam had never even heard of it—and was always jetting off to Milan, New York, Paris, or some other fashion capital of the world.

"Travel isn't always as exciting as you might think," he said, interpreting her expression. "Oh, come on. I won't get in your way, I promise."

"Joe, it's bad enough having people slam doors in your face without someone else watching. I'll feel self-conscious."

"No you won't. Besides," he poked at her hair, "you've got a lot more to feel self-conscious about than having a door slammed in your face."

Sam smiled. "It's technically my day off."

"Come on, Sam; you know you want to start working this story today. Let me tag along. Please? Or we could just stay home and I'll spend the day giving you a beauty make-over to try out a new shipment of samples I brought."

"You wouldn't dare."

"It'll make up for making me wait at the airport. We can start with a facial and then move to the brow sculptor—"

"My eyebrows are shaped just fine."

"...and then I have this mineral-based powder—"

"Alright, you can come; no need to use scare tactics," she grumbled. "How long did you say you were staying?"

Joe smiled knowing annoyance was Sam's sincerest form of affection and turned the radio up. Diana Ross was wailing out the beginning of "Ain't No Mountain High Enough."

"This reminds me of the time I went to a Diva's Costume Ball on Halloween."

She looked over trying to imagine the visual. "You as Diana?"

"That's *Ms.* Ross to you. And no, I went as Maria Callas and borrowed a friend's bulldog to be Onassis…"

Joe went off on a story-telling roll and by the time they pulled up to her condo Sam's jaws hurt from laughing. The plan was to drop off the dogs and pick up her backpack and a baseball cap.

Joe insisted on waiting in the car. "If I come up now, you'll find an excuse not to go," he smiled sweetly.

Sam found it a little aggravating, but oddly comforting, to be in the company of someone who knew her so well.

* * *

Desert Wash Drive was a littered, faded cul-de-sac on the eastern end of Palm Springs, adjacent to Cathedral City. The homes lining the street were no larger than a two-car garage and while some were well-tended, most reflected a resigned surrender to decay. Perched at the end of the street was an apartment building that loomed jarringly out of place, peering over the small adobe dwellings like a stucco-clad medieval lord. Twenty years earlier the three-story building had been an attractive, middle class dwelling but subtle neglect had taken its toll, leaving it a low-rent option.

The only signs of life were a couple of Hispanic children playing a lazy game of catch in the middle of the street. They barely moved aside as Sam drove past. She parked the car so it faced the apartment but left the engine running.

"I'm glad we didn't have to come here at night," Joe said, looking at a yard cluttered with several dismantled cars propped on cinder blocks.

"Just because a neighborhood is rundown doesn't automatically mean it's dangerous," Sam said, reaching into her bag for a notebook. She shut off the car and slapped it against Joe's arm. "You're the one who wanted to work today—here, make yourself useful."

"And do what, make a grocery list?"

"Take notes."

He bounded out of the car and immediately sagged against the door. "*Jesus Christ.* It's like an oven."

"Welcome to Palm Springs," Sam said with a *serves-you-right* smile, adjusting the baseball cap lower on her forehead.

The Windy Dunes apartment complex was supposed to be a secure building but a gaping hole yawned where the front door lock should have been. Splayed wires poking out of the wall beneath a dilapidated list of apartment codes was all that remained of the intercom system. Inside the foyer a tenant directory was tacked above the row of mailboxes. The manager was R. Goldman in apartment 201. J. Rydell was in 312 and by the cleanliness of the label he was the newest tenant.

"Why do I have the feeling they must have a *lot* of vacancies here?" Joe asked.

"I don't know; maybe because you're a snob."

"You're probably right," he agreed. "Sam, what are you doing?"

Squatting in front of Rydell's mailbox, she used her car key to gently pry the metal door open just enough to peer inside. "There's mail in there."

"It's a mailbox; that's what it's for. You know, I don't like the look on your face."

"Don't sound so nervous."

"Sorry, but the thought of aiding and abetting a felony tends to make me jumpy."

She smiled and gently worked the key up the side of the box, trying to jimmy open the lock.

"You had the same look on your face in high school when you walked into football games with a Diet Coke spiked with rum."

"Stop worrying. I just want to take a quick peek. I'm not going to actually steal anything...probably."

But the chintzy lock was tougher than it looked and no amount of prying would make it spring open without busting the lock entirely. Frustrated, Sam sat back on her heels—this is what she got for leaving her pick tools at home. She considered just breaking the damn thing open—Sam wasn't above a little larceny in the line of duty.

The one rap against Sam at the *Times* was her tendency to get too involved in stories, regularly crossing the thin line between reporting and sleuthing. But she shrugged off the criticism as ill-informed ignorance. Getting the story sometimes meant digging a little deeper, which occasionally meant taking calculated risks. That was simply good journalism. But in this case the risk didn't seem worth the reward.

Sam stood and faced the center courtyard. Potted palms strategically covered a large mismatched square of uneven concrete where a pool once offered a place to cool off. The muted sound of television sets was the only indication any residents were home. Sam was struck by the uneasy sensation they were being watched. She scanned the rows of doors and windows but saw nothing.

Apartment 201 was the first door to the right as they got off the elevator. A tarnished, brass *Manager* sign was nailed above the peephole. Sam pushed the doorbell, and it stuck in its hole. She poked the offending button until it sprang out, emitting a dull *clunk*. Sighing, Joe reached over her shoulder and rapped briskly on the door.

"I was just going to do that," Sam said, snatching her notebook back from him.

The door swung open. A solid sixty-something woman with short gray hair and wire rim glasses filled the doorway. "I heard you the first time, for Chrissakes."

"I'm sorry, we were having a little problem with your doorbell," she explained, ignoring Joe's muttered *We?* "Are you the manager?"

The woman took off her glasses and tapped the plaque. "That's what the sign says."

"Hi. My name is Samantha Perry. I'm a reporter for the *Weekender*, and I wanted to ask you a few questions if I could."

"The *Weekender*? You're kidding. I didn't know they had

reporters actually working there. Well, I guess you learn something new all the time. That's what they say, isn't it?"

"Yes, ma'am, it is," Sam agreed. "I wanted to ask you about Jeff Rydell."

"I figured as much. I've gone years with nobody coming to the door except tenants upset about one thing or another—you wouldn't believe the things people can complain about—and all of a sudden I'm getting visitors by the hour. Well, come on in before all the hot air does."

"Thank you, Mrs. Goldman."

"Call me Rose."

Rose Goldman's apartment was a packrat's dream. Every nook and cranny was filled with a stunning variety of knick-knacks and tchotchkes. Magazines were stacked neatly on each end table, and three checkerboards adorned the coffee table. A string of Christmas lights framed the picture window, fitted with blue velvet Roman shades, overlooking the courtyard. Although the apartment was clean, the smell of old paper still hovered in the air.

Sam and Joe huddled together on a maroon velvet love seat that coughed a delicate puff of dust when they sat down. The cushions were worn down toward the middle, tilting Sam and Joe towards each other.

"It's been a circus around here today," Rose exclaimed, easing into her chair, "what with the police and all."

"I can imagine," Sam said, suspecting Rose was more excited than upset at being involved in a murder investigation. "How long had Rydell lived here?"

"Four months going on five, the fifteenth of next month. He rented out one of the furnished apartments—said that's what attracted him to the place—and always paid on time, unlike some of the others who live here. Seemed like a nice enough young man. But was kind of strange, too."

"In what way?"

"Well, he kept odd hours. Not that I was checking up on him, but I'm old and don't sleep too good anymore. Out my front window, I can see his apartment because it's opposite mine a floor up. So late at night if I hear the elevator, I make sure it's someone who's supposed to be here. I just haven't gotten around to fixing the door downstairs. Every time I do, someone just rips it out again so why bother? Tenants come in drunk or boyfriends kick the door in because their girlfriends won't answer the buzzer. It never ends."

"I'm sure it's hard keeping up." Sam steered Rose back to the present. "So Jeff was strange. Was he a problem tenant in some way?"

"No, I told you, nothing like that. But he was a bit skittish, though, if you know what I mean."

"I'm not sure I do."

"He seemed nervous lately. Like when I'd see him coming home, he was always looking over his shoulder, like he thought someone might be there behind him. Or maybe watching him."

"You *were*," Joe said under his breath. Sam's elbow jabbed his ribs.

"Did you ever see anyone else with him? Did he have any friends who came over?"

"Not at night. I might have seen him leaving with a friend once or twice, but I don't pay attention to people's comings and goings in daytime. Mostly he seemed to keep pretty much to himself. He wasn't one to sit out on the walkway and get to know the other neighbors. Now, a few tenants did mention to me that Jeff and George had some run-ins but it happens."

"Run-ins as in arguments?"

Rose nodded. "Tenants can get on each other's nerves, like any neighbors can."

"And who is George?"

"George Manuel in 308."

"Any idea who got on whose nerves?"

She shook her head. "Nobody said and I never saw it myself."

"When he rented the apartment, did he have to fill out an application?"

"All the tenants do. Before we'd run a credit check on 'em but now the owner don't want to spend the money. He's glad for anyone who'll put up with this place."

"Would it be possible to take a look at the application?"

"The police took the original. What would you want to look at it for?"

"Maybe he listed some family member I could call who might talk to me about Jeff. I think people should be remembered for who they were and what they did in life, not how they died."

"I never thought of that. I imagine it's not easy finding someone's family." Rose hesitated then heaved herself out of the chair. "Well, management policy says tenant information is supposed to be confidential, but I don't suppose it matters now with Jeff being, you know, dead and all. Like I said, the police took the original, but I always keep an extra copy or two."

While Rose shuffled through a legal portfolio filled with papers, Sam rocked to her feet. The sudden redistribution of weight upended Joe onto his side. Stifling a laugh, Sam walked over to Rose's desk. "Did Jeff ever say what brought him to Palm Springs?"

"Not to me. Like I said, he was pleasant but not chummy. Polite young man, though."

"Did he mention what kind of work he did?"

"Not that I ever heard."

"I assume the police have already gone through his apartment."

"Come and gone. Didn't look like there was much in there."

"Can we see it?" Joe asked.

Sam frowned, annoyed that he asked first.

Rose handed her Rydell's application and mulled over Joe's question. "Well, they didn't say *not* to. I guess there's no harm in that, either." She opened the desk drawer and pulled a key off a large ring, "Here. Just bring it back when you're done. I would come with you, but my program's about to start."

"That's okay," Sam took the key. "Thanks."

In the elevator Joe asked, "Did I do something wrong?"

His contrite tone evaporated her peevishness. "No, you didn't do anything wrong. I'm just obsessive sometimes." She caught his raised eyebrow. "All right, most of the time."

Sam hesitated before opening up the door to Rydell's apartment, turning to see what Jeff's view of the world had been. Directly across from his apartment was the elevator bank. In front of the apartment to the left, two bikes leaned against a tower of stacked milk crates. The door to the unit on the other side of the elevator was open, the blue flicker of a TV set reflecting off the screen. One floor below was Rose's velvet-covered windows and looking further down Sam could see the foyer and mailboxes. All in all, it was a depressing scene.

Joe used the toe of his shoe to straighten Rydell's doormat, a bargain basement reject imprinted with a goose holding a *Welcome!* banner in its beak. "No wonder someone killed him."

Sam laughed and opened the screen door, growing silent when she saw the front door was ajar.

"What?" Joe asked.

"Something's not right." She pushed the door open slowly. "Shit."

The living room had been completely trashed. Seat cushions from the couch and chair sliced open letting loose a snowfall of foam; the drawers of two hollow-core side tables lay smashed on the floor with papers spread around like confetti; overturned lamps rested like perfect bookends on either side of the couch; and the carpet had been pulled away from the wall in each corner.

Sam and Joe stepped across the threshold. Sam wondered if the intruders found what they were looking for.

"You'd think the police would clean up after themselves," Joe said.

"The police didn't do this. And if they found it like this, they'd still be here."

"I was afraid you were going to say that."

The window shades were all closed and the dim lighting elevated the creep factor. "Rose is going to have to call the police to file a report for insurance," Sam told Joe. "I just want to take a quick look around first."

She took a cautious step forward. Off to the left was a compact kitchen, down a short hall straight ahead was the bedroom. She assumed the closed door on the left side of the hall was the bathroom.

Joe pulled at his shirt. "I can't believe how hot it is in here."

Sam was too preoccupied to be uncomfortable. "You stay here. I'm going to check out the bedroom. Make sure not to touch anything."

The bedroom was equally torn apart. Rydell's few belongings lay in heaps on the floor. Shirts had been ripped off their hangers, jeans dumped, and underwear scattered. The mattress was pulled off its frame and sliced open in several places, puffs of stuffing bulging out like sprouting mushrooms. The drawers of a small desk had been ransacked although the computer on top seemed untouched.

Tacked to the wall above the monitor was an *Elect Ellen Konrad* poster. Hanging beside it was a photo of Rydell and the candidate in a cheap store bought frame. The inscription read: "*Thank you Jeff for all that you do and all that you are. Ellen.*" Sam looked at the photo and shook her head. "Phil Atkins is a damn liar."

Even in a snapshot, Ellen Konrad merited a double-take. Sam stared at her smile; it looked warm and genuine. But then again, she *was* an actress.

Sam put the photo in her bag and recorded the scene with her Nikon. There was always something a little sad about poking through a dead person's home, but the atmosphere in Rydell's place was particularly gloomy.

She crossed the room, carefully stepping over clothes and a pile of empty plastic DVD covers, to open a door on the far wall. It was a linen closet, empty except for an old pillowcase hanging from a hook inside the door. She smelled a familiar scent and ran her hand over the middle shelf. She smiled in recognition at the white residue on her fingers.

Sam closed the door and went over to Rydell's desk. She sat down and turned on the computer, hoping there was an address book installed on it. There wasn't. Over the beeps and blips of Windows shutting down, Sam thought she heard voices coming from down the hall and assumed Rose had come to check up on them—until she heard a thud and the brittle sounds of breaking glass.

"Joe!"

Sam sprung out of the chair but tripped on the mattress and pitched forward, her right knee smashing into a clothes drawer lying on the carpet. Shaking off the jolt of pain, she scrambled to her feet and rushed into the hall just as the front door slammed shut. Her pursuit ended abruptly when she heard Joe moaning in the bathroom. She found him propped against the wall holding his nose with one hand and the side of his head with the other. The medicine cabinet mirror was shattered, and bits of glass sprinkled the floor. Blood covered the fingers of both his hands and spotted the front of his shirt.

"Oh my God, Joe, are you alright?"

Joe shook his head, dazed. "I'm not sure at the moment."

Sam found a washcloth and soaked it with cold water. She gently pried Joe's hand away from the front of his face. "Just lean back."

Joe winced as she applied pressure to stop the bleeding. "Is it broken?"

"I don't think so."

"What happened?"

Joe gingerly touched his rapidly swelling eye. "I'm not sure."

"Just take it slow. What did you do when I went to the bedroom?"

"I went to the kitchen and got a drink of water…I sat down to wait for you…then I had to go to the bathroom. The light didn't work but I went in anyway. Before I had a chance to unzip my pants, somebody jumped out."

"From where?"

"I guess they were behind the door, or maybe the shower curtain. We struggled. I think his elbow hit the mirror. I turned my head to avoid the glass and lost my grip, and he was able to push me down. My head hit the side of the tub."

"You're sure it was a man?"

Joe's good eye glared at her. "I know I'm not Mr. Macho, but I think I could handle a woman coming at me. Yes, it was definitely a man, and he was wearing Paco Raban aftershave."

"Did you see what he looked like?"

"No, he was wearing a cap." Joe looked down at the bloodstains on his shirt. "I just bought this, too."

"I'll buy you a new one. I'm so sorry. I should have never brought you here."

She helped Joe to his feet, worried he might still be woozy. But he was surprisingly steady. "What's going on, Sam? Do you have any idea what're they looking for?"

"I have a feeling once I know the answer to that I'm going to have one hell of a story."

* * *

They waited in the manager's apartment for the police to show up. Rose fussed over Joe, applying cold compresses to his bruised and swelling face.

"I feel responsible," she said anxiously, refilling his glass of iced tea from a sweating pitcher. "I should have never let you go in there."

"I would have figured out a way to get in there regardless," Sam assured her, suspecting Rose had visions of litigation dancing through her head. "I'm a reporter and it comes with the territory. Joe's fine, so don't worry. Besides, *we* asked to go in," Sam reminded her, looking at Joe pointedly. "I'm more concerned why someone tore the place apart."

"You think it was the killer?" Rose asked, alarmed.

"I think it was probably just a looter," Sam lied, trying to allay her fears. All she needed was for Rose to have a heart attack.

"Well, this scares me, I have to tell you. To think a murderer could be lurking around here."

A sharp knock on the door made all three of them jump. Sam stood as Rose let Detective Larson in.

He stared in surprise. "You again," he said dryly.

"Like a bad penny, I'm afraid."

Larson sat on the arm of the couch and took a brief statement from Joe. He tucked the small notepad in his shirt pocket and looked at Sam. "Any particular reason you were up there in the first place?"

"Just researching a story. It wasn't a restricted crime scene nor was it marked off limits."

"And I'm going to have a talk with some people about that," he grunted. "You're really taking your job at the *Weekender* seriously, aren't you?"

"Yeah, well...helps pass the time."

The detective stood to leave. "Mrs. Goldman, if you hear or see anything suspicious call us right away. I'd be surprised if the intruder came back but you should have the locks to that apartment changed in any event." He turned to Sam. "Try not to get in over your head."

After Larson left, Sam helped Rose clean up then motioned Joe it was time to go. "I'm sorry for all the excitement Rose," she apologized, picking up her bag. "Promise me you'll call if anything out of the ordinary happens. It doesn't matter what time of day it is." She pressed her business card into Rose's hand.

"Oh, I will. Don't you worry about that."

The elevator was stifling, the air so heavy it was uncomfortable to breathe. "I don't understand how people live in this heat," Joe said.

"You must be feeling better; you're complaining again."

The door creaked open, and Sam stepped out first. She stopped so abruptly Joe bumped into her.

"Damn," she swore softly.

The door to Rydell's mailbox hung off its hinges, everything inside gone.

CHAPTER THREE

Sam slapped the snooze bar three times before finally sitting up in bed at 5:54 a.m. What she really wanted to do was go back to sleep for another slovenly but blissful hour. As usual, though, guilt won out—if she didn't go to the gym in the morning, she wouldn't work out at all.

She turned up the radio and lay back down to organize her thoughts and her day. Music always helped Sam think; silence was the complete distraction. By 6:15 she was sufficiently motivated and got out of bed, knees cracking in protest. She changed out of the shorts and T-shirt she'd slept in and put on workout shorts and an old T-shirt. She stuffed her clothes for the day—black shorts and black T-shirt—into her gym bag. By the time Sam finished taking the dogs on their morning walk she was looking forward to the exertion to come.

After class, during which Sam knee-lifted, V-stepped, and half-hop turned herself into a cardio frenzy, she showered and dressed on automatic pilot while reviewing what precious few facts she knew about Rydell. She was still puzzled over the mailbox—what would somebody be looking for in the mail of a dead man?

Sam asked the same question aloud an hour later in her editor's modest office. Marlene was in her fifties with short dark hair and an expressive, triangular face that always made Sam think of a Keebler elf. Despite having lived in California for thirty years, you could still hear Marlene's New York roots when she talked. While she liked to foster the image of a harried, overwhelmed editor as a way to disarm people, she missed nothing. Marlene chain-drank coffee while Sam sipped on a Diet Coke.

"Forget the mailbox a minute; is your friend alright?"

"Joe's fine. Surprisingly so. He's always had a flair for the dramatic, but this time he's gone all Clint Eastwood on me and is shrugging it off."

Marlene's concerned eyes peered over her glasses. "Please be careful. It's possible whoever broke into the apartment knew Rydell wouldn't be there."

"They didn't break in. Well, maybe they picked the lock, but there was no sign of forced entry. Either the police left his door open, or whoever was in there had a key. If there were no keys on the body, I guess it's possible the killer took them."

Marlene digested that a second. "What do we know about Rydell?"

"Not much, but I'm still hoping to jog the collective memory over at Konrad's campaign."

"Just because you found a button, a picture, and a poster?"

"That, and because of the reaction I got at the headquarters yesterday. I know omission when I see it. What does our competition say about Rydell in today's paper? I haven't had time to look yet."

"Just the usual: dead body, identity being withheld until authorities notify relatives, yadda, yadda, yadda. And no, nothing about the victim being in any way associated with the Konrad campaign. Apparently, the police haven't made the connection or decided not to let that tidbit out."

"Well, I wouldn't count on it lasting," Sam said, assuming the *Palm Springs Tribune* reporter had police sources. On the other hand, the murder of an apparent transient might not draw enough editorial attention for anyone to start digging. Regardless, Sam felt a familiar pressure to get busy. "I'd like to have an old contact of mine, an investigator, get some information for me."

Marlene raised her eyebrows. "All legal, I trust."

"I miss the good old days when journalists could pull credit reports and medical records with impunity, don't you?" Sam sighed nostalgically, deftly evading Marlene's question.

"You're too young to miss the old days."

"I miss them in theory. Don't worry; I just want to try to find out where he lived before—"

Marlene cut her off with a wave of her hand. "Go ahead and do whatever you need—within reason and the law. I'm going to hold this story for the print edition and maybe give the *Tribune* a run for its money."

As Sam headed for the door Marlene asked, "Need any help? I could pull someone else in."

"I haven't been out of the field that long," Sam said dryly. "No, I'm fine."

"You're going to pop a vein," Marlene smiled. "Don't get insulted. I just meant if you need a body to do any legwork, let me know. Only trying to help."

"Did I hear you say you needed help?" Steve Leon asked, sauntering into Marlene's office with a too-hip-for-the-room breeziness.

Sam inwardly cringed. At their first introduction, the soft flesh behind her ears tingled in alarm. Steve exuded buddy-buddy friendliness, let-me-help-you earnestness, and you-can count-on-me sincerity, but Sam knew trouble when she met it. Or at least her ears did, and what she heard was the sound of a knife slicing into the small of her back. Someday, somehow, this man would prove to be bad news.

"I saw the murder on the story list this morning. I'd be glad to give you a hand on it."

"If I get in over my head, I'll let you know," Sam said with a surprising lack of sarcasm.

"Okay, kiddo, you do that." Steve slid his hands into his pockets. "Marlene, I have to run out to have my brakes checked. I'll finish that article on the drought when I get back."

"Fine, fine."

Marlene waited until Steve was gone before dropping her forehead onto the desk. "Drought-shmrought. The first bars must be opening. That man is going to be the death of me yet."

Sam excused herself to let Marlene vent in private and spent the rest of the morning on the phone. Her first call was to the Department of Motor Vehicles' media services office. After providing her old access code from the *Times*, the operator checked for registrations listed to Rydell. There were none.

That meant he was driving a car registered to someone else or, more likely, had come from out of state. Many people didn't bother to reregister their cars in a timely manner after relocating. Of course, that was assuming Rydell had actually intended to stay in California.

Next, she dialed the number for Data Search. Officially, the company was created to help find missing relatives and heirs via real estate records, utility records, and other publicly accessible means. Unofficially, it was a valuable research tool for tracking down people who weren't readily, or willingly, found. Data Search claimed to have addresses for 90 percent of American households.

"Data Search, may I help you?"

"Michelle, hi; it's Sam Perry."

"Sam! My God, it's been ages. I was just thinking the other day about you. Where'd you retire to again?"

"I'm still working. I just moved to Palm Springs."

"Oh, that's right—to rub elbows with the rich and famous."

"So far, the old and infirm is more like it."

"Just remember to wear sunscreen."

"Don't worry. I'm a walking oil slick. Although I doubt it matters much once the heat reaches inferno stage. Anyway, I need some help."

"Are you back on the beat?"

"Appears so."

"Where you working?"

"At a local paper called the *Weekender*."

"Oh, that's great," Michelle said with the enthusiasm of the uninformed.

"It's so nice talking to someone out of state. So listen, can you get me a list of every Rydell family, that's R-Y-D-E-L-L, in Riverside County? Then another list of Rydells in California." It was possible Jeff had relatives in the area. No guarantee they'd have the same last name but it was a place to start.

"Of course."

"And how fast can I have it?"

Michelle hummed in thought. "How about a half hour?"

"Great. I appreciate it." She gave Michelle the *Weekender*'s fax number and billing address. Places like Data Search preferred sending their information the old analog way rather than via hackable computers.

"It's good to have you back. I need the money."

"Thanks for the sentiment," Sam said. "I'm so touched."

She heard Michelle laughing as she hung up.

Sam's desk was located in a secluded niche conveniently situated outside the break room. To her left was a thick supporting wall. Behind her was a picture window overlooking the south end of Palm Canyon Drive. To her right was the common wall with the break room, decorated with a framed lithograph from the 1984 Los Angeles Olympics Sam had brought from her LA condo. On the wall opposite her, which was only five feet away, were shelves filled with various reference books. Although it wasn't technically a private office, it was as close as one could get without installing doors. Leaning her chair back against the supporting wall, Sam used the desk phone to call Rose.

"Hi, it's Sam Perry."

"Oh, hello dear. How's that friend of yours?"

"He's fine. He's out buying shirts color coordinated to his bruises."

Rose laughed, thinking Sam was making a joke. "I wish he'd shop for me."

"Listen Rose, I was wondering about something. Does your complex have a parking structure?"

"It's around back, but there's only enough room for one car per unit bedroom. So there are lots of cars that have to go on the street. People get upset, but what am I supposed to do?"

"Do you happen to know if Rydell's car is parked in his space?"

Through the earpiece, Sam heard the volume of Rose's

television go down. "It's funny you should ask. Just this morning I noticed his space was empty when I took out the garbage. I hope nobody else notices, or I'll have fistfights between tenants trying to take it over."

"Do you know what kind of car he drove?"

"Well, from what I remember it was an old clunker. Nothing special about it except for the stickers."

"What stickers?"

"Oh, all kinds, you name it. Is it important?"

"When you don't know what you're looking for everything is important." Sam sat up and grabbed a pen. "Can you specifically remember any of the stickers?"

"I never paid that close of attention," Rose apologized, "and then he covered them all up with those Konrad stickers except for the one on the back window that said Ruby Falls. I remember that because I thought it was a strange name for a college. Probably some community place. But getting through any college is an achievement to be proud of..."

Sam let Rose run out of verbal gas then ended the call and swung her chair around, staring out the window. *See Ruby Falls*— there was a sticker she'd never seen on the West Coast.

Sam was raised in Indiana and growing up had taken several vacations to Florida, both as a kid with her dad and sister and as a teenager on spring break with friends. The road to the Sunshine State was Interstate 65, which ran through Chattanooga, Tennessee, the home of two tourist must-sees. The first was Lookout Mountain, where you pay for the privilege to gaze down upon the invisible point where Alabama, Georgia, and Tennessee meet.

By comparison, Ruby Falls—advertised as an underground waterfall in one of the area's more accessible caves—sounded like an exotic adventure. Everywhere you looked were signs promising one of nature's awe-inspiring wonders. Twenty years later, she still remembered the excursion vividly. Her sister was off at college so it was just Sam and her dad that summer.

After donning an industrial-strength yellow rain slicker with hair-flattening hood, a no-nonsense guide called their group to order and issued stern warnings not to get too close to the waterfall. The implication was clear: to do so was to take your life into your hands. A rattling elevator lowered everyone into an unremarkable, dank cave. Instructed to put on the hoods, walk single file, watch one's step, and not to wander off alone the intrepid spelunkers made their way along a stony corridor that led to a vast chamber. And there, dramatically lit, was Ruby Falls—a pathetic trickle of runoff water.

Sam smiled, remembering her dad muttering, "Hell, I can drool more than that."

The acoustics being superb, Dad got a big laugh from the group, the guide hustled everyone back to the elevator, and *See Ruby Falls* forever thereafter took the place of *bullshit* in his vocabulary.

There were three possibilities: Rydell had seen Ruby Falls himself while on a trip; the sticker was put on by a previous owner of the car; or he had lived in the Chattanooga area at some point prior to moving to Palm Springs. The number of Southern California residents who had Disneyland stickers on their vehicles made Sam lean toward door number three.

More puzzling was what Rydell had done, or become involved with, in the few months he had been in town that would warrant such painful final hours of life. Sam connected her Nikon to the computer and studied the photos from Rydell's apartment. It looked like the aftermath of a hurricane. The place had been torn apart in a frenzy of unbridled fury—the same kind of rage behind Rydell's brutalization. Knives were used in both instances. It wasn't much of a stretch to suspect the same person was involved in both instances.

Through the white noise of office hum, Sam heard the fax machine beep. She walked into the file room where Monica Gold, the *Weekender*'s editorial assistant, was paper clipping the fax pages together.

"Here you go." Monica handed her the pages.

"Thanks."

There were fifteen Rydell families in Riverside County, 132 statewide. "Could be worse," Sam decided. She sat down at her desk and called all the Rydells listed in the county. Of those who answered, none had heard of a Jeff or Jeffrey. Sam straightened the pages and locked them in her desk drawer. She'd plod through the out-of-county Rydells later.

Sam stuck her head into Marlene's office. "I'm gonna stop by the police station and see if Detective Larson has anything he'd care to share with me."

Marlene motioned her to go. "Call me later."

Sam was almost out the door when Monica stopped her. "Sam, you have a call on line one. You can take it here if you want."

Sam leaned against the desk and punched the blinking light on Monica's phone. "Hello?"

"Now on top of everything else, I think I have sun stroke," Joe announced.

"It's angst a minute with you," Sam smiled. "What happened?"

"I fell asleep in the pool. I was on your float—you know I've owned a waterbed for years so I'm conditioned. When I woke up I looked half albino, half Indian."

"I think any reference to 'red skin' is now politically incorrect. The term is epidermally challenged."

"Samantha, it's not funny. I'm in pain."

"Sorry. Listen, why don't we go for an early dinner, and I'll ply you with pain-killing alcohol. There's a nice Italian place on Indian—"

"As long as it's air conditioned and has a liquor license, I don't care what kind of food they serve."

"Good. I'll pick you up about a quarter to six. And try not to fall down the stairs or something in the meantime."

"Your compassion is touching."

* * *

The Palm Springs Police Station was east of downtown in the middle of the civic "district," a two-block area of city government buildings cloned from the same genius tract-housing mind that invented mini-malls.

A lone female officer manned the front counter. Short and

round, she was perched on a stool, her chin resting in the palm of one hand while the other idly turned the pages of a *People* magazine. Sam glanced at her nameplate as she neared the counter.

"Officer Jacobs?"

"Yes?" She sprung to attention but to her credit made no attempt to squirrel away the magazine. "Can I help you?"

"Is Detective Larson in?"

"Is he expecting you?"

"No, but I was hoping he could spare me a few minutes. Tell him it's Sam Perry from the *Weekender*."

Officer Jacobs disappeared through the security door and when she returned gave Sam a closer look. "Sam Perry the writer?"

She nodded, feeling self-conscious.

"How about that? I really liked your book…as much as you can like a book about a psychopathic killer. But you make cops look good. I appreciate that."

"Thank you, Officer Jacobs."

"Please," she waved a finger at Sam, "you call me Rolanda," and opened the door leading to the back. "Larson's the last desk on the left."

The detective was on the phone when Sam peeked around the corner of his cubicle. He waved her towards a folding chair that gave her a perfect view of the pegboard on the wall beside his desk. Assorted snapshots of a woman and two kids were tacked up next to the schedule of the Palm Springs Power, a summer collegiate baseball team. Below that was a chart of the state's most wanted criminals.

He hung up and leaned back in his chair. "What's up?"

"I was wondering if you located Rydell's next of kin yet. It'd be nice to talk to someone who knew him; otherwise it's going to be a very short story."

Larson shook his head. "No, we have not located any relatives. What I can tell you is he has no criminal record and got his first California driver's license four months ago without surrendering an out-of-state license."

"So he either just started driving after moving to California, chose to take the full driving test rather than turn in his out-of-state license, or lost his old license."

"Right."

Sam saw no reason to share Rose's observations about Rydell's odd behavior or the argument with George Manuel, but to show good will and the spirit of cooperation she offered Larson a bone.

"It's possible he dabbled in small time drug dealing."

"What makes you think that?"

"In his bedroom was a small digital scale, the kind dealers use to weigh out drugs. And in an empty linen closet I suspect you'll find cocaine residue on the middle shelf."

Larson's chair squeaked as he sat forward and wrote on a legal-sized yellow note pad. "You saw a scale?"

Sam *had* seen it, just not in person. It showed up in one of the photos taken at the apartment, visible thanks to the flash. "It's on top of the dresser in the bedroom."

"Apparently we missed it. Or somebody didn't think it was important."

"Maybe your officers don't share my same checkered past."

Larson smiled. "By the way, Tom McDermott says hi."

Sam was surprised into momentary silence. Tom McDermott was the first cop who befriended her in those early, anxiety-filled months of her crime-beat career. Thanks to his acceptance, other cops trusted Sam and so began her network of police sources. Besides giving her credibility, Tom taught Sam much of what she knew about police procedure and cop psychology. Now in his fifties with a weakness for Guinness, Tom was straight out of a dime novel and knew it, never missing a chance to play up the stereotype.

"You know Tom?"

"We have some mutual friends," Larson explained vaguely.

"In other words, you were checking up on me." Sam kept her voice level.

"Can't usually trust you media types."

Sam detested being referred to as *the media* and its tacit insult. She gave Larson a cool stare. "That's funny; a lot of people feel that way about the police."

Larson tensed for the briefest of moments then relaxed and nodded, "Fair enough. Look, I've come across a lot of irresponsible writers, just like I'm sure you've met some bad cops. There's nothing I hate more than finding out about a case by reading it in the paper. I don't like being shown up, which some newspaper guys seem to live for. But Tom assures me that's not your style, so I'll help you whenever I can as long as it doesn't compromise an investigation. You just need to follow the rules and play fair with me."

Something in his tone put Sam on edge, but she resisted the temptation to say what she really felt—that she was too experienced and proven to hear lectures about playing nice and he could shove the rules up his ass. Instead, she stood to go and said, "Thank you, Detective, I appreciate it."

Her next stop was the Palm Springs library. Actors like Konrad were used to signing autographs so it would be second nature to use her full name. But the photo in Jeff's room was signed simply *Ellen*, indicating a more personal acquaintance between them. Rather than dick around with Atkins, Sam decided to go to the source. But first she wanted to know more about the charismatic woman who was using her considerable charms to woo local voters. She spent the next several hours scanning old newspaper interviews and articles, putting together a profile of the actress and the woman.

As Sam rewound the last microfilm, two things struck her. First, she was intrigued by Konrad's decision to retreat from acting to focus on small town politics. Although she accepted occasional film roles and high profile TV guest spots, politics currently seemed her primary interest.

And now little more than a year after moving to Palm Springs she was running for mayor and, according to polls, enjoyed a double-digit lead over her opponent.

Sam looked at a recent news photo of Konrad. She had turned thirty-six in April but could easily pass for someone at least ten years younger, a blessing no doubt due in part due to her well-documented passion for exercise and fitness, to the point of religious fervor.

"Yeah, that and really good genes." Sam stared at the astonishing face smiling back at her. It was easy to see why Ellen was regularly named to various Most Beautiful lists.

Both her children were attractive enough teens but neither possessed the stunning looks of their mom. Ellen was one of those women who grew more gorgeous as they aged, their features becoming more defined. Especially for her daughter Anne, it had to be tough growing up in Konrad's high-wattage shadow.

Rubbing her achy eyes, Sam also found it curious how little had ever been written about Konrad's childhood and youth. Just that she was from Indio and was an only child home-schooled by her parents who died within months of each other shortly after she moved to LA when she was twenty-one. Sam went into the bathroom and called Monica.

"Could you please do some quick research for me?" Sam asked her to have the *Weekender*'s library clerk pull clips on Konrad's early years.

"Do you want the clips left on your desk?"

"No. Just hold onto everything and I'll call you back. I'm going to try and talk to her later this afternoon."

"Got it. Also, you have a message from Rose. She said you had the number."

"Okay. One last thing. I need you to call a friend of mine named Mike Lewis who works at AT&T." After reciting the number from memory she added, "Tell him that Alpha and Omega miss him and that I need a favor."

"Is that some kind of code?"

"Yeah, they're my dogs. That way he'll know the request really is coming from me. I need Ellen Konrad's home phone number and address."

"What if she doesn't subscribe to AT&T?"

"Won't matter. He's a world-class hacker for hire."

"And why am I calling this hacker instead of you?"

"Because he's also a world-class talker, and if I call, he'll keep me on the phone forever. If you call and tell him I'm in the field waiting, he'll give it to you within minutes. So thank him for me, and tell him his case of wine will be delivered shortly. Just put me on hold while you call."

Sam left the bathroom to get a drink from the water fountain then leaned against the wall to wait. The library was fairly full; mostly elderly readers taking advantage of the magazine racks or the computer terminals. She wondered if this was a sneak preview of her own future forty or fifty years down the road: alone except for library reading buddies.

"Kill me now."

"What?" Monica was back on the line.

"Nothing—just having one of my Black Irish moments." She wrote down Konrad's information. "Thanks much."

"You're welcome. Also, the library said they don't have any childhood background on Konrad, only recent information."

Sam breathed out an irritated sigh. She forgot the *Weekender*'s limited resources. "Okay, never mind. I'll check in later." She started for the exit then impulsively went back into the bathroom and called the Motion Picture Academy's film library in Beverly Hills. She asked for the research desk and told the librarian, Mrs. Ingles, what she wanted and was told to call back in fifteen minutes.

She killed the time by reading the bulletin board and checking to see if the library carried her most recent book. It didn't. She thought of the box of books in her storage bin and made a mental note to anonymously donate a copy. After waiting an extra five minutes, Sam called Mrs. Ingles back.

"Hi, this is Sam Perry calling about the Ellen Konrad material."

"Yes, Ms. Perry, I'm afraid we can't be of much help."

"Why?"

"I can't find any family background material at all, other than what you already have."

"You're sure?" Sam asked more out of frustration than thoroughness.

"Quite sure, dear. It's as if Ellen Konrad didn't exist before she made her first movie."

CHAPTER FOUR

Sam turned the air conditioner on full blast and adjusted all the vents to point at her face. The inside of her car felt as if molten lava had recently passed through.

"Remember, you're the one who always said you love hot weather," Sam muttered as she checked her neck in the rearview mirror for heat rash.

She sat back wondering how a famous movie and television star could go through public life without some busybody reporter, such as herself, digging up her pre-Hollywood family history? It was probably because, despite having serious box office clout, Konrad was never a tabloid darling. She lived a scandal-free, normal life—at least as far as celebrities go. There were no ink-worthy affairs, no diva demands on the set, no marital drama, no conspicuously excessive lifestyle, no rehab stints, no embarrassing relatives. With a little digging, Sam could probably excavate the story of Konrad's early years in Indio and made a mental note to talk it over with Marlene as a possible profile—especially if Konrad won the election. Local girl makes good...and good again.

But that would have to wait until she finished the story at hand. She wrestled a windshield shade into the back seat then took out her notebook and called Konrad's house. The first ring had barely faded away when a woman answered.

"Hello?"

"Hi, is Ellen Konrad in?"

"This is she. Who's this?" she asked with polite curiosity, her voice colored with warm tones.

"My name is Samantha Perry, Ms. Konrad. I'm a reporter here

in town and was hoping it'd be possible to stop by today and talk to you for a few minutes."

Sam was well aware how *so* not-by-the-rules this was. Protocol demanded you call a publicist who in turn called the candidate who in turn scheduled a time when such a meeting could take place—usually in the presence of said publicist.

"I'm sorry, Ms. Perry," Konrad apologized, slipping comfortably into the polished tones of a politician. "My schedule is so full I really don't have the time. But I am planning to hold another press conference next week, so I hope your questions can wait until then. Just have your paper call, and we'll add you to the press list."

"I don't want to talk to you about the election, Ms. Konrad. I wanted to speak to you about Jeff Rydell's murder. I know you were personally acquainted with the victim," Sam told her. "I assume you want the opportunity to be quoted directly and not through some hired mouth piece."

Sam listened to Ellen's even breathing and could hear music playing softly in the background. Sam waited patiently for Ellen to say something—then again, patience was never one of her virtues. "Ms. Konrad?" Sam heard the click of a door being closed.

"I'm sorry, I was distracted by someone for a moment," she said. "I don't mean to be rude, but I've already spoken to the police about this, and I'll tell you what I told them: I have no idea who would want to hurt Jeff."

"That's not what I'm looking for. It's not my job to find the killer, but it *is* my job to make Jeff Rydell more than some faceless murder statistic," Sam explained. "I'm trying to write a story about the person who was murdered. But I can't do that if I don't have some sense of the man. And I can't have *that* if nobody who knew him will talk to me. I need you to talk to me. At this point, you're honestly all I've got."

"I'm curious what makes you think I know anything that would help you?"

"Because all good actors see the world in terms of character and emotion, and by all accounts you're an exceptional actor. If you spent any time at all with Jeff, I suspect you have unique insight into who he was," Sam told her, hoping it didn't come across as shameless pandering. "Please share that insight with me, so I can bring him to life for the readers to make his death matter, even if just a little."

There was another beat of silence before Ellen cleared her throat. "Well, I don't know if I'm giving into flattery or not, but why don't you come over around 4:30," she said, adding dryly, "Since you have my private phone number I assume you know where I live."

Sam thanked her and hung up. She had time to kill and knew just the way to spend it.

* * *

Ted's was a nondescript bar and grill on Indian Drive with a predominantly local clientele. It's faded and peeling outer facade did little to attract tourists but soft lighting, polished wood, and a genial atmosphere made it a favorite watering hole for a wide cross section of desert regulars. There was also a covered patio for those who couldn't get enough of the heat, or nicotine. Sam said hello to the hostess, Sharon, on her way into the enclosed bar area where Dinah Washington was playing over the bar speaker. Felder, the day bartender, pushed a napkin in front of Sam as she slid onto a stool.

"There she is. You want a 'Sam'?" he asked.

"Please. And put some ice in it. Lots of ice."

"Hot outside?"

"Any hotter and I'll sprout red horns."

Felder smiled as he poured a glass of champagne into a chilled flute. After adding just enough crème de cassis to turn the sparkling wine a blush pink, he added a twist of lemon peel and set the glass in front of Sam. She took a sip and sighed appreciatively.

"Perfect. Hey, what do you know about Ellen Konrad?" Before moving to Palm Springs, Felder had bartended at several A-list restaurants in LA. "What was the dirt?"

Felder folded his arms. "A couple friends of mine worked with her on a few films. A real pro on the set and crews loved her. Sorry to disappoint you but there really was no dirt. Lily white."

She downed the rest of her drink, paid her $6 bar tab with a ten, and slid off the stool. "No such thing, Felder."

* * *

Ellen Konrad's home was located at the end of a picturesque, well-tended cul-de-sac—the polar opposite of Desert Wash Drive. Tall, thick hedges bookended two intricately designed wrought-iron driveway gates customized with a smoky-gray PVC backing to ensure visual privacy. Separating the gates was a stone wall with a pedestrian entrance, the door made with the same wrought iron pattern.

A state-of-the-art security system with video camera, monitor, and intercom was installed next to the door. Sam pressed the intercom bell and the light on the camera briefly glowed green. A moment later the door clicked open and Sam stepped into the pages of an *Architectural Digest* photo spread. The expansive front lawn was landscaped with ornamental and exotic cacti set among earth-toned decorative gravel. Citrus trees lined the left side of the property, rose bushes adorned the right. To the left of the house Sam could see a three-car garage and behind it what looked to be a guest cottage. On the right, a gated eight-foot, wooden fence extended from the front corner of the house to the wall on the far edge of the property. Sam assumed there must be a pool and spa hidden from view.

The house itself was two sprawling stories of stone and wood that somehow managed to be both understated and exquisite. A short, smiling woman of indeterminate age opened the front door, and Sam introduced herself.

"Yes, please come in," the woman said in a pronounced French accent.

"Thank you."

"I am René. Please come this way."

The décor and furnishings inside were designed for comfort and enjoyment. This was no showcase residence, Sam thought; this was unmistakably a home.

She followed René past a curving staircase and down a long hall that opened into a large corridor. A set of wood and glass partition doors to their left were open to a large kitchen. A matching set of doors to the right were closed. Directly ahead was a room. René opened the door and stood aside so Sam could pass. "Please, you wait here in the study, yes?"

The study was clearly Konrad's office. The first thing Sam noticed was a small but beautifully stocked bar.

"You wish something to drink?" René asked.

"You have no idea," Sam muttered under her breath. Louder she said, "I'll take some iced tea, if you have it."

"Of course." René walked behind the bar and retrieved a pitcher of tea from a small refrigerator. "Would you like to sit on the couch?"

"No, I'm fine here." She perched on a bar stool and glanced around the room, wondering if the Oval Office were as big. It certainly could not be more scenic. The back wall was a row of French doors that looked out over the desert, the view of the mountains through them spectacular. Konrad's mahogany desk was in the back left corner, positioned so the front faced the room and the computer table was flush against the side wall.

On the opposite side wall was a granite shelving unit. In the center was a display case holding Konrad's Golden Globes, Emmys, BAFTA, and several other awards Sam didn't recognize. The shelves around it were filled with more books that were less literature and more guilty pleasure in nature. Browsing the titles revealed Ellen was partial to biographies, popular fiction, and true crime although Sam didn't see any of *her* books among them.

"First the library, now this."

René looked at her curiously. "*Pardon*?"

"Sorry; just talking to myself."

"Ah."

Her tolerant smile reminded Sam of the way some people humor the very elderly—or the mentally infirm.

René placed a large tumbler of iced tea on the counter along with small bowls of lemon wedges, Stevia, and sugar cubes. "*Madame* Konrad will be right in." She smiled at Sam again then left, closing the door soundlessly behind her.

Sam downed half the tea in one long drink as her eyes wandered back to Konrad's desk. The flat screen computer monitor was powered off but several manila file folders were on top of a large day planner. As she leaned closer to see if the files were labeled, the study door flung open, and Ellen Konrad strode through, a cinematic vision in white Armani.

"Damn," Sam blurted out, "dramatic much?"

Ellen froze and stared at Sam a split second before laughing. "My kids are always telling me I still know how to make an entrance," she said, nudging the door shut with her foot. "That's fine for an actress, but I suppose a politician should enter softly, as they say." She walked over and extended her hand. "Hi, I'm Ellen."

Konrad had a warm, welcoming grip and an unsettling, scrutinizing gaze. Her stunning cobalt blue eyes expressed open assessment as she held onto Sam a split second longer than necessary. Staring back, Sam noticed random specks of violet in her irises.

She thought, *You could drown in those eyes*; she said, "Well, at least you got the handshake part down."

"Thank you," Ellen smiled, revealing delicate dimples. "Now if I could only stop swearing in public like a Marseilles whore and learn to act like I really enjoyed kissing strange babies."

Besides an arresting physical beauty, Ellen possessed a commanding presence and undeniable charisma that made it that much harder for Sam to tear her eyes away.

Ellen gestured towards the glass. "That looks good. I think I'll have some, too."

While Sam grabbed a notebook and pen from her bag, Ellen walked behind the bar, looking all leg in high heels. Her hair was a rich golden blonde with sun-kissed streaks. She wore it pulled back in a loose ponytail that served to showcase her eyes. A few layered strands framed her face, casually accentuating the high cheekbones.

Tall and toned with no discernible jiggle of flab anywhere, even in person she could easily pass for a woman in her mid-twenties at first, and second, glance. Only her watchful eyes hinted at a longer, or possibly harder, lived life.

"I hope you weren't waiting long."

"No, not at all."

"Good." Ellen glanced up with a sly smile as she cut some fresh lemon wedges. "I learned a long time ago you should never leave a journalist alone in your room."

Sam smiled back, guilty as charged. "Well, any journalist worth her salt."

"Which you clearly are. What made you leave the *Times* for a local also-ran?"

The question surprised Sam. Ellen obviously spent the afternoon doing some research of her own. Sam didn't mind but felt compelled to defend her paper.

"*Also-ran* sounds so, I don't know…"

"Pathetic?" Ellen teased.

"Thanks a lot," Sam laughed, "but yeah. So for the sake of my fragile writer's ego could we say *up-and-coming*? I think the owners aspire to make the paper more of a *Village Voice* or *LA Weekly* alternative than traditional broadsheet. As to why I'm here…," she shrugged. "I wanted a change of venue. My old editor from *SoCal* magazine is running the *Weekender* now, and she offered me a job after I decided to live here full-time."

Ellen added some Stevia and lemon to her tea. "And considering how much they paid you for the film rights to your last book, you could easily afford to change career paths."

"Something like that." Sam pointed to the bookshelf. "Remind me to send you a copy."

"No need." Ellen walked to the desk and opened the top drawer. She pulled out a dog-eared hardback of Sam's last book and placed it back on the book shelf. "I thought your name sounded familiar. I was just refreshing my memory about your writing."

Sam was ridiculously flattered. "Do you go through this much bother any time a reporter wants to talk to you?"

"Of course not. But it isn't every day I'm interviewed about a murder by a noted crime journalist."

"I'm afraid *noted* is a bit of a stretch. Lucky is more to the point. Right place, right time—like they say: timing is everything."

Ellen regarded her with candid interest. "Your humility is very refreshing."

"Trust me; humble I'm not—just honest."

Konrad sat on the stool next to her. "Is it okay if I call you Sam?"

"Please do." She resisted a sudden, powerful urge to let her leg brush against Ellen's. "Usually the only time people call me Samantha is when they're annoyed with me, serving a subpoena, or about to write me a speeding ticket."

Ellen smiled and sipped the tea, her eyes never leaving Sam's face. "You know, my campaign manager thinks I'm insane talking to you at all."

"Because…?"

"Because that's the way campaign managers are. Not too unlike most publicists I've had who think the road to hell is littered with journalists."

"Funny, I've always had the same thought about publicists and campaign managers." Sam countered, eliciting an amused chuckle from Konrad. "Anyway, thank you for agreeing to see me over his objections."

Ellen swiveled the stool so her left arm rested on the bar. "What would you like to know?"

Can I just sit here and stare at you a while first? "Can I get some background first, like how long Jeff worked for you?"

"Jeff became a campaign volunteer about eight months ago. Not too long after the new year, maybe late January."

"Meaning he wasn't paid."

"He was not paid to help with the campaign, that's correct. We do supply our volunteers with sandwiches and drinks but they are not on payroll."

"Do you have many volunteers?"

"Enough. A lot of them grew up watching me on television, so they get a kick out of working for the campaign. Whatever gets them involved in the process is fine with me. At the campaign office, Jeff pitched in wherever he was needed: stuffing envelopes, passing out literature, doing phone solicitation, that sort of thing. He was especially helpful when it came to computers. He was quite a whiz, actually."

"Seems like he'd have been a familiar figure at the office, then."

Ellen took another sip of tea and didn't respond to the non-question.

Sam elaborated. "I'm sure you know I stopped by your headquarters yesterday, interrupting a heated discussion between your son and Mr. Atkins. Your campaign manager wasn't terribly forthcoming about knowing Jeff Rydell. In fact, the argument could easily be made that he outright lied. Any particular reason?"

Ellen flicked an invisible piece of lint off her skirt. "Phil is very protective of the campaign. He's also my former personal manager so as I said, very wary of reporters on my behalf."

"Because of all those skeletons rattling around your cedar-lined closet?" Sam smiled lightly.

Ellen laughed softly and smiled back. "Nobody's found any yet."

Sam glanced at her notebook and followed a hunch. "You said Jeff wasn't paid to help with the campaign."

"That's correct."

"So, what *was* he paid for?"

Ellen considered Sam a moment. "You *are* good."

"Yeah, well…I have my moments."

She took a sip of tea before answering. "He worked for me as a kind of…" she hesitated, searching for the right word.

"Go-fer?"

"I always hated that term on sets but yes, I suppose that's what he did: odd jobs around the house, running some personal errands, things like that. He also set up a computer network here. We have every program you can think of although I'm still not sure why."

"When did that start?"

"During the spring."

"Was that well known among the other volunteers?"

"It wasn't exactly a secret, but no, we didn't advertise it either. I thought it best to keep the two separate as much as possible. Volunteers can get possessive, like fans, and I didn't want to be seen as playing favorites. All my volunteers work hard, and I appreciate every one of them."

"Just like parents say they love all their children."

"Much like that," Ellen agreed, adding somewhat ruefully, "Of course what most parents don't admit is that while you love all your children equally, you might not like them all the same."

Sam took a sip of tea, making a mental note to pull backgrounds on the Konrad kids. When she looked up Ellen's eyes were focused intently on her. Sam met the penetrating gaze and felt something shift deep inside her gut. She cleared her throat and forged ahead, ears radiating heat.

"Between working for the campaign and working here, it sounds like you were a full-time job for Jeff."

"I guess so."

"Do you mind if I ask how much he was paid?"

"Not much at all. Maybe $150 or $200 a week depending on the hours."

"Why him?"

"What do you mean?"

"I'm sure a lot of your volunteers would jump at the chance to work for you on a more personal level. Why was he the chosen one?"

Ellen paused then spoke slowly, measuring her words. "He broke my heart. Jeff seemed so very alone and desperately wanted a place to belong. I admired his passion over causes and the way he threw himself into projects, his intensity. Maybe I saw some of myself in him, someone trying to rise above the cards they were dealt in life. One day he mentioned he was having a hard time finding steady work and asked if there were any odd jobs I needed done. That's how it started. But it wasn't a handout. Jeff is very—" Ellen's voice caught, "I mean Jeff *was* very diligent."

"Where was he from?"

Konrad took another drink, lifting her shoulders in a small shrug.

"He never once mentioned where he grew up?" Sam pressed, her tone politely skeptical.

"Maybe it says something unflattering about me, but I didn't initiate conversations about his past." Ellen put her glass down and leaned forward. "I try to live my life very much in the here and now so that's what our primary interaction revolved around: what needed to be done that day, what needed to be organized, what could be gotten ready for tomorrow. We didn't have heart-to-hearts in front of the fireplace. I just don't go there with people, even people under my own roof."

Sam heard the echoes of regret. "Sounds like that could get lonely." When Ellen didn't respond, she asked, "Did Jeff have a steady girlfriend?"

"Not that I know of." Her voice gave noting away but her body language subtly tensed.

Sam considered the obvious: Ellen and Jeff had been intimately involved. That would certainly explain why Phil Atkins was so nervous about journalists poking around. Sam tapped her pen on the notebook, wanting to phrase the question as respectfully as possible.

"I'm sorry, but I have to ask—"

"Were Jeff and I lovers?" Konrad cut her off, sounding weary. "Of course that's what the assumption is going to be, isn't it, regardless of whether it's true or not. I guess I shouldn't be surprised, especially when there are people under my own roof who assumed the same thing."

"I'm not assuming anything," Sam assured her calmly, wondering who in Ellen's inner circle had thought she was having an affair and why they cared even if she was. "I just need to ask the question."

"I know." Ellen looked at Sam evenly but spoke with unexpected emotion. "No, Jeff was *not* my lover. There was no sexual relationship, or sexual contact, of any kind between us—not a kiss, not a grope, not a brief encounter, not a fleeting touch, not so much as a wet dream."

Her intensity made Sam lean back on the stool. "I'm pretty sure wet dreams fall into the *too much information* category, even for the *Weekender.*"

Ellen instantly relaxed and took an audible breath. She pulled off the hair band, put it around her wrist, and gave her head a shake, sending the blonde tresses falling below her shoulders. "Sorry," Ellen apologized, adding wryly, "and as far as wet dreams go, I guess I can honestly only speak for myself."

"Well, thanks for sharing. That's certainly the first time I've had *that* visual during an interview."

Ellen coughed out a self-conscious laugh, "My pleasure, so to speak," and checked her watch. She went around the bar, pulled a bottle of Pinot Grigio from the refrigerator, and held it up. "Would you care to join me?"

"Very much. Thank you."

Sam stood and twisted to stretch her back, which cracked loudly in complaint. Ellen glanced up. "Someone clearly needs a chiropractor."

"Nah, I'm just getting creakier with age."

Ellen took off her jacket and tossed it across the counter, eyeing Sam's leanly muscled body with open appreciation. "How old are you, if you don't mind me asking?"

"Thirty-two, but a few of the joints are going on sixty. Old basketball injuries," Sam explained. She watched Ellen lean over to use a cork puller attached to the back of the bar. "How tall are you?"

Ellen glanced up, curious about the question, "Five-ten in stocking feet. I would think we're about the same height."

"Almost, on days I'm not slouching." Sam sat back down. "So do you wear Achilles-straining stiletto heels because you like them, are a masochist or otherwise kinky, or because you know a woman pushing past six feet will intimidate old boy politicos who are otherwise far more interested in looking down your blouse than hearing your views?" she asked, her eyes brushing over the breasts in question.

"That's very perceptive of you," Ellen acknowledged, aware of the discreet glance. "It's tricky. You want to be taken seriously by the local party power base, so yes, I don't mind being a little intimidating in that sense. But you also want to be accessible to the people you're supposed to be serving, so you don't want to present yourself in too rarefied air." She peered at Sam. "*You* don't find me intimidating, do you?"

"Not at all…even if I do feel like a slug standing next to you in those heels."

"I like slugs."

"Thanks. I think."

Ellen smiled and after a beat asked in a playful tone, "So, you think these heels are kinky, huh?"

"Only if used to squash slugs."

Ellen laughed out loud. "To tell you the truth, I don't like high heels very much and rarely wear them, but I was at a Chamber of Commerce luncheon where I knew photos would be taken. Stature conveys certain qualities, so I just dressed the part today. Personally, I can't wait to change into my jeans and boots."

"As one who believes every day is casual Friday, I'm heartened to know you don't normally wear your designer duds to hang around the house."

"Trust me—Donna Reed, I'm not," she winked.

A *zing* went through Sam's body, causing her arms to erupt in goose bumps. *This is getting embarrassing*, she thought, flustered by her reaction to this woman.

Ellen handed Sam her wine and sat back down. She reached over and lightly *clinked* their glasses. "It's good to meet you, Sam Perry."

"It's good to meet you, too." Sam touched the counter lightly with her glass then took a sip, wondering how much of this repartee was genuine or just an actress playing the role of congenial hostess.

She moved her backpack to make room for the wine glass, causing the envelope of photos with *Rydell* written on it in black marker to slide out onto the counter. She quickly shoved it back in.

"So, did Jeff have any friends you know of?"

Ellen ignored the question, staring at the backpack. "You have pictures of him?"

"I visited his apartment and took some shots, just to keep a visual record for myself when I write the story," Sam hedged.

"Can I see them? I'd be curious to see where he lived."

"That's not a good idea."

"Why?"

"Because," Sam explained, feeling ever-so ghoulish, "I had my camera with me at the crime scene."

"You mean there are pictures of him? Of his body?"

"Some."

Ellen reached for Sam's arm. "Can I *please* see them?"

Sam understood the request. Humans have a primal need to see death in order to believe it. For surviving friends and family, it's the first step in dealing with the finality of it. Even so, she felt uncomfortable being Ellen's Kubler-Ross conduit. But the blue eyes reeled Sam in, and her resolve quickly waned. She sighed in surrender.

"Do you ever take no for an answer?"

"Not often."

She hesitated, still conflicted. "Are you really sure you want to look through these?"

"I'm sure."

"I'm probably breaking some major code of ethics, but…," she handed her the envelope.

Ellen pulled out the prints and went through them one by one. The first few were of the apartment and her eyebrows knitted in dismay. "I can't believe he lived like this."

Sam sat forward. "When we went to the apartment, somebody had broken in. That's why it's such a mess."

"He was robbed?" Ellen repeated. "What was taken?"

"Who knows?"

"Do you think it's related to his death?"

"Possibly."

Ellen slowed as she got to the next series of shots, which were different angles of Rydell's sheet-covered body, one burned and bloodied arm sticking out, the broken fingers of his hand bent in obscene angles. Her jaw clenched, but she otherwise maintained composure until the last photo when her eyes welled.

She stacked the pictures and replaced them in the envelope. "I'll never understand how anyone could hurt another person like that regardless of who they were or what they'd done." She handed the envelope back to Sam. "Do you ever get used to seeing such cruelty?"

Sam put the photos in her bag before answering. "No, of course you don't. You just try to keep some professional distance."

"That's got to be a fine line. You can't constantly confront violent death, even as a career choice, and not be occasionally haunted by it."

"Let's just say insomnia can be an occupational hazard."

"And what do you think about lying awake in the dark?"

Sam ran her finger slowly around the top of the iced tea glass, eyes fixed on its movement. "You see the terrible things people do to others and it's awful. But in a weird way, that's the least of it. What stays with you is the ripple effect of grief one death causes for so many people. The victim's pain is over, but the survivors' agony is just so…raw. You try not to imagine that loss and personalize it, but it happens anyway. And I think that's the real price you pay for getting immersed in the human element of the story."

"What about the price others pay?" Ellen moved closer, well into Sam's personal space, her eyes intense. "What if in finding your story, you hurt innocent people?"

Sam felt the warmth of her breath and inhaled the scent of her perfume. She reined in her overactive senses and sipped some wine before answering.

"If by innocent you mean family members or significant others of a victim or a killer, the public's right to know outweighs their embarrassment or discomfort. And so does the victim's right to justice." It was an old debate and Sam's voice reflected it. "When you write about murder a certain amount of privacy will be lost for everybody involved. That's a given. So I suppose sometimes innocent people do suffer, but at least *they're* alive to feel it."

Ellen put her hand over Sam's. "I wasn't trying to put you on the defensive, even though it probably sounded like it."

"And I didn't mean to sound defensive," Sam cleared her throat, "even though I probably am."

Ellen nodded and squeezed her hand before letting go. Sam suddenly felt very shy and blushed. *This is fucking ridiculous.* She averted her eyes and flipped to a fresh page in her notebook.

"When was the last time you saw Jeff?"

"That would have been Friday, around dinner time. He took my car to get it filled up and washed. I drove to Los Angeles Saturday morning to attend a fundraiser for breast cancer research that evening then had brunch on Sunday with some friends before driving back."

"What—no driver?" Sam teased.

Ellen grimaced. "I hate the whole notion of being driven. Always did. And yes," she added dryly, "I've had enough therapy where I can fully accept it's a control issue. It's funny; I never even sat behind a steering wheel until I was eighteen, had absolutely no desire."

"So you really did come to Los Angeles on a Greyhound bus?"

She smiled at the memory. "Actually, I did, corny as it sounds. But after I moved I realized I had no choice but to drive if I wanted to get around. Once I learned, I loved it and would drive for hours all over LA, just to be on the road." She refilled their wine glasses. "When I was on the series, I always drove myself to the set or location because besides wanting to be in control of the car, it was time to myself. Between work and kids and fans it was hard to find solitude. Even now, though the kids are grown and I don't really have fans milling around out here, it's still a challenge," Ellen paused, surprised she had veered so off-topic. "So anyway, yes, I drove myself to Los Angeles."

"Alone?"

"Alone."

"I'm surprised Atkins let you."

"It not his call," she said pointedly, "but why?"

"For security reasons. You're running for office, plus you're Grade-A stalker material—rich, famous, and beautiful. So I suspect you've had a lot of unwanted attention over the years."

"Sure, I've had some stalker incidents, but they ended up being more sad than dangerous. There are some very lonely people in the world. But I can't let any of it dictate my life. That said, I usually travel with my assistant, Lena Riley. But not Saturday."

"Solitude is seriously underrated," Sam commented.

"Yes, it certainly is," Ellen nodded, staring into her wine. Sam again sensed Ellen's loneliness. She couldn't imagine what it would be like to live such a public life. No wonder the woman took to the road solo. "Just out of curiosity, what kind of car do you drive?"

"What would you think I drive?" Ellen challenged coyly.

"Well, let's see…probably something sporty. Definitely a convertible—your tan is natural and I doubt you have much time to spend lounging around the pool these days, so you must get your sun while driving. Mercedes are way too user unfriendly, Volvos are too boxy. Possibly an XK but Jags are temperamental and my guess is you'd get impatient with that and want something just as sleek but with a tougher constitution, like the latest BMW M series. How am I doing?"

Ellen stared. "My current car is a BMW and my previous car was a Jag. You had to already know that; there's no way you could guess that, Sherlock."

"It wasn't guesswork at all, my dear Watson. I noticed that on the far end of your bookcase you have some driving manuals stacked on the bottom shelf. You don't seem like the Cadillac or Celica type. The Jag manual was several years old, and I assume you trade your cars in every three years or so. Plus, on the table in your hallway was a set of keys, and I noticed a car key from a BMW. My mother owned a gas station, so I spent a lot of time around cars growing up. One of my favorite jobs was to make duplicate keys."

"Why did you think the M series?"

"It just suits you. It's stylish, classy…"

"Thank you for the compliment."

"No thanks necessary; just stating the obvious."

"Are you always so observant?"

"Are we talking about you or the car?"

"My ego's not *that* big," Ellen laughed. "About the car."

"I'm afraid so."

Ellen twirled the wine in her glass and regarded Sam thoughtfully. "Perceptive *and* observant…I'm sure your editors love that about you, but I suspect your intimates might find it challenging."

Sam shrugged and met Ellen's unwavering gaze, "Only if they're trying to hide something."

"I'll consider myself forewarned," she said, her smile enigmatic.

It was like playing 3-D chess, Sam thought, feeling seriously outmatched. She glanced at the clock on Ellen's desk, surprised it was almost 5:15. "I really didn't mean to take up this much of your time. I just have a few more questions."

"There's no rush," she waved off Sam's concern. "Besides, you need to finish your wine."

Sam picked up her glass and pointed toward the lighted case of awards. "Nice hardware."

For the first time, Ellen seemed uncomfortable. "Thank you."

"Is that an embarrassment of riches I detect?"

"Exactly," she admitted, surprised by the insight. "Don't misunderstand; I'm very proud of the work those awards represent, but I think the awards themselves should be personal mementoes, not trophies per se. But my assistant feels they should be prominently displayed in keeping with my so-called stature. We compromised putting them here instead of the living room. It's still a bit showy, though, isn't it?"

Sam glanced up at the pin-light illuminated awards then back to Ellen. "The only thing missing is an oil portrait of you hanging over the case."

"Oh, dear God," Ellen laughed, "please don't give her any ideas!"

The intercom on the phone beeped. "Excuse me." She walked

over to her desk and picked up the receiver, her voice light with lingering amusement. "Yes?"

Although Sam couldn't make out specific words, she could hear the agitated tone and wondered who was making Ellen's smile fade.

"That can wait...Because, I'm in the middle of something... Yes, she is...Of course it's not...Well, it really isn't up to you whether I do or not." She sat on the front edge of the desk, her jaw twitching as she listened. After a few more moments, she held her hand up. "You know what? We're going to have to talk about this later." She hung up and blew out a small sigh. "Sorry for the interruption."

"That's okay. Sorry if you're getting flack for talking to me."

To her credit, Ellen didn't deny it. "The irony is, this is the most relaxed I've felt in weeks. Months. There are just a lot of tense people around me who are very focused on this election, and to be honest, they are *making...me...crazy*. And now with this happening to Jeff..." She looked at Sam, debating. "Were Luke and Phil really arguing yesterday?" she finally asked.

"It wasn't arguing, exactly. More like, unhappily engaged in an intense discussion. Your son looked pale, and your campaign manager looked ready to eat glass. Unfortunately, the closed door made eavesdropping impossible."

"That's too bad."

Her candor intrigued Sam. "Is everything okay?"

"Be careful what you ask; I just might unload on you."

"Then Atkins really would eat glass. So, please—unload away."

Ellen laughed softly and shook her head. "You're bad."

Sam could happily talk to this woman for hours but forced herself back to work. "I need to ask if Jeff ever showed up for work drunk or stoned."

"Never. Jeff didn't do drugs."

"What makes you so sure?"

Ellen walked back to the stool. "You don't spend a lot of years on Hollywood sets without learning to recognize when someone is stoned."

"Okay, but just to play devil's advocate, isn't it possible he could have done drugs out of your presence, even just recreationally?"

She considered the possibility a moment before resolutely rejecting it. "That's just not who he was, Sam. To be honest, he could have used a little loosening up. Jeff was very serious-minded, so to him it would have been irresponsible."

"Serious-minded or single-minded?"

"Both. When he committed to something, he was dedicated to see it through, whether it was volunteering, building a door, or running your errands. There was an endearing nobility about him."

Sam regarded Ellen a moment. "Do you have any enemies?"

"Me?" she paused. "I'm sure I do, but why does that matter?"

"Sometimes it's easier to hurt someone indirectly through someone they care about."

Ellen gazed pensively at Sam and touched the backpack where the photos were. "In other words, is someone I know responsible for that?" She shook her head slowly. "I pray to God nobody in any aspect of my life is capable of such a thing. It would be devastating."

Sam snapped her notebook shut and rocked to her feet. "Thank you very much for seeing me on such short notice and letting me bypass the normal red tape."

"You're very welcome." Ellen opened the study door and walked Sam down the hall. "Feel free to call me directly if you have any more questions. You have my number," she smiled, "don't be shy about using it."

"Thanks, I appreciate it." She reached into a side pocket of the backpack for a business card and wrote her cell number on the back. "Here, in case you think of anything. Or ever need to unload, off the record. I'm a good listener."

"I just might take you up on that," she warned, briefly resting her hand on Sam's shoulder.

"I hope you do."

Walking to her car, Sam glanced back at Ellen's house. A reflection of light from an upstairs window caught her eye, but by the time she turned to get a better look, all she could see was a swaying curtain settling back into place.

CHAPTER FIVE

Sam stopped by the office to make a phone call before picking Joe up for dinner. Nate Joseph was a private investigator whose specialty was retrieving personal records such as credit reports. When talking about the dead, it was not an issue—the right to privacy expires at death. The living, however, were another matter entirely, so Sam never asked how he obtained the information she requested. If she ever had to plead plausible deniability, the less she knew the better.

A soft voice with a heavy Brooklyn accent answered the phone with a rapid fire, "Joseph here. Who's this?"

"Hi, Nate. It's Sam Perry."

"Sam! I thought you dropped off the face of the earth, movin' to some God-forsaken desert or something livin' the life of leisure." He said it *leeshuh.*

"Well, it's not exactly the Gobi, Nate. I'm in Palm Springs."

"Same thing. So what's up? You back workin' graveyard?"

"I am. And I need you to do a background check."

"Who is it?"

"Who was it is more like it."

"Oh, body bag time. Who's the stiff?" From anyone else it would sound affected, but the clichés that tumbled from Nate's mouth were the genuine article.

"His name was Jeff Rydell."

"I'm assuming death by unnatural causes."

"I think torture, stabbing, and bludgeoning fit that category."

Sam gave Nate the few details she knew, including birth date and the social security number Rydell had given Rose. A social security number was probably the single most important piece of data when trying to piece together a person's life. Nearly everyone had one, and they never changed although some less scrupulous people might use a second, fraudulent one.

"So what you want me to do?"

"Everything. I'd like to know who this guy is. Was."

"Regular mystery man, huh? The kind I like. I'll get started on this right away."

"And Nate, I want you to run another name. Ellen Konrad."

"The actress? Hey, she's a real looker."

"You should see her in person." Sam gave him Ellen's birth date and address.

"What's up with her?"

"I don't know yet. That's why I pay you the big bucks."

"You writers are such jokers."

* * *

The Patio at Vallarta was only half-full, but Joe insisted on sitting directly under the misters. Sam positioned herself as far as possible from the constant rain of fine spray, but she could still feel her hair sprouting wings.

Joe's bruises had taken on the colors of a wonderful desert vista at sunset, a nice counterpoint to his crimson face. Despite the sunburn, Joe seemed oblivious to any discomfort as he cheerily poured himself another margarita—his third. He topped off Sam's drink—her first—with dregs from the empty pitcher.

"You know," she warned, "nothing's worse than waking up with a sunburn *and* a hangover. Maybe we should order some food before you break into your Carmen Miranda impersonation."

"Why? Is there a sarong and basket of fruit close by?" Joe asked brightly then swatted away her concerns with a flip of his hand. "Sam, I've had a hard twenty-four hours, so don't nag. These drinks aren't that strong, and the glasses are small. Besides, it's your fault. You said this was an Italian restaurant."

"It was, last week."

"So you say." He downed half the drink and sat back with a satisfied sigh. "Have you nailed my assailant yet?"

"I'm not the police. Ask them."

"Yeah, but you'll find out quicker because you're smarter—"

"Stop trying to butter me up."

"…and because you've got a personal interest in it—namely me."

"Actually, my personal interest in this story is my weekly paycheck."

"All $300 of it," Joe snorted. "You work because you're driven to, not because you need the pittance they pay you at that rinky-dink newspaper."

"You don't know *what* they pay me—" Sam stopped when the waiter appeared at their table. She ordered chicken fajitas for them to share, and Joe ordered another pitcher. When the waiter walked away, she added softly, "It's $700."

"Must have broke the bank," Joe drawled without skipping a beat, making Sam laugh. "So tell me, what's Ellen Konrad like?"

She thought a moment, moving the margarita glass in small circles on the table. "Smart. Charismatic. Funny. Gorgeous. Intriguing. Great hair. Even better legs. Killer smile. But other than that nothing special."

"She sounds like a catch," Joe observed. He popped a guacamole covered chip into his mouth and joked, "Maybe you should ask her out."

"I wish," Sam said absently.

Joe stared, surprised. "I meant as a friend, but that works too." Sam blushed, and he leaned forward. "My God, you really *are* smitten with her. Well, it's about time."

"What's that mean?" she asked defensively.

"It means I'm glad you're finally keeping an open mind. Listen, it couldn't turn out any worse than Olaf."

"Jens."

"Jens, Hans, whatever." Joe knew the name, but loved ragging Sam about her ex-boyfriend. "You're far too independent, far too stubborn to spend your life being an emotional fluffer. You need a peer, a partner, an equal—everything Gustav…"

"Jens."

"…whatever, was not."

"An emotional fluffer?"

"Stop changing the subject. All I'm saying is, you can do better. You deserve better." He paused while the waiter delivered the fresh pitcher on their table then leaned forward. "Do you remember me asking you in high school if you were attracted to Pam Magnin?"

"I remember. I lied and said I wasn't."

Joe sat back, feeling vindicated. "Why didn't you just tell me instead of keeping it a secret? I told you everything about me."

"Yeah, but you were comfortable with yourself. I was afraid of what other people might think, so there was no way I could admit it to you or anyone. Plus I hate the idea of being labeled. As it was I knew there were people who assumed I was gay because I wasn't exactly the frilly type." She studied Joe a moment. "Did you?"

"I thought it was possible but not because you didn't wear dresses. You just didn't seem that attracted to guys. I knew the difference because I *was* attracted to guys."

"That's not totally accurate. I was, and have been, attracted to men."

"Alright, but I bet you've always been *more* attracted to women."

There didn't seem to be much point in denying it. Sam's one serious relationship, with Jens, lasted almost eight years before fading away over accusations that she was more interested in murder and mayhem than having a private life. She angrily denied it but had since wondered if there might not be more truth to it than she cared to admit. Dealing with the dead was heartrending but decidedly less complicated than dealing with the living—especially when you hadn't openly acknowledged certain fundamental truths about yourself. Her years with Jens had confirmed what Sam had long known—she had no significant emotional connection to men, romantically speaking. On the other hand, she found women endlessly beguiling.

"That's probably why I started dating Ross," she mused, "to prove I fit in. But that was then; now it just doesn't seem like a big deal anymore." She took another sip, adding, "And before you ask, no, nothing has ever come of it."

"Aren't you at all curious?"

"Sure," she again moved her glass in circles on the table, "more than just curious. But since the only women I've been attracted to were all straight—"

"Or so you thought. There are a lot of lipstick lesbians in the world."

"Yeah? Where?"

"You are so cynical."

"The bottom line is the situation never presented itself. And however intrigued I might be, you know I'm not one to pursue *anyone*, regardless of gender."

"But if a woman you found attractive came on to you now, would you go for it?"

"I don't know. Maybe. Depends who."

"If you went to a lesbian bar at least you'd know the women there are—"

"No, thank you," Sam waved her hands. "I have no desire to be part of any meat market pick-up scene, straight *or* gay, anymore. Those days are over. Been there, done that, over it."

"Then how are you ever going to meet anyone?" he asked, exasperated.

Sam shrugged. "I don't know, Joe. I guess they'll have to find me."

Before she could turn the tables and ask Joe about his love life, he veered the conversation back to Ellen. "So tell what else about her."

"Well, she's holding back."

"How do you know?"

"I can just feel it."

"What's she lying about?"

"I wouldn't say lying exactly; it's probably more omission.

Whatever it is, she's not being completely forthcoming about Rydell. I just feel it. Plus, look," she reached down and pulled an envelope out of her backpack. "Here's a copy of Rydell's phone bill for the last month—"

Joe snatched the sheets out of her hand. "How'd you get these?"

"Through keen reporting."

"Seriously, how'd you get these?"

"Rose called as I was leaving the office tonight. She took Jeff's mail so it wouldn't get stolen again and wanted to know what to do with it. I told her I'd be happy to take it off her hands. It was a bunch of junk mail and his phone bill."

"Is it legal for you to have this?"

"Technically?"

"Never mind; I don't want to know." He handed back the pages. "This is very interesting, but what does it mean?"

"The only thing it means for sure is that Jeff Rydell spoke with someone at Ellen's house—at length—nearly every day. That's her home number there. Tomorrow I'll check to see who the other numbers belong to. What's curious is that he received many more calls from the house than he made to there."

"So are you thinking they were lovers?" Joe sounded skeptical. "Somehow, Ellen Konrad doesn't seem the type to go slumming."

"From the expert on slumming?"

"Very funny. Very brave. Very true."

Sam smiled and stretched her arms over her head, setting off a series of muted cracks along her spine. "She denies being involved with Rydell—rather colorfully and convincingly. And my gut believes her; I don't think that was a performance. But the closer you get to the truth the more of a reaction you get. Rydell is a definite hot button, but why? Maybe he was blackmailing her."

"For what, minimum wage? He sure wasn't spending money on fabulous living quarters." Joe drained his margarita just as the waiter brought their fajitas, and the conversation veered off to Joe's account of a recent trip to Mexico where he took a tour identifying indigenous flora known to be hallucinogenic.

After dinner, they walked into the balmy night, the temperature hovering around one hundred degrees. Sam was parked near the post office on Calle Encilia, a block east of Indian Drive. During the day the street was busy, but at night the area was dark and deserted.

"We need to stop at the drugstore," Joe told her.

"Why?"

"I ran out of aloe. Actually, *you* ran out of aloe."

She looked at him before stepping off the curb to cross Calle Encilia. "You used that entire bottle—"

"Sam! Watch out!"

She turned toward the sound of a gunning engine to her right and was aware of a dark shape hurtling towards her. Joe yanked her by the arm, causing her to fall backwards onto the sidewalk just as a large black car zoomed by so close Sam could feel the heat of exhaust fumes as it passed.

"Samantha, are you all right?" Joe's burnt face was strangely pale.

Sam rolled to her feet, brushing off the seat of her shorts. "What the hell was that?" she asked furiously. Whenever Sam was frightened, it caused an immediate anger response; the bigger the scare, the bigger the knee-jerk ire.

"That car almost ran you over."

"No fucking shit," she snapped. Despite the heat her skin felt chilled, which helped douse her indignation. "I'm sorry. What did you see?" she asked more evenly.

Joe took a deep breath. "Just as you stepped off the curb a car that was parked right there suddenly took off," he pointed to a now-vacant parking place. "It was heading right at you. Sam, it missed you by inches."

"Its lights weren't on," she said, remembering the sound of a car accelerating but not seeing it. They stared at each other a minute. "I think somebody's trying to send me a message," she finally said.

"And I think I need to change my underwear."

* * *

Sam walked into the house. Ellen was sitting on the steps, dressed in jeans and leather boots.

"You were supposed to meet me at four."

"I couldn't find my keys."

"You know the door is unlocked."

Sam followed her to the office. Inside, part of it had turned into a bedroom. Ellen sat sideways on the desk, smiling at her. She had changed into a blue silk robe that matched her eyes.

"You need to listen, Sam."

"I'm trying to."

Sam walked behind the counter to get some wine, and when she looked up they were in a ship's cabin. Ellen opened the doors and stepped out onto the balcony. Sam joined her, and they jumped into the water. It was only waist deep and very warm. Sam took off her shorts.

"Did you find what you were looking for?"

Sam wasn't sure what she meant. They stood close to one another. Sam could smell Ellen's perfume. They kissed. Her lips were soft, her tongue gently assertive.

Ellen reached into the water. Sam felt the touch of fingers between her legs, sliding in, then out. Ellen pulled her under the waves as an exquisite surge of pleasure rushed through her body…

She sat up, heart racing, body still electrified. Disoriented, her initial reaction was embarrassment at having lost control. She was also mortified that Joe might have heard her. But once Sam's head cleared and her libido simmered down, those concerns eased. She closed her eyes, reliving the vivid sensations, savoring the unfamiliar emotion of it. This wasn't the first time she dreamed of kissing a woman. But this *was* the first time a kissing dream had made her climax. And made her yearn.

Sex with men had always offered basic physical release but lacked genuine passion. Rather than directly confront the glaring implications of that, she spent her adult life escaping into work and sublimation took precedence over introspection. Except she couldn't escape her dreams.

In the instant before she fell back asleep, her last thought was of Ellen's smile.

* * *

"Oh Monica, could you come here a minute?" Sam asked sweetly.

"Uh-oh, I know what that means—more work for Monica."

"Am I that transparent?"

"Uh-huh."

"Yeah, well…subtlety never was my strong suit." She handed Monica the phone bill. "I need to know everybody Jeff Rydell called."

"Please say you're kidding."

"Don't panic. It's not as bad as it looks. Call Mike Lewis again. He should be able to track down who these numbers belong to. Tell him I will be forever grateful—and that two bottles of single barrel scotch will be there by the weekend."

"That's all?" Monica asked hopefully.

"Not quite." Sam handed Monica the Data Search list of Rydells. "While he's doing that, I'd like you to see if any of the numbers on the bill match any of these numbers."

Monica slowly flipped through the pages. "I hope my scotch is in the mail, too," she commented with an arched eyebrow.

"If you scan both the phone bill and the list of Rydell numbers as editable text files and merge them into a directory, it'll be easy to see if there are any duplicates."

Monica made a face. "I should have thought of that. I'll get right on it."

Sam tapped on the door jamb of Marlene's office. Her editor waved her in. "Come in, come in. So when can I expect to see the Rydell copy?"

"How late can I go with the deadline?"

"Five o'clock Thursday."

"Then you'll probably see something around 4:55 Thursday," Sam smiled.

"Is turning in copy early against your religion or something?"

"I have no religion."

"No wonder it's impossible to put the fear of God into you," Marlene smiled back.

"That's not necessarily true," Sam said slowly. She recounted the experience of nearly being reduced to human road kill the night before.

Marlene slumped back in her chair. "Were you hurt? Do you need to see a doctor?"

"No and no. Thanks anyway."

"This just doesn't happen in Palm Springs, except back when the college kids used to invade us for spring break. You think there's a connection between what happened last night and your investigation?"

Sam did but played it down. "It's possible although it does seem a bit melodramatic."

"Well, for God's sake—and mine—please be careful. No story's worth getting run over for. By the way, how *is* the story coming?"

"Fine, thanks." San stood up and headed toward the door.

"Do you think you'll be doing a follow up?"

"I don't know yet."

"Can you at least give me an idea of how many column inches you think the story will be?"

"You'll be the first to know, as soon as I figure it out."

Marlene sighed and pulled an economy-sized bottle of Rolaids out of her desk. "Writers. God love 'em."

* * *

Despite Ellen's adamancy, Sam wasn't convinced drugs could be completely ruled out yet as a factor in Rydell's death. His reported run-ins with George Manuel prompted her to see if the neighbor had a known history with drugs. It took calls to the DMV, Nate Joseph, and a cop friend in LA before she had the answer and was on her way back to Desert Wash Drive.

The idea in Palm Springs is to get errands done early to beat the afternoon heat. But when it's already 105 degrees at 10:00 in the morning, that plan gets shot to literal hell. The forecasted high for the day was 118, with warmer temperatures expected tomorrow.

Visitors either stayed inside with the air conditioner running nonstop or neck deep in a pool outside. Residents just soldiered on with sunscreen and water bottles in hand to stave off skin cancer and dehydration. Sam found it fascinating that despite having already drunk two quarts of iced green tea this morning, she had yet to go to the bathroom once.

Walking into the Windy Dunes lobby, Sam noticed a shiny new aluminum mailbox making a gleaming spectacle of itself among the older copper-colored doors. She took the elevator to the third floor where wind-blown desert sand crunched under her cross-trainers. Sam wondered if that's how the building got its name.

She opened the screen door to George Manuel's apartment and tapped out a friendly *rat-tat-a-tat-tat, tat-tat.* From behind the lightweight front door, she could hear the faint sound of music. Sam waited a full minute then knocked again, this time with enough insistence to make her knuckles sting.

A sleepy voice called out from behind the door, "Yeah?"

"Hey George, it's Sam."

"Sam?"

"Yeah, you know…"

A dead bolt lock turned, and the door opened. Sleep-puffed eyes squinted at her. "I don't know you."

"You would if you read the right paper."

George shook his head, as if his ears were plugged with water. "Man, who are you, and what do you want?"

Sam wedged her leg and shoulder just inside the doorjamb. "I'm Sam Perry. I'm a reporter for the *Weekender,* and I want to talk to you about one of your neighbors, Jeff Rydell."

George's foggy brain cleared, and he was instantly alert—and wary. "I don't know anything about that." He tried to close the door, but Sam's body was an effective doorstop.

"I think you'd rather talk to me than the police."

"Why would I be talking to the police?"

"Local cops are always interested when a convicted drug dealer moves into their area, Jorge."

Once again, a social security number had proven to be her best friend. Sam used Manuel's name and address to get his birthdate from the DMV; she gave Nate his name and birthdate to get a social security number; and then she asked her cop friend to run the social through the law enforcement data base. The name Jorge Diego-Manuel popped twice in Beverly Hills. Both arrests were pot busts with intent to distribute. The first case was dropped when the drugs disappeared from the police evidence room, and he received probation on the second after pleading down to a misdemeanor.

"When did you start Anglicizing your name, Jorge?"

"My name is George now," his eyes darted nervously. "I'm not that person anymore."

"Look, I'm not out to get you busted," Sam assured him. "All I want is to ask you some questions."

He rubbed his face. "Fine, come in."

"No thanks. I'd rather we talk here. Don't worry, I'll speak quietly." Although she had occasionally walked into potentially dangerous situations during her career, she wasn't foolhardy. No reason to go into a stranger's apartment as an unwelcome guest when you could talk publicly in front of a slew of nosy neighbors.

"Goddamn," George glared at her. "Then wait a minute and let me get my shirt."

He left her at the front door and disappeared down the hall. Sam peered into Manuel's apartment; it was the mirror-image of Rydell's but in layout only. The living room boasted a state-of-the-art stereo in a solid oak entertainment cabinet—this was obviously not one of Rose's furnished units. Resting on top of the cabinet was a brand-new television.

"The drug business must be booming," Sam muttered.

George's taste in art leaned toward cinematic pop culture, with what looked to be vintage posters of *Clash of the Titans*, *Mighty Joe Young*, and *Beast from 20,000 Fathoms* visible. Sam found it curious that Manuel had enough money for expensive furniture and electronics and yet chose to live in a rundown building in a low-income neighborhood.

George came back five minutes later, looking surprisingly put together. He'd shaved, combed his hair, and looked downright collegiate in his jeans and T-shirt. Sam thought the gold Virgin of Guadalupe medallion was a nice altar boy touch.

"Now what?" he asked in a decidedly un-collegial tone.

"No need to be surly, George. I just want to know what was up with Rydell. I personally don't care if you deal coke."

"You're dreaming, lady. If you know I got busted then you know it was for pot."

She took out her cell phone. "So if the police searched your apartment they wouldn't find any evidence of coke or meth in your apartment?"

"Put that away," he hissed. "And don't talk so loud. Look, sometimes I'll do people favors. About a month ago Jeff asked if I could get him some blow for some girl he was hot and heavy with. Said she got really wild when she was high, and he wanted to keep her happy and horny. So I did. But that was it. I just did a favor. Why are you hassling me?"

"It's what I get paid for."

"I thought reporters got paid to write."

"That, too. But I need information before I can write. I know the two of you had a falling out. And then he turns up dead. So you can see why I'm curious."

George kicked the carpet. Sam waited. Finally he sighed, "Jeff owed me money. That's what we argued about. I was really blown away when I heard he was, you know…I still can't believe it."

"How'd you know he was dead?"

George looked at her in surprise. "Rose, how else? She told everybody. And she told everybody about being interviewed for the paper."

"How much money did he owe you?"

"Five hundred."

"He owed you that much for coke? Sounds like more than a favor."

"He didn't owe me for drugs. It was a loan."

"A loan for what?"

"I'm not sure."

"You lent someone $500, and you didn't even ask?"

George shoved his hands in his pockets. "He said he had a chance to do a deal and make a lot of money. He just needed an ante."

"And you didn't mind the idea of new competition?"

"I *told* you; I don't deal. It's too risky."

"Did Jeff do drugs?"

"Not that I know of. That's one reason why I trusted him and lent him money. I knew it wouldn't go up his nose."

"That the only reason?"

George looked away. "He was going to give me an extra $250 back."

"So what happened?

"I don't know. When I asked him for the cash, he put me off but promised he'd have it in a couple of days. I got pissed because I needed the money."

Sam nodded towards his living room. "Doesn't look like it."

"It's called credit card debt. Look, I move just enough pot to put myself through night school, okay? I'm almost finished now, so I won't have to do it much longer. Good thing, since I never could spot an undercover narc."

That, she believed. "I don't suppose he told you the name of his girlfriend?"

George shook his head.

"When's the last time you saw Jeff?"

"Last Friday. I caught him coming home, and that's when we argued. I never saw him again after that."

Sam took some generic notes, using the time to think. Assuming George was right, it was conceivable Rydell was the victim of a drug deal gone bad. She wondered if the girlfriend was still breathing.

"Did Jeff ever mention where he was from?"

George shook his head. "He never talked much about anything."

"Do you know if he had any local hangouts?"

"I ran into him once or twice at the Village Pub on Palm Canyon. Other than that, I don't know. We really weren't that tight."

Sam capped her pen and flipped her notebook closed. "Thanks, George. I appreciate you taking the time to talk to me," as if she'd given him much choice.

George fingered his medallion. "You're not really going to talk to the police about me, are you?"

"No. They'll have to find you on their own."

"Thanks."

Sam started to walk away then stopped and looked back. "By the way, what're you studying in school?"

George blushed. "Law."

CHAPTER SIX

Fielder spun a napkin in front of Sam and carefully placed the daiquiri on it. "Starting the hard stuff early today, eh?"

"It's not early. It's got to be, what—ten past noon?"

It was so hot out Sam wanted the coldest drink she could think of. When the icy slush hit her throat the searing pain of brain-freeze shot through her jaw into the back of her head. "That's really good, Felder," she rasped, eyes watering. Once the throbbing subsided, Sam flipped to her notes from Sunday and motioned Felder over. "What do you know about the Crazy Girl in Indio?"

"Now there's a fine establishment," he said, doing a W. C. Fields impression. "Live nude girls who'll dance for a song and a $50 bill. Being a happily married man, I know this only by reputation."

"I won't tell Sharon."

"Planning a change of career?" he smiled, absently smoothing down his well-manicured beard.

"Somehow I think my earning potential at the Crazy Girl would be severely limited. By some miracle, do you know any bartender or server who works there?"

"I don't, but I *do* know someone who probably does. A buddy of mine named Jim Pearson works in Indio at a joint called Tracks. He's lived in Indio his whole life, poor fellow, and has tended bar since he was old enough to pour. You could say he's the doyenne of the Indio liquor service industry, so I'm sure he knows somebody who works at Crazy Girl in some capacity. It's been there a long time. Jim works the day shift at Tracks, so he'd be there now if you want to call him."

"I think I'd rather stop by in person."

"I'm sure he'll be delighted to help you. Tell him I said hello. And remind him he still owes me for that Super Bowl pool."

"He still owes you from January?"

"No, the Raiders-Redskins game. I told you—he's an *old* buddy."

* * *

Sam drove down Ramon Avenue to the I-10, heading east toward Indio, blaring the local country radio station on her stereo. The sky was a brilliant blue, but the ground was brown and brittle. The flowers that covered the desert in spring with vivid colors were now seared wisps crumbling in the sun. Marlene swore there was usually at least one good thunderstorm per summer, but Sam knew her editor's sick sense of humor.

With the help of her cell phone's navigation app, Sam found Tracks with no trouble. She parked illegally in an alley so her car would be in the shade and walked across the street where a neon sign blinked *Welcome.*

Sam strode through the door and stopped, blinded by the darkness. Once her eyes adjusted she saw a pub pretty much like every other local pub she'd ever been in. The bar was on the right; to the left were tables covered in red and white checkered plastic tablecloths. In the back was a pool table and a pinball machine so old it probably played five balls for a quarter.

Two older men hunched over the bar, staring at her. She nodded in their direction as she slid onto a stool. The bartender was watching a soap opera on a small portable TV. Slim and petite, he wore wire frame glasses, a vest, and a bowl haircut.

"Excuse me. Are you Jim?"

He turned around and smiled. "You must be Miss Perry. Felder called and warned me I'd better do right by you, or I'd have him to answer to." His voice was soft but had a distinctive throaty quality to it. "However, he refused to tell me what you needed, just to irritate me."

"Felder thought you might know somebody who works at the

Crazy Girl."

"May I ask why?"

"Sure. A man was murdered in Palm Springs a few days ago, and I'm hoping to track down anybody who might have known him. It's possible he hung out there."

"Do you work for the police?"

"No, just a reporter for the *Weekender* trying to do a story."

Jim nodded. "You know, someone just mentioned that place to me the other day, lemme think. Can I get you a drink?"

"I'll take a split."

He grabbed the champagne and a chilled glass from the cooler and didn't talk until he popped the cork and poured. "If I'm not mistaken, a girl who used to work here got a job tending bar at the Crazy Girl. My girlfriend, Terry, and Alison—that's the girl—got to be pretty close, and they keep in touch. I'm pretty sure Terry said that's where she was working."

"Do you know Alison's last name?"

"Peters." One of the men at the end of the counter, draped over an empty glass, raised his hand and wiggled two fingers at Jim. "Excuse me. If I don't give 'em their drinks fast they'll go into DTs."

Sam quickly finished her drink and stood up when Jim returned. "Listen, thanks for everything. What do I owe you?"

Jim shook his head, "Nothing. Just tell Felder I'm still waiting for the money he owes me for that Super Bowl game."

"Raiders-Redskins?"

"Hell, no. Jets-Baltimore."

* * *

The Crazy Girl was a converted warehouse wedged between a body repair shop and a wholesale mattress outlet. There was no sign in front, and the street number on the curb was barely visible. It was not the kind of place you'd likely happen upon by chance. Sam knew; she'd driven right past it her first time around the block. She pulled into the club's fenced-in lot and parked near the lone light post a few yards from the door. At night, the outer reaches of the lot would be a mugger's paradise. She wondered how many businessmen had been rolled after an evening of naughty pleasures.

Even though it was only 2:30 on a weekday afternoon, there were at least two-dozen cars in the lot. According to a placard on the door, Crazy Girl's hours were from noon 'til 2:00 a.m. seven days a week, 365 days a year. "And who wouldn't love a Crazy Girl Christmas show?" Sam grinned, opening the front door.

The cashier's booth in the foyer was closed; a sign in the barred window listed a $10 cover from 8:00 p.m. until closing. At the end of the foyer was a pair of dingy red velvet curtains that muted the music playing behind them. Sam slipped through the drapes and stepped into a surprisingly clean and well-kept main showroom.

A large stage with a silver pole dominated the center of the room. The stage was elevated enough so that the sides and front doubled as counter space for the customers who sat bug-eyed in the chairs lining the perimeter. The rear of the stage was draped with black curtains that spanned the width of the room. The bar was located to Sam's left against the far wall. Past the end of the bar was another set of faded, red drapes she assumed led to the lap dance room. A circle of ledges bordered the room, with tables and comfortable chairs on casters filling the rest of the space.

Over the stage was a light grid filled with strobes spinning small spotlights of color on the walkway near the black curtains. The curtains opened and a blowzy, big-breasted bottle blonde *click-clacked* down the stage in pink stilettos, twirling the belt of her silk, pink robe. Sam wondered what the woman's stage name was. Underneath the ton of make-up…*Pink Lady?*….had to be well into her forties. But her legs were solid, and when she spun out of her robe, huge silicon-inflated breasts guaranteed few men would spend much time looking at her crow's feet and frown lines.

Sam thought anyone doubting we were descended from apes only had to take a look at the hooting horde watching the show to be convinced. She had to admit, though, it *was* some show. *Blondie?*… now clad only in those life-threatening shoes and a pink G-string, pulled the robe through her tightly closed thighs. Sam assumed her expression was supposed to depict erotic pleasure, but it looked more like she was giving herself a nasty cloth burn.

"Can I help you?" asked a cheerful waitress who looked young enough to be in high school. Her name tag said September. Like the other waitresses and bartender, she was modestly dressed in jeans and a Crazy Girls T-shirt. "I hope so. Is Alison here?"

"Uh, we don't have an Alison here."

"You don't have a bartender named Alison who used to work over at Tracks?"

"Why do you want to know?" she asked suspiciously.

"I'm visiting from out of town and thought I'd surprise her," Sam said, which in and of itself was true.

"Oh, so you a friend of hers?"

Sam thought it better not to complicate the issue with the truth. "I'm so stupid because I don't have her phone number with me. Last I heard she was at Tracks, but the bartender there told me I could find her here. I guess I misunderstood, or he was just blowing me off."

"Oh, no, he told you right," September told her. "I just had to be sure. Hang on; let me see if anyone knows when she's coming in."

Sam perched on a stool to wait. The stage lights dimmed and the mirror ball spun into action. *Lady Godiva*?...caressed her breasts, which looked as supple as over-inflated tires, then risked injury doing a shoulder shimmy. Next...*Gypsy Rose Wannabe*?...climbed three feet up the pole, flung her arms out like a debauched trapeze artist and flipped upside down, held in place by vice-like thighs. Sam could see she was still smiling like a pro despite the hair hanging in front of her face.

Defying all laws of gravity, her breasts sagged nary an inch.

Realizing she was sitting there with her mouth open, Sam snapped her jaws shut and saw September walking briskly toward her.

"I'm sorry, Alison isn't working tonight. She won't be on until after six on Thursday."

"Damn," Sam said under her breath. "Well, thanks anyway. By

the way, is September your real name?"

"No way!" she laughed. "All the girls here use aliases. Alison goes by Kona. That's why I figured you must of been a friend 'cause you knew her real name. This place gets a lot of horny guys, and you don't want them to know who you really are. Want a drink anyway?"

"No, I'd better be going, but thanks again."

Disgruntled, Sam exited through the red curtains. The story was due Thursday afternoon. She'd just have to find Alison today.

Sam checked in with the office first, realizing she hadn't told anybody where she was going—a beginner's stupid mistake.

"Any calls?" she asked when Monica picked up the phone.

Sam heard the rustle of the message book. "Let's see, your crazy friend Joe called. He said something about re-styling your dogs... Nate called back, said he needs to talk to you...and Rose called. That's it. I called Mike Lewis, and he'll email you the information by 6:00 tonight, and I finished comparing those phone numbers. None of them match."

"Of course not, that would be too easy. Okay, would you tell Marlene that I'm in Indio trying to track down someone who might know Rydell? If she needs me, I'm on my cell."

Sam decided to call Joe later, dreading to think what her dogs might look like when she got home. She punched in Nate's number.

"Hi, Nate, it's Sam."

"So here's what I found on your guy. First off, he's got bad credit. Not that he'd ever had a lot, but over the past two and a half years what few cards he had, he bailed on. They are all closed now, and he has no current cards, nor does it look like he's applied for any credit in the past year. There were a couple of judgments against him, one for a bum check to a grocery store."

"Sounds like he fell on hard times."

"Yeah, easy to do. Now here's the best part. I got a former address in some backwater place called Cattle Hill, Tennessee."

"Great work, Nate. Do me a favor and email the address to my home account."

"You want me to send the other stuff on him at the same time?"

"Just hang on to that in your files," Sam said. The *Weekender's* in-house attorney would implode if he caught her with a credit report, even if Rydell *was* dead. "Nate, could you do one other thing for me?"

"It'll have to be tomorrow. I've got tickets to the Mets-Braves game. Just email me what you need, and I'll get on it first thing. I should have the other information you wanted by tomorrow, too."

She thanked him, hung up, and called Rose. "Hi, Rose, it's Sam."

"Oh, I'm so glad you called. I've been cleaning out Jeff's apartment. It's so sad, seeing all his things scattered all over. It's just…you know."

"I do know." Sam reclined her seat until it was almost flat and closed her eyes. This could take a while.

"He was such a nice young man. I didn't really know him, but he *seemed* so nice. But then again, if he really *was* that nice, why would someone want to kill him? I mean, it wasn't like he was killed by accident, know what I mean? Who really knows what he was up to, right? Anyway, I spent most of the day trying to make the place presentable again to rent. The police said it was okay. I mean, I told them I couldn't afford to have an empty apartment just sitting around."

"No, that wouldn't be fair to you." Sam felt herself almost drifting off. If she ran out of gas and the engine died while she slept, she'd roast in minutes.

"Anyway, I called Goodwill to take the furniture and put his clothes in a box, but I'll probably just leave those on the curb in case somebody in the neighborhood wants them. I didn't know what to do with his computer, but I was thinking maybe it was time I learned QuickBooks if nobody claims it. But I'm really not sure what to do with all these papers of his."

Sam's eyes opened. "What kind of papers?"

"Oh, I don't know. It just looks like business papers, receipts, and things like that, a few pictures."

"Where'd you find them?"

"A couple of envelopes fell out when the Goodwill men were

moving out the bed. I guess they'd fallen behind the headboard and got stuck."

Sam released the seat and was bounced upright. Not stuck; more like hidden behind the headboard. "Rose, just hang onto those papers and I'll stop by later today, okay?"

"I'm not going anywhere, so you can come over whenever you want."

Sam ended the call and placed the phone in her console cup holder. At the very least, maybe the papers would lead to his family. She'd make Joe come with her to run interference with Rose to make up for whatever he'd done to her dogs.

She stopped at a 7-11 for some water and a bathroom break then called directory assistance. There was no Alison Peters listed, but there were two A. Peters. She wrote down the numbers and called the first. Voicemail clicked on, playing dialogue recorded from *Valley of the Dolls*. Sam listened to Patty Duke having a drug-induced breakdown.

"And you think you're having a bad day, what about poor Nellie?" a flamboyant male voice said. "So dolls, Adam and I aren't home, but leave your number, and one of us will get back to you."

"Joe would so appreciate that," Sam smiled, dialing the next number.

"Hello?" This voice was young and feminine.

"Hi, is this Alison?"

"Who is this?" The voice turned wary and suspicious.

"My name is Samantha Perry. I'm looking for the Alison Peters who used to work at Tracks."

A pause. "Why?"

"Jim at Tracks thought you might be able to help me."

"You're a friend of Jim's?"

"Friend of a friend. I'm a reporter in Palm Springs and need help with a story I'm working on. I'd really appreciate it if I could talk to you in person for a few minutes. I won't be offended if you want to call Jim and check me out."

"That's okay, I'm not *that* paranoid," Alison sounded sheepish.

"You just can't be too careful these days."

"So I keep hearing."

"What kind of story are you writing?"

"The kind I'd rather not talk about on the phone. I *am* that paranoid," Sam joked.

Alison gave it a couple seconds thought. "Okay. Let me tell you how to get here."

Ten minutes later Sam parked in front of the small duplex where Alison lived. A black cat with white paws sat in the driveway and fell in step behind her as she passed, mewing softly. Alison opened the door as Sam climbed the steps. "Hi, come on in. You too, Mitts." Once inside, the cat wound in and around Alison's legs. "Can I get you something to drink?" she asked, picking up Mitts.

"No, I'm fine." Sam sat in the nearest chair and pulled a copy of Rydell's driver's license photo from her notebook. "Do you know this guy? I was told he hung out at the Crazy Girl."

"Yeah, I recognize him." Alison settled on the couch with Mitts. "That's Jeff. He's tight with Money."

"Who's Money?"

"One of the girls. He's always following her around. She's really into him, too."

"Do you know anything else about her?"

"I think she's a bit of a cokehead or something. She's got those crazy eyes, know what I mean?"

"I do, actually. Are they dating?" Sam asked, wondering if *dating* was perhaps dignifying the relationship more than was warranted.

Alison shrugged. "It wouldn't surprise me. Technically it's against the rules for the girls to date the customers, but they do it anyway. You know, hoping to find someone to take them away from that place and take care of them. Same old story. And then there's those guys who think they're some white knight who's gonna save some girl from a life of lap dancing," Alison gestured towards Rydell's photo. "That's the way Jeff seems, like he's looking for somebody to save."

"What's Money's real name?"

"I don't know. She's not real talkative about her life outside of work. So what's this all about, anyway?"

"Jeff was murdered over the weekend. They found his body on Sunday."

"Oh, God." Alison put her cat on the floor and sat on the edge of the cushion. "What happened?"

"He was bludgeoned. Was Jeff at the club this weekend?"

"Saturday night. This is just so bizarre," Alison sat forward, hugging her knees. "I've never known anyone who got murdered before. Do you think it was someone from the club?" Fear pinched her face.

"I have no idea. That's for the police to figure out. I'm just trying to find people who knew him. The authorities haven't been able to locate any family members. Is there anyone else you can think of who might know Jeff personally?"

"Anyone else? Sorry, I'm just blown away."

"Don't be nervous. This is just between you and me," Sam promised. "Did anything happen out of the ordinary Saturday?"

Alison bit her lip. "It's probably nothing, but I was working the bar and Jeff was there with some other guy. I didn't recognize him, and it was obvious he was uncomfortable being in the place."

"Obvious in what way?"

"His body language and just his vibe. Plus, he hardly ever glanced up at the girls. This guy and Jeff got into an argument. It's real loud in there, especially at night, so I couldn't hear what they were saying, but the guy kept poking his finger in Jeff's chest."

"What did Jeff do?"

"Nothing. He tried to walk away, but the guy grabbed Jeff's collar, said something right in his face, then stormed out."

"What did this guy look like?"

"I didn't really get a good look at his face because he was at Argo's end of the bar and was wearing a baseball cap pulled pretty low."

"Who's Argo?"

"The other bartender. But I do remember he was tall and

slender. His clothes looked expensive."

"How tall?"

"Tall, like over six feet."

That eliminated George Manuel, who had been eye level with Sam. "What did Jeff do after the guy left?"

"He went into the lap dance room."

"What time was this?"

"It was probably around 10:30 or 11:00."

"Did you see Jeff leave?"

Alison shook her head, twisting her hair. "Do you think this guy killed Jeff?"

Sam gave a noncommittal shrug. "What did Money have to say?"

"About what?"

"About the argument."

Alison put her hands up, as if to ward off any more questions. "Look, I don't really want to get involved in this."

"I have no intention of involving you," Sam assured her. "Nobody, including the police, can make me reveal your identity. This stays between us, and you're being more helpful than you know. So, please...did you talk to Money about what happened?"

"When Money came to the bar for a drink I told her I had seen that guy getting all over Jeff and asked if everything was okay," Alison recounted reluctantly. "She said they were fighting over money and laughed, as if it was some big joke. She said the guy who left was jealous because Jeff was coming into a lot of cash, and when it happened, they were going to go away together."

Sam wondered just how many people Rydell borrowed money from. "What time did you have this exchange with Money?"

"It had to be before midnight because Lavender had just gone on."

"Lavender's another dancer?"

Alison nodded. "She's real popular and makes a mint in tips. Lavender and Money don't get along. When Jeff first started coming to the club, he was really into Lavender, buying her drinks and some table dances."

"The dancers are allowed to drink while working?"

"Most of the time we just pour them a plain soft drink, but the guy still pays full price," she explained. "But if a dancer says to 'make it strong' that lets the bartenders know they really do want alcohol in it. The club doesn't mind as long as they don't drink too much."

"I imagine falling off the table wouldn't be good for business," Sam joked, trying to ease Alison's discomfort. "So Jeff spent a lot of time with Lavender?"

"At first but then he started paying total attention to Money. It's funny, though; he never bought Money drinks. And I never saw him take a lap dance with her. The few times I had to go back there, he'd be standing off to the side. But some guys get off by watching, you know?"

"What's Lavender's real name?"

"I don't know. She stays to herself. On stage she's all energy and is really outgoing with the customers but off, she's a totally different person. Kind of weird to turn it on and off like that."

"How long have Money and Lavender been working at the Crazy Girl?"

"Lavender's been there a couple of years from what I hear. Money's the new girl. She's only been dancing for the last four or five months. That's another reason she's popular; she's something new for the guys to watch, plus she can get *really* wild. I hear they line up ten deep for her lap dances. The dances are done at private booths and it's real dark in there. But you can still tell what's going on, and believe me, she's doing a lot more than just dancing. She's totally full contact. She supposedly goes through a box of condoms a night."

"Nobody worries about losing their liquor license over dancers turning tricks in the club?"

Alison snorted, "Like any of the guys are going to complain to the manger? And as long as they're spending hundreds of dollars a night, the owners are happy to look the other way."

Sam put the picture in her notebook and stood. "I better get going. I really do appreciate your help. I'll let you know what happens."

Alison walked her to the door. "You're not going to tell Money I talked to you are, you?"

"I don't plan on it. Why?"

"You don't know her. She's crazy. If you come in, just pretend you don't know me, okay?"

Sam finally understood. It wasn't the cops Alison was afraid of. It was Money.

CHAPTER SEVEN

It was after 5:00 when Sam sat down at her desk, but the newsroom was still busy with layout people working on the upcoming issue. Her eyes felt gritty, so she tossed her old lenses and put in a fresh pair. As she blinked to settle the lenses in place, Steve Leon sauntered over.

"So how's it going, kiddo?"

"Just fine," Sam glanced up briefly but avoided eye contact, not wanting to invite conversation.

Steve was a one-time *Philadelphia Inquirer* columnist who settled in the desert after an escalating drinking problem and a run-in with an underage female source caused him to take an abrupt hiatus from big city journalism. The incident had not left a lasting ethical impression. He'd been caught at the *Weekender* going through notebooks left unattended, so his efforts to insinuate himself in the Rydell story made Sam even more territorial than usual.

"How's that murder story coming along? I have a couple of cop buddies I could call."

"Thanks for the offer, but I'm okay." She stood up. "I've got to go talk to Marlene before she leaves."

Steve blocked her way. "I worked the police beat here for a long time and know a lot more people than you do. It's not like LA. You need to work it from the inside. Some slick spiel won't cut it down here."

Sam put her backpack in the bottom desk drawer and locked it before answering. There was a time, in the not too distant past, when she would have responded to such patronization with a road-rage level of anger. But getting upset took too much energy, was too indulgent, and wasn't nearly as satisfying as cutting people off at their knees.

"I don't use a spiel," she responded calmly, stepping around him. "I find reporting much more efficient. You should try it some time."

Sam went into Marlene's office and sat on the window ledge by the corner of her desk. "You never told me Steve used to work crime here. When did he stop?"

"What difference does it make?"

"None, if he stopped a year or two ago."

Marlene got up and shut her office door. She walked back and leaned against the front of her desk, speaking quietly. "Mind you, the paper didn't cover that much crime when I got here because they were a much softer publication. And there wasn't the gang crime like we now have in some parts of the Valley. But the old man's sons who hired me want to make the paper a contender, God help us. I decided we could *may*be get noticed if we took an in-depth look at crime in the Valley, if we made that our specialty, and I originally gave Steve that plum."

Marlene looked out the window, "He was all right, but what he wrote just didn't…*grab* me," then brought her gaze back to Sam. "That's because he's lazy and wants to phone it in. He wasn't giving me what I wanted, and I was trying to figure out where to go from there when you called, said you were moving, and here we are."

"Except he thinks he got shoved aside to make room for me."

"He *was* shoved aside," Marlene conceded, "but that was going to happen regardless. Look, even if I hadn't already decided he was better suited covering the Shriners' convention, am I going to have you doing sports? Please. I know you said you needed a break from the blood and guts, which is why I figured I'd give you enough time to get settled in, chase away a few demons, and then get you back doing some serious work. I mean, how many old folks' bingo scandals can you really stomach?"

Sam looked at the carpet. "Yeah, well, you've got a point there."

"Don't let Steve's sour grapes get to you. You haven't cost him anything. He's done it all by himself." She walked around her desk and eased back into her chair. "So, where are we?"

Sam updated Marlene. "The obvious scenarios would be: a drug deal gone bad, he welched on loans, or he just got rolled. My biggest issue at the moment is finding some background on Rydell. I finally have some promising leads thanks to Alison. I'll also check with the police to see if they've found any relatives."

Marlene stood and stretched, "Sounds good. Just put together whatever you have on Thursday then keep working on it for a follow-up story if you think there's enough to warrant it."

The office had thinned considerably by the time Sam walked back to her desk and called home.

"Ms. Perry's residence."

"You really haven't been answering the phone like that, have you?"

"Of course not…because nobody else has called. Don't you know *anybody* here?"

"Not really."

"And to think, I knew you when you were popular—way, *way* back when. So, did you do anything fun today?"

"You have no idea. I'll tell you all about it over dinner. But I've got some stuff to do here first. Is an hour okay?"

"An hour? I better start getting ready. Oh Scarlet, whatever shall I wear?"

"If you dare touch the curtains, I'll kill you."

"Even I'd be hard-pressed to make anything fashionable out of vertical blinds."

Sam hung up smiling. She actually hadn't realized how much she missed having company until he showed up. Maybe Joe was right; maybe she was getting too used to being alone.

"So, on that cheery note…" Sam logged on to her computer and opened Nate's email that simply said, *4 Rosman Road, Cattle Hill.* Nate never sent more information than necessary.

She called Veronica Flowers, who ran another investigative service—Sam liked spreading the work around. Veronica's voicemail picked up, saying she was gone for the day but to please leave a detailed message.

"Hi Veronica, it's Sam Perry. Could you please get me a current phone number and listing for 4 Rosman Road, Cattle Hill, Tennessee? And while you're at it, could you get me the phone numbers of the nearest neighbors? Thanks."

Sam could have looked in a cross directory herself, but that would exclude any unlisted numbers, and she was pressed for time. Sam couldn't remember it ever taking so long to track down next of kin.

She retrieved a new memory key from her bag and wrote EK on the outside of it. She plugged it in and downloaded Ellen's vital statistics from IMDb.com onto it. Next, she connected an external hard drive to her computer that contained California's voter registration list. A contact she made while doing a series of articles on voter fraud several years earlier sent her an updated list every January. And every January Sam treated the source to a night out at Matsuhisa, LA's top sushi restaurant. It was $300 well spent because the list gave Sam a quick and easy way to locate current home addresses, privacy laws be damned.

She picked up the phone and called Nate, waiting for the message machine to pick up. "I'm going to send you some names via email. I need all past known addresses for them, plus any vital stats you can come up with."

She located Phil Atkins' listing and copied down his address. Then she did a search for Lena Riley. She was surprised to see it was Ellen's home address. *A live-in personal assistant?* "That's so Hollywood."

She referred back to the IMDb page and typed in her last entry: William and June Konrad. Indio. Deceased.

Sam wasn't sure why she was spending her time, or the paper's money, on digging into Ellen's background, but something she said nagged at her.

Maybe I saw some of myself in him, someone trying to rise above the cards they were dealt in life.

Sam's gut told her that wasn't an idle comment although she had no clue what its significance could be. She talked to Joe about it over their first cocktail in the bar of a steak house called St. James Club. Between them was a large plate of calamari. "Somewhere there's a thread," Sam said. "Ellen was originally from Indio. Jeff spent a lot of time at the Crazy Girl in Indio. Maybe she used to work as an exotic dancer as a young girl, he found out, was blackmailing her—"

"And in her Armani sweat suit Ellen Konrad ran through the desert after him with a butcher knife?" Joe asked skeptically.

"Okay, that does sound like a scene out of a bad Faye Dunaway film."

"Or a good one, depending on how you look at it."

"True," Sam laughed. "Besides, I confirmed she was in Los Angeles."

"She could have hired someone," he suggested.

"I suppose," she conceded, not remotely believing it. "Or I *could* see Phil Atkins getting violent. Jeff told more than one person he was about to score big money. To me, that means either drugs or blackmail or some other illegal enterprise. People like Jeff Rydell don't have that many legal moneymaking options, especially when their primary social haunt is an exotic dance bar."

"So, follow the money."

Sam nodded. Murder usually came down to a few simple human basics: love, money, sex, control. In this case she suspected it was a combination of all the above. "Money does seem to be at the heart of it. He was arguing with someone about money the night he was killed. He owed George Manuel money. He was allegedly coming into money. But of more immediate concern to the story due Thursday is simply finding out who this guy was. I suspect once I know that and what brought him here, it might be easier to figure out why he ended up on the wrong end of a boulder."

"Maybe he was just trying to start a new life and went about it the wrong way," Joe observed.

"Maybe."

"By the way, how'd you like the dog's bows?"

Sam frowned. "It was a little hard to tell since they refused to come out from under the bed."

Joe swirled the ice in his empty drink "So, your tawdry tale from today got me thinking: why don't we go to the Crazy Girl tonight? It sounds like a hoot."

"Speaking of gender preferences that aren't you," Sam pointed out.

"I wasn't speaking of the titillation factor—it's so fun using that word when talking about a girlie bar—but maybe you'll find out something interesting. Or at least check out the nighttime crowd. I can be your escort. Besides, I just love stiletto heels."

"That's because you don't have to walk in them."

Joe speared some calamari with his fork. "Says who?"

The more Sam thought about it, the more she warmed to the idea of checking the club out and getting a look at Money. Going during the day was one thing, but even she would be hesitant to go there by herself at night so Joe's offer was a good opportunity to do some more digging.

"Okay, let's do it. But I still need to stop by Rose's before we go out there."

The drinks and calamari filled them up, so they skipped ordering dinner. While Joe paid the bill, Sam took out her cell phone and called Rose again. And again there was no answer.

"Where the hell is she?" Sam stared at her cell phone with a worried look. "She said she'd be home."

"It's only eight o'clock," Joe said, joining her. "You know, *some* people actually have social lives."

They walked out of the restaurant into a swirl of warm air, the breeze picking up as the desert floor slowly cooled. White spotlights attached to the palm trees lining the sidewalks illuminated the fronds and gave the street a festive appearance. As they crossed the street Sam glanced up at some light pole banners promoting voter registration. Since Ellen was an overwhelming favorite among the under-forty crowd, Sam assumed Konrad's campaign was behind the push to recruit younger voters. She wondered how receptive Ellen would really be if she had the nerve to call her just to talk.

Some of the retail shops and art galleries they passed were closed for August, but all the gift shops were open for business. Joe amused himself by walking through the aisles looking at kitschy souvenirs.

Sam led Joe to a display of snow globes and pointed to one depicting a desert diorama populated by a cowering tortoise and scraggly coyote. When shook it turned into a blur of beige. "This one's a sandstorm. Gets you all warm and fuzzy, doesn't it?"

Joe's bark of laughter sounded loud in the hushed shop. "This is just too much," he said, enthralled. "I have to have it. And they say California has no true culture."

* * *

Back outside, Joe looked at his watch. "Since we're waiting on Rose why don't we go have another drink?" Joe suggested. "The cabbie today pointed out a place I want to try."

"What place?"

"It's over this way. Just come on."

They cut over to Indian Drive and he led Sam to Arenas Road, home to more than a half-dozen gay bars and restaurants.

The bar was called Rafters and was the size of a warehouse. On the right were several pool tables. Two fortysomething women dressed almost identically in white polo shirts tucked into tan shorts played at one table, two young Latino men at the other.

Directly in front of the entrance was a large rectangular bar. Most of the stools were filled—all with men—and the murmur of friendly conversations and laughter mingled with music videos playing on flat-screens positioned throughout the bar. The back wall was lined with an assortment of pinball machines and video games, mostly classics like Space Invaders and Centipede.

Joe motioned Sam to follow him. "Let's go in there."

To the far left was another room connected by a revolving door. Above the entry a neon sign read: *The G* Spot.*

Sam slowed down. "Joseph Sapone…what are you up to?"

He turned around laughing. "Get over yourself. We're only going to have a drink."

"The cabbie told you about this?"

"Or maybe I found it on lesbian.com. Just come on."

He pushed her through the revolving door and they emerged into a completely different atmosphere. The room was half the size of the video bar, with low lighting and the scent of candles in the air. The bar and liquor shelves behind it were bathed in a soft red accent light. There were no stools at the counter. Instead, low cocktail tables with cushioned chairs were scattered throughout the rest of the room where a couple dozen women sat in pairs or small groups.

Tucked in the back corners to the right and left of the entrance were plush couches behind sheer, red netting hung from the ceiling. The draping created an illusion of privacy, even if there was none in reality. Sam watched two women kissing lazily on one of the couches.

"This isn't so bad, is it?" Joe asked, breaking her reverie.

"It's very nice," Sam agreed.

"I have to go to the bathroom. Why don't you get us a drink?"

Sam made her way to the bar aware of interested glances as she walked past, aware the attention was not unpleasant. The bartender was a very attractive woman in her twenties wearing a black T-shirt with *G* Spot* embossed in red on the front.

"Can I help you?" She had the smiling demeanor and the physique of a college cheerleader. Sam half-expected her to do a cartwheel in greeting.

"A Jack and Diet and a vodka tonic."

She scooped ice into two glasses. "I haven't seen you in here before. Are you visiting?"

"No, I live here. A friend suggested we stop in."

"What's your name?"

"Samantha, but people call me Sam."

"Hi. I'm Jennifer. I like it when we get new faces." She reached under the counter and came up with a flyer. "Here's our schedule. We have something different going on every night. Our Sunday barbecue is really popular. It's packed because we do bingo afterwards."

Sam looked around. "A little dark for bingo."

"We hold it on the outside patio," Jennifer gestured toward a door in the back corner. Next to it was a red neon *dance floor upstairs* sign pointing towards some stairs. The place was deceptively big.

Sam looked over the schedule while Jennifer poured the drinks. The bar catered to a wide range of tastes: salsa dancing, pool tournaments, a movie night.

Jennifer put the drinks on the counter. "Karaoke's another popular night."

"Dear God," Sam folded the flyer and put it in the back pocket of her jeans. "What is it with drunk people and singing?"

Jennifer reached under the bar counter again and this time held up ear plugs. "And it's always the ones who shouldn't, isn't it?"

Sam laughed and handed her a $20, telling her to keep the change as a tip. She watched Jennifer walk to the cash register, wondering if she was gay or worked in a lesbian bar because it was preferable to Hooters. She didn't strike her as gay, but then again, what the hell did gay look like anyway?

Sam studied her reflection in the bar mirror. Her 33-year-old body was lean and strong from years of going to the gym. While not busty, she was far from flat-chested. She stared at the face she'd been told many times was pretty although she had her doubts.

Perhaps because you're always scowling when you look in the mirror.

Sam wondered if people assumed she was gay because she didn't wear make-up and preferred shorts and jeans to skirts and dresses or if it was something more innate. When Joe came back they found a table and she asked him the same question.

"There are many worse things than people thinking you're gay."

"Obviously," she agreed, "like people thinking I'm Republican. I'm not saying it was a bad thing; I just wondered what makes someone look gay."

"I've told you; it has less to do with your lack of make-up as it does your lack of hormonal-driven interest in men. Tonight at the restaurant our waiter was doing his best to flirt, and you were completely oblivious."

"He was?"

"Thank you for proving my point *so* succinctly."

"You know I've never been good at that kind of thing. I'm not wired that way. I don't know how to flirt."

"Oh, please," Joe chided, "You flirt."

"I don't."

"You might not bat your eyes or flip your hair, but you flirt. Your way of flirting is through humor. You can actually be quite charming when you want to be."

Sam rolled her eyes.

"I saw you talking to the bartender over there."

"So?"

"When was the last time you made small talk like that?"

"Yesterday with Ellen."

"Interviews don't count."

Was that all it had been, Sam wondered, *just an interview?* The thought depressed her. "Your point being?"

"Maybe the reason you can't find someone you connect with emotionally is that you're looking in the wrong places. Or in your case, not making yourself available in the right places. Don't be so stubborn; you know you're interested."

She scanned the room with a reporter's eye, taking in details and atmosphere. There was no particular type in the room. The women varied in age, race, and size but most were feminine and traditionally attractive.

While Sam enjoyed people watching and felt a certain thrill being among women who loved women, she was still preoccupied by her visceral reaction to Ellen. And it wasn't just her physical beauty; it was the tantalizing glimpse she had seen of the person inside. But she wasn't about to admit any of this to Joe. He would think she had lost her mind finding a straight woman to pine after, especially one so clearly unattainable.

"I hear you, Joe. I'll eventually figure it out. Or not."

"Okay, enough about you."

"Thank you."

He laughed and moved his chair closer. "I'm thinking of moving to California."

"You mean opening a boutique out here?"

"No, actually relocating. That's another reason for this trip. I'll also be spending some time in Los Angeles before going back to Chicago."

Sam was stunned. First, because he was only mentioning this now three days into his trip, but mostly because she knew how much Joe loved Chicago.

"Part of it is simply business," Joe explained, reading Sam's mind. "But part is personal. I've met someone who lives out here, has very close family ties out here, and I would rather be in California with him than in Chicago without him. There are just a few things to work out first."

"Joe, I'm really glad for you," Sam said, meaning it. At the same time she felt excluded that he was in such a serious relationship she knew nothing about. "So what's his name? What does he do? How did you meet? You know I need all the particulars."

Joe shook his head, "Not yet, Sam. I want you to meet him first. But his name is Kevin, and we met when he was in Chicago on extended business."

"So how come you're down here staying with me instead of with Kevin in Los Angeles?"

"He's away on business right now, but you'll be meeting him sooner rather than later. Just be patient for once."

"Have you met me?" Sam muttered.

They finished their drinks and decided to head back to the St. James Club where the car was parked. They crossed at Indian and passed by Konrad's campaign headquarters. Sam stopped when she saw it was still open. "Let's go inside a minute."

The front was deserted, but the office door in back was ajar, and the light was on. Sam heard the faint sound of a toilet flushing. Soon after a young woman flipped off the light and closed the door. She looked up and jumped when she saw Sam and Joe, uttering a breathless, "Oh, God!"

"I am so sorry if we scared you," Sam apologized, recognizing her as the same girl she spoke to on Sunday. Once again, she was wearing baggy clothes and hiking boots.

"I thought everyone had gone," the girl said quietly, regaining her composure. "Is there something I can help you with?" she asked, walking quickly to her cubicle.

"I was here on Sunday—"

"I remember you," she said, gathering papers into a haphazard pile. She kept her head down, avoiding eye contact.

Sam walked over and extended her hand, forcing the girl to look up. "I don't think I ever introduced myself. I'm Sam Perry."

The girl hesitated then shook Sam's hand. "My name's Annie."

"Hi Annie. This is my friend Joe."

The girl nodded in his direction.

"How did you get stuck having to be the last one here?" Sam asked.

"I always close up."

"How long have you worked for the campaign?"

"Since the beginning."

"How's it been going?"

"Fine." Annie closed her black and gray leather messenger bag and slipped it over her head. She grabbed the handlebars of the bike propped up against the wall and started walking to the door. "I don't mean to be rude but I really need to go."

"I'm sorry. We didn't mean to hold you up. Thanks for your time."

Sam and Joe walked out and turned towards Palm Canyon. At the light, Sam looked back and saw Annie riding her bike down the sidewalk toward Indian Drive. She made a right when she got to the corner and disappeared.

"Strange girl," Sam said. "And people say I underdress."

"You do. And while that girl might look like a shlub, her clothes aren't. Those were $400 boots she was wearing, the pants were Lacoste, the mountain bike is worth at least $3,000, and that leather bag is $200. She might not have style, but she's got good taste. Well, expensive taste, anyway."

"She's probably some trust fund baby working for a cause."

Sam's cell phone vibrated. She pulled it out of her jeans pocket and answered.

"I'm so sorry," Rose sounded contrite.

"That's okay. I was just getting worried."

"Oh, I'm fine. I made plans to go play Bingo, and it completely slipped my mind when I talked to you earlier."

"Is it still okay if we stop by? We could be there in no more than fifteen minutes."

"Of course, dear. I'll be up watching my programs."

"So where was she?" Joe asked when Sam hung up.

"Bingo. Hey, did I tell you about the story I did on weighted bingo balls…?"

* * *

When they got into the car, Joe laid his head back and rubbed his temples. "Who knew there was so much to know about bingo balls and that anybody would *ever* want to share that information in such painful detail."

"Did I tell you I also did a follow-up story?" She started the car and smiled as Joe moaned and put his hands over his ears. Her phone rang again. "It's probably Rose wanting to know if she should whip you up a batch of cookies."

"All things considered, I'd rather she whip me up a Valium with a double martini chaser."

Sam answered laughing, "Hello?"

After a brief pause she heard Ellen's amused voice. "Are you always so happy to get a phone call?"

Sam's stomach did a mild flip, and she smiled in surprise. "Says something really tragic and telling about my social life, doesn't it?"

"Maybe I can help with that."

"Well now, you really are looking to be the full service mayor, aren't you?"

Ellen laughed softly, her voice playfully seductive. "Depends what kind of servicing you have in mind."

Sam let the clutch out too fast, and her car stalled with a screech. She dropped her forehead against the steering wheel with a self-conscious laugh. "Do you always try to intentionally fluster people over the phone?"

"No, but in your case I'm making an entertaining exception," Ellen admitted cheerily. "Is it working?"

"Well, let's see…my ears are embarrassingly hot and my clutch is nearly stripped. You be the judge."

"You really are easy, aren't you?"

"And apparently getting easier by the minute," she sighed, restarting the car.

By now, Joe was sitting sideways in his seat openly eavesdropping.

"I hope I didn't interrupt anything."

"Not at all. I just finished telling my friend Joe here, who's visiting from Chicago, about my *Weekender* investigation of the weighted bingo balls scandal, so he for one is actually quite grateful you called."

"Lord, I can certainly see why." Sam heard the *ting* of crystal, the creak of a door hinge, and a muted *pop*. "I don't know how much it'll help your social life, but I'd like to invite you to a cocktail party I'm throwing tomorrow evening."

"Absolutely," Sam said, outrageously pleased. "So you're getting an early start now with a glass of Pinot Grigio while hiding out in your office claiming to be on a business call?"

There was a moment of silence. "Do you always show off your observational prowess over the phone?"

"No, but in your case I'm making an entertaining exception."

"Touché," Ellen chuckled. "I better learn to be careful around you, huh?"

"Don't worry. I'm harmless."

"Oh, I certainly hope not." Her voice held a smile and a challenge.

Not knowing how to respond, Sam changed the subject. "So what's the cocktail occasion?"

"I'm hosting a get-together here at the house for supporters and others we want to endorse the campaign. I bet your bingo ball stories will be a big hit among some of the older constituents we're courting."

"That's it, pimp me to the AARP crowd."

"They always say politics makes for strange bedfellows."

"Thanks so much for *that* visual."

Ellen laughed again. "So you'll definitely come?"

"Wouldn't miss it."

"Good. It starts at 6:00. And please bring your friend."

"Really? That's very kind and hospitable of you. I'm sure he'd love it."

Joe perked up. "A cocktail party? Now I really do have to go shopping tomorrow."

"Tell him it's California casual; there's no need to be formal."

"No, you don't understand. Joe lives to accessorize. That's the difference between us: he looks forward to being fashionable, and I simply look forward to an open bar."

"And I look forward to your company. Come find me when you get here, okay?"

"I will. Goodnight."

"Goodnight, Sam. Sweet dreams."

Sam smiled. *If Ellen only knew the half of it.* She hung up and saw Joe grinning at her. "What?"

"I just enjoy watching you flirt."

"What's with you and the flirting? I wasn't flirting."

"You most certainly were. Sounded like you were both flirting."

"That wasn't flirting. It was...friendly banter."

"Whatever it was, it becomes you."

"Oh, please."

"All I'm saying is you need more friends here. Even one friend would be a start. It sounds like you and Ellen have a rapport, so you should be open to a friendship there."

"I am," Sam said, "but it's hard to imagine it will happen."

"Why not?"

"For a lot of reasons."

"Because she's famous?"

"That's one."

"Because you don't run in the same social circles?"

"That's another."

"Because you're attracted to her and it scares you?"

Sam was quiet for several moments. "It doesn't scare me, and it wouldn't get in the way. I wouldn't let it. But what does scare me is that I'm working on a story that for all I know might involve her. I need to stay objective."

"I understand that, but how many people in the world do any of us find really appealing and interesting? So when we come across someone who grabs our attention, we should give it a chance."

Sam knew there was a fundamental truth in what Joe was saying. She also knew it was rare for Joe to be openly philosophical. "Please tell me you're not dying or something."

He smiled. "No, I am disease—and parasite—free."

"More imagery I could have lived without," Sam sighed, pulling up to Rose's apartment building.

Joe reached in back for her bag. "I'm not lecturing, Sam. I'm just saying don't forget to actually join in life and not just report on what others are doing in theirs."

Sam turned off the car unsure how to respond, so she just said, "Point taken."

CHAPTER EIGHT

Rose answered as soon as Sam knocked and hurried them in, grabbing their sleeves and pulling them through the door. "I don't want the cool air to get out." The ancient window air conditioner rattled as if on life support but still managed to spew out enough cool air to keep the living room comfortable.

On the coffee table were two large manila envelopes and a tray holding a pitcher of lemonade and two ice-filled glasses. "Rose, thank you so much." Joe went over and gave her a hug.

This is why he made a mint as a salesman, Sam thought. He can turn it on like a faucet.

Joe filled both glasses with lemonade while Sam opened the first envelope. She dumped a pile of receipts onto the table, quickly sorting them into three stacks: credit card receipts, cash receipts, and miscellaneous. They told a mostly mundane story—grocery store, gas, *lots* of fast food, a drug store, office supplies, a few movie stubs—except for one.

"Look at this." Sam held it out.

Joe leaned closer to read it, "The Spy Shop." It was dated May 31 of that year. "Isn't that like an electronic toy store for adults?"

"Yes and no. It started as a novelty store, and I'm sure a lot of people still go there to buy stuff for fun. But I know a lot of reporters who won't leave home anymore without their tie clip video cameras. They also sell nanny-cams and other surveillance devices."

"Security is a great business," Joe agreed, sitting back. "What did he buy?"

"I have no idea. These model numbers on the receipt mean nothing to me. But I suspect the one for $500 was more than a novelty. He spent almost $700 altogether. That's a lot of money for someone who was doing odds jobs here and there to get by. Unless he was buying it for someone else."

There were only a handful of credit card receipts, most from restaurants and grocery stores. There were also several cash advance slips from ATMs using the same Chase account. While the purchases were unremarkable the name on the card left Sam shaking her head—Jeff Rydell. "This makes no sense. Rydell didn't *have* a credit card so how could this be in his name? And these go back to April."

"How do you know he didn't have a credit card?"

"I. Just. Do." She shot Joe a *not in front of Rose* glance, and he obediently let it drop.

Sam stacked the piles and put everything back in the first envelope. The second envelope contained a potpourri of apparently unrelated items. There was a dog-eared local map, some fast-food coupons, two postcards showing vistas of Palm Springs, several empty letter size envelopes, some newspaper clippings, a promotional flyer for discount computer programs that had the bottom torn off, a copy of the photo in his bedroom of he and Ellen, a candid snapshot of some houses, and a folded piece of paper that Sam picked up and opened.

"It's a letter." She smoothed it out on the coffee table then read it out loud.

> *My J –*
>
> *I was so happy to hear the sound of your voice last night. I've missed you so much. It seems like forever. Waiting has been a terribly hard cross but I never stopped believing you would come back to me. I understand why you had to see it through for yourself and for us. I know it's been hard on you, too. Know you are righteous. They brought ruin unto themselves. You deserve all the bounty that is coming to you. I'm counting the hours until we can begin the rest of our lives together as one. One heart. One soul. Remembering how your naked body feels against mine is making me want you so bad. I can't wait until next Sunday. - Your L*

"So who's L?" Joe asked.

Sam reread the letter silently then sat back. "Take your pick: Lavender? *Lena*? Hell, it could even be phonetic for *El* as in Ellen or someone we don't even know."

"Lavender?" Joe interrupted.

"She's a dancer at the Crazy Girl. That's her professional name."

"And from the sounds of it, she probably *is* a pro. By the way, don't be so closed-minded. Who says L doesn't stand for Larry or Lance?"

"Or Lucas. That's the name of Ellen's son. But to be honest, this doesn't sound like a guy—gay, straight, or otherwise." Sam sat tapping her glass of lemonade with her finger. "Judging from the postmark, the Sunday she's referring to is the day they found Jeff."

Rose suddenly looked worried. "Do you think the murderer wrote the letter?"

Sam thought it doubtful. "The person would've had a rather dramatic change of heart. That's certainly happened before, but I'm not sensing that's the case here." She picked up the letter. "*They brought ruin unto themselves*. That wording seems very…"

"Biblical?"

"*Fundamental* is more what I'm thinking. Although the bit about Jeff's naked body does seem a bit naughty for the religiously conservative crowd." Sam set the letter on the coffee table. "The overall phrasing doesn't sound like the writer is from this area."

"You don't think the murderer is going to come looking for that letter, do you?" Rose asked.

"Rose, I truly don't think this letter was written by the murderer," Sam assured her. "And I certainly don't think you are in any danger. Besides, I'm going to take the letter so if anyone wants it, they have to come looking for me, okay?"

Sam checked her watch then stuffed everything back in the envelope. "You know, it's probably better if I organize all this at work. Besides, it's getting late."

"Oh, don't worry about that, dear. I never go to bed until after the news and my crossword." It sounded like Rose didn't want to be alone, but Sam didn't have time to babysit, which is why *she'd* never be salesperson of the year.

"Thanks, Rose, but Joe and I have a couple of other errands to run. Don't get up; we'll let ourselves out." Sam walked to the front door while Joe took the tray with the pitcher and their glasses into the kitchen. "By the way, did Jeff have a storage area here?"

"Not one of his own. We have a locked space out back on the side of the carport that anyone can use on a first come basis. They just have to get the key from me, and he never did. It's pretty full, anyway. Why?"

"No real reason. Just wondering." Sam opened the door as Joe walked back in the room. "Take care, Rose."

On their way down the creaking elevator, Sam took out the Spy Shop receipt and called the store's phone number.

"Spy Shop. This is Robert," he announced enthusiastically.

"Hi. How late are you open?"

"We're here until 10:00."

Sam got directions and hung up. It was a little after 9:30. "It's not too far from here. Do you mind if we stop by on the way to the Crazy Girl? I'm curious to see if we can find out what Rydell bought."

The street outside the apartment was deserted and creepy. Joe looked around. "Don't you wonder why someone would have picked to live here? There has to be other places just as inexpensive that aren't so bleak."

Sam started the car. "I wonder where he lived before moving to this apartment. According to Ellen, Jeff started working for the campaign around February, not long after she announced her candidacy. But Rose says he didn't rent here until April. I suspect he didn't show up in town with much cash, so maybe he lived in one of those rent by the week places."

"How can you find out?"

"Good question." She put the top down then made a U-turn. "The man had to talk to *somebody*. I just need to find them."

Driving down Highway 111, the dark desert sky seemed enormous. In Los Angeles, the city lights blocked out all but the brightest constellations and planets, but here the night sky was ablaze with a blinking array of stars. It never failed to make Sam feel cosmically insignificant.

Joe twisted in his seat to face Sam. "Why did you ask if there was a storage unit at Rose's?"

Sam turned down the radio. "Almost everybody has keepsakes and mementoes that are important to them: pictures, books, letters, diaries, a bible, porno, or whatever. Jeff Rydell came to Palm Springs from somewhere else by himself, and yet in his apartment there was nothing personal, except a generic photo of him and Ellen in front of an *Elect Konrad* backdrop and the letter from L. There was no reminder of any past life or times, and I think that's unusual."

"Maybe he wanted to forget his past."

"Maybe," she agreed. "But there is a difference between putting your past behind you and running away from it. A lot of people achieve the former but not many succeed in the latter. I'm thinking he kept stuff in his car. I suspect the only reason the letter was still in his apartment was because he wanted it nearby so he could reread it and feel close to whoever L is."

The Spy Shop was located in a mall on the far side of Rancho Mirage. Sam pulled into the shopping center lot at 9:45 and found a parking space directly in front of the store. The Spy Shop's display windows were papered in black and decorated with painted eyes peeking through Paul Bunyan-sized keyholes. Once inside you were transported into a digital wonderland. The interior design was black chrome and neon. Along each wall were monitors transmitting images from various hidden cameras in the store.

Sam went to find a salesman while Joe entertained himself at a night vision goggle display. She waited at the counter until a young man with multiple body piercings walked up. "Hi, my name is Jason," his pierced tongue visible when he talked. "Can I help you find something?"

"I'm hoping so." Sam pulled out the receipt, wondering how Jason ate with the rings looped through his lip. "I have this invoice, but it only has model numbers on it. I need to know for my business records what exactly was bought. Could you look these up for me?"

"Sure," Jason took the receipt and studied it. He had a diamond stud in his nose, a bar through his eyebrow, and when he pushed the hair back from his face, Sam could see he had several gold studs forming an arc along his left earlobe.

He looked up the model numbers on the computer then handed back the receipt. "Would you like me to show you what the items were?"

"That'd be great." Sam followed him to a large display of spy cameras. They came in all sorts of creative shapes and sizes. Sam picked up a baseball cap camera that attached to a micro recorder, which could be worn in a pouch around the waist, all for just $513. Jason stopped in front of a glass case that held an array of sunglasses, pocket protectors, and pens.

"This is our wireless selection. The more powerful ones can transmit up to a mile away, depending on building interference."

"So what was bought?"

Jason picked up a pen designed to resemble a Mont Blanc. "This is our top-of-the-line pen spy cam. It has a wireless receiver and can be connected to a monitor and recorder."

"So this receipt is for the pen spy cam and wireless unit and a receiver?"

"That's right. They opted against the monitor, most likely because they used a laptop."

Suddenly, a little credit report or two didn't seem quite so invasive. Sam thanked him and went to get Joe. She found him in the disguises aisle. She heard him snickering as she walked up. He was standing in front of a board of fur patches.

She read the sign. "Fake chest hair?"

"I could put one of your dogs down my shirt and it would look more realistic."

On the other side of the aisle were wigs, and on the end was a black mullet, which Joe held up in two hands. "I thought the point of a disguise was to blend in so nobody would remember you."

"God, that looks just like the haircut my freshman gym teacher

Miss Winters had, remember?"

"How could I forget? It complimented her flannel shirts *so* beautifully."

Joe opened the store door and held it for Sam as they walked out. "So do you think Rydell was a jealous lover, a blackmailer, or just a perv?"

"Perv as in strategically leaving his pen in Ellen's bathroom?"

"Or on the floor beneath her desk, on her night stand, whatever. Except at these prices it would have hardly been a cheap thrill."

Sam seemed doubtful. "My impression is that Ellen would be sensitive to that kind of creep factor. So, no, I don't think he was trying to get crotch shots of her. But yeah I do think Jeff was spying on someone. Maybe for blackmail, maybe for some other reason."

"Maybe he was making secret recordings of girls he had over."

"It just seems like a lot of money when you could buy a $150 video camera and hide it behind a few books on the desk." Sam unlocked the car doors. "What I want to know is where did all this equipment go? His desktop did not have wireless, so I'm betting he had a laptop. But neither it nor the car has turned up, which leads me to believe whoever killed him took the car and dumped it somewhere. If they did and the equipment was in there, we may never know what he was up to."

There were just so many more questions and loose ends than answers. But Sam knew from experience the only thing to do was keep tracking down each lead and see where it led. And right now, it led back to Indio.

CHAPTER NINE

Although the streets around Crazy Girl seemed exponentially dodgier at night than during the day, the club itself looked almost festive with its garish neon sign and the white lights strung along the top of the front wall. Sam drove through the gate into the fenced-in parking area and looked for the closest spot to the entrance. There had to be at least one hundred cars in the lot, so she settled for a space next to the fence because it was slightly more illuminated from the street. She popped the trunk and retrieved a steering wheel lock. After securing it, she locked the console and glove box then grabbed her bag.

"Ready?"

Joe stared at her. "No barbed wire car cover?"

"I just don't know the neighborhood."

"You do realize you've always had an unhealthy attachment to your cars?" he asked as they walked in. Joe stopped and looked around the dilapidated foyer.

"It's really not as bad inside." Sam handed him a $20. "Here, I'll let you go pay the cover charge."

He took the money. "This is truly a first."

While he was at the cashier's booth, Sam wandered over to a bulletin board covered with notices. There were flyers urging people to fulfill their potential and earn $10,000 a month working from home, house cleaning ads, moving sale announcements, credit card applications, and rental listings. Except for the 800-numbers listed to call for penile enlargement and in-home "therapeutic" massage, it was pretty much the same stuff she saw posted on the bulletin board outside her local grocery store.

A flyer in the lower left hand corner caught her eye. It offered an array of high-end professional software for an on sale price of $150. Lesser titles were offered for $69 and under.

Sam remembered there had been a similar flyer among Rydell's papers. She opened her backpack and found it in the second envelope. They were identical except the bottom of Jeff's flyer with a phone number and instruction to "Ask for Argo" was torn off.

Joe walked up. "What are you looking at?"

Sam held up the flyer in her hand and pointed to the board. "That flyer is the same as this one that was in Jeff's stuff. Ellen told me Jeff had installed a bunch of programs on her computers at home, and I'm thinking this might be where he got them. Especially since Argo is the name of a bartender who works here. If he did business with this Argo and they knew each other from the club, then maybe Argo is someone who can tell me something about Rydell. It's certainly worth talking to him. Let's go see if he's here."

Sam put the flyer away and led Joe to the red velvet curtain. The doorman stamped the inside of their wrists with the initials *CG* and waved them through.

Joe looked around. "It looks like a lot of gay bars I've been to. Well, except for that," he gestured toward the stage.

A slender redhead with small breasts and deathly pale skin was joylessly grinding her hips to an old Donna Summer song. She would periodically touch herself with all the eroticism of a self-breast exam. Although a few men had dollar bills in their hands, the majority of those in the ringside seats looked indifferent. Sam didn't blame them; the young woman was either bored, drugged, jaded, or some combination of all three.

"She really needs a new choreographer," Joe observed.

He grabbed them two seats at the bar. They had a clear view of the stage but were far enough away from the speakers that they didn't have to yell too loudly to be heard. The song ended and there was a polite smattering of applause. The girl retrieved her few tips then disappeared behind the curtains. The stage lights went out, the DJ turned down the volume, and a Blake Shelton song came on.

Sam was waiting to order when a waitress walked up with a tray of empty glasses. September looked at her and smiled. "Hey! I recognize you. Did you ever find Kona?"

Kona? Sam's memory kicked in. "You mean Alison. Yes, I did. It all worked out. Thanks for your help."

"So you came back to see the show?"

Sam swiveled around so September could see Joe. "I have a friend in from Chicago, and he was curious to check it out. Joe, this is September."

"What a lovely name," he said.

"Oh, thanks. Well, you came at a good time. Our two most popular dancers are up next."

"Together?"

"I don't *think* so," September laughed and rolled her eyes. "No, Lavender is on next then Money performs after her. That's why the stage seats are already filled. The guys come early to get seats just to watch them. I hear Money's breaking in two new songs tonight so it should be pretty good."

Sam motioned toward the nearest bartender. "Alison told me to make sure to introduce myself to Argo. Is that him?"

"No, Argo only works weekends now 'cause he started some other job. Lucky him. Hey, can I get you guys a drink? The show is about to start."

"Yes, please." Sam ordered a Jack and Diet for herself and a vodka tonic for Joe.

"So that isn't Argo?" Joe asked.

"I'm afraid not. I'll call the number on the flyer tomorrow and see if he calls back. It's just easier to make someone talk face to face."

"Sure, because on the phone they can hang up when you badger them."

"I don't badger, exactly. I'm…persistent. But maybe I can still corral Lavender or Money. Speaking of which…"

The strobe lights made swirling patterns on the stage and Christina Aguilera's "Fighter" blared from the speakers. Lavender came through the curtains, and the crowd broke into cheers that were somehow louder than the music. Tall and pretty with short dark hair, she was dressed in purple silk boxers and matching robe with purple boxing gloves hung around her neck. She strutted down the runway in time to the music.

Some of the younger men in the audience danced along to the song, as did the bartender behind them, making the atmosphere more dance club than strip club. Joe leaned over again. "Do you suppose performers have any idea their songs are used for this? I think K-Tel should put out the Girlie Bar Collection."

Lavender pulled off the belt and put it around her neck, the robe falling open just enough to show flashes of cleavage. Unlike the sickly first dancer, Lavender radiated health. She looked to be in her early thirties, with clear eyes and a smooth complexion. Sam wondered what circumstances led her to work here.

The next song was an old disco classic, "Come to Me," by a one-hit wonder named France Joli. Joe sat forward on the stool. "I love this song."

Lavender showed off some obvious dance training, mixing spins, kicks, and jazz moves into her routine. Halfway into the song, she walked the perimeter of the stage, collecting money, occasionally exchanging a few words with the customers, and once good-naturedly wagging a finger at a man who tried to put his hand up inside her boxers.

When the music changed to the hard rocking beat of Def Leppard's "Pour Some Sugar on Me," Lavender ripped off the robe and threw it into the crowd. She had a slim body with slender hips, a lean torso, and surprisingly generous breasts. Sam glanced around. Some men watched with fascination, some with casual interest, and some stared with lust-hardened eyes.

During the chorus, the DJ turned up the volume and the crowd sang along with lusty fervor.

"Pour some sugar on me..."

Lavender shimmied out of the boxers revealing a purple thong. Pointing to a group of customers at the foot of the stage, she ran her other hand over the front of her thong slowly and suggestively to the lyrics—*I'm hot, sticky sweet; From my head to my feet*—then winked and walked away laughing.

Seductive, sexy, and in total control of herself and the crowd Lavender interacted with the customers, graciously fueling their fantasies. Sam noticed even Joe seemed mesmerized. There was so much money being shoved into her thong that she had to take some out to make room for more. The cheering continued long after the music stopped and only ended when Lavender disappeared behind the curtain.

"She was hot," Joe announced.

"She was fun to watch."

"Not your type?"

"I don't have a type."

Joe took a sip of his drink before answering. "Everyone has a type."

"Well then, I suppose breathing and ambulatory would be high on my list." She stood and stretched, ignoring his exasperated expression. "Watch my bag. I'm going to find a bathroom."

"Make sure to use the sanitary seat cover."

The restrooms were located through the lap dance room, so low lit it was positively murky. Sam looked around at all the activity. To the far left was a short bar. Along the wall in front of her was a row of high-backed booths. Apparently each was set up with its own directional speakers because the music volume changed as Sam walked past each table. The going rate was $25 for your basic table dance and $50 for a lap dance, but the price no doubt went up the more contact the dancer allowed. Sam wondered how much cash Money pulled in a night for her special "dance" moves.

Just beyond the backstage entrance was the women's restroom, which was surprisingly clean and smelled of pine. When she got out of the stall Sam was surprised to see Lavender standing at a sink trying to get a lash out of her eye. She still had on stage makeup and was wearing lace panties and a see-through purple lace camisole.

Sam hesitated then walked over to the sink next to Lavender's.

She made eye contact through the mirror as she turned on the water. "Hi."

Lavender nodded politely in response.

Sam dried her hands. "You're Lavender, right?"

She nodded again, her brown eyes suddenly wary.

"I promise I'm not a stalker. And I know this is an odd place to meet, but my name is Samantha Perry. I'm a reporter and was hoping you'd be willing to talk to me about a story I'm working on."

Lavender rubbed her eye and finally turned to face Sam directly, "A story about what?" Her tone was curious, not hostile.

"Jeff Rydell."

She looked surprised. "Why would you be doing a story on Jeff?"

"He was murdered over the weekend."

Lavender stood motionless for several moments then put her hand up to her mouth, leaned over the sink, and closed her eyes. Sam tensed, thinking she was going to be sick. When Lavender opened her eyes she stared into the mirror. Two large tears ran down her cheeks, streaking her face with mascara. Without looking at Sam, she asked quietly. "What happened?"

"He was found out along Highway 111. He was apparently killed by a blow to the head."

"Do they know who did it?"

"No. The police are still investigating. I understand you and he were friendly. I'd really appreciate it if you'd talk to me for just a few minutes."

Lavender turned the water on and washed off the mascara. She didn't say anything until she turned off the faucet. "Okay, but not here. I can meet you in about an hour. I'm supposed to mingle and do a couple table dances."

"You name the place because I'm not really familiar with this area."

"Consider yourself lucky." Lavender dried her face. "There's a local bar over by the freeway entrance called the Galaxy. It's quiet, and people leave you alone. I'll meet you there at 12:30."

"Thank you."

Lavender just nodded and walked out.

Joe's legs were draped over her stool when she walked up. "Do you know how hard it was keeping this seat for you? People were circling like sharks." He pulled the stool out for her. "I was getting worried maybe you got swept away by the atmosphere and decided to give lap dancing a try."

"Trust me, I'm not that limber."

When the lights in the main bar went out, a palpable energy radiated through the crowd. Sam picked up her drink and swung around to face the stage. "So let's see what all the buzz is about."

The spotlight was fixed at the center of the back curtain and the intro to some Beyoncé song blared from the speakers. Money pushed the curtains apart and exploded onto the stage. She was wearing a man-tailored red silk night shirt over a black strapless bustier with black garters, fishnets, thong, and five-inch stiletto heels.

The physical opposite of Lavender, Money was short—Sam estimated she was probably only 5'4" or so—and curvy. Her blonde hair was pulled back into an Evita Peron-style chignon, and her eye makeup was Cleopatra-esque. Walking down one side of the stage and up the other, Money reached out and touched the hands of the men reaching out for her. Some were already offering up bills in their fingers, which Money plucked and stuffed in her corset. She moved to the end of the stage dancing, arms undulating over her head.

Sam squinted, trying to see her more clearly. "Who does she remind me of?"

"Julie Newmar as Catwoman?"

Money sauntered back towards the curtain as the first song faded out, and the sultry, haunting melody of Fiona Apple's "Criminal" now pulsed through the club. Money shrugged off her night shirt, executed a slow pirouette, and then walked provocatively toward the pole.

Crazy eyes indeed, Sam thought, as Money leaned against the pole, sliding into a squat. Her figure was voluptuous, but her soft belly and rounded face betrayed her youth. Sam doubted she was much past legal age. Money gracefully rolled onto the floor and pulled herself along the stage to the delirious encouragement of the crowd. When she was almost close enough for them to touch her, she slid away, making them yell even louder. Unlike Lavender, who playfully teased the audience, Money's energy was more adversarial, as if they were an enemy to conquer.

September walked up to the service bar and motioned toward the stage. "That's one of her new songs. Pretty good, huh?"

"She's something," Sam said diplomatically.

The show Money put on with her last song, Nine inch Nail's "Closer," was a Freudian's field day. With her hair down, she was an erotic Sheena prowling the stage. She spun on the pole, rubbing her leg against it, inching further up her thigh with each turn. She pivoted and braced herself against the pole, legs spread in a wide stance. One hand caressed her breasts, the other slipped inside the thong. Her skin glowed with a light sheen of perspiration, and her breathing quickened. Oblivious of the crowd, eyes closed, she swung around and straddled the pole, hips moving with rhythmic urgency.

The sheer overt sexuality of her exhibitionism made it hard to watch but impossible not to. The song faded out, but Money kept going until she shuddered in release then slid to the floor with a deeply primal groan, her eyes glazed and oddly lifeless.

The lights went out, leaving the club in stunned blackness.

CHAPTER TEN

There was a brief moment of edgy silence as the audience collectively regrouped, followed by a cascade of wild cheers and stomping. When the lights came back on Money was gone, but appreciative patrons threw bills onto the stage. The men around the bar clapped in syncopated unison, calling for her to come back and get their tips. A few jokers called out for an encore. But the stage lights went off, and a big man in a Crazy Girls security T-shirt came out and picked up the cash littering the stage. A rumble of disappointed *boos* greeted him, but the DJ turned up the house music, making it clear the show was over.

Joe and Sam looked at each other. "Watching that together is the closest you and I will ever come to having sex," she decided.

"I feel like I should be having a cigarette." He took a long swallow of his drink. "You know I'm not a prude, and in fact if Kevin were here we'd probably be out in the car right now, but there was something disturbing about that."

Sam nodded. "She was completely detached from the experience. Of course, maybe that's to be expected when your partner is an aluminum pole."

"Whatever it was, she kind of scared me."

"Money seems to have that effect on people. I wonder if it's just part of her act or she really is nuts." Sam stood up. "I'll be right back. I'm going to see if I can find her."

"Just remember not to shake her hand. We *know* where it's been."

Sam made her way back through the lap dance room. Every table was in use, and several dozen men anxiously milled around the bar, apparently waiting for their turn. Money was obviously very good for business. The area had assumed a musky scent that Sam didn't want to spend too much time dwelling on. She walked to the backstage entrance and poked her head through the curtain, coming nose to nose with a surprised security guy.

Sam stepped through the curtain. "Hey, I was wondering if it would be possible to get back there and talk to Money for a moment. We have a mutual friend, and I just wanted to say hi."

He gave her a friendly smile. "Sorry, can't do."

"Well, can I just wait for her here?"

"Could, but you'd be waiting a while. Not that I'd mind the company," the smile getting friendlier and flirtier.

Sam was oblivious. "Thanks, but I have a friend waiting at the bar, and I've really got to be going. Any idea how long she'll be?"

The guard accepted the turndown graciously. "Actually, Money's already gone. Took off right after the show. Musta been in a hurry because she left just wearing her robe." He pointed a thumb towards the lap dance room. "Lotta those guys gonna be disappointed tonight."

* * *

Inside the Galaxy they found a cozy room with a friendly atmosphere. Jukebox music was playing, and most of the patrons were engaged in quiet conversation, with only a few curious glances cast their way. Lavender was sitting in the back corner booth, eating soup. She nodded at Sam and eyed Joe curiously as they approached.

"Hi Lavender. This is my friend Joe."

"Nice to meet you," Joe shook her hand then turned to Sam. "I'm going to go sit at the bar and give you two some privacy. Do you want me to have the waitress bring you something?"

"Sure, I'll have a Diet Coke. Can I get you anything?" Sam asked Lavender.

"No, I'm fine. If you're hungry they have a small menu. There's not much of a selection but what they have is usually good."

Sam slid into the booth. "Sorry we're a little late."

"That's okay. I figured you stayed to watch Money," Lavender said, biting into a cracker. With her face freshly washed and wearing a linen jacket over her camisole and jeans, Lavender was the picture of modesty. "What did she do to shock the patrons tonight?"

"Let's just say her last song built to a climax, and in some states she'd have to marry the pole now."

Lavender's eyes widened. "You're serious? That's kind of out there even for her. I don't think I could make myself get off on that stage if my life depended on it. Hell, it's hard enough when I'm by myself, if you know what I mean," she said with a wry, tired smile. "I usually fall asleep half way through."

Sam again wondered what circumstances had brought her to the Crazy Girl and a solitary midnight dinner. "How long have you worked at the club?"

"It'll be two years next January. Feels a lot longer, though."

"Do you mind if I ask how you ended up there?"

"I don't mind." Lavender tilted the bowl for the last spoonful of broth then took a sip of her red wine. She sat back and looked at Sam with a steady gaze. "My husband got busted trying to sell a truckload of pot to an undercover cop and got sentenced to three years in prison."

"He was a dealer?"

"No, he's a carpenter—and a really good one. But he got laid off his construction job when I was pregnant with our second kid and panicked."

Sam involuntarily glanced towards her slender hips. "You have two kids?"

"Both C-sections. The thong covers the scar."

"So he was gone when you gave birth?"

"Right. He's never been able to hold his son yet. So stupid," her voice was edged with frustration and anger. "I moved in with my mom, but that didn't work. An infant and a three-year-old were too much for her. I needed my own place and a reliable car, which meant I needed to make big money fast, but I also wanted to be home during the day. When I saw an ad in the paper for dancers and what they said you could earn, I applied. The first time I had to strip I thought I was going to throw up, but I just kept thinking I needed the job for my kids. I make almost $2,000 a week so it's worth it."

Sam watched Lavender take a drink of wine. "You actually seemed very comfortable on stage. Did you ever model or act?"

"I took dance lessons and stuff as a kid," she smiled. "After Mitch and I fell in love all I ever wanted was to be with him, have a family, live a quiet happy life, work at a fun job with nice people, and have good friends. That's still what I want."

"Does your husband know where you work?"

"No, that's why I moved out of Indio to Palm Springs. It's kind of a long drive home late at night, but when Mitch gets out, hopefully we won't run into anyone who knows me from the club." Lavender sat forward, resting her elbows on the table. "I know people think I'm standoffish or cold, but the truth is I don't want to get to know anybody there or get too close. When Mitch is released I'll go back to bartending part time, he'll find work, and this chapter of my life will be *over*."

Sam grabbed a pen from the side pocket of her backpack and wrote Sharon's name and the phone number for Ted's on the back of a business card. "Here. I have a friend who owns this pub in Palm Springs. They periodically need bartenders, so when the time comes you should give them a call. Or call me and I'll make the introduction."

Lavender took the card. "Thanks. I appreciate that."

"You obviously won't make nearly as much money there, but they're really good people. I never knew dancing in a club could be so profitable."

"I could be making even more, but I only do table dances. I won't do lap dances. I couldn't do that to Mitch. He'll get over me dancing on stage or on a table, but he'd never be able to deal with me touching a guy one on one. Besides, I don't have a habit, so I've been able to put *a lot* away in savings. That's going to be our safety net in case we ever hit another rough patch again."

The waitress brought the soda over and cleared the soup

bowl, wiping the table. Sam took a sip and waited for her to leave. "So, Lavender—"

"Please, my name's Kim; Lavender's not who I am outside that place."

"Okay, thanks. So, how well did you know Jeff?"

Kim's smile faded, her expression turning melancholy. "I just can't believe somebody killed him. Do they know why?"

"The police are still trying to figure that out. Is there anything you can tell me about him? Like where he was from or why he came to Palm Springs in the first place? I have to tell you, there are some people in that club who think you and Jeff were romantically involved."

"I couldn't care less what anybody there thinks, but I never slept with Jeff. It never came up. He was the only man in that place that didn't look at me like he was fucking me in his head. We actually *talked.* You know the phrase 'a gentle soul'? That was him. I think the only reason he bought table dances was because he knew about my situation. It was his way of helping. That's why it's so unreal he would end up murdered, unless he was killed helping someone."

"Did he ever say where he was from?"

"Not specifically. But the few times he talked about *back home;* he made it sound far away."

"Do you remember when you met?"

"Yeah," she glanced away, thinking. "He started coming in shortly after Money began working there, so that was probably around April. After a while I noticed he was only there on the nights she worked."

"How often is that?"

"She works three nights. I work every night but Sunday, so I know all the regulars by sight."

"Do you know what Money's real name is?"

"No. Sometimes I wondered if the owners hired Jeff to shadow her. She's a cash cow but completely unpredictable. She has pissed off quite a few guys big time."

"Did it seem like he had a crush on Money?"

"Not at all," Kim said. "If anything, he seemed protective towards her. She was always really touchy-feely with him, but he was always a gentleman."

"So they were not involved?"

"You mean like boyfriend-girlfriend?" She shifted in her seat. "No."

Okay," Sam said slowly, alerted by Kim's body language. "Did they ever hook up?"

Kim pressed the palms of her hands together, covering her nose and mouth, obviously conflicted. Sam waited. Finally, she sat back with a sigh. "He made me promise never to tell anyone, but I guess it doesn't matter now."

"This is about Money?"

She nodded. "I never saw Jeff drink, except for one night in the middle of May. I remember because it was right around my birthday. I had a bottle of wine backstage and talked him into having some with me. He was a real lightweight and got a major buzz. He was very funny, in a silly kind of way. We really had a great time," she said, smiling softly at the memory. "Then all of a sudden, he checked his watch and jumped up, saying it was time to go babysit Money and earn his keep."

"That's the word he used? Babysit."

"Yeah. Later that night he came back to my dressing room and was just a mess. Upset. Really crying. He told me Money talked him into having more drinks then insisted he buy a lap dance. Except it went way beyond that."

"They had sex?"

"Right in the booth. Honest to God it seems Money can put any guy under a spell."

"Why was he so upset?"

"That's what I wondered. I tried to tell him it was no big deal. They were both adults, but Jeff was inconsolable. He kept talking about his betrayal. That was the night he told me he had a girl back home. But I got the impression his upset went lots deeper than just cheating on his girlfriend."

"As in, it wasn't so much what he did but who he did it with?"

"More like what he did *and* who he did it with. Also, I don't think he was very experienced sexually, so maybe it just freaked him out."

Sam mentally circled back to the babysitting comment. "Did Jeff ever get any more specific about his relationship with Money?"

"No. But after that night, it was like Money had some weird control over him. She'd make him stand there all night watching her give lap dances. I also know she made him buy her drugs at least once because he came to me in a panic, needing to know where to get some."

"What did you tell him?"

"To ask one of the bartenders. They always know who's carrying."

They sat in silence a few moments, sipping their drinks. "It almost sounds like she was blackmailing him," Sam said.

"That's exactly what it seemed like to me, too," Kim agreed. "One time, I was backstage and overheard Money threaten to tell their *secret* if he wasn't nice to her. She said it in a jokey way, but I know she meant it."

"The secret being they had sex, and he bought her drugs?"

"I guess."

"And who would she tell?"

"I assumed his girlfriend."

That would mean Money knew who his girlfriend was and how to reach her.

"Do you remember her exact words?"

Kim closed her eyes, remembering. "Let's see how much she wants you around after I tell her about our little secret."

"How did Jeff react?"

"He looked like he wanted to cry," she said softly. "God, I felt so terrible. If he hadn't been buzzed, he would have never let himself get in that situation."

"I don't think you should blame yourself. It seems like it was only a matter of time before Money got him under her control one way or another."

"Maybe," Kim shrugged. "She was definitely obsessed with him."

"And Jeff only started coming to the club *after* Money started working there."

"Right."

"Did he knew her before or did they meet at the club?"

"I just assumed they met at the club, but I don't know for sure. I never asked and he never said."

"Did Jeff ever mention going into some kind of business or that he was planning on leaving the area soon?"

Kim turned sideways in the booth, stretching out her legs. "The last few times we talked he said he was ready to go back home but had some personal business he needed to finish up here first. I told him he should just go now and get away from here. But he said he had to make some things right before he could move on. When I asked what, he said he couldn't tell me yet but would later." Kim's eyes moistened. "I wonder if that's what got him killed."

Sam looked at her watch. "I know you probably need to get home. I just have a couple more questions. When was the last time you saw Jeff?"

"Last Saturday," she said quietly. "But I never talked to him. I was backstage doing a table dance when I saw him and Money over by the bar."

"What time was this?

"It had to be after 12:30 because I had finished my last stage set."

"What were they doing?"

"It looked like they were arguing. She seemed to be angry at him, and he seemed to be trying to reason with her. He kind of grabbed her by the shoulders, but Money pushed him away and walked off. I remember thinking how sad he looked."

"Where'd she go?"

"To the main room. The next time I glanced over, Jeff was gone." Kim looked at Sam. "Do you think it's possible Money killed him?"

"I really have no opinion."

"I think she's more than capable of it," Kim admitted. "There's just something not right about that girl."

Sam didn't disagree. "One last thing: did Jeff ever talk about any other friends he might have confided in? Any name he ever mentioned?"

Kim gathered her purse and scooted to the edge of the bench, thinking. "Once or twice he mentioned some guy named Jerry. But he never went into detail."

"Did he talk about Ellen Konrad?"

"I think he was a bit star-struck there," she smiled. "One day coming into to work I walked past his car and saw the bumper stickers and the signs in the backseat. That's when I found out he did volunteer work for the campaign. When I asked about it, all he said was that she was a great lady and would make a great mayor. I know I'm voting for her."

Sam suspected Ellen would be pleased to know she had the local stripper vote. She pulled out her wallet and insisted on paying Kim's check, courtesy of the *Weekender*. She motioned to Joe, and the three of them walked out together. Kim got into an Audi that had two child seats in the back.

"Thanks again," Sam said. "I hope everything works out for you."

She watched Kim drive off and wrote down her license plate number in case she needed to contact her again.

Sam got in the car and stared out the window, lost in thought.

Joe put his hand on her shoulder. "What are you thinking?"

"That Jeff Rydell was a man with a whole lot of secrets, and one of them got him killed."

CHAPTER ELEVEN

Sam didn't get to bed until almost three in the morning, but her brain pulled an all-nighter with a vivid working dream that kept repeating the same images and situations, as if on an endless loop. She woke up before dawn, edgy and exhausted.

She tried to fall back asleep, but images of Ellen kept intruding her thoughts. It was the memory of watching her mouth when she talked, the scent of her perfume, the intelligence and humor in those eyes that twisted Sam's gut with yearning.

She turned on her side, a folded pillow wedged between her legs. Sam imagined Ellen was next to her, their skin touching, hands exploring. Her hips rocked, pressing against the pillow, but in her mind it was Ellen's caress sending her to the edge…

Sated and strangely comforted, Sam quickly dozed back off, this time to a dreamless sleep.

* * *

Sam moved her glass of iced tea to the corner of the desk and pushed her notebooks off to the side. She opened the envelope containing Rydell's receipts and dumped them out. Once again she separated them into piles, this time sorting them by type: fast food receipts in one pile, gas in another, and so on. She picked up a credit card receipt and called Nate.

His voicemail picked up. "Hey, it's Sam again. I'm sitting here looking at credit card receipts apparently belonging to our recently departed friend from Tennessee. The only way he could have this card and it not show up in his report would be if this was a reloadable card, which it is not, or he's not the primary account holder. If that's the case, I'd like to know who is. So I'm hoping you might be able to get the info from the card number." Sam read the number off to him, along with its expiration date. "As usual, the sooner, the better."

Still holding the receiver, Sam reached into the second manila envelope and retrieved the software flyer. She punched in the phone number doubting she'd get a live person on the other end. Her pessimism was aptly rewarded. An automated recording announced: *The party you are calling is not available. Please leave your number at the tone.*

"Hi, Argo, my name is Sam. I saw one of your flyers at the club and was interested in getting some more information. Please give me a call at your earliest convenience. Thanks." She left her cell phone number and jotted down in her notebook the day and time she called. She opened the other envelope and took out the local map. She went to the file room copier and made an 11x17 enlargement of the area from the tram to the sharp turn where South Palm Canyon turns into East Palm Canyon and heads towards Cathedral City. Sam put the copy on her desk and chose red and blue Sharpies out of her drawer. She went through each stack of receipts and further separated them by date—those before April 1 and those after—and put them in two piles.

Sam picked up the *after* pile first and went through each receipt, marking the location of the business with a blue dot and writing its name down in her notebook along with the number of receipts. She went through the same procedure with the *before* pile, except with those she used a red dot. Any receipt that was from outside the designated area Sam ignored and set aside.

After notating each receipt, she studied the map. The blue dots mostly started from the area near Konrad's headquarters and moved east, the direction of Cathedral City. But the red dots were concentrated on the right side of the map, west of the tram turnoff, south of Racquet Club. Of particular interest to Sam was where the blue and red dots overlapped: the Desert Diner.

Sam numbered the businesses from least frequented to most

frequented in her notebook then rolled up the marked map and secured it with a rubber band. She locked the receipts in her desk drawer, turned off the music, and headed out. Her plan was to stop by the places Jeff frequented and see if anyone knew him. If she was lucky, she'd find Jerry.

Preoccupied with her thoughts, Sam grabbed the car door handle and let out a yelp, shaking her hand in pain. The metal handle was scalding hot. The display on the bank across the street read 112 degrees, and it was moving-in-molasses muggy. She used the bottom of her shirt as a mitt and gingerly opened the door, stepping aside to avoid the blast of searing air rushing out of the heated interior. She covered her leather seat with a towel before getting in.

At Vista Chino, she turned right and slowly navigated the streets of her targeted area, making a mental note every time she located a store from the receipts. She also jotted down the name of three motels she passed that looked like the kind of place a shallow-pocketed visitor might choose. She decided to work her way through the list of businesses from the least frequented to the most frequented.

The first two were gas stations. Sam couldn't imagine the numbing boredom of sitting in a six-foot square cubicle for eight hours, so it didn't surprise her when the cashier at the Shell on Racquet Club was unhelpful and uninterested. The second gas station was a mom-and-pop place called Gas 4 Less, a few blocks from where Palm Canyon turned into Highway 111. It had a large, well-kept mini-market and an attached do-it-yourself car wash. The cashier was a middle-aged lady wearing a shirt monogrammed with the name Marge. She exuded the no-nonsense demeanor of a bowling alley cocktail waitress or truck stop server. Sam waited until the customer left before introducing herself and showing Marge two photos of Rydell.

His DMV photo had all the personality of a mug shot. The other headshot was cropped from his photo with Ellen. In it, he looked proud and full of life. Sam wondered if it was from doing work he thought was important or from simply standing next to someone like Ellen.

Marge nodded in recognition, "Sure, I know him. He's one of my regulars although I don't know him by name, just by sight." She handed the photos back.

"His name is Jeff Rydell, and he was killed early Sunday. I'm writing a story about it and am trying to find people who might know something about him."

"You're saying he was killed just this past Sunday? Killed how? Car wreck?"

"He was murdered."

Marge's eyes widened briefly then narrowed. "What time did it happen?"

"The police estimate he was killed sometime in the early morning hours Sunday."

"I knew something wasn't right!"

"What do you mean?"

"That night—" She stopped when a customer entered to get their change. Marge practically threw the money on the counter to hurry them out. She waited until the door closed. "Saturday night I worked the four-to-twelve shift, but my overnight guy ran late, as usual, and didn't get here until almost two o'clock. Claimed his wife had some kind of emergency but I think he's got a new girlfriend on the side. Anyway, right before he showed up that fellow stopped in for gas," she pointed at Jeff's picture. "I remember thinking *This is unusual*, because I had only ever seen him during the day."

"Did he say anything to you?"

"Nothing other than to say hi when he paid. But he seemed kind of odd."

"Odd in what way?"

"Kind of…excited. And a little edgy."

"Scared?"

"No, not that. Just hyped up. I remember he looked over his shoulder a couple times at the other car."

"What other car?"

"A black car pulled in right after he did and parked over by the air pump. It must have been waiting on him to get gas because when your guy finished and drove off, it followed him."

"Which way did they go?"

Marge pointed towards the open expanse to her right. "Out Highway 111."

The information was significant; it meant that other than the killer, or killers, Marge was probably the last person to see Jeff alive. "Could you see the driver of the black car?"

Marge folded her arms and stared off in thought. "It's real dark at night over there. I never got around to replacing the light bulb in that lamp post. It looked like a man was driving, clean shaven, and from what I recall had dark hair and was wearing a white shirt."

"You're very observant."

"Well, in a business like this, you learn to keep an eye out. Twenty-four years and we haven't had one robbery," Marge rapped the counter with her knuckles. "There was some blonde woman with him. Even in the dark you could see she was blonde, hair in a long pony tail, well past her shoulders. Couldn't tell you how old she was."

Sam noticed two cars pull up to the pumps. "One last question: could you tell what kind of car it was?"

"Sure could," Marge smiled. "It was an older model Lincoln Town Car, maybe ten years old. My late husband loved those cars. Called them his little piece of heaven."

Before leaving Sam filled her tank, remembering how much she loved spending time at her mother's gas station as a kid. In some ways, it held the same appeal journalism did. You met people from all walks of life, every day was different, and you weren't stuck in a nine-to-five existence. Of course, there were marked differences, too. The biggest traumas faced at her mother's gas station were a blown transmission or the cost of oil going up, and the biggest danger was walking into the men's bathroom after a busy holiday weekend. You didn't encounter many murders.

Back in her car, Sam updated her notes. The description of the woman passenger in the black car certainly fit Money. If Money was the killer she must have had an accomplice, presumably the driver. Sam doubted a small woman like that would be able to physically overcome a man Rydell's size and age in a one-on-one, hand-to-hand confrontation.

She could have had a gun, Sam thought, playing devil's advocate with herself.

"So then why not just shoot him?" she argued back.

Too loud. The echo would reverberate against all that rock.

"So, she held a gun on him with one hand and with the other hoisted a sixteen pound rock and cracked Jeff on the skull with it?" Sam responded skeptically.

The other possibility was that *she* was the accomplice. "Which brings us back to the question, who's the dude driving the damn car?"

Sam glanced over and saw the woman pumping gas on the next island watching her curiously. Embarrassed, she nodded at the woman and drove off.

The next business on her list was a twenty-four-hour Rite-Aid with the world's most confusing layout. It was like a rat's maze. The aisles slanted in various directions, some meeting at a point, others intersecting perpendicularly. Sam showed Jeff's picture to the cashiers on duty, but nobody recognized him. The same was true at the office supply store, several fast food joints, and the grocery store.

It was lunchtime when she walked into the Desert Diner, the last entry on her list. Sam sat at the counter and looked around. Most of the inside booths were filled by people eating alone. The outdoor patio was a third full with smokers who'd rather brave the heat than go half an hour without a cigarette. Misters blasted the patio with a rain of spray that left the tile floor wet. Sam wondered how it was possible to keep a cigarette lit at all.

The smell of grilled onions filled the air and made Sam's stomach growl. She ordered a turkey sandwich on toasted whole wheat with melted pepper jack, a side of cottage cheese, and a large iced tea. Her waitress was a friendly young woman with shoulder length brown hair and glasses named Kylie who kept her drink refilled and brought Sam a copy of the *Tribune* to read over lunch.

She ate slowly, and by the time she finished, the diner crowd had thinned to just a few customers.

"Would you like some dessert?" Kylie asked, clearing Sam's plate.

"No, thank you. But there is something else I'm hoping you might be able to help me with." Sam pulled out the photos of Rydell and placed them on the counter. "By any chance do you recognize this person?"

Kylie glanced at the pictures then looked at Sam. "Why? Are you with the police or something?"

"No, I'm a reporter. My name is Samantha Perry." She handed the waitress a business card. "I'm working on a story and was hoping to find someone who knows him."

"A story about what?"

Sam hesitated; being the bearer of bad news was getting old. "About his death."

"Oh, no…" Kylie slumped onto the stool next to Sam's. "What happened?"

"So you do know him?"

"Jeff was one of my counter regulars. What happened?" she asked again.

Sam heard the noise level in the diner fall as customers within earshot picked up on their conversation. "Listen, can you take a break so we can talk more privately?"

"Sure. Of course." Kylie spoke quietly to another waitress then led Sam to the furthest corner booth. Sam sat with her back to the wall so that Kylie faced away from the room.

"So what happened to Jeff?" Kylie asked again, sliding onto the seat.

"He was found murdered last Sunday."

"Murdered? Oh, my God." Kylie shook her head in disbelief. "Do they know who did it?"

"No, the police are still investigating. I've been having a hard time finding out much about him. I know he was relatively new in town but not much else. Is there anything you can tell me?"

"He's been eating breakfast at the counter since at least

Valentine's Day."

"How do you remember that?"

"Because we were having a special of heart-shaped pancakes with fresh strawberries, and he asked me a couple times if the strawberries were really fresh. He couldn't believe fresh strawberries were available in February. He told me all they had during winter in Tennessee were frozen berries. The conversation just stuck in my head; you don't usually get customers excited about fruit," she smiled.

"He specifically said Tennessee?"

"For sure."

Why would Rydell tell a waitress where he was from but not Ellen or Kim, Sam wondered. The man was a frustrating cipher. "Did he ever talk about why he came to Palm Springs?"

"No, not really. Breakfast and lunch are the busiest times around here, so there's not a lot of opportunity to get into conversations. It's always just small talk."

"How did you find out his name?"

"For a long time, I *didn't* know. Usually you find out a customer's name when they use their credit card but he always paid cash in the beginning. And he never introduced himself the way most guys do. I think he was just really shy. Then a few months ago he came in with some mail. I teased him and said something like, *Well, now I finally know what to call you.*"

"Do you remember what the envelope looked like? Was it long like a letter, or square like a utility bill?"

"No, it was a big envelope. You know, the size of a piece of paper but thick, like there must have been a lot of stuff in it. What first caught my eye was that it had *Confidential* stamped on it in red ink."

"You said this was a couple months ago?"

"Maybe a little longer. It could have been before Memorial Day. That's when we got new uniforms, and I'm thinking I was still wearing the old apron, but I can't be 100 percent sure. Sorry."

"There's nothing to apologize for. You're being very helpful. I know I'm asking a lot, but is there anything else you remember about the envelope? Its color, if the address was printed or handwritten?"

"It was white," Kylie said slowly, trying to visualize. "It must have been a printed label or else it wouldn't have been so easy to read."

"Was there any kind of identifying mark, like a logo or picture on it?"

"There might have been some kind of mark by the return address…." Kylie's eyes grew focused. "There was! I remember now; it was green because that and the red *Confidentiality* made me think the envelope had Christmas colors on it. The logo design was interconnecting letters, but I don't remember what now."

"Did Jeff ever say anything about a job or family?"

"Nothing about family but he did work. At first, he came in pretty early for breakfast nearly every single day. Then maybe a month or two after Valentine's Day he only came in a couple times a week, usually later in the morning. Sometimes almost at the end of my shift."

"Which is when?"

"I get off at one. Anyway, I mentioned to Jeff I noticed he wasn't coming in as often. He said he'd moved to a nicer place a little further away. He also told me he was doing some work that kept him out late, which was why he was eating breakfast at noon. But he never said what he was doing exactly, and I never thought to ask."

"Did Jeff ever mention anyone named Jerry?"

"Not that I can think of."

"Was there *any* friend he ever talked about?"

"He didn't talk *about* anybody but there's a guy he'd meet for breakfast every now and then. That's the only time Jeff would sit at a booth."

"I take it this person isn't a regular."

"Oh, no, he is. But he sits outside, and I only work inside."

"Is whoever works those tables still here?"

Kylie turned around and looked. "No, I don't see her. Her name's Marie, but she's new. She's only been here a couple of weeks, and I'm not sure she's had a chance to get to know the regulars that well yet."

Sam let out a small sigh. Nothing was going to come easy on this story. "Do you remember the last time you saw Jeff?"

"I think it was last Friday. I remember thinking he looked tired." Kylie stared at the table.

Sam recognized the look. People inevitably wonder if they could have changed fate by somehow intervening. She took out another business card and jotted *Very important. Please call ASAP about Jeff Rydell* on the back. She handed it to Kylie. "I have a huge favor to ask you. If you happen to see the man who Jeff had breakfast with, could you please give this card to him? It's really important."

"I will. I promise."

"Thank you." Sam gathered her backpack and slid out of the booth. "Sorry to keep you after work like this. I'm sure you're tired. This seems like a busy place."

"It is," Kylie agreed. "Actually, I have to come back and work the evening shift. The cashier called in sick." She glanced at the pictures of Jeff in Sam's hand. "Guess I shouldn't complain, though. There are lots worse things."

CHAPTER TWELVE

Parked in the shady alley behind the Desert Diner, Sam glanced at the clock on her dashboard. In four and a half hours she'd be at Ellen's house, and the thought made her stomach flutter in anticipation. Was Ellen really making an overture, or was Sam reading way too much into what was very likely a professional courtesy? More importantly, could she remain objective?

Sam was convinced that Ellen was hiding something. Not about Jeff's death but about his life. Was she protecting herself in some way or someone else? If so, then who and why? She reread the notes from their interview, but nothing jumped out to shed any new light. She idly ran her finger over Ellen's phone number. Impulsively she reached for her cell phone and called the house.

"Konrad residence," a curtly efficient voice answered.

"Hi, is Ellen in?"

"I'm afraid she's busy. Would you like to leave a message?"

Sam hesitated. "That's okay. I'll just catch up with her later."

She hung up, feeling foolish. She tossed the phone onto the passenger seat and flipped through her notebook to the page with the list of motels to check out. As she shifted into first gear, her phone vibrated and played the incoming call tone: the opening notes of the *Hawaii 5-0* theme song.

"Hello?"

"Hey, I'm sorry about that," Ellen apologized, sounding slightly winded.

Sam put the car back in park. "I didn't mean to interrupt you."

"The only thing you interrupted was my indecision between egg salad and yogurt for lunch."

"And the egg salad no doubt won out."

"I'm not even going to ask how you knew that," Ellen said genially. "Do you mind if I eat while we talk? I'm starved."

"Of course not." Sam heard a door close and Ellen sigh as she sat down. "Do you always have people screen your calls?"

"Not if I can help it. But Lee sometimes gets…let's say, overly protective."

"In other words, she saw who it was on your caller ID and didn't want the riffraff bothering you."

"Something like that. Except you're not a bother at all and hardly riffraff. How's your story going?"

"Well, so far there are a lot more questions than answers. Jeff Rydell was a man with a lot of secrets."

"Like what? Or can't you say?"

Sam debated a moment. "Did you know he was moonlighting at an exotic dance club in Indio?"

"Doing what?"

"He apparently was paid to look after one of the dancers."

"You mean like a bodyguard?"

"More like a handler. To make sure none of the patrons got out of line with her and that she didn't break their heads open for trying."

"When was this?"

"Up until the night he died. In fact, he was killed within hours of leaving the club."

"A strip club?" There was a pause and a squeak, probably from Ellen leaning back in her chair to absorb the information. "That's honestly the last place I would picture Jeff."

"Why?"

"He wasn't very sure of himself or assertive, which a job like that requires, I would think. Plus, he seemed a bit repressed and inhibited to be comfortable hanging around strippers."

"As in born-again Christian repressed?"

"No, more like, never-been-laid-much inhibited."

"Maybe he was never-been-laid-much inhibited because he was

born-again Christian repressed. God, maybe he killed himself."

"You really are bad," Ellen laughed softly, then became serious. "I always got the sense Jeff was trying to figure out who he was so he could find what would really make him happy."

"Aren't we all?"

"I suppose to varying degrees we are. Sometimes it's just a matter of reclaiming the pieces of ourselves we lose along the way."

Sam sensed Ellen was speaking as much about herself as Rydell. There was so much beneath the surface of this woman she craved to know.

"Well, it seems Jeff decided going back home to be with his girlfriend would make him happy," Sam said.

There was a pause. "He had a girlfriend?"

"You sound surprised."

"He never mentioned being involved with anyone. I wonder why he would keep that a secret."

"There's a lot I wonder," Sam said. "Why he was willing to be away from her for so long? What brought him here? What kept him here? Why was he killed once he decided to leave and go back home to his mystery girlfriend? I just wish I could talk to her."

"Where is she?"

"I have no idea because I don't even know her name yet. I do know that before coming to Palm Springs he lived in the bustling metropolis of Cattle Hill, Tennessee. Ever hear of it?" she asked casually.

"Has anyone? It almost sounds made up."

"Well, it's not as bad as Deadhorse, Alaska, or Monkey's Eyebrow, Arizona."

"Those are real places?"

"Just like French Lick, Indiana, and Dildo, Newfoundland."

"Must be those long Northern winters."

"Or serious wishful thinking."

Ellen chuckled then grew somber. "You said the strip club was in Indio; so how did he end up dead out in the desert?"

"He drove there. I talked with someone who saw him heading

that way late Saturday night. I'm pretty sure he knew his killer, or killers, but why it happened I have no clue. I'm still just trying to get a picture of who this guy was. It's like a moving target because he seems to have been a different person to everyone who knew him. I haven't found the common thread that ties all these different Jeff Rydells together. He *was* up to something, though, and I think that's what got him killed. But *what* he was up to, I can't say."

Ellen was quiet a moment. "You know, when you work on a character in a script, the first thing you're supposed to do is create their backstory, which is where you find the character's current motivation. Once you figure out Jeff's backstory, you'll be able to tie all the different Jeff Rydells you see now together into the individual he really was."

"Let's hope or there's going to be a lot of empty space in this week's edition." Sam sighed. "So on one hand you have people trying to run interference for you, screening who gets through, and yet you haven't even asked the reason I called."

"Was there one?"

"Not really. I guess I just wanted to talk."

"That's reason enough," she said warmly. "I've been thinking about you, too."

Sam felt exposed and flustered. Unnerved, she moved to safer ground. "So, how's your party set-up coming along?"

Ellen groaned. "Mostly, I just stay out of the way so the caterers and rental people can do their thing, and everyone else can fight it out."

"Who's fighting what out?"

"Lee and René are always at odds, mostly because Lee tries to micromanage the kitchen along with everything else. René is French, so it's not just a personal affront but an assault on her heritage. It's a good thing Lee doesn't understand French very well, or I'd really have a war on my hands."

"So you're hiding out in your office?"

"With the door locked."

Sam smiled. "Who knew a cocktail party could have so

much drama?"

"You think you see violence? The last thing they were arguing about were the bar stations. René thought both bars should be full service; Lee wanted one beer and wine, the other mixed drinks. I honestly thought they were going to come to blows."

"Split the baby: let both be full-service, but pick one bar to have an express beer-and-wine-only line as well."

There was a moment of silence. "Observant *and* diplomatic."

"Oh, so not," Sam assured her. "Well, I better get back to work. I hope things calm down there so you're not too stressed for your party."

"I'm going to go be boss and pull rank now. That's always a good stress reliever."

I can think of better, Sam mused.

"You know, I can hear you thinking," Ellen said, "and it's no wonder you blush so much."

"Busted again," Sam laughed. "And on that note, I really better go. I'll see you in a few hours."

"I'm really looking forward to it. And Sam? I'm very glad you called."

"Me, too."

Sam hung up, energized and optimistic. *Maybe…*

There was truly nothing she wanted more than Ellen Konrad in her life in whatever way possible. But before that could happen in earnest, there were questions that still needed to be answered.

* * *

Sam worked through the list of motels. It was a bust. Although the clerks tried to be helpful nobody recognized Jeff. Nor did they have a record of anyone by that name in their registration ledgers. She made one last sweep and passed the Sandy Dunes Inn, which sat on a dusty stretch of Indian Drive just outside her original target area. Journalistic due diligence compelled her to stop in.

When Sam walked in, a chime rang in the deserted lobby. A

slender, balding, middle-aged man with a comb-over emerged from an office behind the front desk.

"Can I help you?" he asked with clipped efficiency.

"I hope so," Sam smiled, noticing he didn't respond in kind. She introduced herself, briefly explained her assignment, and held out the pictures. "I'm just wondering if this man ever stayed here."

"Why exactly do you want to know this?"

"Because I'm trying to write an obituary and nobody, including the police, have been able to locate next of kin."

The man regarded her coolly. "Are you going to quote me?"

Sam's gaze narrowed to match. "Do you have anything quotable to say?"

"I'm not sure I want my name bandied about in the paper."

"Actually, I don't even know your name."

"It's Benjamin Hayes. I'm the proprietor."

"Well, Ben, I'm not much of a bandier. I only quote people if they've given me their okay. Right now, I'm just looking for information that might help me write an accurate article. So, to your knowledge, did this man ever stay here?"

"You mean you don't want to quote me?"

With an effort, Sam refrained from grabbing his throat and kept her tone amiable. "I would be happy to quote you, if you have anything pertinent to say. Certainly, if he stayed here, I would mention that in the article as well."

"That would be good. A little publicity never hurts, right?"

Sam just smiled, debating whether she would use *hellhole*, *squalid*, or *fetid*. "So, *do* you recognize him?"

"I do. He stayed with us for several months earlier this year."

"Did he ever talk about family or why he came to Palm Springs?

"Not to me. I don't fraternize with the guests."

"Can you tell me what kind of lease he was on? Was it by the day, the week, the month?" Sam suspected this place probably rented by the hour as well.

"I believe he was on the weekly special, which is the daily rate minus 15 percent."

"When he checked in, did he have to fill out a registration form?"

"Yes, we require that of all our long-term guests. I suppose you want to see it."

"That would be most helpful. I appreciate it."

Benjamin Hayes disappeared into the back office and returned in under a minute to hand the file to Sam. He pointed to the receipts. "It appears that he paid a full month, which is the daily rate minus 20 percent, his first two months here then started renting by the week thereafter."

The first receipt was dated January 26; the second, February 23; and the rest dated at seven-day intervals until the last receipt, dated April 13.

The registration form listed his Cattle Hill address although the phone number line was left blank. His emergency contact was Larissa Dodds, with an 865 area code phone number.

"Hello, L," Sam whispered.

"Did you say something?" Hayes asked.

Sam ignored the question by pretending she didn't hear it. "Do you have a copier? I need a copy of these receipts and registration. The police need to notify next of kin." Although both statements were absolutely true, the inference was not. The copies were really for her, but Sam knew Benjamin Hayes would feel more important thinking they were official police documents.

"Of course," he held out his hand. "I'll do that and put them in an envelope for you."

Sam gave him the file. "And please make sure to put your name down on the envelope in case they need to contact you."

Benjamin almost smiled but couldn't quite get there.

It was nearly 2:30 by the time Sam was finally on her way back to the office. She really did need to call Larson and give him Rydell's emergency contact information. But she didn't necessarily need to do it this second. Instead, Sam mentally replayed her conversations with Ellen, Kylie, and Kim. The portrait of Rydell taking form in her mind only served to create more questions than answers. Why would someone like Jeff be associated with an apparent loon like

Money? He had obviously gotten in over his head with something, but Sam increasingly doubted it was drugs. It just didn't feel right that he was dabbling in a life of crime, although she certainly couldn't hang a story on intuition.

Something else bothered her. She pulled over to the curb in front of the Denny's on North Palm Canyon and flipped through her notebook. According to Kim, Money and Jeff had their confrontation, or whatever it was, sometime after 12:30. Just a half hour earlier, Alison said Money was talking about running away with Jeff as soon as he made some kind of major financial score.

Sam eased back into traffic wondering what had happened within that half hour to piss Money off. From the sounds of it, Money could switch moods on a whim, but Sam thought it significant that Money wasn't driving with Jeff when he stopped for gas. She was with the mystery man in the black Lincoln. Sam pulled over to the curb again. She looked up Alison's phone number and called.

She answered with a friendly, "Hello?"

"Hi, Alison. It's Sam Perry."

"Oh, hi."

"Listen, I have a really quick follow-up question."

"Okay. What?"

"You told me you talked to Money last Saturday around midnight, right when Lavender started her set, about Jeff's run-in with that guy, right?"

"Right."

"And that she bragged about going off with Jeff once he came into some big money, right?"

"Right," she dragged the word out, sounding warier.

"I've heard from other people that Jeff and Money got into an argument Saturday after Lavender's set was over. And that she was pretty mad. Do you know anything about that?"

The silence answered the question.

"Why didn't you tell me?" Sam asked gently, not wanting to give Alison a reason to hang up.

"You asked me the last time I saw Jeff. You never asked me the last time I saw Money."

She's right, Sam thought grudgingly. But it still felt that Alison intentionally withheld the info. "So, you *were* aware Money had words with Jeff after she talked to you the first time?"

Alison sighed unhappily. "She came out to the bar and was ready to spit nails. Whenever she's like that we try to stay out of her way. Well, except for Argo. He's about the only one who can talk to Money."

"What do you know about Argo?"

"Not much. He's a fun guy to work with, but we've never gone out or anything. Like a lot of people there, he doesn't talk about his life outside the club."

"But he's friendly with Money?"

"Argo's friendly with *everybody*. But yeah, I'd say he talks to her more than anybody else. They seem to get along. They kind of hang when he's on break and stuff."

"Have you ever seen them leave the club together?"

"I think once or twice he gave her a ride home because her car was in the shop or something."

"So obviously they know each other outside the club. Or at least, he knows her well enough to know where she lives."

"I guess. One time he said something about them going way back, but that was all he'd say."

"So what happened Saturday?" Sam pulled into the *Weekender* parking lot and kept the car idling.

"She came out of the lap dance room and went straight to Argo. They were over in the corner by the waiters' station, so I couldn't hear what they talked about. But whatever it was put Argo in a weird mood. He said that Money wasn't feeling well, and he needed to drive her home because they'd driven to the club together. Right at our busiest time, too, so it kind of pissed me off."

"And you never saw Jeff leave."

"No. He probably went out the back door. That's the same way Money and the other girls usually come and go, so they don't have to pass by too many customers."

"Do you have a phone number for Argo?"

"No. The only person I talk to outside the club is Jenny."

"I assume that's September."

"Yeah. But as far as everyone else, that's the kind of place you just do your job and mind your own business."

"I hear you." Sam knew she had pumped this well dry. "Thank you so much, again. Just one more thing: do you know what kind of car Argo drives?"

"I've only ever seen him on a motorcycle."

"What about Money?"

"It's some kind of small car that still looks too big for her."

Sam hung up, frustrated. *So whose Lincoln is that?*

* * *

Monica handed Sam her phone messages when she walked in. "And some faxes came in, too." She opened her desk drawer and pulled out a Manila envelope. "I didn't think you'd want these left on your desk with Mr. Read-Over-Your-Shoulder on the prowl. Marlene wouldn't let him leave early so he's in one of those foul moods."

"Thank you," Sam gave Monica an appreciative bow. "I'll start collecting for your Christmas bonus now."

Sam glanced into Marlene's office, saw she was on the phone, and decided to bring her up to speed later. She sat at her desk and read her messages. The first was from Nate saying most of her order was on the way, the rest would be over by the end of the day. The second was from Joe. She called the condo but no answer. As threatened, he had rented a car and was probably on his second round of shopping.

Leaning back in her chair Sam's body sagged with fatigue, a mid-afternoon slump she suffered whenever she didn't get enough sleep the night before. She idly picked up Rydell's Palm Springs map still tucked under her keyboard and studied the creases. Originally the map folded in half, then thirds, exposing the front and back covers. But there was a second set of creases. Sam folded the map to match those. Where the back cover should have been was the section of map that included the area where Rydell's body was discovered.

"I simply do not believe in coincidences," Sam muttered, staring at the map. The vast area east of Highway 111 from the tram to the 10 Freeway was a flat expanse inhabited primarily by energy producing windmills. But on the west side were a couple of roads that led up into the foothills of the mountains. "What the hell were you up to?"

She logged onto a paid service that supplied address information as well as tract and parcel numbers. She typed *Palm Springs* in the search box and an aerial map of the city loaded onto the page. She moved the cursor where Highway 111 turned into Palm Canyon and double-clicked. The map zoomed in to show more detail of that area. It was like Google Maps on steroids. She kept going deeper into the map until she could see structures. She clicked on the Gas 4 Less and a window popped up showing the owner—Margery Black—and the real property information.

Sam zoomed out and located the turnoff nearest to where Jeff's body was found. Devil's Canyon Road snaked up the mountainside past a small trailer park and dead-ended into two large commercial buildings both identified as belonging to Environmental Tech Services, Inc.

Sam opened a second browser and searched until she found a detailed topography map of Palm Springs and zoomed in on Devil's Canyon Road. She adjusted the degree of zoom on both windows until they were the same proportions then printed them out, the property page a fast draft so it would print lighter and the topography page best quality so it was darker. She put the property sheet on top of the topography sheet and held them up to the window. They told an interesting story.

The two buildings were situated on a bluff directly above Devil Canyon Wash, a deep channel that ran down the mountainside east, back towards Highway 111. On the other side of Devil's Canyon Road, to the north, was a visible trail that curved over a relatively low tor. Sam guessed it was a makeshift road created by ATV riders or a long-existing Indian trail. However it was formed, following that path led almost directly to where Sam found the jacket—an exposed expanse that would make someone running for their life easy prey. Sam stapled the two pages together and set them aside.

Next, she did a fictitious business name search for Environmental Tech Services. The listed owner was a limited partnership called ETS. Looking statewide, Sam saw there was another Environmental Tech Services office near San Francisco. Sam called local directory assistance and asked for a listing.

"I have two," the operator said. "One is in Palm Springs on Devil's Canyon, the other is in Cathedral City on Via Rancho."

"Can I have both please?"

Sam wrote down the numbers then called the listing on Devil Canyon. There was no answer so she called the Cathedral City location.

A female voice answered, "ETS."

"Hi, I was wondering if you could tell me what kind of business this is?"

"We're a recycling company," the woman responded politely.

"Where I can drop off my paper and bottles?"

"No, we do industrial and technology recycling."

"Oh, I see. Well, thanks anyway."

Sam minimized the window on her screen and leaned back in her chair. Technology recycling included old computers, surplus inventory, overstock software, discarded cell phones, and other related materials. It was a thriving Information Age cottage industry.

She closed her eyes and assimilated this new wrinkle into the facts as presented.

Ellen called Jeff a computer whiz.

There was a flyer for software stashed in his papers.

Not far from where his body was found is a building in the business of computer recycling.

He borrows $500 from George as seed money for some business venture, maybe drug-related but maybe not.

He tells Kim he's heading home but has business to finish

here first.

Kylie sees him reading papers from an envelope marked confidential.

Jeff's map is folded to the area where the buildings are located.

Marge sees him drive off in that direction followed by a big black car similar to the one that came close to making her human road-kill.

Jeff gets into a verbal confrontation with Mystery Man A at Crazy Girl.

Their argument elicits amusement from Money.

A half hour later, Jeff and Money get into an altercation that leaves her furious and driving in a car with Mystery Man B, possibly Argo.

Jeff ends up dead in the desert.

His car, laptop, and surveillance equipment are missing.

Rather than dwell on it, Sam cleared her head and left it alone. Eventually, some nugget of information would ignite a chain reaction of deduction, and in a moment of synaptic fission the picture would come clear. Until then, she just had to keep investigating.

She called Larissa Dodds—no answer, no voicemail, or machine. Sam saved the number on her cell phone to call later. She also saved the numbers for Ellen and Detective Larson.

Sam made another copy of the motel receipts and registration, put them in a fresh envelope, and wrote *Attn: Detective Larson* on the front. She put the envelope in her backpack then opened the email from Veronica Flowers listing the nearby phone numbers of Rydell's former Cattle Hill neighbors along with their names. Like Nate, Veronica kept her emails cryptic, leaving off the area code and just listing the local number. It was going on 6:15 in Eastern Tennessee, a good time to reach people at home.

Sam pulled out her laptop, attached her headset, and opened Skype. As soon as a call connected, she had an app that automatically recorded the conversation. The laws on taping phone conversations varied from state to state. California was a two-party state, meaning both parties' consent was required; to secretly tape record a phone call was a misdemeanor. If Sam worried the person on the other line might resist, she simply shuffled some papers while asking, "Do you mind if I tape some notes?" In all her years, only one person had ever noticed she was saying *tape* instead of *take.*

Sam looked up Tennessee law and discovered it was a one party state so she could tape with legal impunity. And she felt no ethical qualms about taping without asking.

The first number she called was Jeff Rydell's former house. It only rang twice before a woman of indeterminate age answered. Sam glanced at the page. "Hi, is this Mrs. Pangburn?"

"Yes it is," she answered without a trace of wariness.

"My name is Samantha Perry. I'm calling from California. I'm trying to track someone down, and I'm hoping you might be able to help me."

"California! I certainly don't know anybody in California."

"I'm looking for Jeff Rydell. I believe you bought your house from him."

"Jeffery Rydell, that's right. But we didn't know him. We never even met him. Everything was handled by the real estate agent."

"Did the agent ever mention why the house was on the market?"

"He said that Jeffrey's mother had recently died after a long illness, and he needed to sell the house to pay off bills. The house wasn't in the best of shape, to say the least."

"Do you know if any of your neighbors have stayed in contact with him?"

"I wouldn't," she apologized. "I haven't gotten to know the neighbors very much, what there is of them."

Mrs. Pangburn couldn't remember the name of the real estate agent, "I've blocked all that from my memory," but suggested Sam call later to talk to her husband.

There were three other numbers Veronica had designated nearest neighbors. To infer from Mrs. Pangburn, these people could live miles away, but Sam was hopeful Cattle Hill wasn't *that* rural. There was no answer or machine at the first number. A service picked up on the second number, but Sam didn't want to tip her hand by leaving a message. The last number belonged to a Mrs. D. Monroe. The voice that answered sounded elderly but lucid.

"Is this Mrs. Monroe?"

"Yes, that's me. Who is this?"

Sam introduced herself by name, not profession. "I'm trying to track down relatives of Jeff Rydell and was hoping you might be able to help me."

She clucked her tongue. "I don't think so, dear. He doesn't have any left."

"So you know Jeff?"

"Only for all his life."

Sam sat forward. "Mrs. Monroe—"

"Oh, it makes me feel so old when people call me that. Please call me Dorothy."

"Okay, Dorothy. So his parents are dead?

"Yes, Stan and Vicky have both passed away. They were each only children, and Jeff was an only child so there aren't many Rydells to be found in these parts anymore. Why is it you need to know this?"

Sam originally intended to lie because she didn't want to risk any friends or relatives learning about his murder through gossip. But if Dorothy was right, there wasn't much point in being circumspect. And since she wasn't next of kin Larson couldn't bust her chops.

"I'm afraid I have some sad news. Jeff's been killed."

"Oh, no. Dear God bless his soul," she whispered. Sam visualized her making a sign of the cross. "Are you with the police?"

"No. I'm a reporter in Palm Springs working on a story about his death. I've been trying to find someone who knew him to get some background information. He never told his acquaintances here much about where he was from or his life."

"No, I don't suppose he would have," she sighed, sounding shaken but holding it together.

"Why do you say that?"

"Jeff went through some hard times in recent years taking care of his mama. She had liver cancer, and it took her a long time to pass. Terrible thing. But he was devoted to her. His daddy died right after Jeff graduated from high school, and he took the responsibility of being the man of the house to heart. Instead of going on to college he stayed home, got a job, and supported Vicky. Then when she got sick he took care of her that way too."

"So to your knowledge, he has no living relatives?"

"Well now, that I can't be sure of, no, because Jeff was adopted, you see. So who knows if he has any blood kin left, but this line of Rydells died with him. What happened? Was it a car wreck?"

Sam hesitated, still digesting the fact Jeff was adopted. "No, it wasn't an accident. Jeff was murdered last Sunday."

Dorothy gasped. *Please don't drop dead of a heart attack*, Sam prayed. But when Dorothy spoke she was stunned but steady. "I've never known anyone who was murdered. Who did it?"

"The police are still investigating, but right now they're not sure who killed him or why. Maybe he was just in the wrong place at the wrong time," a scenario Sam didn't believe but hoped would deflect any more questions.

"My Lord, I'm so glad Vicky's already dead, or this would have killed her straight away."

"Are you up to me asking you some questions?"

"Of course, dear. Anything I can do to help."

"Thank you. Was Jeff adopted as a baby?"

"Yes, I remember the day they brought him home."

"You and Vicky were close."

"You could say that. We were neighbors and friends for well over sixty years. Her family moved into the house across the way when we were both ten. We were best friends all through school. Then I got married and started a family right away, and we fell out of touch the way you will although we always sent Christmas cards. When my folks died, I moved back into the family home with my husband and kids because it was more roomy, and my older brother didn't want it. Not long after, Vicky and Stan bought *her* family home from her parents who were moving to Florida. So twenty years later we were reunited. It was like no time had passed at all."

"But Vicky and Stan had no children of their own?"

"That was one of Vicky's heartbreaks; she couldn't have little ones. Then like a miracle they got Jeff. She was almost fifty by then, but having that little baby invigorated her."

Sam was surprised a couple in their fifties would be able to get an infant, especially a healthy white infant. "They went through an adoption agency?"

"Oh, no, nothing like that. It was a, uh, private situation."

"They adopted the baby directly from the mother?"

"Something along those lines."

"Were they related to the mother?"

"They really didn't like to talk about it much."

"I can appreciate that," Sam spoke calmly, trying to gain her trust. "Every family has secrets they don't want to share with strangers. But Dorothy, the truth can't hurt them now. And it might help me a lot in understanding what happened to Jeff or at least get a better sense of who he was."

"That sounds reasonable," she conceded, but her voice wavered with uncertainty.

"Was it that a young girl in their family got pregnant and couldn't care for the baby?"

"Something along those lines," she said again, sounding relieved that Sam guessed it so she wouldn't have to say it. "Vicky and Stan were very, very close to another couple over in Sevierville, where they lived after getting married. I met them once when they came during Christmas for a visit. We all had dinner, and it was such a fine time. For the life of me, though, I don't remember their names."

"That's okay. Just tell me about Jeff."

"What I *can* recall, it was the husband's niece who got in trouble. She went to live with them so that nobody back home would know. After the baby was born, she didn't want to keep it. Can't really blame a girl that young. I don't think she got along with her daddy, from what Vicky said. Sad state of affairs." Dorothy's voice sounded distant, lost in memories.

"So this girl's uncle and aunt asked Vicky and Stan if they

wanted the baby?"

"That's right. They couldn't stand the thought of putting it in an orphanage, and they felt they were too old to start a family, even though they didn't have kids of their own either. Plus, they were moving out to California because he got offered a good job out there."

"Why didn't the girl's family take the baby in?"

Dorothy hesitated. "It wasn't a good place for a baby to grow up. There were…problems. I think the girl went with her aunt and uncle out west to get away from the situation."

Sam could only think of one "problem" that would cause such hesitancy. "So her father was sexually abusive?"

"It sounded like it, from what Vicky let on. It had to be bad because she wouldn't tell even me everything."

"Do you remember what town this girl was from?"

"It's not a matter of remembering; I never knew. What little I did know about everything, Vicky swore me to secrecy about. I think they were scared of that young girl's daddy. So once the adoption was done, they never said another word about it. Not a one. Not to me, not to Jeff. Vicky took that secret to the grave."

Sam wasn't convinced. What if Jeff found out he was adopted and tracked his mother or her relatives to California? That would explain why he was here and some of the cryptic comments in L's letter, which reminded Sam.

"Did Jeff have a girlfriend?"

"He did for quite a while. High school sweethearts. Vicky dreamed of having grandbabies and used to tease Jeff about hurrying up and getting married. But then Vicky got sick, and there was no way Jeff could settle down while caring for his mama."

"Do you remember the girlfriend's name?"

"Something like Lisa."

"Larissa?"

"That's it! I heard she moved away, though."

"From whom?"

"Jeff. At his mama's funeral I asked what he was gonna do. That girl, Larissa, got a good job in Knoxville, and he was thinking of moving there with her. I told him to go and not look back. With his parents dead there was nothing to tie him to Cattle Hill anymore. It was time to get on with life and find himself some happiness. That's what Vicky would've wanted, and I told him so."

"When was the last time you talked to Jeff?"

"That was it. About a week later I saw a *For Sale* sign go up in the front yard. Never saw Jeff or that big old car of his again, so I assumed he left to be with his girl in Knoxville." Sam heard a sniffle. "I can't believe anyone would hurt that boy."

Sam had no response that would make sense of the senseless. "I want to thank you, Dorothy. You have no idea how much you've helped me. If I have any other questions would it be okay if I call you back?"

"Of course, dear. You can always catch me at supper time."

"And if you remember anything else, like the names of Vicky and Stan's friends, please call me." She gave Dorothy her number, said goodbye, and called Larissa Dodd's number. Still no answer. Sam would just keep trying, into the middle of the night if need be, until someone answered.

CHAPTER THIRTEEN

Sam stood and stretched, her body stiff from too little sleep and skipping her morning workout. She got a Diet Coke and glass of ice from the break room, hoping to get a caffeine-fueled second wind. Back at her desk, she picked up the faxes from Nate and swiveled her chair around to face the window, putting her feet up on the ledge. The top page was Ellen Konrad's personals, as Nate called them. It showed driving history, including all issued driver's licenses, residences listed in reverse chronological order, real property owned, tax returns, known DBAs, marriages, and divorces recorded.

Sam was impressed by Ellen's extensive, revenue-producing real estate empire. She owned rental properties in Miami, Hawaii, La Jolla, Laguna, Manhattan, and Cannes. She also owned boutique hotels in Los Cabos and Costa Rica. Every property was paid for in full, and each property was a stand-alone incorporated business. She bought the house in Palm Springs for $2.5 million—an absolute steal—and paid cash for it. Sam's father always claimed you could never go wrong putting your money in property because even if the real estate markets occasionally slumped, every year there was less ground to go around. Apparently Ellen followed the same investment philosophy.

Being executive producer on her TV series meant she received a sizable share of the domestic syndication and international sales. That, along with some lucrative cosmetics and clothing endorsements, made Konrad one of Hollywood's richest working actresses.

She also owned a production company with two successful dramas currently on the air, an equity waiver theatre in Los Angeles, a vineyard in Santa Ynez, a stake in a video game developer, and several other limited business partnerships. The woman was staggeringly wealthy.

The second page was Phil Atkins' personals, which were uniformly bland. He was born and educated back east before heading west to attend USC graduate school. He had two DBAs: Greenlight Professional Consulting, Inc. and Pools 'R Us. Sam smirked when she saw three divorces listed. "Big surprise there."

The last sheet was Lena's. Sam leaned her head back, holding the page in the air to read. When her brain caught up with her eyes, she sat upright. The address on Lena's first driving record was Rocky Hollow, Tennessee. Sam had never believed in coincidences and now they were piling up around her like old newspapers in a packrat's hovel.

Sam went online and pulled up a Google map of Rocky Hollow. It was twenty miles from Sevierville in Great Smoky Mountain country. Far enough away that a teenager could go there to sit out her pregnancy in secret but close enough to share the same area code. Cattle Hill was on the other side of Knoxville.

Sam tried not jumping to conclusions. Just because Lena lived in the same general vicinity as Rydell, just because she was the right age to have given birth to Jeff as a teen, and just because she got her California driver's license within two years of Jeff's birth didn't necessarily prove anything.

Sam put her head back to think but immediately started to doze off, so she sat forward again, yawning. "Who in a really small town is going to know everything about everyone else?" she asked just as her editor passed by.

Marlene stopped and put her empty coffee cup on Sam's desk. "I would say a rabbi, a priest, or a hairdresser. Was this a quiz or did I interrupt one of your one-sided conversations?"

"Both. I was quizzing myself." Sam quickly brought her editor up to speed.

When she finished, Marlene picked up her cup. "Nice work."

She disappeared to into the break room. On her way back, Marlene paused in front of Sam's desk again. "Just be careful, for both the paper's sake and the people involved. But I know you know that, so I'll shut up now and get back to proofing the classifieds."

Sam typed *Physicians, Rocky Hollow* and *Tennessee* into Google and three names came up. One was a dentist, the other two general practitioners, both with the same business phone number, address, and name, except one was identified as Junior. She picked up the phone and called directory assistance.

"Hi, for Rocky Hollow, Tennessee, I need a residential listing for a Gerald Crane. Senior, not Junior."

"Here's your listing…"

God bless the traditional GP, Sam thought writing down the number. She braced herself for the brush-off. The whole reason clergy and doctors knew so much is that they had ethical obligations to keep secrets. She wasn't even sure what she was going to say up to the moment a pleasant sounding woman answered the phone.

"Hi, ma'am, my name is Samantha Perry. Is Dr. Crane available?"

"Just a minute, please."

Sam tapped the end of her pen on the desk with a *rat-a-tat, rat-a-tat-tat* cadence, while waiting. Finally a man came on the line. "Hello, how can I help you?"

Visions of Will Geer and *The Waltons* danced in her head, "Hi, Dr. Crane. My name is Sam Perry—"

"You don't sound like a Sam," he joked.

"My dad had a warped sense of humor," she responded easily. "I'm calling from California, and I know this is a real long shot, but I was hoping you might be able to help me. I'm trying to track down an old work associate. I know she was born in Rocky Hollow, but we've lost track of each other."

"Well, if they lived here anytime in the past fifty years, odds are I know 'em. If they're old enough, odds are I might have delivered them too. Who's it you're looking for?"

"Her name is Lena Riley." There was a long silence on the line then the sounds of him talking with his hand over the receiver. "Dr. Crane?"

"Yep, I'm here. I remember Lena. How'd you say you knew her?"

"We worked on a charity together a while back, and I was hoping to recruit her to help with a benefit I'm producing for pediatric diabetes." Sometimes it worried Sam how easily lies came to her when necessary.

"That's a good cause there, young lady," he said, making Sam feel like pond scum for promoting herself as some humanitarian. The karma gods probably didn't like it, either. "It's good to hear Lena's using her time to good use."

"Would you know of any friends or relatives in the area who might know how I can reach her?"

"That's a tough one. She left a long time ago, and I don't think she kept close to her family here."

"Really? Why is that?"

"Lena was, uh…different. Caused her some problems growing up. Things like that still matter in places like this."

"So there's nobody I could call?" the frustration in her voice not an act.

Sam heard more muffled conversation before Crane answered. "There was a cousin of hers she was close to. Belinda Peletier." He spelled it for her. "She lives over in Ashland. If anybody knows where Lena is, it's Belinda. They were birds of a feather, if you get what I mean."

Sam didn't but wasn't about to tell him that. "Thank you, Dr. Crane. I really appreciate it."

"You're welcome. And good luck with that benefit," he added, making Sam cringe.

According to directory assistance, there was only one Belinda Peletier in Ashland Grove. It occurred to Sam that if Lena was still close to this woman, they might be in regular contact so the benefit story would not work. She needed something closer to the truth without being exactly upfront. She thought a few minutes then called Peletier's number.

The phone rang a long time before a woman answered. For what seemed the hundredth time that day, Sam introduced herself. "Dr. Crane over in Rocky Hollow suggested I call you."

"He did? Why?"

"Do you know who Ellen Konrad is?"

"The actress?"

"She's running for mayor in Palm Springs, and I'm researching a profile on her and the main people in her campaign. One of those people is Lena Riley."

"Oh, my God! You're kidding!"

"No. Lena is Ms. Konrad's assistant."

"I'll be damned. I knew she'd gone out West but thought she'd probably left California after everything happened and started over somewhere else."

Sam adjusted her headset and made sure the recording app was running. "Is this a convenient time for you?"

"Sure. What is it you're looking for exactly?"

"Mostly just background to show how she overcame personal adversity to become a successful professional in Konrad's campaign."

"Did she ever."

Sam forced herself to take it from the beginning. "Dr. Crane says you and Lena are cousins. Is that correct?"

"Distant cousins but we were close as teenagers. We never lived in the same town but we always hung out together at family functions. And once Lena could drive she came over a lot."

"Do you remember when Lena moved away to California?"

"It was right after she finished high school. That summer."

"Dr. Crane indicated that Lena had to overcome some problems as a teenager," Sam said, trying to be delicate.

"I'm sure he would say that," Belinda said dryly. "He's a closed-minded old bastard."

"So she did get pregnant?"

"What!" Belinda started laughing. "Boy was he giving you a crock. Lena's the *last* person who'd of gotten pregnant."

"Okay, I'm confused."

"Lena's troubles had nothing to do with boys. It had to do with girls."

"Are you sure?"

"Positive. Lena was in-your-face proud about it."

"In what way?"

"She cruised girls, dressed in Dockers, and refused to even pretend she had an interest in boys. In New York and LA that would be okay but around here…that Neanderthal Dr. Crane actually told Lena's parents they should try to *cure* her by sending her to a mental ward."

Just because she was gay didn't mean Lena couldn't have been Rydell's birth mother, Sam thought stubbornly, unwilling to write Lena off just yet.

"What did her parents think?"

"Not much. They were too busy drinking and arguing to care. They saw her as a lost cause and gave all their attention to her younger brother. I always thought she'd end up an activist or something, so it doesn't surprise me she's interested in politics."

"That's a good angle," Sam said, gently reeling her source in, "showing how experiences in Tennessee shaped her California politics."

"That does sound really good," Belinda said. "This is exciting."

"Do her parents and brother still live in the area?"

"Other than Lena, I was never close to her side of the family. But I heard they moved away after Lena ran off with her girlfriend. It was quite the scandal."

Thank you, Reader's Digest. "Could you give me the long version?"

"I'll try; it was a long time ago. My memory is a bit hazy."

"Even if you can just remember names of other friends, it'll help. Maybe I can track them down."

"I'm terrible with names. Can you hold on a minute?"

The minute turned into five. Sam could hear the television playing in the background, so she knew there was still a connection. Finally, Belinda came back, breathless. "I'm sorry. I ran out to the garage. Lena used to keep stuff at my house because she didn't trust her parents. I still have a box of photos she never came and got. Let me look."

Sam waited some more while Belinda rustled through the

pictures. "Here we go. Nell Overton. Lena was obsessive about writing captions on the back of photographs. So anyway, she was friends with Nell and used to go to her house all the time. I think they got along because they both had crappy home lives. Nell's mom was apparently mental, always in and out of hospitals for depression or whatever, and her dad was just a creep. Actually, it was her stepdad, even though he insisted Nell and her sister call him *daddy*. Is that creepy, or what? Lena said it grossed her out the way he looked at Nell."

"Do you know the stepfather's name?"

"Weird—*that* I remember. His name was Dale."

"So when did Lena start hanging out with Nell?"

"Right after they got to know each other in junior year biology class. When Lena fell in love with Nell's cousin, Lena spent most of her time at Nell's house."

"Why at Nell's house and not at the cousin's house?"

"The cousin lived with Nell. I'm sorry, I'm screwing the story all up."

"No, you're not. Just take it slow. What was the cousin's name?"

After more rustling, Belinda said, "Elisa Bayles."

"Okay. And Elisa lived at Nell's house?"

"Right. Elisa's parents and Nell's real dad were killed in some car accident several years earlier. Elisa's mom and Nell's mom were sisters so that's why she was living there."

"So Elisa and Nell were first cousins, and their mothers were sisters?"

"Identical twin sisters, yeah. So the first time Lena went to Nell's house she took one look at Elisa and fell totally in love. I can see why, too. She was a beautiful girl. Actually, so was Nell," Belinda said. "In these photos they look so much alike *they* could have been identical twins, too."

"When did Nell's mother remarry?"

"I guess not long after the accident. Lena said she only married the guy because she was so whacked. He kept moving them from town to town, like he didn't want them to ever be able to make friends. Again, just a total creep."

"When did Lena and Elisa get involved?"

"The summer before Lena's senior year."

"And how old was Elisa?"

Belinda paused. "I don't want to get Lena in trouble."

"I won't use it if it can get Lena in trouble," Sam promised. "But I can't know unless you tell me."

"Elisa had just turned fourteen in June. There's a picture here of her blowing out the candles on a cake."

"She was just out of grade school?" Sam frowned. "Kind of young for Lena to be lusting after, wasn't she?"

"Yeah, but you sure wouldn't know it to look at these pictures. She was definitely an early bloomer. And remember, Lena was really, really in love and just a teenager herself."

"So is that why they ran away? Because Elisa was underage?"

"No. They ran away because of Nell's stepdad. He'd been molesting Nell for years. After she moved to California to get away from him, he began messing with Elisa and Nell's younger sister."

"What was the sister's name?"

More rustling sounds. "Elizabeth. She was around Elisa's age."

"Jesus," Sam sat back and tossed her pen on the desk. "Where the hell was Nell's mom while her rapist husband was busy molesting everyone?"

"Like I said, she was mental. She'd been in the same car crash that killed her husband and Elisa's parents and went crazy over it."

"Why didn't Lena go to the police and turn him in?"

"She was afraid of getting in trouble. Dale only started messing with Elisa after walking in on them once. So she and Elisa ran off together. A couple months after that Lena called me. She wouldn't say where she was, just that she and Elisa had left and were staying with family friends. The next time I heard from her was maybe a year later when she sent me a note with the newspaper article."

"Article about what?"

"Nell and Elisa were driving on some expressway out in California and got hit by a semi. Nell survived but Elisa died. I haven't heard from Lena since." Belinda was quiet a moment, then Sam heard the sounds of her crying. "It really sucks that stuff like this happens to good people."

"Do you still have that newspaper clip?"

"Yeah. It's in another box in the garage."

Sam still wasn't convinced Lena didn't have some connection to Rydell. Maybe the stepfather assaulted her, too, and gotten her pregnant. Or maybe he got Elisa pregnant. That could be the real reason they ran away.

"Belinda, I have a huge favor to ask. Is there a full service copy place by you?"

"Sure, there's a Kinko's right next to the grocery store."

"Great. I need you to have them scan those photos of Lena, Nell, and Elisa and the newspaper article. Tell them to use best quality. And make sure to have them scan both front and back of the photos. Then I need them to email me the files. We'll pay for it from here, and I'll also reimburse you for your time and gas as well. Can you do this for me?"

"Of course I can. I'll do it first thing in the morning. And don't worry about my time or the gas. I'm just relieved Lena's doing well. Do you think you could put me in touch with her?"

"I'd be happy to," Sam said, knowing it wouldn't be any time soon. "Why don't you email me your contact information, and I'll see it gets to her."

"That would be so great. God, you never know what the day will bring, do you?"

"No, you certainly don't." She gave Belinda her email address and thanked her again before forwarding the call to Monica so she could get the location of the Kinko's to make the payment arrangement.

Sam logged onto the public records search engine she used at the *Times*, wondering when her old editor would think to change the password. She searched birth records for "E Bayles" in Tennessee and came up with Elisa Avery Bayles, born June 21. Her parents were Grace and Thomas Bayles. Sam pulled up their death certificates, which confirmed they died twenty-four years earlier. She also pulled up Elisa Bayles' California death certificate.

Next Sam located Grace and Thomas' marriage license, which listed her maiden name as Grace Tolliver. Sam tracked down her birth records, which listed her parents as Eleanor and Joshua Tolliver. The Tollivers had a second child, Grace's twin sister, Gail—

The phone rang, making Sam jump. "Hello?"

"I know it doesn't take you long to get ready, but do you realize what time it is?" Joe asked.

Sam looked at her watch. It was 5:20. "Oh shit!" She'd meant to be home a half-hour ago. "I got totally absorbed in what I was doing."

"Anything good?"

"Actually, yes. I'll tell you about it when I get home."

She shoved everything into her bag and tried making a fast, unobtrusive exit, but Marlene saw her walking by and waved her in.

"How goes it?"

Sam leaned her head into the office. "The physician was a good suggestion. Right now I'm on information overload. I need to let the mental dust settle then I'll give you an update tomorrow." Sam glanced at her watch.

Marlene peered at Sam over her glasses. "You got a hot date?"

I wish. "I'm going to a cocktail party at Ellen Konrad's tonight, and I'm running late."

"Leave it to you," she smiled, then shooed Sam out of the office, "Go, go. And have a couple drinks for me."

CHAPTER FOURTEEN

Sam parked her Spyder next to the valet umbrella, where a half dozen sweating attendants huddled together. Sam released the trunk and reluctantly tossed in her backpack, Joe insisting she not look like a reporter.

"I really feel naked," she complained.

He was unmoved. "If something comes up, like Lena confessing to murder, you've got a near photographic memory. You don't need to pull out a notebook."

"I won't know what to do with my hands."

"Sure you will. Hold a drink."

"I meant my other hand. I won't know where to put it."

"Well, you could have carried a tasteful little clutch purse," he taunted.

"I'd rather cut my hand off first." Sam gave her keys to the valet. "You know I've never owned a purse, clutch or otherwise."

"My point exactly."

The valet gave Sam a claim ticket, which she slipped it into her breast pocket. She was wearing lightweight, dark gray Bistro pants and a salmon colored raw silk shirt, the sleeves folded so they hung loosely above her wrists. Joe was decked out in black cargo pants, a sea-foam green shirt, and a gray linen jacket that was miraculously wrinkle-free.

Guides wearing black T-shirts with *Elect Konrad* embossed in green on the front directed guests toward the gate leading behind the wooden fence to the right of the house. Sam steered Joe past the crowded check-in table and stepped through the gate into a huge side yard. The centerpiece was a freeform pool, big enough for laps. It was currently filled with bouquets of floating candles. The attached Jacuzzi resembled a small lagoon, a verdant oasis nestled beneath a waterfall. Past the pool was a spacious lawn of lush forest-green waterless grass—artificial grass that looked and felt like so real it was impossible to tell the difference. Sam knew this because there was a display by the gate that told her so. The entire yard was secured by an eight-foot redwood fence that ensured privacy, as did the smattering of small palms and citrus trees planted along the perimeter.

This side of the house was all French doors, which opened onto a stone patio that ran the length of the yard. Three separate electric awnings shaded the patio, where four tables of food were set up. There were two bars, one in each far corner of the yard. Keeping the food and booze on opposite sides kept people flowing back and forth, preventing human logjams. Sam smiled when she saw a sign next to the closest bar that said *Beer & Wine Only Line.*

Redwood patio chairs and lounges were positioned around the near side of the pool and by both bars. The deck on the far side of the pool was covered by a long tent shading a row of bar tables and stools. Strategically positioned around the backyard were six outdoor cooling systems, the kind used by professional and college football teams on the sidelines during games played in August and September. It had to be at least twenty-five degrees cooler back here than out in front. Before moving to Palm Springs, Sam would have never believed ninety degrees could feel so refreshingly cool.

Joe took in the surroundings with open approval. "She certainly is the hostess with the mostest. Unbelievably classy."

"Unbelievably expensive."

"But unbelievably tasteful. Let's hit the bar."

Even though it was only a quarter after six the place was already filled with people. She spotted Ellen talking to a group of men in business suits sitting at one of the bar tables under the tent. She wore white jeans over low-heeled boots and a sleeveless, sapphire blouse that showed off gym-toned arms. Wearing no jacket, her figure was fully visible, and the men she talked to were having a hard time keeping their eyes from drifting below her neckline. With her hair down and loose, sunglasses propped on top of her head, she looked just like the movie star she was.

"She is an exquisite real woman," Joe murmured.

"As opposed to what? A drag queen?"

"I mean she's not a skinny stick like so many actresses I've met. She's hot *and* healthy. To have that face and body plus talent seems patently unfair to the rest of us mere mortals."

Sam put her hand on his back. "Oh, I always thought of you more as a demigod."

"Well, yes, but bragging is so gauche."

They made their way to the bar in the corner furthest from the front gate because it was the best vantage point to people-watch. She propped against an unoccupied patio chair and scanned the crowd while Joe got their drinks. Other than supporting Konrad for mayor and wanting a piece of her time and attention, the only thing the disparate guest list seemed to have in common was a hearty appetite and a thirst for booze, leaving the caterers and bartenders mobbed and sweating profusely.

Considering the line, Joe was back in a relatively quick ten minutes and handed her two drinks.

"These are both for me?"

Before he could answer, Phil Atkins appeared beside them radiating naked aggression. Feeling like a bit of a freeloader, Sam lowered her drink-filled hands, holding the rims by her fingertips. "Hello Mr. Atkins," she said genially.

He did not return the pleasantry. "What exactly do you think you're doing here?"

Sam nodded toward the nearby air conditioning unit. "Enjoying the breeze?"

He stepped closer. "This is an important gathering tonight. The last thing we need is some reporter sniffing around here disturbing our guests."

"Well, I haven't pushed anyone in the pool yet although the night *is* young."

He pointed his finger at her. "Your being here is inappropriate."

Sam remained amiable but didn't bother to hide her sarcasm. "You need to brush up on your vocabulary skills, Phil. Pulling out my murder mystery party game would be *inappropriate*; me just standing here is simply *innocuous*."

Sam sensed someone move behind her. She caught a scent of perfume in the fan-stirred air and knew who it was without having to look.

"Is there a problem here?" Ellen asked lightly, directing the question at Atkins.

"It's under control. I was just about to escort these people out."

She put her hand on Sam's shoulder. "These are my guests. They're not going anywhere."

Atkins' surprise quickly morphed into resentment. "I don't remember seeing her name on my list."

Sam suspected this tension had deeper roots than a just cocktail party guest list. Ellen gave her shoulder a quick squeeze then led Phil several steps away. Sam could still hear them clearly and wondered if that was the point.

"I would have never approved this," he complained.

"I don't need your permission," she reminded him calmly.

"I'm your campaign manager. This is what I get paid to do."

"You get paid to help run my campaign, Phil, but not to make my decisions or run my personal life."

"Your personal life? I'm telling you, you're making a mistake."

"And I'm telling you, this is my house." She never raised her voice but the words were suddenly razor sharp. "Your opinion is noted and appreciated but I will invite whoever I want into my home whenever I want. And they will be made welcome. I hope that's understood." Ellen did not wait for him to respond. She walked back, stood next to Sam, and exhaled softly. "I am so sorry about that."

"Not a problem." She watched Atkins stomped off. "Is it just me or doesn't he seriously look like Mr. Spacely?"

Joe snorted. Ellen folded her arms, one hand covering her

eyes, laughing softly. The more she thought about it, the harder she laughed until she was practically doubled-over. She finally composed herself and straightened up, wiping tears from her eyes. "You are very bad."

"I do my best." Sam gestured toward Ellen. "Joe, this is Ellen Konrad. Ellen, my friend Joe Sapone."

They shook hands, and Joe pointed at her watch. "The Tangara is one of my favorite Piaget designs."

"Thank you. Are you a jeweler?"

"No, he's just a snob," Sam joked, sipping from one of the glasses.

Ellen glanced at the drinks in her hands and raised an eyebrow. "Two-fisted, huh?" she teased. "You weren't kidding. You really do go for the open bar."

"This wasn't my doing." She looked pointedly at Joe.

He shrugged. "You're the one who said you didn't know what to do with your hand. Or where to put it."

Ellen laughed softly. "Sorry I missed out on that conversation. I could offer a suggestion," she waited a beat then flashed a wicked smile, "or two."

Sam shook her head. "I give up."

Ellen gestured toward Sam's blushing cheeks with a mischievous grin. "Nice to know I haven't lost my touch."

"Too bad I can't say the same about my dignity," Sam sighed, making her laugh. She drained the glass and set it on the accent table next to the pool lounge chair. "One down…"

"What do you drink?" Ellen asked.

"Jack and Diet."

"Good choice." She looked past Sam and waved at someone. Emerging through the crowd was her son Luke. She grabbed his arm and held it close to her side. "I want to properly introduce you. Luke, this is Joe Sapone."

"Nice meeting you," he said, flashing Joe a Hollywood politician's son's smile.

"And this is Sam Perry."

"Actually, we've already met," Sam said as they shook hands.

"That's right." Luke's smile dimmed as though suffering a power outage. "You're the reporter."

Ellen watched their interaction closely, her son's discomfort obvious. "Is everything okay with Phil?" she asked.

"Sure. Why wouldn't it be?"

"I don't know. You tell me."

"There's nothing to tell." His eyes darted nervously towards Sam.

"He's seems a bit edgy lately," Ellen pushed.

"You know Phil. He gets that way." He patted her hand and disengaged his arm. "I need to go in and check on some things, Mom."

"Has your sister shown up?"

"Not that I know of. I'll see you later."

Ellen watched Luke hurry away. "I wish I knew what's gotten up everyone's ass around here lately."

"You mean besides me?" Sam asked, adding dryly, "metaphorically speaking." Ellen smiled and gave her a friendly nudge. Looking past Ellen Sam noticed a dark-haired woman standing near the pool was watching them. She was dressed in a conservative business suit, wore her hair pulled back in a severe ponytail, and looked to be in her forties. She might have been very pretty once but permanent frown lines and tension now etched her face. She walked up to Ellen, giving Sam and Joe a perfunctory, and subtly dismissive, nod.

She pointed in the direction of the tables. "The head of the Chamber of Commerce is here waiting to talk to you."

"Okay, just a second. Sam, Joe, I'd like you to meet my assistant Lena Riley."

It took all Sam's will power not to grill her on the spot. "Hi, I'm Sam Perry."

Lena shook hands briefly and regarded her coolly. "I'm aware who you are."

"A *Weekender* fan?"

"Hardly. I have to tell you, I don't think your presence is

appropriate tonight."

"Is that why you removed Sam's name from the final guest list?" Ellen asked with a smile that didn't reach her eyes.

Lena didn't flinch. "I have no idea what you're talking about." She turned back to Sam. "I just hope you won't involve our guests in the story Ellen tells me you're working on."

Sam bristled at her officious manner but smiled cordially. "For as etiquette-challenged as I may be, Ms. Riley, since I'm here socially and not professionally, the other guests can breathe easy. Unless of course I spot someone wearing an *I murdered Jeff Rydell* T-shirt; then all bets are off."

Lena recoiled away from Sam. "That's offensive."

"So is assuming I'd be disrespectful of Ellen's hospitality."

Lena chose not to respond. "We really need to go," she said again and walked away expecting Ellen to follow. She stopped and turned around when she realized Ellen hadn't moved.

Joe leaned close to Sam. "You really do have a unique way with people."

"You've noticed?"

Lena came back and grabbed Ellen's arm. "You really shouldn't keep him waiting."

"I said I'll be right there," Ellen pulled her arm free. "You can talk to him until then."

Sam waited until the assistant was safely out of earshot. "You know I'm on a roll when people I've never even met before already dislike me."

Ellen placed her hand over her heart in a gesture of apology. "I'm sorry—"

"Don't be," Joe stopped her. "Sam delights in getting under people's skin."

"I do not," she demurred, without much conviction.

"Samantha O'Shea Perry, of *course* you do. Because people who are agitated are more apt to say or reveal things they might not otherwise."

A look of understanding crossed Ellen's face. "I was wondering why you didn't just tell Phil I invited you."

"I would have. Eventually. But it was entertaining to let him think I was a crasher. He was so angry his comb-over was standing on end."

Ellen laughed, "You really are bad."

Sam glanced up and saw Lena staring at them, her expression a mask of umbrage.

Ellen followed Sam's gaze and said quietly, "Thank you for putting up with my complicated life." She gave Sam a brief, friendly hug then straightened her shirt and took a steadying breath. "I better not keep Mr. Chamber of Commerce waiting."

After Ellen left, Joe took his jacket off and draped it over the back of the nearest lounge chair. "Lena sure doesn't look like a lesbian, wild-child lady killer."

"Apparently she underwent a personality transplant."

"Removal seems more like it. I'm going to grab us some food. Do you want to get us another round?"

"Sure." Sam put her still half-full glass on the accent table next to the chair with a napkin over it, hoping an overzealous caterer wouldn't take it away. As she stood in line for the bar, Sam studied Lena, who hovered around Ellen. Joe was right. She looked like a prim, proper, asexual bookkeeper. And every fiber of her being screamed discontentment. Sam wondered why nobody in Ellen Konrad's inner circle seemed very happy. It certainly helped explain why she seemed desperate for outside company.

While Sam waited for the bartender to fill her order, she watched Ellen say goodbye to the Chamber head. Before Lena could pull her away, two women approached carrying babies. One handed her child to Ellen and pulled out her iPhone to take a picture. Ellen turned around briefly, made eye contact with Sam, and mouthed *Help me.* Sam laughed out loud.

"Sounds like you're enjoying yourself."

She turned around and saw Detective Larson, casually dressed in a polo shirt with a PSPA logo.

"What a surprise," she smiled, picking up the drinks. Larson motioned for her to wait while he got a beer then followed as she navigated back to the lounge chair.

"Why a surprise?" he asked.

"I guess I wasn't expecting to see a local cop at a political meet-and-greet."

"Cops vote, too."

Sam leaned against the chair. "So you're here in a personal capacity?"

"Not really. I'm the head of the local Police Association. We've officially endorsed Ellen for mayor. But what brings you here?"

"Ellen invited me. And after meeting some of the people she works with, I suspect it's primarily for comic relief. They're a tense bunch."

"Well, you can't blame them, especially with someone like you poking around. And I mean that as a compliment."

"Thanks, but shouldn't they be more worried about someone like you, as in the police, poking around?"

"Only if one of them committed a crime, and there's nothing to indicate they have. Unless you know something I don't."

"Actually, I was going to call you tomorrow." Sam knew she should have brought her backpack in. "I have some things you ought to see."

Larson moved a step closer and asked quietly, "Such as?"

"The name and phone number of Rydell's girlfriend and some other background material. Bottom line is his parents are both dead. He was an only child and adopted, so as far as I can tell the girlfriend is the only next of kin left."

By Larson's expression, all this was news to him. After a brief internal debate, she added. "I'm looking into whether he came to California in search of his birth mother and just who that might be. So, how's your investigation coming along?"

He took another swallow of beer. "I don't suppose you'd be willing to tell me how you tracked all this down?"

"Detective, you know I can't reveal my sources," she said, hoping she sounded appropriately apologetic.

Larson was disgruntled, but Sam did not take it personally. While cops had better resources and the power of authority behind them, it was easier for journalists to establish personal relationships with hesitant sources. People who helped the cops might find themselves called as witnesses, and the average person shied away from that kind of involvement.

"I'll drop the package off to you tomorrow morning. Or I can email it."

"Thanks." He fished a business card out of his wallet along with a small pencil Sam associated with playing miniature golf. He wrote his email address and another number on the back. "That's my cell phone number. I always have it with me so if anything especially important or urgent comes up, call that number."

"Thanks."

Larson left to mingle as Joe came back, setting plates down on a small table next to the lounge. He pulled napkins from one leg pocket of his cargo pants and silverware from another.

They spent the next half-hour eating, people watching, and discussing the day's story developments in more detail, including Rydell's map being folded to the area where he died.

"So what does it all mean?" he asked.

"I'm not sure yet how it all ties together. And as much as I'd like it to be her on principle, why would Lena give a rat's ass if she had a son come out of the woodwork or the son of her dead lover?"

"Look at her," Joe pointed to where Lena was steering Ellen to another group of constituents, "she seems the more ambitious of the two. Desperately ambitious. Maybe she was afraid if the truth about her past came out, such as running off with an underage girl regardless of who was pregnant, it might reflect badly on Ellen. Or more to the point, Ellen would have to fire her. She would lose her position, her prestige, her power base, and her only claim to fame. People have killed for a lot less."

Sam considered another possibility. "Or, while in Palm Springs looking up his birth mother he got involved with some unrelated scheme that got him killed, maybe something at the Crazy Girl."

Sam thought back to her conversation with Ellen. "Then again, maybe everything is connected because it was all part of why he came here and stayed here."

"It just doesn't make much sense."

"As Sherlock Holmes said, 'When you have eliminated the impossible, whatever remains, however improbable, must be the truth.'" Sam stood and stretched off a mild wave of fatigue. "I need to find a bathroom."

"Me, too," Joe also stood and neatly piled the dishes. "Time to go explore."

CHAPTER FIFTEEN

They walked toward the set of open French doors behind the food tables. A sign posted on an easel pointed to the restroom, which was in the hallway just to the left. About a half-dozen people were already waiting in line, so they passed the time with Joe rhapsodizing about the artwork on the walls.

Sam wandered down to a door and peered in to see a large library furnished with plush chairs and pillowed divans, the walls covered floor-to-ceiling with bulging bookcases. One section of visibly old books was in a temperature-controlled case. Sam realized Ellen was more than an avid reader. She was a book collector, something none of the articles about her mentioned. She wondered how much else the woman had been able to keep private over the years.

Out of the corner of her eye Sam saw a familiar face walking past.

"Bonjour, René. Ça va?"

René recognized her and smiled. *"Je suis bien. Et vous?"*

"Bien. La nourriture était merveilleuse."

René pointed toward what Sam assumed was the kitchen. "*Vous aiment autre chose?*"

"God, no," Sam patted her stomach. "*Je suis pleine.* But, uhm," she had to think of the words, "*Excusez-moi, mon français n'est pas très bon. Je voudrais une ligne plus courte.*"

René looked at the people waiting to use the guest bathroom. "Ah. *Suivez-moi*," she whispered.

As they followed René past the others in line, Joe tapped Sam on the shoulder. "Impressive."

"Oh, please. I know you're fluent. My French sucks."

René turned around. "Oh, *Madame*, you don't suck. It is quite good, for an American."

It intrigued Sam how the French always seemed to compliment you and insult you in the same breath.

René led them into a large den with a gleaming wooden floor. In the corner to the right of the door were a bookcase, divan, and floor lamp making for a cozy reading spot. The French doors along the right wall, which faced the yard and pool, were closed to prevent access by party guests. René pressed a button on the wall and the glass in the doors turned dark and opaque so people couldn't see in, either.

"I want those doors," Sam said.

Joe rolled his eyes. "You are such a gadget geek."

Ahead of them in the right front corner was a teak wood bar with matching stools. The shelves behind the bar were lit from underneath, casting a pleasant glow on the extensive selection of spirits. René turned on the lamp positioned at the end of bar, adding to the room's soft lighting. Next to the lamp was one of Ellen's Academy Awards. In front of it was a Magic 8-Ball.

There was another set of French doors on the far wall leading out onto a balcony. The desert beyond was already turning dusky; being so close to the mountains meant early-falling evening shadows.

René walked over to a door in the back left corner of the room. "*Voici la salle de bain*," then walked out with a big smile.

Sam told Joe he could go first and wandered around the room. She opened one of the doors leading to the balcony and walked out. There was nothing behind Ellen's house except the foot of the mountains. About thirty yards out was a channel approximately fifteen feet wide that spanned her field of vision. Sam assumed it was an ephemeral stream—more commonly called a wash by desert residents. These streambeds only carried water during rainstorms as runoff flowed down from the mountains.

Joe stepped onto the balcony, "Your turn." He looked out at the desert, painted orange and rose by the setting sun. "There was always something about deserts that kind of scared me. They seem so unforgiving."

Sam left Joe to his primal fears and used the bathroom, furnished with a Jacuzzi tub, separate shower, private bathroom stall complete with bidet, and make-up vanity. Out of curiosity she turned on the bidet and jumped back when a powerful stream of water shot three feet out of the bowl. "Who'd need a pillow with one of these?" Sam muttered. Before leaving, she tried calling Larissa, but again there was no answer. When she came back into the den, Joe was playing with an elaborate remote control.

"What are you doing?"

He glanced up. "I'm looking for my favorite dance satellite station and making sure I don't turn it on through the whole house." With a *harrumph* of success, Joe found the channel. He moved to the middle of the room and held his arms out. "Come here, Sam. It's been too long."

"You've got to be kidding," she groaned but dutifully walked over, unaware Ellen had come through the backyard gate and onto the balcony. Not wanting to interrupt and a little curious, she leaned against the railing and settled back to watch and listen while eating her plate of shrimp.

Joe and Sam danced and reminisced about nights spent bar-hopping and not getting home from Chicago until well after dawn. When the song finally ended, Joe dipped Sam almost to the ground. She squinted up at him. "If you drop me, you're such dead meat."

Laughing, he spun her around one last time then gave her bear hug. "We've still got it."

Ellen walked in smiling. "You two should take your act on the road. You dance well together."

"I made Sam enter a dance contest with me years ago when we were nineteen. I was going through my salsa phase," Joe explained, "and she is still complaining about how much we rehearsed. But, of course, we won."

"But, of course, the acid helped," Sam deadpanned.

"I'm not always sure when you're kidding or being serious," Ellen admitted.

"When it comes to hallucinogenics, I rarely kid," she sighed nostalgically.

Smiling, Ellen went behind the bar and plucked a bottle of Knob Creek from one of the shelves. "What would you like?" she asked Joe.

"To be nineteen again, but for now a vodka tonic would be great, please."

Joe took a closer look of Ellen's Academy Award. In front of it was a small folded card that read: *Ask Uncle Oscar.* "This is too funny," he said, picking up the Magic 8-Ball.

Ellen glanced up. "That's my kids' doing. I'm sure AMPAS would not be amused, but Luke and Annie find it entertaining."

Joe shook the ball, "Okay, Uncle Oscar…will Ellen win the election?" He turned it over and read the bottom.

Without a doubt.

Joe raised an eyebrow and shook the ball again. "Are you sure about that?"

Yes—definitely.

"Could there be an upset and she lose by a vote?"

My reply is no.

He eyed the ball suspiciously.

Ellen smiled. "It is *my* Oscar, after all."

"Will I stay in Chicago?"

Outlook not so good.

"Will it snow tomorrow?"

Don't count on it.

"Will Phil Atkins stop wearing a comb-over?"

My sources say no.

"Will Sam ever find true love?"

You may rely on it.

"Finally!" Joe said. "A wrong answer."

"Oh, fuck you."

"Oooh," he shook the ball vigorously, "will she?"

It's highly unlikely.

"Would you put that down," Sam said, reaching for it.

"Just one more," Joe promised. "Will Sam know when she finds her true love?"

Better not tell you now.

Joe leaned over and whispered in Oscar's ear so Ellen and Sam couldn't hear. "Is the person in the room right now?"

It is certain.

He set the Magic 8-Ball down with careful reverence. "That thing is more than a little freaky. I wouldn't be surprised if it started spewing pea soup green vomit and scream for Father Merrin."

"*Exorcist V: The Magic 8-Ball,*" Sam said, imitating a movie trailer voice-over.

"*Ask, at the risk of your soul,*" Joe finished.

Ellen laughed. "My kids will love you two." *Because*, she thought in amusement, *it's like having two more adolescents around.*

Sam eyed Joe. "So, what was that last question?"

"Oh, nothing. But I'm so happy for you," he pinched her cheek. She grabbed his thumb and bent it back, making him let go.

"Hey, watch the digits."

Ellen walked around the bar with the other two drinks. She handed one to Sam and slid onto the stool next to her. They touched glasses. Sam also tapped the bar counter with her glass before taking a sip.

"You did that the other day, too," Ellen observed.

"You always have to bless the bar," Sam explained.

"I never heard of it until Sam, either," Joe told Ellen. "Some weird Celtic pagan ritual, I'm sure."

Ellen shrugged, "Who doesn't like pagan?" and touched the bar counter before sipping. "So, is Kevin the name of your boyfriend?"

It took Sam a moment to realize Ellen was talking to her. "Mine? *Nooo.* Kevin is Joe's freshly minted would-be life partner. And from the sounds of it, I think they're way overdue for some quality time together."

"I'm sure it's no surprise to hear I was always much more interested in spying on the boys' locker room than the girls'. And as for Sam, thank God she finally dumped her Aryan boyfiend Otto…"

"Jens."

"...whatever. Now she's living in emotionally unencumbered but lonely solitude."

Sam rolled her eyes. "I'm not exactly Howard fucking Hughes."

"True. You have much better hygiene."

Ellen raised an eyebrow. "Aryan?"

"Jens was born in Germany, but he grew up here. He enjoyed going out and having a good time, but when it came to self-awareness and the world at large, he could be a bit...humorless."

"Mmm hmm," Joe muttered, "and Joseph Goebbels was a bit opinionated."

"I can't at all imagine you with somebody humorless."

"Yeah, well, neither can I. Now."

"So what was the attraction?"

Joe snickered and held the palms of his hands approximately eight inches apart.

Ellen smiled and clarified, "Emotionally speaking."

"Thank you. I keep telling Joe size is overrated."

He dismissed the notion out of hand. "You'd think differently if you were a man."

"Only because then I'd be thinking with my dick instead of my brain."

"Mee-ow!" he snapped and they all laughed.

"Anyway, the primary attraction with Jens was that he pursued me," Sam admitted with a self-conscious laugh. "And he did have an amazing body. Of course, at the time I didn't realize it was borne out of an equally amazing level of self-absorption. But in the beginning it was a lot of fun and just so carnal. I'd never had a relationship quite like that before, not that I had much to compare it against."

"She was a virgin until twenty-two," Joe announced. Sam shot him an annoyed look. He shrugged, unconcerned. "Well, you were."

"Why don't you just broadcast it over the house intercom system?"

Joe studied the remote. "Is there a microphone attachment?"

"Play nice," Ellen intervened mildly, amused at their sibling-like squabbling. "A lot of people prefer to wait until they're older," she said to Joe then admitted to Sam, "although it does surprise me you did."

"Why?"

"You come across as a very sensual person and in my experience sensual people tend to have robust libidos."

"I did, but in high school and college it just seemed more efficient and less complicated to take care of myself...myself."

"You're awfully forthcoming," Ellen commented.

She shrugged. "I spend my professional life asking people questions so it'd be kind of hypocritical not to answer some on occasion."

"Sam's life is an open book," Joe explained. "The chapter on her relationships however, is exceedingly short and sad."

"So true," Sam agreed.

"Why?" Ellen asked.

"I never really dated. The whole notion of getting-to-know-you dating gives me hives. If I was horny enough and buzzed enough I'd go home with someone I met at a club or party, but once it was over I got the hell out as fast as I could."

"You must have broken a few hearts," Ellen observed.

"Me?" Sam snorted dismissively. "The only heart I broke was my own."

"Day-after remorse?"

"Always. I never felt anything in here," she tapped her chest, "so it just left me empty. It was like having an itch you could never quite reach."

"Maybe you should have found a woman to scratch it," Joe suggested pointedly. To his surprise, Sam simply shrugged.

"Yeah, well...I didn't know any who'd want to."

"You certainly didn't look very hard, then," Ellen commented.

Sam had no idea how to respond, so she didn't.

Ellen found her shyness very appealing. "You must have felt very relieved when Jens came along."

"That's exactly what I felt. He was the first person I spent the entire night with. We were friends first, so I was comfortable with him."

"That was the beginning of her nympho phase," Joe said.

"Let's just say I made up for lost time with a vengeance."

"Maybe sexually," Ellen observed, "but you still weren't in love."

Sam met her gaze, aware she might have met her observational match. "You're good, too."

"I also have my moments."

Joe felt as if he were suddenly eavesdropping and was loving every moment. Sam turned to lean back against the bar, her leg settling against Ellen's. "For a while I wanted to think I was in love. But even at our closest, I was always aware something fundamental was missing. So as time went on the sex began to feel like glorified mutual masturbation and eventually I avoided it altogether. So ironic considering how the relationship began."

"Why did you stay?"

"I'm not big on change. Rather than make the effort to extricate myself, we started living very separate lives, and I delved into sixteen-hour work days. When he finally moved out it was all rather anti-climactic."

"And you haven't been involved since?"

"She won't even look," Joe complained.

"I just don't think you can force it. If it happens, it happens."

"Trust me," Ellen predicted with a soft smile, her eyes an inviting warm, blue bath, "when you least expect it someone will walk into your life and change absolutely everything,"

"Maybe so," Sam said, drawn in by her gaze. "Anyway, thank you for inviting us tonight. Cheers."

"Thank *you* for being here." They all touched glasses, then the bar. "You two are lucky to have each other as friends."

"Yes, we are," Joe agreed, "especially since nobody else wants us."

"Well, consider yourself wanted here."

"Be careful," Sam warned, "You might never get rid of us."

"Maybe that's the plan," Ellen smiled, tapping her boot

against Sam's.

Between the company and the bourbon, Sam felt unusually content. She gestured towards the pool area. "Looks like there's still quite a party going on out there."

"I hope so. I wanted people to relax after doing business, myself included."

"So that's why you're hiding out in here?"

"Partly. I need time where I don't have to be in candidate mode. It's so nice to talk about something other than politics and to have great company." Ellen absently brushed her hair back, leaving it sexily tousled. "How long have you known each other?"

"Since high school."

"You two must have been a handful together in class."

"They pretty much kept us on opposite sides of the room," Sam recalled, "especially after we discovered a mutual love of Tennessee Williams."

"Mendacity!" they said in unison.

Joe pulled up the third stool and explained, "Big Daddy was my favorite Burl Ives role of all time."

"Personally, I was always partial to Sam the Snowman in *Rudolph*," Ellen smiled.

"Big Daddy was his best *role,* but the snowman was Burl's greatest *performance* of all time. Let's face it: his rendition of "Holly Jolly Christmas" is a classic. And the way he did it without ever moving his little snowman face or changing expression was unequaled... with the possible exception of Elizabeth Berkley in *Showgirls*."

Ellen laughed out loud then caught herself. "Actors rarely have control over the finished product."

"Spoken like a true politician."

"I've always wanted to do *Cat on a Hot Tin Roof* on stage," Ellen said. "Or *Streetcar Named Desire*. Blanche is a great character. *What you are talking about is desire, just brutal desire*." Ellen's accent was magnolia perfect as she abruptly transformed into Blanche, her body loose and languid. "*I don't want realism. I want magic! I do misrepresent things. I don't tell the truth. I tell what ought to be truth*."

"That was my last boyfriend's philosophy, too," Joe said dryly, making Ellen laugh.

"I see you more as Maggie," Sam told her.

"I strike you as being immersed in mendacity?" Ellen asked lightly then leaned closer. "*I get lonely...very. How long does it have to go on? This punishment? Haven't I done time enough, haven't I served my term, can't I apply for a pardon? You know what I feel like? I feel all the time like a cat on a hot tin roof...But I can stay on it just as long as I have to.*"

Then just like that, Ellen was back. "God, I love Williams."

"It's like sitting next to Sybil," Sam told her, referring to the famous multiple personality case.

Ellen smiled, flattered. "Oddly, that's one of the nicest reviews I've ever gotten."

"So, when your kids were little," Joe asked, "did you have fun freaking them out by becoming different people at the dinner table?"

"Only on holidays."

Laughing, he stood up. "I left my jacket outside, and I hear the prime rib calling me for seconds. I'll be back."

Ellen held her hand out for Sam's glass and went behind the bar to make them another round. Sam walked onto the balcony and stared out at the desert, dimly lit by the moon. Lost in thought, she didn't hear Ellen approaching and instinctively flinched when she touched her arm to hand over the glass.

"I didn't mean to startle you," she apologized.

"Old reflex."

When Sam didn't elaborate, Ellen prodded, "You don't like being touched?"

"That's not it at all." Sam poked at the glass in her ice. "Mommy Dearest's penchant for dragging me out of bed in the middle of the night left me a bit skittish about someone coming up behind me when I'm not expecting it. You must have been a cat in a previous life."

Ellen leaned forward so that their foreheads briefly touched. "I'll try to be noisier next time," she promised and then raised her glass. "Cheers."

They touched glasses. Sam also touched the railing.

Ellen paused. "I thought it was bless the bar."

"The bar…the railing…whatever. At home, it's usually my dogs. Blessing knows no bounds."

Smiling, Ellen touched the rail and took a sip. She could smell Sam's scent. "What perfume are you wearing?"

"Amarige."

"I like it very much."

"Thank you. I notice you wear Bal à Versailles."

"Not many people would recognize it," Ellen said, pleased they shared another connection. They stood in companionable silence, staring out at the night sky, the sounds of talking and activity drifting over from the yard. Ellen tried to remember the last time she felt this at peace, this content, and couldn't. She turned to face the rail, so their arms touched.

"This is a great view." Sam pointed toward the mountains. "I never knew there was a wash here."

"It doesn't look like much now but you should see it during a storm. You know the sound a strong earthquake makes?

"That roar?"

"Exactly. Before you can see the water you can feel and hear its vibration coming down the mountain. When the water comes down at night it's like a freight train outside your window. I don't know if you can see now, but the only things growing in the channel are high up on the sides because anything on the bottom gets completely washed away."

"The desert's not a place I'd want to be out alone in at night, rainy or otherwise." The air around them was hot and thick. Sam blew down the front of her shirt. "I'm going to start carrying around a portable shower if this weather doesn't break soon."

Ellen took a deep breath. "It smells like it's going to rain. We're overdue; we haven't had a thunderstorm in probably six months." She turned around so her back rested against the railing and stretched out her legs. They were face to face, their arms again resting against one another. "I'm really glad you're here, Sam. Thank you for coming."

"Thank you for having me. I'm glad I'm here, too. Tonight's been a lot of fun."

"Is O'Shea really your middle name?"

She nodded, taking a sip of her drink. "My paternal grandfather came over from Ireland, so it was supposedly a nod to my Gaelic heritage. I personally suspect it was just an homage to his favorite pub."

"Whatever the origin, it fits you. It's unique and unexpected."

Sam looked at her thoughtfully. "You're not what I expected, either."

Ellen twirled the ice in her drink. "When's your birthday?"

"February 21."

"A Pisces, huh?" she smiled. "That's interesting."

"Why?"

"My makeup lady on the series was always telling me Pisces are the most compatible with us Cancers."

"Maybe that's why I feel so at ease with you." Even though Sam could hear the sounds of talking and laughter from the party, it felt as if they were the only ones in the world at that moment. "At the risk of sounding silly, it's as if I knew you before we ever met."

"It's not silly at all. I feel the same way," Ellen assured her, briefly cupping Sam's face. "Would you like to go to dinner tomorrow?"

"I'd love to. You're not worried about getting grief for consorting with a known journalist?"

"Not remotely. It's been a long time since I met someone I feel so comfortable talking to. And what you said the other day is true. It does get lonely. Maybe it's time for some heart-to-hearts."

Sam grinned. "You show me yours, I'll show you mine?"

Ellen raised an eyebrow. "We can do that, too."

"Uh-oh…I think my face is smoldering."

Ellen's smile faded at the sound of footsteps walking briskly across the den's wooden floor. Sam turned her head and saw Lena approaching, her face inscrutable but her posture stiff with irritation. She straightened up, but Ellen didn't move other than to take another sip of her drink.

Lena stopped in the doorway and looked from one to the other, then addressed Ellen. "You should really come out to say goodnight to your guests."

"If you'll excuse me," Sam gestured toward the den, "I need to use the bathroom."

"Don't leave," Ellen lightly tugged at the hem of her shirt. "I'll be right in."

Sam closed the bathroom door and let out a long breath. She washed her hands and rinsed her face with cold water. The idea that she and Ellen could be friends and confidantes thrilled her. She was well aware her attraction to Ellen went beyond friendship but unconsummated desire was a small price to pay to have the woman in her life.

When Sam came out of the bathroom Lena and Ellen were still on the balcony speaking in low, clipped tones. Although she couldn't hear what they were saying, their body language was strained. She strolled over to the fireplace and browsed the pictures lining the mantel. Many of the photos appeared to be from past vacations. Several showed Ellen and a man she assumed was her late husband along with two young children who were all grins and youthful energy.

Sam remembered reading at the library that Ellen had married cameraman Seamus Evans right after she turned twenty-two and they adopted a little boy and his younger sister within a month of their marriage. Sam could see why they had been considered Hollywood's golden family. Seamus had been killed in a traffic accident six years earlier.

Beside the older family photos was a more recent picture of Luke posing with friends on a boat that was positively Kennedy-esque. Next, there was a group shot of young people Sam didn't recognize, but the picture after that brought her up short. It was a family Christmas portrait from two years earlier of Ellen and her now-grown kids. Sam was surprised to realize that Annie from the campaign headquarters was Ellen's daughter, Anne.

"Talk about keeping a low profile," Sam muttered, studying the picture. Despite the festive occasion Anne's eyes were remote, head held at a downward angle as if trying to disappear into the background.

Reexamining the group picture of high school-aged youths, Sam was now able to pick out Anne. It was like looking at two completely different individuals. This Anne was smiling, head held up, her eyes engaged with whoever was behind the camera.

"Where did you go?" Sam wondered. Anne was hugging the arm of the boy standing next to her. He wore a mustache and projected the cocky aura of teenage testosterone. Something about him seemed familiar but Sam couldn't place it.

"I'm sorry about that," Ellen said, walking in from the balcony. She joined Sam by the fireplace. "For as big as this house is it can still be ridiculously difficult to have a conversation without getting interrupted."

"Don't apologize." Sam saw the balcony was empty, Lena apparently exiting through the rear yard gate rather than come back through the den. She sat on the arm of the couch. "I know we were joking earlier, but seriously, is there a particular reason Lena is so hostile? Part of it is clearly directed at me, but there's a whole lot of free-floating ill will toward the world at large there, too."

Ellen sat across from Sam and absently twisted the watch on her wrist. "Lee's very focused, so she comes across as off-putting to a lot of people. But you shouldn't take it personally."

"Even when it's directed at my person?"

"That's probably in part because you're a reporter," she acknowledged, "and in larger part because you make me laugh more than anyone has in a long while."

"That's a bad thing?"

"Obviously, to me it isn't. I really enjoy your company, but she sees it as a distraction. Lee thinks I should devote 100 percent of my thoughts and energy into the campaign. I don't agree it has to be all-consuming, so that's where we butt heads, which I'm afraid is what you got the brunt of this evening."

"Why does she get such a vote?"

Ellen hesitated, choosing her words carefully. "She's been with me a long time and feels she's earned the right to express her opinion. But you need to know in the end I make my own decisions, okay?"

"Okay." Sam pointed toward the mantel. "I didn't realize that was your daughter."

"You've met?"

Sam was surprised that Ellen sounded *this much* concerned. "Twice, actually. The first time was when I stopped by your headquarters on Sunday. She's the one who directed me to talk to Luke and your delightful campaign manager, Darth. Then last night Joe and I were walking by after dinner, and I stopped in again."

"Why?"

"To show Joe but mostly just to see if Phil was there for me to antagonize," Sam admitted. "I just love the way that vein pops out on his temple when I talk to him."

Ellen laughed at Sam's unabashed glee in provoking Phil. "You really are bad, you know that?"

"Yeah, and that's what makes me so good. But anyway, she was the only one in the place, so I introduced myself before leaving. She said her name was Annie, but I didn't make the connection, so on second thought I'm obviously not *that* good. She seems very ...introverted."

"Anne used to be very outgoing. Running was her life." Ellen stood up and looked at the pictures. "That's her with the high school cross country team. But as she got older, she became more and more withdrawn. She quit the team and quit running. That was the beginning of...it was a rough time for her." She sat back down on the coffee table, facing Sam. "Can I ask you something?"

"Of course."

"That jacket in the photos you showed me, how did you happen to have a picture of it? It didn't look like it was taken where the other shots were."

Normally, Sam would circle her journalistic wagons, answering a question with a question. But with Ellen she was navigating on pure intuition. "I found it in the desert about a half-mile from the crime scene. His driver's license was in it, and one of your campaign buttons was pinned to the front pocket flap. That's why I showed up at your headquarters."

"You called me on the basis of a button?" Ellen asked, fascinated at the whimsy of fate.

"No. I called you after I saw the photo he kept of you and him in his apartment. It seemed obvious you meant something to him beyond just a preferred candidate. And your inscription on the picture indicated more than just a passing acquaintance. Why did you ask about the jacket?"

"Because it was Annie's."

Sam slid onto the couch to be eye level with Ellen, their knees touching. "Are you sure?"

"I'm sure. For Christmas one year she bought all the members of her team that same jacket. During the winter they would often still be training after dark and were always dodging cars. The streets in our part of Beverly Hills, up in Coldwater Canyon, were not well lit, but those racing stripes could be seen a mile away and made them all feel safer."

"So why would Jeff have it?"

"Right after he started working for me he was here late one evening, and it had gotten chilly. He was wearing a T-shirt and didn't have a coat with him, so Annie took the jacket from her closet and gave it to him. She joked it would protect him."

"Are things better for your daughter now?"

"I think she's turning a corner in her life. I hope so. Earlier this year she got her own place in town with a roommate although she still stays here a couple nights a week." Ellen stood, glanced at her watch, and sighed. "As much as I'd rather stay in here talking to you, I need to go make a final round."

"I'll walk out with you. Joe must have made some new friends."

As they went out onto the balcony, Sam's cell phone rang. Ellen waited by the back gate while she answered it.

"Hello?"

"I'm looking for Samantha Perry."

"This is she. Who's this?"

"My name is Gerald Alvarez. Kylie at the Desert Diner gave me your card. She also told me about Jeff. I'm in shock."

Abruptly shifting gears from cocktail happy-and-relaxed to journalist-focused was a little jarring. Sam mentally hustled to organize her thoughts. "Thank you so much for calling. Listen, I know it's kind of late, but is there any chance you can see me this evening?"

"That would be fine. Let me give you the address."

Sam automatically reached for her notebook before remembering she didn't have it. "I'm sorry. Could you do me a favor? I don't have a pen handy, so would you mind calling this number back and leaving the address on my voicemail?"

"Sure. What time did you want to meet?"

"How about a half-hour?"

"I'll be expecting you."

Sam waited until her phone rang again before putting it back in her pocket. Ellen watched with interest. "You have to work tonight?"

"This should be interesting; nothing like doing an interview with a buzz going."

"Does this have to do with the story?"

"Actually, yeah." Sam walked over to the gate.

Instead of opening it, Ellen hugged her. "I mean it," she squeezed for emphasis, "you're welcome here anytime."

Sam squeezed back, her heart hammering. They held onto each other a moment longer then with a sigh, Ellen gave Sam a final squeeze and opened the gate. The yard was still filled with people although the crowd had noticeably thinned.

"I'm going to find Joe and then hit it out of here."

"Hold on." Ellen took Sam's cell phone out of her pocket and programmed in a number. "I just wanted you to have my cell," she said, handing it back. "Call me tomorrow."

"Thanks. I will."

"You better." Ellen raised her hand in goodbye. She had only taken a few steps before being engulfed by a group of people wanting a piece of her time.

CHAPTER SIXTEEN

Sam found Alvarez's address in the middle of a well-tended block a block off Indian Drive. It was a modest house located directly next to a small Catholic church on a dark, people-deserted street.

Joe looked around in exasperation. "This city doesn't believe in street lamps, do they?"

"No, actually, it doesn't. They prefer people being able to see the stars." Sam grabbed her backpack and tossed Joe the keys. "I'll be as quick as I can."

She walked up the sidewalk and rang the doorbell. While waiting, she glanced over at the church and noticed the doors were padlocked. She remembered when churches were open 24/7. Apparently, she thought dourly, people needed to have their spiritual or personal crises during business hours. Because Sam was still silently decrying the limitations of organized religion in the modern world, she was particularly thrown off balance when a priest answered the door.

"Hi..." she hesitated, wondering if she had the wrong address. "I'm looking for Gerald Alvarez."

"I'm Gerry Alvarez. You must be Sam. Please come in."

He led her to a small but comfortable living room. "We can talk in here. Can I get you anything? Water, a soft drink, some wine?"

"Actually some ice water would be great. Thank you."

The priest excused himself, and Sam took in her surroundings. Except for a crucifix on the wall, and a stack of the Catholic magazine *America* on the end table, the home was devoid of overt religious trimmings.

Alvaraz returned with two glasses and handed her one. "Please, sit." Sam settled in a well-worn chair, and he took a seat on the couch to her immediate right. "Is there anything you can tell me about what happened to Jeff?" he asked somberly.

Sam gave him a brief rundown of the basic facts as she knew them, concluding with what she needed for her story. "Today I talked to a family friend of Rydell's parents, but it's been difficult finding anyone who really seemed to know Jeff and his life in Palm Springs. Was he a parishioner here?"

"No, Jeff was not Catholic. We struck up a conversation one day at the diner and developed a friendship. We found it very comfortable talking to each other." He took a drink of water. "You seemed surprised I was a priest."

"It's just that Kylie never mentioned it."

"She probably doesn't know," Alvarez smiled. "I don't usually wear my collar out when I'm on personal time. Some people are put off by it these days, but Jeff was never judgmental. Although he was not a church-going man, I found him to be very spiritual. A genuinely good soul."

"You're not the first person who described him that way."

"How specifically do you think I can help?"

Even though Alvarez was not his pastor or official spiritual advisor, Sam assumed a priest would still be reluctant to break confidences. This was one of those times she needed to be completely upfront.

"Father Gerry, this is what I know. I know Jeff was adopted. I know he hung out at a strip club in Indio. It's possible he was paid to watch over a dancer there. I know he had a girlfriend back in Tennessee. He was very likely spying on someone. He was apparently expecting to come into some significant money. I know he was unusually committed to Ellen Konrad. But what I don't know is how all these things tie together and which of these things, if any, are related to, or resulted in, his murder. It's been difficult getting a clear picture of who he was or what he was after because Jeff was a man with a lot of secrets."

Alvarez leaned forward. "One thing you learn quickly as a priest is everybody has secrets—even priests. It's complicated because secrets are inherently dishonest. But the question you have to ask is whose secret is being kept and why. Are we keeping a secret to prevent others from finding out we are being hurtful or untruthful in some way? Or is the secret being kept on behalf of someone else we are trying to protect from some kind of harm?"

"In other words, the devil is in our motivation."

"Yes. If Jeff was secretive, I suspect it was to protect others. However, the danger is that no matter how good the intentions, when too many secrets collide they have a tendency to isolate people from one another. Often more damage is done than if the secret had been revealed to begin with."

Sam digested his words. "But obviously Jeff didn't have trust issues. He trusted you, didn't he?"

"Yes, I knew Jeff was adopted. He only found out after his mother died. He came across his original birth records buried in the bottom of an old trunk in the attic. As you can imagine, it was quite a shock. Jeff was grateful he'd been raised by such good people, but even though he loved his parents very much, he was still curious about his birth parents. I don't think his intent was to disrupt anybody's life. He just wanted to know where he came from. That's simply human nature. By the time we became friends his questions had been answered, and he seemed quite at peace with it."

"Did he say who it was?"

"No, he didn't. And I didn't ask, either."

Sam swore under her breath. She gave herself five seconds to pout then pushed her disappointment aside. "Is that why he stayed in Palm Springs, because of his birth mother or father?"

"Actually, I don't think so." Alvarez looked thoughtful. "Are you familiar with *rumspringa*?"

Sam nodded. "That's when Amish teenagers leave their community to go experience the sex-drugs-and-rock-n-roll ways of the secular world."

"Right. Palm Springs was Jeff's *rumspringa*. He came from a small town in a relatively conservative area then found himself in Palm Springs and was taken in by the wealth, the clubs, the movie stars you see walking the streets. He was so impressed getting to meet Ellen Konrad, somebody he had watched on TV. This was a different world, and Jeff was suddenly in a position to explore who he was without anyone looking over his shoulder. He could be whoever he wanted to be. He could reinvent and start over."

"So what did he discover about himself?"

Father Gerry's smile was sad. "That he wasn't ready for that much freedom. He told me he had decided to go home and settle down with his girlfriend. I'm drawing a blank on her name."

"Larissa."

"That's it. And I'm sure a part of him wanted just that. But I also think part of his decision was based on guilt."

"Over what?"

"Jeff explored his sexuality while here," the priest revealed. "I think it proved too much for him to handle."

"Because he didn't like what he did," Sam asked, "or because he liked it too much?"

"Self-awareness doesn't always lead to happiness. It takes a lot of courage to be who we really are, especially if it puts us at odds with those we love or our upbringing."

"Or our religion," Sam added. "Did he ever mention anyone specifically?"

Alvarez sat back. "No. He was vague."

"Did you notice any change in his behavior over the last couple of months?"

"Not then, but now in hindsight I can see that there was something on his mind. He was more distracted the last several times we spoke. But he was also making plans to go back home so I assumed it was that, until two weeks ago."

"What happened then?"

"This." Alvarez reached behind the couch and lifted a small wheelie bag, grunting with exertion. He set it on the floor by Sam. "He asked me to hold this for him. He joked that in case he got hit by a bus, he wanted to know it was in the right hands."

"Do you know what's in there?"

"Some papers, some computer disks, one of his laptops."

"One of them?"

"He had one of his own, and Ellen Konrad gave him an old one of hers."

Sam stared at the bag, convinced it held the answer to a lot of questions. "Father Alvarez…"

"You want to take this with you."

She nodded, worried she'd sound too desperate if she spoke.

The priest rested his elbows on his knees, hands folded beneath his chin in a pose of reflection. "When Jeff gave this to me, I was puzzled by his choice of words, that he wanted this *in the right hands*. In light of what's happened, I think what he really meant is that he trusted me to find those right hands." He sat thinking, eyes closed. It occurred to Sam he was praying. She waited, the clock on the end table sounding loud in the silent room. Finally he asked, "If I entrust this to you, will you promise to return any personal belongings to Larissa when you are done?"

"Of course."

"And you will let the police know if you find anything relevant to their investigation?"

"I will."

Alvarez stood. "Then I would like you to take it."

"Thank you." She got up and released the bag's retractable handle. "I have a friend waiting in the car, so I should be going."

He walked Sam to the door and shook her hand. "Thank *you* for trying to find justice for Jeff."

"That's for the police to do, Father. I'm just trying to honor his memory in words."

"I don't think the two are mutually exclusive. And by the way, if you ever start going to church again you're always welcome to come to Mass here."

"How did you know I was raised Catholic?"

The priest just smiled and closed the door.

"Well, shit," Sam muttered, "that's really annoying."

She pulled into her parking space at 9:30. Joe lifted out the wheelie bag from the back seat and set it next to the car.

"Since you'll be busy I'm going to take the rental to Arenas for a nightcap."

"Good idea."

"Do you want me to take this upstairs for you?"

"No need." She hugged him goodnight. "Go have fun."

By the time Sam walked the dogs, gave the bird fresh water, said hello to Hamlet the hamster, fed her sea horse Sea Biscuit, took a quick rinse-off shower, changed into sweat pants and tank top, and got herself a glass of iced tea, it was almost ten o'clock when she finally sat down at her desk and unzipped Rydell's bag.

On top of his pile of possessions was a high school yearbook. She leafed through it, marveling at how hairstyles were as specific as carbon dating for pinpointing an era. Toward the back, among the photos of the incoming senior class, was an envelope. Sam took it out and saw that underneath it was the senior class studio portrait of Nell Overton. The picture confused her, but the document inside the envelope was a punch in the gut.

She opened her notebook and logged back onto her public records database. She typed in "Gail Tolliver," the maiden name of Nell's mother and searched for marriage records. There were two. The most recent was to Dale Overton. No surprise there. But it was the first marriage that told the story. Sam sat staring at her computer screen for a long time. Finally she picked up her cell phone and placed a call.

Sam printed out the marriage records and put those sheets and the envelope back inside the yearbook, which she tossed in her bag. She put on a workout bra and slipped on a long-sleeved shirt over her tank top. After a moment of indecision, she grabbed the wheelie bag and headed out. On the drive over, Sam wondered if Ellen would ever want to see her again after this visit.

She parked on the right side of the cul-de-sac and put the top up before getting out. The air was uncomfortably muggy without a breath of breeze. Not even the crickets were chirping. Sam noticed a dark bank of clouds gathering over the mountains.

The gate buzzed as she walked up to it, and Ellen opened the front door, waiting. She was wearing yoga pants and a sleeveless jersey with a towel draped over one shoulder. Her hair was in a loose ponytail. "Do you always work out this late?"

"No, but I was wound up after the party. I have a small gym upstairs where I can take out my aggressions. Comes in handy a lot these days," she said wryly. "Let's go in the den."

As they walked under a hallway light, Sam noticed a crescent-shaped mark by Ellen's right eyebrow. "Did you smack yourself?"

She absently touched the mark. "No, that's an old scar."

"I never noticed it before."

"It's usually hidden under a dab of concealer, plus it's more prominent when I work out. I fell climbing a tree when I was fourteen and was gashed by a branch on my way down. Lucky it wasn't a half-inch over or I'd probably have lost my eye. I forget it's there."

"Still climbing trees at fourteen?"

Ellen smiled. "I was playing hard to get."

The rooms downstairs were quiet but Sam heard the sounds of a television drifting from upstairs, and the kitchen lights were on. Once in the den Ellen pulled the door half closed and turned on a lamp behind the couch. "What is it, Sam?" she asked, sitting down. "Something in your eyes tells me this isn't a casual visit."

Sam sat beside her. "That interview I went to tonight was with a friend of Jeff's who had some of his personal belongings. The friend gave them to me to look through. In there was this."

She set the yearbook on the coffee table. Sam flipped to the page with Nell Overton's picture. Ellen glanced at it but showed no outward reaction. Sam handed her the envelope. She opened it and took out the document inside. It was Jeff's birth certificate, which listed Ellen Konrad as his natural mother. The space for the father's name was blank.

Sam showed her the printouts of Gail Tolliver's marriage licenses: one to Dale Overton, the other to a David Konrad. "I didn't understand what the connection to the yearbook was until I found these and remembered that Nell is a common diminutive for Ellen in certain parts of the country, including the Appalachians."

When Ellen didn't say anything, Sam talked to fill the silence. "After your mother married Overton, I'm guessing he wanted you and your sister to go by his name. That's why people knew you as Nell Overton. Then you went back to your legal name, Ellen Konrad, after you moved to California to get away from Dale."

Sam stared at the photo. "You've changed somewhat in appearance…maybe just grown into your looks. Do your children know about this?"

"No."

When she didn't elaborate, Sam closed the yearbook. "I understand why you didn't but I wish you could have told me; been honest with me. You didn't have to lie to me."

Ellen's eyes met Sam's. "I have never lied to you."

"How can you say that? You told me you didn't know anything about Jeff's background."

"No," she raised her hand in objection, "I told you I didn't know about his childhood, and that's the truth. You never asked me if I knew anything about the circumstances of his birth."

Sam rolled her eyes in irritation because Ellen was right. It was the kind of deft omission she regularly employed herself. "Okay, maybe you didn't outright lie, but you weren't exactly forthcoming. It's still dishonest."

Ellen's words were strained. "You don't understand."

"What's not to understand?" Sam asked harshly, expressing her disappointment and hurt through anger. "That a story like this in the middle of an election wouldn't be the best timing?"

Ellen grabbed her arm. "Do you really think that's my primary concern here? Being elected?"

Sam tried to read the emotion in Ellen's eyes. "No, probably not," she admitted, still stubbornly listening to her gut. And her heart. "Then explain to me what *your* motivation is."

"I can't," her voice was weary. "But it isn't what you think."

"Meaning what?"

"I wish to God I could tell you, but I can't."

"Was Rydell trying to blackmail you?"

"Jeff would never do anything like that."

Sam slapped the couch in frustration. She was missing something. There were too many loose ends. Who were Bill and June Konrad? Where was her sister Elizabeth now? What was Ellen still afraid of? The answer was in front of her but just beyond her grasp. Go back to the basics. Journalism 101. *Start at the beginning. Don't assume the obvious. Double check all your facts. Ask the right question. Follow your instinct.*

"Ellen, was he your child?"

"You've got the paper that says so."

"That's not what I asked. Did you give birth to Jeff Rydell?"

She pulled the hair-band off and closed her eyes. "Please Sam—"

"*God dammit!*" Sam abruptly stood. "Why can't you talk to me?"

Ellen pulled her back down and brought one leg up on the couch so they were face-to-face. She spoke quietly but with impassioned urgency. "Because I promised. Because there is so much that can never be undone or fixed or made right. Because too many people might get hurt."

Sam was equally emotional. "Somebody already *has* been hurt."

"I swear to you that I had nothing to do with Jeff's death."

"I believe that. To me, that's not even a question."

"Thank you," she whispered.

Sam ignored the lump in her throat and kept pushing. "If Jeff was here to find you, then you need to at least consider the possibility that it might be related to his death in some way. While I personally don't think it would matter to most people that you gave a child up for adoption as a teenager, especially with the abuse involved, perhaps there are people in your own camp who it *would* matter to."

"I refuse to believe anybody under my roof is involved."

"I'm sorry, but that's not something I can just accept on your blind faith."

Ellen sat quietly a moment. "So you know about Dale."

Despite being intimately familiar with the long-term emotional effects of physical abuse, Sam couldn't begin to imagine the ignominy of sexual abuse. "I know he molested you and your sister and the cousin who came to live with your family after the accident."

"*Molesting* always sounds so sterile," Ellen said in a distant voice, absently rubbing her shoulder. She shook off her reverie and leaned forward to emphasize her words. "Dale Overton was a serial rapist."

"Jesus, I am so, so sorry." *For what he did to you. For not having the words to take away your pain. For not having been there to stop it. For what I'm putting you through now.* Sam hesitated but had to confirm the obvious. "Ellen, Overton was Jeff's father, wasn't he?"

She didn't answer and just sat staring at the floor. Feeling like an abuser herself at the moment, Sam put the birth certificate and printouts back in the envelope and stuffed it inside the yearbook. She leaned closer and tried again. "You know I can't just let this go."

"I know that."

"And whatever the whole story is, I'm going to figure it out, sooner or later."

"I know that, too."

Sam reached out and grabbed her hand. "Then why can't you trust me enough to tell me yourself? I'm only looking for the truth. Help me find it—for Jeff's sake. And if it turns out to have nothing to do with his death, I will take what you tell me to my grave."

Ellen intertwined their fingers. "You don't know what you're asking me to do."

"I'm asking you to trust me. You have to know I'm not out to hurt you."

"I do know that." Her eyes were a storm of conflict and her resolve was visibly wavering.

"Please," Sam whispered, "let me help you while I can, before it's out of my hands." She was skirting a dangerous professional line but didn't care. *Her* primary concern now was not the story but to protect this woman. "Listen to me. Things *can* be made right because ultimately truth wins out."

Ellen gazed at the yearbook, her eyes a sea of deep blue regret.

She took a deep breath. "I don't know where or how to begin."

Sam brushed a stray strand of hair away from her face. "Just take your time."

"What is going on here?" Lena demanded to know, standing in the doorway.

Sam and Ellen both jumped and sat back from each other, startled at the intrusion. When neither answered, Lena repeated the question. Sam looked at Ellen, whose eyes now filled with silent apology, and knew the moment had been lost. She didn't want her pit bull assistant and long-time best friend to know what she was going to reveal.

Sam stood and faced Lena. "Not that it's really any of your business but I needed to ask Ellen a couple of questions."

"At this hour?"

"I have an early deadline tomorrow," Sam lied. She picked up the yearbook and tucked it under her arm so Lena didn't have a clear view of it. She glanced down at Ellen. "Thank you for taking the time." She nodded at Lena as she walked past. "Good night."

Ellen got up and followed her to the front door. "Can we please talk tomorrow?"

"Of course." Sam saw Lena still watching them from down the hall. "Call me; maybe we can go for a drive."

They exchanged silent goodbyes, but before Sam could walk away the door opened back up. Ellen came out and hugged her tightly, "Please don't give up on me," she whispered and impulsively gave Sam a lingering, emotion-fueled kiss on the mouth before running back into the house.

* * *

Disjointed and unsettled, Sam sat in her car, trying to get her mental bearings. She could still feel the touch of Ellen's lips, the press of her body. She wanted to just stay there in her car and relive the sensations. But there'd be plenty of time to obsess later; right now she needed to concentrate on the work at hand and tried to decipher Ellen's cryptic comments. What was Ellen trying to tell her? Maybe Lena had blackmailed Ellen all these years. But what did any of this have to do with the Crazy Horse and the black sedan? And why would any of these people be out running around in the middle of a desert?

Sam knew she wouldn't be able to sleep until she went through the rest of Rydell's bag and made an impromptu decision to go to the office. She drove with the top down, the tropical night air still warm. But dark clouds blotted out the stars, and a steamy breeze had begun to blow.

Even though Marlene gave her keys the first week she was hired, Sam had never been to the office after hours, much less late at night. The parking lot of the business center where the *Weekender* was located looked desolate and foreboding at this hour, with its limited lighting and the long shadows cast by palm trees bunched along the perimeter. Inexplicably edgy, Sam scanned the doorways as she walked to the building, the sound of the wheelie bag rolling over the asphalt obnoxiously loud.

She opened the outer door, which automatically relocked during non-business hours. Sam usually used the stairs, but the thought of the stairwell at night was not remotely appealing. She took the elevator to the second floor, acutely aware of each creak and groan.

"I am so creeping myself out," Sam said, unsure where this self-torture was coming from.

Her unease dissipated once she was in the office with the door securely bolted behind her. She got a cup of ice and a Diet Coke from the refrigerator before sitting down at her desk. She put the yearbook and the birth certificate in her bottom drawer for safe keeping then opened Rydell's bag to sort through the rest of his belongings. There were numerous newspaper articles, a half dozen computer software programs in packaging that had been opened, another flyer from Argo, an envelope with snapshots, a manila folder filled with some papers, a few mini DVDs, and a laptop.

Sam stretched her legs, knees and ankles cracking in protest, and reached for the newspaper articles. All dealt with the same subject, giving Sam a crash course on the growing problem of grand scale software counterfeiting. One Department of Justice official observed to *The Washington Post*, "Organized crime is now involved because the profit margins are as great as they are for drugs but with few penalties even if caught."

The head of security for the world's largest computer software enterprise summed up the problem for the *Los Angeles Times.*

> *"Theft and leakage out of the supply chain are our greatest threats. Our current efforts to reduce piracy is focusing on areas such as replication plants, where stampers have gone missing, and recyclers, who sometimes resell 'scrap' products—overruns and other surplus product—which are then in turn sold on the black market. Also of great concern to the entire software industry is the theft of Certificates of Authenticity. Those are just like currency."*

After she finished reading, Sam reached for the stack of software, all copies of the same expensive business productivity program. She spread them out on her desk.

"You kept these for a reason. What was it?"

She examined the disks. At first glance, they appeared legitimate, until she turned the discs over and realized each disc had the identical identification number stamped on them. They were also missing hologram characteristics found on all modern disks.

"You're all counterfeit," she concluded triumphantly then sighed, "but so what?"

Jeff was certainly not the first person to buy illegal software. In looking at Argo's flyer, which offered too-good-to-be-true prices on expensive brand name programs, it seemed obvious where he had gotten the fraudulent discs.

"But why buy so many copies of the same program?"

One obvious answer was that Rydell was turning around and reselling them for a fat profit. *Nobility-schmobility*, as Marlene would say. Sam repackaged the discs and set them aside along with the flyer, making a mental note to call Argo again tomorrow since he hadn't returned her call from earlier today.

Next, she opened the packet of snapshots, digitals printed off a home computer. Sam spread them out and stared at pictures of parked cars. All were expensive sedans and all were parked in the same location with the license plates clearly visible. As she studied the pictures more carefully, one photo gave Sam a jolt—it was a black Lincoln Town Car.

She was reminded of being a kid and trying to work out the logic problems that came in crossword puzzle books. Cryptic statements of fact were given and you were supposed to figure out the problem based on pure deductive reasoning. Sam always found them frustrating because she inevitably missed one last leap of logic necessary to solve the problem completely. She felt a similar frustration now.

She rolled her head in a wide circle, beginning to feel very tired. But she wanted to finish before leaving. She got another soda from the coffee room and sat forward in her chair, afraid she'd doze off if she got too comfortable.

Inside the folder were letters from several top software manufacturers giving general instructions on how to file a claim of suspected piracy. On one of the letterheads was a green logo of interconnected letters, no doubt what Kylie saw him reading.

In a separate envelope was correspondence with the mega-brand whose counterfeited products Jeff had in his bag. The first was a glorified form letter.

> *Mr. Rydell –*
>
> *Thank you for your inquiry. Yes, our company's reward incentive remains in effect for anyone who supplies information leading to the arrest and conviction of those engaging in software counterfeiting and piracy. Naturally, the amount of the award depends on a number of factors. Please contact our security department for further details and information on how to file a report.*

The next letter was more personal.

> *Dear Mr. Rydell –*
>
> *This is to follow up on your phone call earlier today. After*

reviewing the matter with my supervisor, we would like to arrange for a representative from our security department to meet with you at your earliest possible convenience to review the documentation in your possession.

The last letter, sent from the Los Angeles regional office for the Department of Justice, was urgent in tone.

Mr. Rydell

This is to confirm our meeting on this coming Sunday. I need to reiterate that for your personal safety, we strongly advise that you cease any further information gathering at this time and let the proper authorities take it from here. Please contact me as soon as possible.

K. A. Mallory

Special Agent Digital Investigations

Sam noted the letter was dated just two days before Jeff's murder and was confident the *why* of his death was answered in its three, short sentences. The discs in the bag were Rydell's proof. So were the photos. He planned to turn in the people who sold him the counterfeit software and collect a large reward but something had gone horribly wrong. It seemed likely his adoption had nothing to do with his murder after all.

Sam's first instinct was to tell Ellen, but it was well after midnight, too late to call. Plus, she didn't want to take a chance of Lena eavesdropping. Needing to share the revelation with someone, she called her condo. Sam muttered a quiet curse when her voicemail answered, mentally kicking herself for neglecting to input Joe's new cell phone number yet. She hung up and stared out the window into a wall of black, thinking. She needed to turn over the bag and its contents to Larson tomorrow, so she gathered up everything from her desk and made copies, which she added to Rydell's file and put it back in her desk.

The last items from the bag were the laptop and two mini DVDs in jewel cases, labeled June and July. Sam turned on the computer and inserted the June DVD. There was no audio but the video feed said plenty.

On the screen was a wide-angle view of a warehouse, the camera moving towards the entrance. It took Sam a moment to make the connection; the video was taken with the spy pen camera Jeff had bought.

For the next hour she watched the inner workings of a major counterfeiting operation. Some segments showed rooms filled with cases of brand name software, movies, and music stacked to the ceiling, others showed disks being separated out from the original packaging by people she did not recognize. There were also shots of duplicating machinery.

In most of the video, it was apparent Jeff was walking next to somebody. Once or twice the person came into frame but only from the neck down, revealing little except his shirt and a gold pendant. She wondered if he had been working with an inside informant whose identity he wanted to protect, or if Jeff just didn't want the person getting too close a look at the pen. Another thought nagged her. Who had she just seen wearing a chain? But her tired brain was drawing a blank.

Sam yawned again. "I really need sleep."

She repacked the laptop in the wheelie bag and stashed it under her desk. She went to the supply room for an extra-large envelope and put the articles, pictures, program disks, letters, and DVDs in it, wondering why there wasn't an August DVD. She stared at the software flyer for several moments before adding it to the other items and locking the envelope in her bottom desk drawer.

Sam leaned back in her chair and swiveled to the right so she could fully stretch out her legs. She gazed at the Olympic poster and its overlapping rings. It occurred to her that the shadowy Argo was similarly interconnected—to the Crazy Girl, to Jeff, to Money, and to illicit software.

Argo. Sam had to give him credit for picking such a catchy nickname. As a kid she dreamed of owning a golden retriever and naming it Argo in homage to *Jason and the Argonauts*. To this day she'd sit enraptured anytime she watched the DVD, especially the skeleton scene that took special effects guru Ray Harryhausen four months to film for just three minutes of screen time. Although Sam also loved Harryhausen's other films, particularly the campy *Clash of the Titans*, in her opinion *Jason* was the best of his special effects extravaganzas—

"Fucking hell." Sam stood up so abruptly that her chair tipped over backwards. She quickly did a mental double-take, standing with one hand propped against the desk and the other pressed against the side of her head as the pieces fell into place. "Holy shit."

She picked up the phone and called home.

Hi, I'm not in right now…

"Dammit!" She looked at the clock. It was almost 2:00 a.m. Apparently Joe was making a full night of it. She waited for the beep. "Joe, it's Sam. I'm still at the office, but I'm getting ready to leave. I think I know who killed Rydell."

Just needing to hear it out loud, she gave Joe a quick rundown of her conclusions and was convinced she was right. "Anyway, we can talk about it when I get home."

When she opened the building's front door, droplets of rain splashed onto her face. The wind had kicked up considerably, and the back of Sam's shirt whipped out like a flapping cape. As she stepped off the curb Sam spotted Joe's rental turning into the driveway. Surprised, she stopped and watched him pull to a screeching stop behind her Eclipse.

"What are you doing here?" she called out when the car door opened.

But the gusting wind rustling through the palm trees was so loud she couldn't hear if he answered her or not. She started walking toward the car but froze mid-step when Joe got out, brought his arms up, and pointed a gun directly at her.

CHAPTER SEVENTEEN

"Stop where you are!" Joe yelled out.

Sam didn't feel fear, just sheer bewilderment. Her thoughts were sparking in random, incongruous flashes. *Where would Joe have gotten a gun? He hates the whole idea of hunting. More to the point, he knows how much I hate guns. When did Joe change into a black shirt? That's got to be a toy gun. Maybe he had one drink too many, and this is his inebriated idea of a joke. But he sure doesn't look drunk...*

She held her hands out, palms up, in a display of incredulity. "Joe, what the hell are you doing?"

"Sam, move!"

Stop. Move. For God's sake. Sam was losing her temper. "What the *fuck* is going on?"

At that instant, she realized Joe was actually looking past her. Before she could turn and follow his line of vision, a forearm grabbed her around the neck from behind. Her head's lateral movement was stopped by the muzzle of a gun pressing into her temple. Sam felt an icy calm and the sense she was having an out-of-body experience. A loud roar *whooshed* in her ears. She initially mistook the sound for the swirling wind, but it was just blood rushing to her head.

Sam's senses were on heightened overdrive, and she was keenly aware of everything around her. The cold metal against her skin, the smell of cologne coming off the arm gripping her, the apprehension in Joe's eyes, the dryness in her mouth, the rain dotting the windshield of her car, the weight of the keys in her hand, the assailant's hyper breathing. Time took on a dreamlike relativity. Her brain processed each sensation in methodical, slow-motion detail that in reality took only a fraction of a second. Einstein's theory in living proof.

"Put the gun *down*," Joe called out, holding his weapon steady.

"You've got that backwards. You put the gun down unless you want to see her brains all over the pavement."

In Los Angeles, Sam had been on constant guard, ever mindful of her surroundings. But Palm Springs, with its resort quaintness and small town atmosphere, had lulled her into misguided complacency.

So fucking stupid.

She naively and carelessly underestimated her exposure by leaving her name on the message to Argo.

The second he heard me calling, he knew I was getting close even, if I didn't.

She wondered how he had known she was at her office. "Have you been following me, Argo? Or do you prefer I call you George?"

George Manuel flexed his arm tighter around her neck. "You can be too smart for your own good, you know that?"

"This isn't the first time I've been told that," Sam responded, finding that talking provided a welcome distraction from the gun digging into her head.

"Well, it's going to be the last."

"Let her go," Joe moved slowly to his left. "We can work something out for you."

George yanked on Sam's neck so hard he almost lifted her off the ground. "If you come any closer I swear I will blow her head off. Put the gun *down*."

Sam's brain went momentarily AWOL, zoning out while the men with guns exchanged ultimatums. She couldn't grasp why Joe was acting with such an aura of authority. Who was this *we* that was going to work something out? Sam considered her meager options. She was a brown belt in Ashihara karate, but the muzzle gouging her scalp was strong incentive to do nothing rash.

Apparently, Joe came to the same conclusion. "Okay, I'm putting it down." Holding the gun out to the side, he leaned over and set it carefully on the ground.

"Slide it over to me," George ordered. Sam wondered if a gun could go off skidding across the asphalt. "Now your car keys."

Joe complied, and George steered Sam forward to where the

gun and keys had come to rest. He abruptly pushed her away, the unexpected motion causing her to stumble painfully onto her knees. Joe rushed over to her while George picked up the second gun.

"Are you okay?"

She could feel blood sliding down the front of her leg. Rather than instill fear, the pain made her angry. And anger was an emotion she could function efficiently within. "I'm fine," she said, rolling to her feet. She refrained from interrogating Joe, but her furious glare drilled the questions home.

"I'll explain everything later," he promised, sounding contrite.

"That's assuming there *is* a later."

George circled so they were between him and the front of Sam's office building. He turned his head to watch a car drive past on Palm Canyon, the driver oblivious to the drama unfolding. He motioned towards Sam's hand. "Throw those keys over here." She reluctantly obeyed, tossing them at Manuel's feet. He put them in his pocket then pointed to the side of the building. "Start walking."

"Where we going?"

"Don't you *ever* stop asking questions? Shut the fuck up and move."

The rain was now coming down in a steady mist, turning the dark night into a murky haze. He herded them around the building and parked in back was the black Lincoln Town Car. George popped the trunk using his key remote. "Okay big guy, get in."

Joe hesitated.

"If you'd rather me just shoot you now I will."

Cursing under his breath, Joe climbed into the truck, having to draw his knees up in a fetal position to fit. "Don't try anything stupid, or I'll shoot your girlfriend here." He closed the trunk and faced Sam. "Get in. You're driving."

She slid behind the wheel of the spacious car. It was like sitting in an easy chair. It made her think about how much Alpha and Omega loved sleeping on the chair in her bedroom, and for the first time tears welled in her eyes. She closed them and took several deep breaths. This was not the time to lose it. She needed to keep her anger fueled, fearful sheer panic would set in otherwise. George got in and handed her the key.

"Go down Indian."

After adjusting the seat and mirrors, she turned on the windshield wipers and pulled onto the road. George opened the glove compartment and Sam saw a baggie filled with small amber bottles and a pair of night vision binoculars, explaining how he was able to find Jeff in the dark desert. George admired Joe's gun. "This is a real nice piece. I always wanted my own government issue."

Government issue?

He shoved his smaller pistol inside the glove box along with Joe's keys and shut the door. Sam concentrated on driving, not letting her imagination stray too far ahead. The mist had turned into a shower, turning the streets shiny with water, the lights from the closed businesses they passed reflecting colorfully off the wet asphalt.

She glanced over her right shoulder to change lanes and saw a black and gray messenger bag in the back seat. Sticking out of the front zipper pocket was a red shirt. Sam's breath caught and in a flash of understanding the connections snapped into place. It had been right in front of her all along.

Sam adjusted the mirror again to sneak a quick look at George. His eyes were glassy, the irises wired, black pools. The silence in the car was ominous.

"Was it your idea for Anne to use the name Money at the Crazy Horse?"

George's head snapped around, and for a moment she thought he was going to hit her. Instead, he laughed. "You want to interview me some more? Sure, why not. It'll be the last great story you never write. Nah, that was all her idea."

"A strip bar in Indio's a long way from running cross country in the streets of Beverly Hills." Sam thought of the cocky youth standing next to Anne and tried to remember if his eyes had looked this cruel in the picture. "I saw your class photo at her mother's house. I was there earlier this evening."

"Ah, right, the great Ellen Konrad. Now there is one fine piece of pussy."

Sam's jaw clenched. "Not that *you'd* ever get any," she taunted, anger momentarily trumping common sense.

To her surprise, he agreed. "Dude, you got that right. Turn here and get on Palm Canyon."

She fought down a wave of nausea and kept talking. "Were you Anne's boyfriend?"

"Her boyfriend?" his voice was bitter. "You know why I had a Beverly Hills address? My mother was the live-in maid for Annie's next door neighbor. They patted themselves on the back for giving us a place to live: a tiny, three-room guesthouse behind the garage. But I learned to play nice, and Annie adopted me, like I was her little pet. She'd come running over anytime she had a problem, which got to be all the time as we got older. She was so needy, always crying, wanting to know if she were as beautiful as her mom, which of course she wasn't. For fuck's sake, what does she think? She's adopted. To end up winning the lottery by living that kind of life and she's complaining."

George shook his head in disgust. He opened the glove box and took out a bottle from the bag. He unscrewed the top, filled it with white power, and snorted it.

Sam could see the sheen of sweat on his face.

"It got to the point where she was just nuts. She couldn't even sit still. But I have to admit, she was a lot more fun, too."

"Being unstable?"

"She wasn't unstable when it came to sex. She became *insatiable*, dude. She wanted to be fucked whenever, wherever, however. She let me do anything I wanted and some things I hadn't even thought of. I could barely keep up with her. She fucked girls, too, but said they were too soft. She liked it rough. I heard her mom caught Annie taking on three guys at once, and that's when they finally sent her to the hospital. Of course they kept it all hush-hush."

Sam was amazed Ellen had managed to keep it out of the papers and wondered if that's what prompted the sudden move to

Palm Springs. "When did you and Anne reconnect?"

George did another bump from the bottle. "I emailed her after I moved here. Told her what I was up to but never heard back. Figured she was embarrassed. Then a few months ago she comes in the club out of the blue, and it's just like old times. We fucked in the car during my break and afterwards tells me she wants to be a dancer, so I hooked her up. Annie always wanted to act but never had the balls to try. Too afraid she wouldn't live up to mommy. But at the club…dude, she's the star."

Lightning crackled in the sky above the mountains to their left, followed a few seconds later by a low rumble of thunder. They passed Gas 4 Less and Sam saw the night clerk watching a small television inside. A few minutes past the tram, George told her to slow down. "Not this turn but the next one, make a left."

Sam knew from the map they were driving up Devil's Canyon Road. Knowing she was retracing Rydell's movements on his final night of life made her stomach twist. "Did you meet Jeff through Anne?"

"He was her latest play thing. Except, he wouldn't play. She actually thought they were going to live happily ever after. Typical Annie delusion. When he set her straight, told her he was getting married, she lost it and came crying to me like always."

The rain and lack of streetlights made it hard to see. Sam drove slowly, in no hurry. As long as they were driving and talking, she and Joe were okay.

"So everything you told me about him borrowing money from you was a lie?"

"You shouldn't believe everything you hear. Think you of all people would know that," he smirked. "But he *was* always crying broke, so as a favor to Annie I brought him in to sell software. Next thing I know he's buddying up to Marco, showing off how much he knew about computers. He should've never gotten greedy."

"By sucking up to the boss?"

"By planning to narc on me," George said angrily. "He wanted me busted and out of the way, so he could take my place here as

Marco's main guy. That's where the real money is. That was going to be his big score." He looked out the windshield towards some lights visible up the hill. "Fucking hick, thinking he could outsmart me. But I got to him before he could set me up."

"How do you know?"

"He would have told me." His eyes glinted with cruelty and Sam pictured Rydell's mangled hand and the knife wounds.

"I meant, how do you know he was trying to get you busted for drugs?"

"Annie told me. He warned her to stay away from me, said something was going down, and I figured it straight out."

George had been right about Jeff's intention but not his motivation. He had no clue the Feds were sniffing around. His narcissism blinded him to the obvious and made him eager to brag about his crimes.

"I can't believe Anne would be happy with what you did."

"As far as she knows, I didn't do anything."

"But she was with you."

"We drove together to the club after she came up to score some blow and get laid. But she took off as soon as we got back, still all weepy because Jeff didn't want to be her playmate. When she called all hysterical the next day after finding out he was dead, I told her he left here right after she did and must of gotten mugged or something. She believes me."

Sam doubted it. The young woman she saw performing on stage was skating on a fragile edge of self-destructive guilt. It probably wouldn't take much to push her over.

The road dead-ended into a parking lot, past an Environmental Tech Services sign. A flash of lighting blazed overhead, briefly illuminating the area. Sam remembered seeing the main building on the DVD. He told her to park under a carport between a motorcycle and an ATV.

George held his hand out for the keys. Aiming the gun at Sam's head, he backed out of the car. "Okay, now you."

Even though they were under the carport, she was hit by a spray of wind-blown rain when she opened the door. Another crackle of lightning flashed. She silently counted the seconds...*two, three, four*... until she heard the thunder. George popped open the trunk, and Joe eased out. "Go inside through the big door right there. Move!"

Pelted by rain, they hurried inside the warehouse. It was filled with boxes, crates, and machinery, looking much as it had in Jeff's recordings. The only light came from a lamp teetering on the corner of a desk positioned to the left of the entrance where a wiry, balding man sat smoking a cigarette. He looked to be in his fifties and seemed completely unperturbed by George holding two people at gunpoint.

"Lou, go grab some chairs in the back for our guests here. We need to have a little chat with them."

Lou nonchalantly stubbed out his cigarette and disappeared into the darkness. "I need to make sure what you've been up to so I can do damage control if necessary. Marco doesn't like loose ends."

George walked to the desk and pulled a hunting knife and pair of pliers out of the top drawer. As if on cue, a rumble of thunder vibrated the building, the rain sounding like rocks on the metal roof. Sam picked up another sound: a car engine revving. Manuel heard it too and looked up.

Keeping the gun pointed at them, he walked towards the door. He got there just as Anne, in full strip club attire, pulled it open. For a split second she made direct eye contact with Sam before George blocked the doorway and pushed her back. He turned his body so that the door rested against his chest enabling him to talk to Anne outside and still keep the gun pointed at Joe and Sam without her seeing it.

"What do you want?" he hissed.

"Georgie, baby, I just needed to get some stuff," she pouted. "You were supposed to leave me some and drop off my bag."

Manuel kept turning his head to make sure nobody moved. When he looked away, Joe motioned quickly toward the knife. "Just be ready," he whispered, taking a half-step to his right. "You take Lou. Use whatever you got."

George pushed Anne again. "It's in my car, in the glove. Just take what you need and get out of here. I have some private business to take care of."

Anne glanced back inside. "What is she doing here?"

George grabbed the side of her neck. "I said get the fuck out of here. Go!" He shoved her and slammed the door closed.

If Marco doesn't like loose ends, where does that leave Anne? Sam wondered if Anne knew how much danger she was in.

Above them the wind howled, and a wall of rain pounded the building. Sam watched Lou walk out of the darkness, carrying a folding chair in each hand and pieces of rope draped around his neck. Outside, a car door slammed, and the engine revved again as Anne drove away. George moved back to the desk, the shadow from the lamp turning his face into a demonic mask. Lou opened the chairs and pushed them behind Joe and Sam.

"Sit," George ordered.

At that moment, a bright light flashed directly outside the windows and a tremendous boom shook the building, accompanied by the sound of shattering glass. Joe shouted, *"Now!"* and dove to his right, grabbing the knife as he rolled past the desk. Sam picked up a chair and swung it. Even though it felt as if her arms were moving in slow motion, she hit Lou hard enough to flatten his nose and split his cheek open but not hard enough to take him down. She crouched and aimed a snap kick at the side of his knee. It landed with a brittle *crack*. He fell over howling in pain and grabbed for his leg.

Sam looked up to see George raising his arm. She darted left toward a stack of boxes, arms raised to protect her head. There was a blast of gunfire and she heard a *whizzing* noise pass directly above her. Squatting behind the boxes, Sam looked down to see that her shirtsleeve was torn. A stream of blood began seeping through, accompanied by a sudden, fiery pain along her right forearm.

He just tried to shoot me. "You motherfucking son of a bitch!" she yelled furiously.

Her enraged outburst distracted George just long enough for Joe to rush him. He hit George full force with a shoulder to the mid-section. They tumbled to the ground. The knife skittered under the desk and the gun slid across the floor, coming to rest where Lou was lying, holding his bleeding right cheek, his left leg bent at an unnatural angle. Joe looked around for the weapon but Lou was already reaching for it. "Sam, run!"

She scrambled to her feet, and they sprinted out the door, nearly knocked backwards by the force of the howling wind and rain. They ran past the gate and onto the road, stopping where it started angling downhill.

"Which way?" Joe asked.

The rain blowing in their eyes made it hard to see. If they took the road, the car would reach them in seconds. To the left was the trail that led over the outcrop. It looked closer and easier to navigate but Sam knew it was a death trap. To the right was a steep, cliff-like slope that led to the large wash below. Sam grabbed Joe's arm. "We need to go this way. This'll take us to the highway." They started running.

The rain had turned the sandy gravel into sludge, and they slipped and slid their way down, stabbing and scraping their hands on sharp rocks and brittle bushes as they made their way to the bottom. They ran steadily, both of them panting hard, breathing in as much water as air. It was pouring so hard the rain stung their faces like pinpricks. They'd been running for at least five minutes when Sam glanced over her shoulder and saw a headlight coming down the hill far behind them.

Joe looked back. "It's got to be the ATV; we need to hurry."

They quickened their pace, Sam swearing she would never complain about step class again if she lived long enough to take one. The headlight was gaining on them. There was no way they were going to outrun it.

"When he catches up, I'm going to distract him, and I want you to keep going," Joe told her.

"Who the fuck do you think you are? Rambo? And what the hell were you doing with a gun?"

"Sam, this isn't the time."

"There might not *be* another time."

The ATV was quickly closing in when a gunshot echoed off the nearby rocks. Joe pushed Sam to the side, and they fell to the ground. Beneath her, Sam felt a fleeting vibration and noticed there was suddenly close to six inches of water in the channel. Joe started to get up, but she stopped him. "What? We've got to keep moving."

The next vibration was stronger. "Do you feel that?"

Sam could hear a low rumble in the far distance. It wasn't thunder. She looked around searching for some scrub, but she could barely see a few feet in front of her. "Come on. We've got to find some bushes. They'll be growing up the sides. This channel is about to flood."

They ran blindly, the ground shifting beneath them as the next waves of the imminent flash flood flowed past. Joe grabbed her shoulder and pointed. "There."

About halfway up the side of the channel was a clump of bushes jutting out from the steep embankment. They managed to crawl high enough to grab the roots then pulled themselves the rest of the way, perching on the thickest branches. Joe wrapped his arms and legs around a sturdy limb, interlocking his ankles and wrists. Sam didn't trust her upper body strength. Keeping her arms inside the sleeves, she lifted the rest of the shirt over her head and looped it around a thick bough like a lasso then crossed her arms in front. But when she saw the ATV roar into view she knew they had run out of time. Sam wondered who would take care of her dogs and hoped Ellen wouldn't think she had given up on her when she didn't call in the morning.

George came to a skidding stop beneath them, his face smug with satisfaction and anticipation. He got off the ATV and stood looking up at them, holding the gun with both hands, the water now up to his knees. He yelled to be heard over the wind and rain and a rumble he was oblivious to. "This is going to be like target practice."

Sam took a deep breath and closed her eyes, bracing for the pain. But the next sound she heard wasn't a gunshot. It was a deafening, unearthly wail as a wall of water crashed into them with so much force that it pulled her body almost horizontal to the ground. She tucked her head trying to ward off a barrage of rocks, sticks, and other debris carried along by the cold water. For an eternity the surge swept overhead, her burning lungs screaming for oxygen, her arms aching with the effort to hold on. Then just like that, the rush leveled off, and Sam was able to lift her head out of the water. She gulped in air, the rain now a gentle shower on her face, the current a steady but manageable flow. For the first time in a long time, she was freezing. She looked over and saw Joe surface, shaking his head to clear his eyes and coughing out water.

Her left hand was numb from how tightly the shirt had been wrapped around her wrist. Sam wiggled one arm out of its sleeve then worked the other arm free. "You okay?" she asked after giving Joe a chance to catch his breath.

"Nothing a tetanus shot and traction won't cure," he winced.

Sam's smile faded when a flashlight beam blinded her. She put her hands up to block out the light, assuming it was Lou coming to finish what George had started. She wasn't sure she had any fight left. But a familiar voice called out from above them. "Is everyone all right?"

"We're okay," Joe yelled back.

"Stay there, Joe," Detective Larson instructed. "We're coming to get you."

Sam looked over. "You have got some serious talking to do."

* * *

With the help of some rope, PSPD officers helped them climb out of the channel and an hour later Sam sat on the trunk of a squad car with a blanket draped around her shoulders, uncomfortable in sodden clothes. She couldn't leave until Larson released her and had spent the last twenty minutes watching the detective talking to a handsome man dressed in black cargo pants and a dark polo shirt. It wasn't lost on Sam that Joe was dressed almost identically.

The warehouse was cordoned off with crime tape and police

cars blocked the parking lot entrance. Sam knew that officers were also posted at the entrance to Devil's Canyon Road, where George Manuel's mangled body had been discovered wedged among some rocks. An advisory alerted all county hospitals to report anyone seeking treatment for a crushed cheek, broken nose, and dislocated knee, but Sam suspected Lou was already in the wind.

Officers had recovered Sam's car keys from George's pocket and on Larson's orders they had been returned to her. She jiggled them in her hand, grateful she wouldn't have to call a locksmith to get inside the condo. All she wanted to do was go home and crawl into bed with her dogs. The storm had passed, and the sky was once again a peaceful canopy of twinkling stars.

Joe walked over and joined her on the trunk. He stared down at his hands. "I'm not sure where to start."

"What were you doing at my office anyway?"

"It's a long story."

"I'll settle for the *Readers' Digest* version for now."

Joe rubbed the back of his neck and rolled his shoulder. "A couple years ago when I was still at the department store, I met with a new European distributor for previous-season designer purses that we sold in our economy departments. His inventory was great, and I placed an order. But when the purses arrived, they were fakes. Good fakes, but fakes nonetheless. He had pulled a bait and switch.

"We notified authorities, and in the course of their investigation, I got to know a few people. One thing led to another, and I eventually accepted an offer to go to work full-time for a special sting department the Federal Trade Commission was forming in cooperation with the Department of Justice. After going through a training course, they set me up in a fabulous Michigan Avenue boutique as a front business, and my job was to ferret out fake art, fake designer clothes, mislabeling, whatever."

Sam was incredulous. "You're a government agent?"

"With a badge and gun and everything."

"And you *never* mentioned it?"

"Sam, I couldn't," Joe groaned. "The whole point was for

people to believe I was just a buyer for an exclusive boutique. I mean, look at me—who would ever believe I was an agent? That's why it was so perfect. But I couldn't tell anybody, not even mom. It was undercover at the highest level. Don't you think I would have loved to tell you?"

Sam was in no mood to be reasonable. Even if his explanation made perfect sense, it still felt like he'd been lying to her. "So why tell me the big secret now?"

"Because it doesn't matter anymore. I'm leaving to start my own security consulting business. There's someone I want you to meet."

The man who'd been talking to Larson now leaned against an unmarked car watching them. Joe motioned him over, and he introduced himself.

"Hi, Sam, I'm Kevin Mallory. I work in the DOJ's Digital Investigations."

She shook his hand, recognizing the name. "K.A. Mallory. You were the one corresponding with Rydell."

Mallory nodded, frowning. "I was supposed to meet him last Sunday at a local diner to get all his documentation. He never showed. It wasn't until I heard from Joe that I found out why."

Sam saw the look that passed between them and finally got it. "This is your Kevin. I should have known by the Bobbsey Twins outfits."

Joe ignored the sarcasm. He'd be lucky if she were speaking to him at all once she heard the rest. "When Kevin told me he was meeting a whistle-blower in Palm Springs, I thought it was a great excuse to come visit and to introduce the two of you."

Kevin picked up the story. "But then Rydell turned up dead. He sent in enough documentation for us to believe there was a major counterfeiting ring operating out of the Valley but not enough to know who was involved or where it was located. He played it very close to the vest. We found his surveillance gear in the trunk of his car."

"Where was it?" Sam asked.

"Stashed in a garage behind the building." Kevin kicked the

ground in frustration. "I don't know why he didn't back off when we told him to."

"I do." Sam rubbed her eyes, desperate to change her contact lenses. "He wanted to make sure he got the maximum reward money. I'm sure he thought that if he gave you a gift-wrapped case to prosecute, he'd get paid sooner." Sam stifled a yawn and turned to Joe. "But I'm still not clear why you didn't tell me what you knew. It might have saved me a lot of leg work."

"Sam, if you knew there was a counterfeit ring working in the Valley, you wouldn't have sat on the story. You would have insisted on investigating it directly, especially if you knew Rydell was an informant. That was too dangerous. Kevin needed to locate Rydell's source of information but had absolutely no idea where to start because Jeff kept everything so secretive. I told him there was nobody who could recreate Jeff's daily life better than you, and he should just wait for you to work your story to find out who Rydell had been close to. Through those leads he could hopefully ferret out the counterfeiters without tipping them off that they were being investigated."

She stared at Joe long enough to make him fidget. "You were passing along my sources?" she asked quietly.

He raised both hands in a defensive gesture. "No, I absolutely wasn't. I swear."

"I wanted him to," Kevin admitted, "for your safety. We argued about it, but he said it was his own safety I'd have to worry about if he compromised even one of your sources."

"He was so right."

"It does not make me less of a man to admit I fear you," Joe said solemnly.

Sam smiled. "So you were just sitting around waiting to read my story in the paper?"

"Basically," Joe nodded. "The plan was to talk to you after your story came out and ask if you'd be willing to share anything that might help their investigation."

"In exchange for exclusive access if and when we busted the

ring," Kevin added. "I have to be honest, though, I didn't like the idea. We'd already lost Rydell, and although we couldn't be positive his death was related to the counterfeiting we had to consider it a distinct possibility. And if that were the case, the odds were high you would end up at risk, too, if you got too close. So I made Joe promise to watch your back and stick to you like glue."

"I blew it." Joe looked stricken. "I thought you were in for the night. That's why I went out. I called Kevin and suggested we meet for a drink just to spend some time together. We sat at Street Bar talking until almost closing. When I drove up and saw your car was gone I didn't know what to think. After listening to your voicemail message I got a bad feeling, and that's why I drove to your office."

Something had been bothering Sam for the last hour. "How did the police know to come up here?"

"He called and told me you guys were in trouble. I got on the horn to our technicians who pinged his GPS then alerted Larson."

"You called from the trunk?" Sam shook her head at the absurdity of it all. "I guess George wasn't the criminal mastermind he thought he was if he let you keep your cell phone. It'd almost be funny except for the fact he was a homicidal maniac." She squeezed her temple.

"Are you okay?" Joe asked.

"I just have a headache." She looked at Kevin. "How'd you know to call Larson?"

"From me," Joe answered. "At the party I told Larson a friend of mine at DOJ might be looking into a local counterfeiting ring and asked for a contact number so they could talk. And no, I never mentioned it had anything at all to do with Rydell," Joe promised.

Sam slid off the trunk and stretched her back, grimacing when she moved her arm, cradled protectively against her stomach. Kevin reached out and held her wrist. "Let me see that. What happened?"

"I got grazed by a bullet." She grunted in pain as he peeled back the sleeve, causing the wound to start bleeding again.

"I'm no doctor but I think you might need a couple stitches there. If nothing else, you should get it cleaned out, especially after being in runoff water. I'll make arrangements to have you taken to a hospital."

This was the last thing Sam wanted to do. "Is he always so take-charge?" she asked Joe sourly after Kevin walked away.

"It's usually worse," Joe smiled affectionately. "He's the one who suggested we start a consulting firm and go into business together."

Kevin came back with Detective Larson, who told Sam one of his officers would drive her to Desert Hospital when she was ready. "How you holding up?"

"I'm fine, or will be, if nobody leaks this to the *Tribune* before I have a chance to go to press on Friday." Between police scanners and loose-lipped cops, no story was ever safe.

"I think you've earned your exclusive on this," Larson assured her, "and I will make sure everyone here understands that."

"Thanks." Sam told Larson and Kevin about the DVDs and photos in Rydell's bag. "I don't know who gets first dibs, so I'm going to let you two figure it out," she said, even though in her experience Federal always trumped local.

"I'll send over a courier tomorrow." Kevin handed her a card. "Just call me on my cell phone when you're ready."

If Larson was perturbed, he didn't show it. Instead, he motioned for the other detective, named Ramon Velasco, to join them. "I'm going to release these two unless you need anything else from them."

Velasco quickly browsed his notes. "So other than the deceased and a man named Lou, those were the only people you saw up here?"

"The only people inside the warehouse were those two," she confirmed in a weary voice, "although on two different occasions George mentioned a man named Marco."

Velasco looked at Joe, who concurred without hesitation. "All I saw in there were George and Lou."

"No other vehicles?"

"The only vehicles I saw were the motorcycle, Manuel's Lincoln, and the ATV," Sam reported. "Otherwise, the parking lot was deserted when we got here."

The detective thanked them and left. Kevin and Larson said goodbye and walked together toward the warehouse. Joe waited until everyone was out of earshot. "That's some careful slicing and dicing of the truth we're doing."

Sam pulled the blanket tighter around her, suddenly feeling chilled again. "Thanks for going along with it, Joe. Anne might be extremely troubled, but I don't see what would be accomplished by involving her in what happened tonight. This part is over."

By the time she got out of the emergency room the sun was up, and other people were just starting their day. Sam thought it ironic that getting grazed by a bullet was less painful than having her arm cleaned and stitched. Joe was waiting in his rental when she emerged from the hospital with her right forearm arm wrapped in a sterile white bandage and a prescription for Vicodin in the pocket of her still-damp sweats.

They went back to the condo and crashed. Sam's alarm clock went off at 11:00. She slapped at the snooze button and turned onto her side, knees drawn up. She was so tired she felt sick to her stomach. Alpha and Omega lay very quietly, chins resting on paws, staring at her with worried dog eyes. She reached out and scratched their ears, thinking how close she had come to never seeing them again. Or anyone else. She pulled both dogs close and cried until the pent up fear and rage over what might have been dissipated in a sea of tears.

CHAPTER EIGHTEEN

Joe drove Sam to work, and she walked into the office right at noon. Monica jumped up from her chair and grabbed Sam in a tight hug. "Oh, my God, Marlene told me," she said in a shaky voice when she finally let go. "I'm so glad you're okay."

Sam was surprised at the outpouring of concern and curious how Marlene knew what happened. She'd left her editor a message saying she'd be late to work but not why.

Monica studied her closely. Sam was wearing jeans and a long-sleeved LA County Coroner T-shirt to cover the assorted welts, cuts, scrapes, and bruises that adorned her legs and arms from the close encounter with the wash and George Manuel. Other than her left cheek, which looked like she'd been slapped by an angry tabby, her face was unscathed. But she looked about to drop.

"I think you should be home resting."

"I'm fine," Sam assured her. "Besides, I have a story to write."

Marlene was waiting as Sam turned the corner and ushered her into the office, closing the door behind them. "I hear you went for a little swim last night."

"Who told you that?"

"Like I mentioned before, I have a cop friend. Are you all right? You look exhausted."

Sam sat on the window ledge. "Yeah, I could use a nap but otherwise I really am fine."

Marlene sat at her desk and gazed steadily at Sam, her expression somber. "No story is worth dying over." She spoke quietly to give her words more weight.

"Fortunately, I didn't."

"But you could have."

She leaned her head against the glass. "Trust me when I say it certainly wasn't my intent. I didn't go looking for this; it came and found me, right in this parking lot."

"Care to fill me in?"

Sam twisted to stretch her back. "The short version is George Manuel killed Jeff Rydell because he thought Rydell was setting him up to be busted for drug dealing. But Rydell was actually working with the Feds to bring down a major software counterfeiting ring Manuel was involved with."

Sam's arm was throbbing because she refused to take any painkillers until her story was written, and the discomfort was making her cranky. "I'd really like to get the story written if the lecture's over."

Marlene nodded. "Go do your story, Sam."

When she got to her desk there was a Diet Coke and cup of ice waiting, along with a Snickers. On her computer screen was a Post-it from Monica: *In case you haven't had a chance to eat.* Sam smiled at the gesture and opened the candy bar. "I should get abducted more often."

After retrieving her notebooks and story material out of the desk, Sam turned on the computer and spent fifteen futile minutes trying to compose an opening paragraph. Frustrated, she exited Word. There was no way she could write the story of Rydell's death until she had more information about Rydell's life. There were still just too many holes.

She pushed all the counterfeit material aside and opened her files on Ellen and Lena. Monica appeared at her desk holding an envelope. "I'm so sorry. I forgot to give these to you when you walked in. I was holding them in my desk for you."

"Thank you." Sam held up the Snickers. "And thank you for brunch."

Inside the envelope were three faxes: two from Nate and one from Mike Lewis. The fax from Mike detailed the numbers on Rydell's cell bill. The calls made to Kevin Mallory's office gave Sam a pang. There were calls to George Manuel, calls to the Konrad headquarters, calls to the house, and to Father Gerry. But it was the numerous calls to Phil Atkins that caught Sam's attention. "Why would Jeff be calling Ellen's campaign manager?"

That question was answered by Nate's first fax. Rydell's pre-paid credit card was ordered through Greenlight Professional Consulting. No wonder Atkins was so antagonistic. He didn't want Ellen to know just how much he was keeping from her. But was he doing it to protect Ellen, the campaign, or himself?

Sam suddenly realized she hadn't checked her email yet. She logged on and felt a rush of energy when she saw seven emails from Kinko's. The first file was a copy of the brief newspaper story about the accident that killed Elisa Bayles. The headline was *Highway Horror, Highway Miracle.* A gas tanker had gone out of control going east on Interstate 10 and slammed into a car. The tanker and the car went off the road and down a steep embankment. The driver of the car was ejected and miraculously survived. But the trucker and the car passenger died instantly when the tanker exploded on impact. Names were withheld pending next of kin notification.

Sam closed her eyes and massaged her temples. The details of the accident in the newspaper account didn't make sense. She had the same thought after downloading the photographs and their captions. At first glance, she assumed the photo captions had been matched to the wrong photos. But after double-checking, she confirmed they were correctly paired. Sam studied each picture a third time, enlarging them to fill her computer screen. There was no mistake.

A slow smile of understanding spread across her face. "I'll be damned."

When she read the second fax from Nate—the personals on June and Bill Konrad—Rydell's circle was complete. There was only one final question to answer.

Sam printed out the pictures, captions, and a couple copies of the article. She set them aside then opened her notebook. She banged her bandaged forearm on the front edge of the desk but was running on adrenaline and barely registered the pain. She logged onto the public records database that eventually led her to an old newspaper article and the final pieces connecting Ellen Konrad's past and present snapped into place.

Invigorated by a lightness of spirit and armed with the full truth, Sam told Monica to hold all her calls, straightened her keyboard, and began to write.

> *It started as an optimistic search for beginnings; it finished as an untimely end in a lonely stretch of desert. Although the answers he came looking for proved elusive, in between his hopeful arrival in Palm Springs this past January and his senseless murder last Sunday, Jeff Rydell proved that the essence of family transcends blood ties. He leaves a legacy of compassion, integrity, and decency among those whose lives he touched during his all-too-brief time in the Valley. And with a final act of courage, he brought a criminal enterprise to its knees.*

The words flowed easily, and Sam wrote as if in on autopilot, rarely referring to notes, and stopping only to take an occasional sip of her soda. In little more than three hours she finished a five thousand-word feature that recounted Jeff's lethal association with George Manuel, beginning with their fateful meeting at the Crazy Girl. The feature ended in Devil's Canyon with police hauling the killer's flood-ravaged body out of the wash, a victim of nature's karmic wrath.

She kept the narrative focused on Jeff and George's fatal dance. Although Sam quoted Ellen praising Jeff's character and talents, nowhere did she bring up the name on his original birth certificate, Anne's association with Manuel, or the fact Argo used to be Jorge Diego-Manuel, the former boy next door of the mayoral front runner.

It was a little after four o'clock when she emailed Marlene the story and printed herself a copy, which she put in a large manila envelope along with the photos and captions from Belinda and the newspaper articles. She pulled Rydell's wheelie bag from beneath her desk and put all his original documentation back in it then zipped it up. She stashed the yearbook, birth certificate, and marriage documents in her backpack, a subterfuge Sam was confident would have Father Gerry's blessing.

She dialed Monica's intercom extension. "Hey, I've come up for air. Do I have any messages I should know about?"

"Let's see…Joe wanted to know if he should make dinner reservations for tonight. Someone named Kevin Mallory called and said you had the number and would know what it's about. A Detective Larson wants you to call him at your earliest convenience. And," she paused for emphasis, "Ellen Konrad called for you."

"Did she say anything?"

"She'd like you to call her at home, it's important. And she said to be persistent. As if you *weren't*," she added sassily under her breath.

"Anything else?" Sam asked, smiling.

"She asked if you were alright."

News sure travels fast down here. "What did you tell her?"

"That other than being understandably ornery, you seemed fine. I offered to tell you she was on the line but she didn't want to interrupt."

Sam disconnected the intercom and found her cell phone under a stack of papers. She speed- dialed the house line and Lena answered, "Konrad residence."

"Is Ellen in?"

"Who's calling?"

"It's Sam Perry."

"I'm afraid Ellen is busy at the moment."

"Lena, I'm returning her call. She said it was important. Can you please tell her I'm on the line and let her decide if she's too busy?"

There was a curt pause. "Just a moment."

Sam stretched again, her body creaking and cracking everywhere in protest.

"Hey," Ellen said softly, "how are you?"

Her concern sent a geyser of warmth through Sam. "To be honest, the left side of my body feels like someone worked me over with a baseball bat. I fear I'm going to wake up tomorrow looking half-Smurf."

"It's good to hear your sense of humor came through intact."

"Waterlogged, but intact."

"How bad is your arm?"

"It's just a graze. We can either credit my lightning fast reflexes or the other guy's lousy shooting while being stoned out of his mind for that. Who told you?"

"Frank. He stopped by to let me know you identified Jeff's murderer, a man named George Manuel, and were nearly killed in the process. Dear God, Sam," her composure suddenly cracked. "Getting shot, almost drowning? It scared the hell out of me."

"It scared the hell out of me too," she admitted, Ellen's raw emotion breaking down her defenses and bravado. Sam leaned back in the chair and closed her eyes, remembering the surreal sensation of thinking she was going to die. "When we were in the wash and George had us trapped, I thought about my dogs and what would happen to them. And I thought about you."

"What about me?" she asked quietly.

"I shouldn't have left last night without telling you that I don't give up on people who matter to me—ever. And you matter to me, more than I can say...more than I really understand...so I'm not going anywhere." Having just been rudely reminded exactly how too-short life can be, Sam didn't care if she was being embarrassingly emo. "What I'm trying to say is, I'm afraid you're stuck with me."

"I'm counting on it," Ellen said. "There's a lot I should have said, too. After you left, I stayed up most of the night thinking and decided you were right. It's time to let the truth play out, whatever the consequences. I don't want any secrets between us. I want you to know it all."

"There are some things I need to tell you, too, before the story comes out."

"Like what?"

Sam turned her chair towards the window. "Like, George Manuel's real name was Jorge Diego-Manuel, your old neighbor."

There was a heartbeat of stunned silence. "Jorge murdered

Jeff? And tried to kill you? Are you sure it's the same person?"

"Absolutely sure."

"My God, how did he even know—" Ellen froze when she made the connection. "Is Annie involved?"

"Not intentionally."

"What's that mean?"

"She came up to the warehouse last night in the middle of everything. George kept her outside, but I know she saw me."

"What was she doing there?"

Sam hesitated.

"Please...whatever it is, I'd rather hear it from you."

"She was getting coke. Manuel was her dealer and sometime hookup."

Ellen's silence was painful to hear. "I really thought we had turned a corner," she finally said. "I wonder why Frank didn't tell me."

"He doesn't know."

"You didn't tell the police?"

"She needs intervention, not interrogation."

"So Annie's not going to be in your story?"

"No, and neither is what we talked about last night. But there are other things you need to know about your daughter, and some of it is going to be upsetting."

"Annie seems to have a knack for that." Ellen sighed wearily. Sam heard voices in the background. "I'm sorry. Phil is here, and we need to conference in a call."

"That's okay." Sam swung her chair back around. "I'd rather talk in person anyway."

"Me, too. Come over whenever you like. I'll leave the driveway gate open. Can we go get a drink or still grab a bite together?"

"Yes and yes. I'll be there within the half-hour."

"Great. I can't wait to see you."

Sam gathered what she needed and locked up her desk. Toting the wheelie bag behind her like a rheumatic flight attendant, she stopped by Marlene's office. "Is it okay if I take off?" She realized the perfunctory nature of the request since it was obvious she was packed and ready to go regardless. "Feel free to edit the story at will if it was too long."

Marlene waved her over. "It *was* long, but we're adding pages to accommodate it. Layout isn't happy but Craig Lowe is thrilled and plans to syndicate it. He wants you to know that you'll get a bonus percentage from any reprint sales."

"That's awfully generous of him."

"He knows a cash cow when he sees one. He's only being generous because he's afraid you're going to come to your senses and go back to work for a real newspaper."

"Regardless, tell Mr. Lowe I said thanks and that I'm not planning on going anywhere."

"That's what I was hoping you'd say, but he doesn't need to know that," she smiled. Marlene peered over her reading glasses. "It's a powerful piece, Sam. Good work. Since both Rydell and Manuel are dead, I doubt legal will need anything from you. So go home, and take tomorrow off. I'll see you Tuesday."

Sam waved goodbye. She parked the wheelie bag next to Monica's desk. "Two more big favors? Can you please call Kevin Mallory back and tell him this wheelie bag is ready for him to pick up? And can you please have this package delivered to Detective Larson over at the police station?"

"Of course," she said, phone already in hand. "You just go home and take care of yourself. And if you need anything, you better call."

"Thanks, Monica."

Between the breeze and bone-dry air it was a comfortable hundred degree day. The heat wave was officially over. Sam put the top down and headed towards Ellen's house. She called Joe who picked up on the first ring. "Waiting for Kevin to call, I see."

"Am I getting as transparent as you?" Joe sounded happy. "They're ready to make some arrests based on documents they found at the warehouse, meaning he has to work tonight. So we're going to meet for happy hour."

"Happy hour?" Sam knew Kevin wouldn't drink before serving arrest warrants. "Is that what they're calling afternoon quickies these days?"

"And you wonder why I had to keep some distance the last couple of years. You always figure everything out. I'm sure the people at the boutique thought I was a raging drunk. Regardless, I should be back around seven o'clock. Did you want to go to El Paseo, or are you too trashed?"

"I'm having dinner with Ellen, if that's okay."

"I think that's wonderful," he said, sounding like a proud parent. "Tell her I said hi."

"I will. See you later."

The Labor Day vacationers had begun trickling in, and downtown traffic was noticeably heavier. Sam couldn't believe summer was almost over. She turned left on Alameda and wended her way through the serpentine streets of the area known as Las Palmas to Ellen's house.

Sam grabbed her cell phone and the manila envelope, leaving her bag in the car. She realized she'd forgotten to return Larson's call and speed dialed his number while walking up the sidewalk. The call failed, and Sam wondered if this was a cellular dead zone being so close to the mountains. The front door was ajar, and assuming Ellen had left it open for her, Sam went in. She had just finished dialing Larson's number a second time when she strolled into a macabre tableau playing out in the Konrad living room.

The seating area was on the right side of the room. Two plush couches were arranged perpendicular to the fireplace. In between the couches was a teardrop shaped wooden coffee table. To the left of the couches were two matching chairs. Phil Atkins and Lena were on the couch closest to Sam, their backs to her. Luke sat on the other couch. Ellen was perched on the arm of the far chair. Everybody was motionless, turned towards Anne, who was backed up against the center set of French doors. She was holding a gun pointed in the general direction of her head.

This is un-fucking-believable.

When Anne saw Sam walk slowly into the room, she leveled the gun toward the door. "What are you doing here?" Her voice was shaking as much as her hands.

Sam heard a voice coming from her cell phone and casually slipped it into her T-shirt pocket, praying Larson wouldn't hang-up. "I'm certainly not here to get shot again. Any chance you can put that gun down, Anne? You might not care about me, but I don't think you want to accidentally hurt your mom or Luke."

She didn't know much about guns but Sam recognized this one, having already been up close and personal with it. She disconnected the call to Larson. "That's George's gun, isn't? You took it out of his glove compartment last night when you got the drugs."

"You're the one who told her, aren't you? It's none of your fucking business what I do or who I see. I am *not* going to be locked up again. I'd rather die first."

Ellen glanced at Sam with a helpless expression. Lena saw the exchange and stood up. "This is your fault," she accused in a brittle voice. "You have no right interfering in our lives."

"Back off and sit down," Sam snapped, suddenly very tired, in pain, impatient, and pissed off. She pointed her finger at Lena, "You do *not* want to be fucking with me right now."

She felt a lightheaded recklessness but no fear. If Anne was going to shoot anyone, it would probably be herself. "At least be honest, Anne," she leaned against the back of the empty chair. "It's not the thought of going to a hospital making you want to die. It's the idea of getting sober and getting well because then you'll have to deal with what you've done, in total clarity."

"I don't know what you're talking about," she said, glancing anxiously towards her mother.

"Sure you do. Jeff told you he was leaving to go back to his girlfriend in Tennessee, destroying your dream of being together. He also warned you to stay away from George, that something was going down. That's what you were arguing about the night he died. First he ruins your life then he tries to tell you what to do? *Fuck him*, right?"

"You don't understand." Anne's voice was ragged and trembling.

"Yes, I do," Sam said quietly. "You felt angry and hurt but mostly abandoned. When he left, you'd have nobody, except for George. When you told him about Jeff's warning, part of it was to get back at Jeff for hurting you, to let George make his life hell for a while. But it was also to get George's approval to make sure he'd still want you. You needed George to keep from being completely alone."

"Please shut up."

"I know you didn't want Jeff hurt. You just didn't realize what was at stake for George. Beyond his freedom it was about money. Jeff was messing with his golden goose. You grew up with money, so you take it for granted. It didn't occur to you that someone like George would kill over it."

"Dear God, Annie," Ellen whispered. "What have you done?"

Anne saw the dread in her mother's eyes and raged at Sam. "Goddam you, shut up! Just *shut up!*" She took a step toward Ellen. "Mama, I didn't do anything wrong, I swear. Please, Mama, you've got to believe me."

"*I've been a bad, bad girl,*" Sam recited softly. "*And I need to be redeemed to the one I sinned against because he's all I ever knew of love.*"

Anne started to cry while everyone else in the room stared at Sam as if she was speaking in tongues. "Those are the words to a song I saw your daughter perform to the other day," she explained to Ellen.

"Perform?" she repeated, confused.

Sam maintained eye contact with Anne as she talked. "She works as an exotic dancer at the Crazy Girl in Indio."

"How? She's only seventeen."

"George was a bartender there and introduced her to the manager. Even if they asked for proof of age, fake IDs are not that hard to come by. Anne calls herself Money, and she's the star of the club. Men pay dearly for her lap dances."

Ellen took a deep breath, gobsmacked.

"I would say it was a secret life except it wasn't," she turned to look at Atkins, "was it Phil?"

"I wouldn't know anything about it," he said calmly.

"Come on, you must have known about Money since you're the one who hired Jeff to keep an eye on her." Sam looked back at Ellen. "He paid Jeff via a credit card applied for through his consulting business."

"That's why Jeff was there watching the show?" Luke blurted out. "Because you paid him to be?"

"You knew about your sister and didn't tell me?" Ellen asked, incredulous, and looking ready to throttle him.

Luke shrank back from her glare. "I just found out. She told me she finally had a job she loved, but that you wouldn't understand. The only way she would tell me where was if I promised not to tell you. I went to check it out last Saturday, and I couldn't believe Jeff was there watching her dance naked, so we had it out."

Mystery Man A, Sam thought, as another loose end was tied off.

"I told Phil about it the next morning," Luke continued pleading his case to Ellen, whose anger hummed through the room. "He said not to worry you with it because he'd take care of it." He turned to Sam for validation. "You saw us. That's what we were talking about when you showed up at headquarters that day."

"I wouldn't be too hard on Luke," Sam told Ellen. "I'm guessing the reason Phil didn't tell you about Anne was that he couldn't. If he told her secret then she might tell his."

Atkins sprang off the couch, his hands flexed into fists and his skin ruddy. His reaction, and the anticipation on Anne's face, convinced Sam her hunch was correct.

"Tell what secret?" Ellen asked, never taking her eyes off Atkins, her demeanor dangerously calm.

"That he treated himself to some of her special lap dances."

Ellen stood and took several steps toward him. "Is that true, Phil?" When he didn't respond, her eyes burned blue fire. "How *could* you? You've known her since she was a child. She's *still* a child."

Lena stared at Atkins, aghast, and moved away from him.

"Oh, please," he said contemptuously, "she was hardly a virgin. Besides, she came on to me. *She* wanted *me*."

"*Oh, please,*" Anne mimicked him and rolled her eyes. "It's always been a mercy fuck. Even at fifteen I could tell you were desperate."

Atkins looked like he was about to implode.

"Get out of my house, Phil," Ellen spoke barely above a whisper, but her words boomed with fury, "before I change my mind and have you arrested."

Atkins tried to stare her down but withered under the ferocity of Ellen's rage and looked away. He reached into his pocket and threw a set of keys onto the coffee table that skidded off onto the area rug. He left without a word. Only when the front door shut did Ellen's anger subside into numbness, and she sat back down. But an uncomfortable silence and growing tension again pervaded the room, and Anne started fidgeting. Just as with Manuel, Sam felt less vulnerable talking.

"It must have been frustrating," she said to Anne.

"What must have?"

"To have the one man you loved turn you down."

"It was her fault," she gestured carelessly toward Ellen with the gun. "He pushed me away because she told him not to. She wanted him to herself."

"Annie," Ellen said patiently, "I've told you, there was nothing romantic going on between us."

"I saw all the times you'd sneak off to another room, all the whispering—"

"You're wrong," Sam cut her off. "Jeff rejected your advances because he had a girlfriend back home he planned to marry, which was a very good thing, too."

Lena tensed. "I think it's time you leave," she told Sam.

"He *would* have wanted me," Anne insisted, ignoring Lena, "but Mama came between us." She looked at her mother. "You have *everything*; you've always had *everything*. Why couldn't you just let me have this one thing?" She was crying again, her face turning splotchy.

"Anne, your mother wasn't trying to hurt you. Just like Jeff, she was only trying to protect you."

"*Bullshit!*" she wailed. "That's bullshit! She's still punishing me for what happened before. She blames me for having to cancel the series. Don't you think I know that? Why do you think we moved to the middle of nowhere? She doesn't want people to know she has a crazy daughter. She's ashamed of me."

"I have *never* been ashamed of you."

"*Yes you are!* How could you not be? Look at me. *I'm* ashamed of me. Why can't you just admit it?"

"I can prove she was only trying to protect you," Sam told her.

"You keep saying that," she snapped peevishly, wiping her nose. "Protect me from what?"

"From this," she held up the envelope.

Anne looked from her mother to Lena, both watching Sam intently. "What's in there?"

"The truth."

"The truth about what?"

"About everything. About Jeff, about your family."

"My family?" Anne repeated, intrigued. "You mean my birth family? What do you know about them?"

"No!" Lena jumped up. "I won't let you do this—"

"Stay out of it," Anne said angrily. "I'm sick of you always trying to run everyone's life around here."

"She's right," Sam agreed. "It's really not your call."

Lena turned to Ellen. "You have to stop this."

"Sit down, Lee. Or leave," she said wearily then looked at Sam. "I should be the one to tell her."

"Let me. Then there'll be no broken promises."

Ellen lightly touched the scratches on Sam's cheek. "Thank you."

"Don't let her destroy us." Desperation pinched Lena's face. "Please."

Ellen's expression was melancholy but resolute. "Lee, we've lived the lie for too long. And look what it's brought us to. Let Anne and Luke hear what she has to say."

Sam opened the envelope and took out the pictures. "By the way," she said to Lena, "Belinda Peletier says hi. She'd like you to call her. Dr. Crane sends his regards as well."

Ellen glanced at her in wonderment while Lena looked as if she had just seen the dead rise.

Sam spoke directly to Anne. "The first thing you should know is that June and Bill Konrad are not your mother's natural parents."

"What?" Luke stared at Ellen. "You were adopted, too?"

Sam held her hand up. "Just be quiet and listen, okay? All your questions are going to be answered."

Luke nodded unhappily, his expression confused.

"Your mother's birth mother and aunt were identical twin sisters whose married names were Gail Konrad and Grace Bayles. Grace had a daughter named Elisa; Gail had a daughter named Ellen. El and El…I assume their names were an homage to their maternal grandmother, whose name was Eleanor.

Ellen nodded.

"Ellen's family nickname was Nell, and her younger sister was named Elizabeth—"

"You have a sister?" Luke asked in disbelief.

"Luke," Sam closed her eyes in annoyance, "what part of *be quiet and listen* isn't sinking in?"

After he apologized again, she methodically recounted the story Belinda had told her: the accident killing the parents, Elisa moving in with Nell's family, Gail's breakdown, her marriage to Dale Overton, and the subsequent molestation of his stepdaughters. "Even though he never legally adopted them, Dale insisted Nell and Elizabeth take his last name, I'd guess mostly as a show of possession."

Sam pulled out a photo of Lena and Nell, sitting on a porch stoop. Lena wore her hair in a short wedge cut. Although not beautiful, she had a pleasant face and exuded a certain vivaciousness that Sam had to admit was appealing. Sam put the picture on the coffee table for Luke and Anne to see, the sheet with the caption placed beneath it. She described how their friendship began after Dale moved the family to Rocky Hollow.

"They became as close as sisters, but there was another reason Lena was a fixture at Nell's house."

Sam put the picture of Lena and Elisa next to the first photo.

They stood with their arms around each other's waist in an obvious romantic embrace, their touching heads turned towards the camera. According to the caption they were standing in front of a "sugar maple by the creek." Although she was younger, Elisa was taller than Lena and from the looks of it already fully developed. Like the young Nell, she was sensual, self-possessed, and beautiful.

"Lena fell in love with Elisa and from the looks of it, Elisa fell in love back."

Whether because the French doors were open or she had a fever, Sam felt flushed and the room blurred. She stopped, rubbing her eyes.

"Go on," Anne prompted, engrossed in the story.

Sam took a step toward her, squinting to focus. "Dale got Nell pregnant when she was barely seventeen and sent her to stay with her great-uncle Bill Konrad, who arranged to have the baby adopted."

Sam glanced at Ellen. "Did anyone at home know about the pregnancy?"

"Nobody knew."

Sam walked over to Luke, who sat with clenched fists. "Nell never went back home. She moved with her aunt and uncle to California to get away from Dale. Once here, Bill and his wife June legally adopted her. And Nell started going by her birth name, Ellen."

"The adoption was Bill's idea," Ellen told Sam. "He didn't want to take the chance Dale would try something."

"Even with grown kids, a new birth certificate is issued when you are adopted," Sam explained to Anne and Luke. "That's why anyone looking will see June and William Konrad listed as Ellen Konrad's parents."

Feeling clammy, Sam pushed up her shirtsleeves. "With Nell gone, Dale turned his attentions to Elisa after he caught her and Lena being intimate." The last photo she set on the coffee table was of Elisa and Nell. "She no doubt reminded Dale of Nell. The two of them looked so much alike they could have easily passed for twins, just like their mothers."

Anne and Luke listened intently as Sam explained how Lena

convinced Elisa to run away and go stay with Nell, Bill, and June in California. Then she handed them copies of the newspaper clipping of the accident that took Elisa's life.

"This is so sad," Anne muttered, tears spilling down her cheeks.

"The problem is, the accident didn't happen the way the article says."

Sam set an enlarged crop of Elisa and Lena's picture on the coffee table for everyone to see. She was again struck by how the picture captured Elisa's natural beauty and made it hard to take your eyes off her. To Sam that had been more identifiable than a fingerprint—or the fresh cut clearly visible by Elisa's swollen right eyebrow.

"If the tanker hit the driver's side, odds are the person thrown from the car to safety was the passenger. That means it wasn't Elisa Bayles who died on the freeway that day. It was Ellen Konrad." Sam gently rubbed her thumb over the scar removing the concealer. "Isn't that right, Elisa?"

She reached for Sam's hand. "They told me it was that one in a million case of not wearing a seat belt saving a life."

"Wait, just wait…" Luke pressed his palms against the side of his head, as if to keep it from exploding. "Just hold on. You're telling us you're not Ellen 'Nell' Konrad? You're Elisa Bayles?"

She met his incredulous, disillusioned stare steadily. "That's right, sweetheart."

He went white. "All this time you've been posing as someone else? Pretending to be your dead cousin? That's like identity theft times ten."

"Mama's still the same person," Anne said, surprisingly calm. "All that's different is her name. Why are you so upset?"

"Because she lied to us," Luke said, biting the words off. He looked at Ellen. "You've lied to us all our lives. I don't understand why you'd ever do that."

"I made her promise to never tell anyone, including you," Lena said. "It was also my idea for her to take Nell's identity. Nell's mother had died a couple months earlier, and Dale had been threatening us."

"About what?" Luke asked.

When she didn't answer Sam picked up the photo. "Lena was over eighteen, and while it might not look like it here, Elisa had only just turned fourteen, so Lena was guilty of statutory rape every time they made love." Sam set the picture back down and said to Lena. "You must have constantly been looking over your shoulders, wondering if Dale would turn you in to authorities."

"When the police came to the door the day of the accident, I thought it was to take Elisa away. When they said there'd been an accident, we rushed to the hospital, not knowing who had survived. It was agonizing, praying that my best friend would be the one dead instead of my lover. You don't know what that's like."

"I wouldn't pretend to."

"Elisa was still unconscious but by the grace of God only had some cuts and a broken arm. When they asked us to identify her, I said her name was Ellen Konrad. Bill, June, and I talked in the waiting room and agreed it was for the best and stuck to the story. When she came to, I made her promise to go along with it. I told her it was the only way we'd be safe."

Sam brushed a loose strand of hair away from Ellen's face. "You used Nell's Tennessee driver's license to get a California ID in her name." She turned back to Luke. "Because they looked so much alike nobody would have questioned it. Your mom simply appropriated Nell's vital statistics to complete the switch and bury Elisa for good."

"I still can't believe you've been lying all this time about who you were. I wouldn't have cared." He sat back on the couch, his petulance turning slowly to stunned understanding as something else sunk in. "Wait a minute. So if you're really Elisa then that means it was you and Lena who were…Oh, wow. Are you still?"

Ellen and Lena hesitated but Anne was amused by her brother's fluster. "Where have *you* been since daddy died? Don't freak, big bro. It's not a big deal."

"You've known?"

"You haven't? Why do you think they fight so much?" She

rolled her eyes. "God, men really are oblivious."

Sam smiled. *She might be crazy, but she's perceptive.* Though Luke hadn't been the only one oblivious to the obvious. Sam couldn't believe she hadn't figured it out either. It wasn't even so much that Ellen and Lena lived in the same house. It was the tension she had witnessed between them. There's a specific acrimony and possessive resentment that is only spawned from having shared a life and a bed.

The realization opened up a world of hopeful possibilities in Sam's heart. She looked down, acutely aware they were still holding hands. Maybe, just maybe, there really could be more between them than just friendship.

Luke picked up the photos from the coffee table then threw them down. "Why was *everything* such a big, dark, damn secret? And what's any of it got to do with Jeff?"

"I was getting to that." Sam rubbed her throbbing temple. "After Nell gave birth, William and June arranged for the baby to be adopted by friends of theirs named Stan and Vicky Rydell."

That had become clear when a previous address in Sevierville had shown up on Bill and June's personals from Nate. Once Dorothy heard the name, she confirmed it.

"When Vicky died, Jeff found a copy of his original birth certificate, which listed Ellen Konrad as his mother. So he tracked down the woman who should have been his birth mother, except you weren't. You were just his second half-cousin. Did you tell him the truth?"

Ellen stared out the French doors. "Part of it. I was stunned because Nell never told us about her baby. But as soon as I saw the birth certificate and his birth date I knew what must have happened. I told Jeff that his mother was my first cousin, and she'd been killed. I said I used her name as my stage name to honor her. I insisted we take blood tests, which confirmed we were not parent and child."

"Did you tell him about Dale?"

She shook her head. "I thought it was more important for him to know his mother was a wonderful person who died far too young and had only wanted what was best for him. He was so compassionate about Nell and genuinely grateful she placed him with such a good family. She would have been proud of the man he became."

"Then why were you so against me loving him?" Anne asked, her face a mask of misery. "Why couldn't you just be happy for me for once? Did you think I wasn't good enough for him?"

"Of course I didn't think that."

"Then what?"

Sam noticed a movement by the French door furthest to her left. She glanced over and saw Larson peering in. He put a finger to his mouth.

"Remember Nell's sister, Elizabeth?" Sam moved slightly to Anne's right to draw her line of sight away from the doors. "With Elisa and Nell both gone, she was on her own with Overton. Not long after Nell left, he got her pregnant as well, but this time, he chose to keep the baby. Dale took Elizabeth out of school and isolated her from her friends. She was essentially a prisoner. After Gail died, Elizabeth in essence became his ad hoc wife. Not long after the birth of their child, he got her pregnant a second time. It's hard to fathom how alone and hopeless she must have felt."

Sam saw Larson move to the second French door, which was ajar.

The last thing in the envelope was a printout of an article from *The Mountain Press* newspaper. Sam hesitated then handed it to Anne. "One day Elizabeth asked a neighbor to babysit her kids for a few hours. Police speculated she shot Dale as soon as he walked in the door then turned the gun on herself. Elizabeth was only 18. She left a handwritten will on the table, leaving the care of her children to the sister who she believed was alive and well in California."

Anne read the article's last sentence. "She is survived by her children Lucas, three, and two-year-old Anne."

As the implication sank in, Anne dropped the paper and began shaking violently. "No…no…*no*! Tell her she's wrong. Please, Mama, tell her she's wrong."

Larson was inching his way in.

Sam took a step closer, trying to draw all of Anne's attention to her. "She can't, because it's true. You, Luke, and Jeff are all Dale Overton's children."

"You're telling me I was in love with my brother? *That I fucked my brother?*"

The agonized keen that came from Anne's core raised the hair on Sam's arms. Ellen reached out, but Anne recoiled from her. "How could you not tell me?" she screamed, choking on her tears. "You knew I loved him, that I *wanted* him. Do you have any idea what I made him do to me? How could you let me do that? You let me defile myself, and him, just to protect your fucking secret? There's something wrong with all of us. We should all be exterminated."

When Anne raised her arms in despair, Luke and Lena ducked, believing she was going to shoot but Ellen sat motionless, prepared to accept her daughter's retribution. Sam instinctively shielded her while Larson rushed in and grabbed Anne's wrists from behind. He pushed her arms up, twisting her hand forcefully until the gun dropped.

"I didn't mean for him to die," Anne sobbed. "Bring him back, God. Please let me die instead. I want to die...please let me die." Her knees buckled, and she collapsed, curling on the floor begging and whimpering for God to make the pain stop and let her die.

"Everyone okay?' Larson picked up the gun and stepped away from Anne. He opened the weapon and rubbed his hand over his face. "It's empty."

Sam doubted she'd been abducted with an empty gun. Anne has unloaded it because she never intended to hurt anyone. She was just screaming for help.

Luke crouched by his sister, cradling her head in his lap and crying. Ellen knelt by the chair, agonizing over her daughter's inconsolable guilt and grief, pierced by her son's anger and disappointment. She leaned into Sam and wept. Sam held Ellen close, rocking her gently. Lena silently stared at them with eyes full of loss and regret then walked out of the room.

EPILOGUE

Sam sat on her patio admiring the mountain vista framed by the towering palm trees of her complex. It was Saturday afternoon, and the sliding glass doors to the living room and both bedrooms were open, allowing her to carry on a running conversation with Joe as he went back and forth between rooms. He had his two suitcases on the guest room bed, and his freshly dried clothes were spread out on Sam's bed in the master, where Alpha and Omega napped on the chair.

"What time is Kevin supposed to pick you up?" Sam was trying to hide her melancholy over him leaving.

"He'll be here in about fifteen minutes, which is why…" Joe disappeared into the kitchen and returned with two glasses, an ice-filled champagne bucket, and a bottle of Mumm Rosé, "…we're going to have a toast now. To friendship." They tapped flutes and the patio table then drank. "I'm going to miss you," he sighed, briefly giving in to sentimentality. "But at least it won't be for long. We should be out here by the beginning of November at the latest, maybe even earlier. Now that we've made the decision to move, I just want to get going with it."

He walked into her bedroom to finish folding his clothes. "So you'll keep an eye out for any units that go on sale here, right?"

"I've already got the resident real estate agent on it,"

He joined her on the patio and emptied his glass in one swallow, checking his watch frequently.

"Getting antsy?"

"We're supposed to have dinner at 7:00 with some prospective clients, and I don't want to have to rush to get ready."

"You don't want to rush through happy hour."

"That, too," he admitted, having the grace to blush.

The intercom buzzed, and Joe jumped up. "That's probably Kevin." He left to go meet the elevator.

Turning to face the mountains again and sipping on her champagne, Sam rocked the chair to the beat of "Low Spark of High-Heeled Boys" playing on the cable music channel. The bluesy melody was an oddly fitting accompaniment for the past week. Sam heard footsteps and swiveled around, surprised to see Ellen standing on the patio holding a vase filled with assorted roses. She was wearing jeans, leather Rainbow sandals, a black form-fitting tank top, and little if any makeup. Even though the emotion and strain of the past couple days were evident in her eyes, she was as beautiful as ever. Maybe more.

"Don't get up." She set the roses on the table and leaned over to give Sam a lingering hug and a brief kiss on the lips. "Hope you don't mind me dropping in unannounced." She sat down. "I wanted to surprise you with these."

"I'm very glad you did. They're beautiful."

Joe came out with another glass, which he filled for Ellen. "Here you are."

"Thank you, Joe."

"Truly, my pleasure." He bowed then turned to Sam. "I'm going downstairs to wait for Kevin."

She started to stand. "Let me walk you—"

"Sit." Joe pushed her back down. "You know I hate goodbyes."

"Tough." She stood back up and gave him an extended hug.

He held her tightly then let go. "Be safe. Be careful. Behave." He took one of Ellen's hands and held it in both of his. "It was really a joy meeting you. I look forward to getting to know you better when I get back."

"I'd like that, too."

He nodded towards Sam. "Please take care of our girl while I'm gone, and try to keep her out of trouble."

"I will. I promise," she glanced affectionately at Sam, "though I suspect it'll be a full-time job."

Joe grabbed his bags, gave a final wave, and left. The sound of the door closing roused the dogs, who suddenly realized there was company. They jumped off the chair and trotted out to the patio, tails wagging in unison. They stood on their hind legs, front paws resting expectantly against Ellen's thigh. She looked down in surprise. "Oh, my God, they're adorable." She picked them up for hugs and teased, "I would have never taken you for a poodle person."

"They're *not* poodles…"

"It's okay, baby; your secret's safe with me. All things considered, it's the least I can do." Ellen put the dogs down and took in the view. "This is so nice."

Sam studied her profile, trying to decipher her thoughts. "Did you see Anne today?"

She nodded. "They still have her on suicide watch. I've never seen such grief. She's suffering so much I don't know how she'll ever survive it." Ellen reached for Sam's hand. "Thank you for staying up with me on the phone last night. I'm not sure how I would have gotten through these last few days without you."

"Like I said, I'm not going anywhere."

Ellen smiled in gratitude then grew somber. "I finally read your article this morning."

"And?"

"It was remarkable," she said quietly. "You really captured Jeff's spirit and the terrible waste of his death. Your editor was really okay with you keeping my background and family stuff out of it?"

"Marlene doesn't know about either. I tend to keep my editors on a need-to-know basis. I find it prevents a lot of backseat writing. I mean, yes, it's a hell of a story, but it's *your* story to tell, if you ever choose to, not mine."

"Thank you. And thank you for protecting Annie."

Sam waved off the thanks. "The only person who should be held publicly accountable for Jeff's death is George Manuel. And I suppose, to a lesser degree, Jeff himself. If he would have backed off the way Kevin begged him to, he'd still be alive."

"I told him that if he ever needed anything to just ask because he was family," Ellen sighed, her expression a mixture of sorrow and frustration, "but he refused to take anything that looked like a handout."

"It was more than just pride," Sam observed. "He was trying to prove himself and do right by his girlfriend, who he obviously felt he had betrayed."

"So his motivation was redemption?"

"I think so. And Ellen, taking money from you wouldn't give him that."

She tapped Sam's leg with her foot. "Would you do something for me?"

"Of course."

"When you called me Elisa the other day, it felt like I had found myself again. Ellen Konrad might be who I am professionally and in public but I never stopped thinking of myself as Elisa in here," she pointed to her chest. "I want her back, and I'd like it very much if you called me by my real name."

Sam lifted her flute. "I'd be honored, Elisa Avery Bayles."

"Thank you, Samantha O'Shea Perry."

They touched glasses and drank to the unspoken sentiment behind the request. Sam refilled her flute. "How's Luke holding up?"

"We're hanging in there." Ellen slowly blew out a lungful of air. "I guess you never know your children as well as you think. I'd have thought that he would be the understanding one and Annie the one full of outrage at learning the truth, but it was just the opposite."

"Maybe that's because since Anne has felt like an outsider most of her life, her identity wasn't tied as tightly to you as Luke's was."

Ellen looked thoughtful. "An outsider with us?"

"With whomever. Mental illness usually makes people feel disconnected from everyone. And I don't think Luke was outraged as much as he was unnerved. Having his foundation rocked scared him, that's all."

"He's still overwhelmed that his adopted mother is also his first cousin once removed."

"He'll get over it. Just tell him hyphenate relatives are a proud Southern tradition."

"Exactly," Ellen chuckled softly. "You know, once he stopped being so angry, he latched onto the fact that we're actually blood kin. It means a lot to him. I spent so many years running away from family I forgot there are others who would do anything to find theirs." She swiveled her chair side to side. "He wants to take over as my campaign manager."

"Really? Are you going to let him?"

"I think I am. He's decided to put off college for a semester then enroll at UC Riverside for the time being instead of Stanford so he can live at home and be close to his sister."

"Well, he's sure to be an improvement over Phil. For one thing, no comb-over." Sam arched her back, still sore from her encounter with the flash flood. "I'm glad to hear you're not dropping out of the race."

"To be honest, quitting was not an option."

"Her hospitalization probably won't remain a secret for long," Sam observed, adding wryly, "not with people like me in the world."

"As far as I'm concerned, it's not a secret. I'm not going to advertise her condition, but if it leaks out, I'm not going to run from it either. Lena wanted her admitted under an assumed name yesterday, and I flat out refused. She's furious with me, but I'm done with the lies. Bipolar affects so many families, and mental illness should be a matter of treatment, not shame."

"Sounds like a stump speech in the making."

"Well, I guess the best ones are those that come from the heart," Ellen said with a weary smile. "I wish you could have known her before. She was so vibrant. I love her more than life, but it's not always been easy." She set her glass on the table. "Sometimes I'll look at her and suddenly see Dale. She looks so much like him and has his edginess."

Sam saw the flash of antipathy cloud Ellen's eyes at the mention of her step-uncle. "I am so, so sorry for what you suffered with him. And I'm sorry I made you relive it."

"No apologies." She briefly touched her finger to Sam's lips. "You were right; the only way to make things better is to have the courage to face what we keep hidden."

"If it makes any difference, you don't need to face it alone."

"It makes all the difference in the world," Ellen assured her. She sat quietly for several moments gazing pensively at the mountains. "I've kept so much hidden for so long and yet, I can remember every detail as if it happened yesterday. The first night Dale came in to my room, he said it was for my own good. That it was time for a man to teach me how to be a *real woman*. He was wearing Old Spice and was drinking a can of Pabst Blue Ribbon."

Ellen paused again, and Sam noticed the pulse in her neck beating rapidly. "I fought him. I was like a wild animal. But he was too strong, and all it did was get him more excited and make him hurt me. He twisted my arm so far back I thought it was going to snap off." She absently rubbed her shoulder. "That's when I realized he wanted me to struggle and beg; that's what got him hard. So I stopped fighting and lay there perfectly still. I guess a lifeless lump wasn't nearly as exciting because it was over very fast after that."

"Jesus, Elisa. How long did this go on?"

"A couple of months, once every week or so. Each time I just closed my eyes and waited for it to be over. I was completely detached. It was like watching it happen to another person from somewhere else in the room. Fortunately, it was usually just a matter of minutes. Once he left, I'd take the hottest bath I could stand."

"Had you known what he was doing to Nell?"

Ellen nodded. "I'd hear him grunting in her room late at night. Then I'd hear her crying. Up to the day she died, Nell had nightmares almost every night that he was coming into her room."

"Why didn't anybody throw this asshole in jail?"

"Who was going to tell the police? There was no adult to intervene. We were just kids coping the best we knew how. It was worse for Nell because she felt betrayed by her mother for not stopping it. My parents were dead; I knew I had to get through it on my own. And I was not going to let him ruin me."

"At least you had the strength to finally get away."

"It wasn't strength. It was cowardice." Ellen slowly traced her finger along the armrest. "Lee once ordered a catalogue from Good Vibrations, and I was fascinated with the idea of women wearing strap-ons. It seemed so empowering." She leaned forward, elbows resting on her knees. "One night Dale was taking a lot longer than usual to finish, probably because he was so drunk. He stank of booze and cigarettes and sweat. To get my mind off what he was doing I started fantasizing what it'd be like to turn the tables on Dale, to overpower *him* against *his* will, to humiliate and hurt *him*." She sat back, tears rolling furiously out of the corners of her eyes, "I don't know how I let it happen…"

"You climaxed," Sam said softly.

"It was horrible. He was smirking, no doubt thinking he had just cured me." Her voice caught. "I felt so *unclean*; so betrayed by my body." She wiped her face. "That's why I agreed to run away. I was terrified it would happen again."

A new stream of tears erupted and Sam's heart broke a little. She wished she had the power to go back in time and personally castrate the bastard. Dale Overton had gotten off with a mercifully quick bullet to the brain.

Sam got a box of Kleenex from the bathroom, and Ellen dabbed at the tear stains on her tank top. "I've never been able to talk about it before to anyone. Ever. I was so ashamed."

Sam knelt in front of Ellen. "You were a child who found a way to survive. You were in no way complicit. Time to let go of the ghosts."

Ellen rocked slowly in the chair as she considered Sam's words. Gradually, the weight of shame that had been her constant companion for so long eased. Complete self-forgiveness would be an ongoing process, but for the first time in a long time Ellen felt a lightness of spirit. She briefly touched Sam's shoulder. "Thank you."

"You're very welcome." A thought made Sam grin. "I just hope the experience didn't turn you against toys."

"Not at all," she smiled, "I still find strap-ons empowering."

"Hey, maybe that should be your new campaign slogan."

Ellen laughed and put the tissues on the table. "Lena would have a stroke." She looked at Sam with an apologetic expression. "I'm sorry I wasn't open with you about my relationship with her that night you came over after the party."

"Why weren't you?"

Ellen leaned forward. "I didn't want to scare you away."

"There was never a chance of that." She sat back in her chair and stretched out her legs so they touched Ellen's. "You've been together for what, like nineteen years?"

"On and off. I tried to end the relationship so many times, but we were held together by all the secrets we shared, even though we kept growing further and further apart. It was like being caught in a trap."

"You're actually just thirty-three now, right?"

Ellen nodded, "My real birthday was last month, July 21," and observed dryly, "I'm the only actress in the history of Hollywood who lies about my age in the other direction."

"Jesus, that means you were only sixteen when you got your first film? No wonder you were always described as baby-faced; you really were one. Did you just blow off high school?"

"Well, yes and no. Bill and June were both teachers so they home-schooled me. I got my GED not long after the accident. You're supposed to be sixteen but I used Nell's ID. After that I took drama classes during the day and night courses in business and pre-law at College of the Desert for a couple years before moving to LA."

"Beauty, talent, *and* brains…be still my heart," Sam grinned.

"You're forgetting sexy," Ellen reminded her in a teasing voice.

Fanning her face, Sam remembered something. "The other night on the balcony you told me you were a Cancer. But your listed birthday is April. I can't believe I didn't notice the discrepancy. Or that you'd make that slip."

"Who says it was a slip?"

Sam stared, the light dawning. "You wanted me to figure it out."

"And you did."

"I did not see that coming," Sam admitted, then asked, "I can see why you might not have wanted Luke and Anne to know all the gory details about Dale's life as the family rapist, but why not let them know you were related?"

Ellen picked apart another Kleenex. "I honestly don't know what I was thinking. Lena was concerned the kids would be traumatized if they found out about Dale and Elizabeth and also what it might do to my career if the truth about our family situation ever got out—that my first cousin was a murderer. She pushed until I gave in. Both times I didn't trust my own instinct, and they became the two biggest regrets in my life." She tossed the shredded tissue onto the table. "I wasn't going to make the same mistake with you. That's why I needed you to find out the truth."

Whatever wrong turns she may have made, Sam admired the substance of character beneath that gorgeous exterior. "I can't believe you adopted Luke and Anne as an eighteen-year-old. That's so much responsibility for someone that young. For someone just starting to make it in their career."

"It was never a question. When we found out about Elizabeth, I felt obligated to take in her kids, the way Aunt Gail had taken me in. I was just lucky that I was already making a good living, so money wasn't the issue."

"What was?"

"Logistics. I wasn't comfortable setting up house with Lee to raise a family."

"Because you weren't out?"

"That some," Ellen acknowledged, "but mostly because I did not want that additional entanglement complicating our relationship even more. By that time, we were only together because of circumstance, not some great passion—at least on my part. I mean, I loved her but she wasn't my soul mate; she would never complete me. I knew Seamus needed a green card, and we came to an understanding: we'd stay married for at least five years then amicably go our separate ways as a couple. We were good friends, and it seemed the best solution."

"Did he know about you and Lena?"

"Of course. I rented her an apartment nearby, and she was over every day."

"Even so, I would have seriously resented you playing house with someone else."

"She did. And she felt excluded. Seamus adored Anne and Luke and was committed to being their dad for the rest of his life. Lee was jealous of the bond I shared with him over the kids. And she was also worried about my relationship with him."

"It wasn't platonic?"

"Mostly."

"Isn't that like a little bit pregnant?"

Ellen responded with a wry smile. "At first we had separate rooms, but on our third wedding anniversary things changed. We went to dinner and had such a great time together; I simply adored him. So when he asked to spend the night with me, I said yes. Eventually, he moved into my room full time. I really did adore him and, I don't know…"

"You wanted to test the waters?"

"Yes, I was curious," Ellen admitted. "Here I had this beautiful family and to the outside world a happy marriage, and I wondered what it would be like to really live it. Seamus was gentle and attentive and the sex was pleasant enough but no fireworks, despite his best efforts. I felt so much affection and love for him, but only as a dear friend. There was just no passion."

"I'm guessing that he was in love with you, though."

"Yes, but I was honest with him. I knew I could never give him what he wanted emotionally or physically. Nor could he give me what I needed. But he said he wanted to stay married until there was a reason to leave, for the kids' sake."

"Was Lena aware?"

"She had to be. It was obvious we were sleeping in the same room. But like a lot of things, we never talked about it."

"And you and Seamus never divorced."

"We would have. He met a makeup artist named Sarah, and he wanted to marry her. I remember being so relieved. He was actually coming back from her house when he had the accident. He'd gone to tell her we were announcing our divorce the next day. Instead, I found myself announcing funeral plans. I don't think Sarah has gotten over it yet. I'm not sure I have, either."

Ellen idly touched the Celtic pendant she wore. "I never got to thank him. Being with Seamus confirmed to me who I am and what I need." A fresh tear slid down her cheeks. "I need passion as much as affection. And it isn't going to happen with any man." Ellen wiped her face. "I am gay, and the love of my life will be a woman. And I don't care anymore who knows it. I'm through with living in the shadows."

"Where does Lena fit in?"

"She doesn't really, not anymore," Ellen sighed softly. "I don't necessarily want her out of my life completely, but I'm not going to keep pretending the relationship is something it hasn't been for a long time. We're not partners; we're not lovers; we're not even really friends anymore. Lee knows we're on the verge of a major change, especially now that the truth is out. I just want to find the most graceful way for us to go about it."

"I guess that means a 'three-day notice or quit' isn't an option."

Ellen gave her a playful smack. "I'd rather it be amicable, so I'm willing to give her some time to prepare for being on her own. She'll accept it; she knows there's no turning back."

"That sounds awfully idealistic," Sam said. "You're all she's got. Do you really think she'll willingly move on?"

"She has to. I've been honest. She is not what I want."

Sam met her gaze. "What is?"

"What I want," Ellen answered in a soft drawl, "is to fall in mad, crazy love; to lose myself in sweaty lust; to laugh and be happy." She leaned closer, the heat in her eyes melting Sam's heart. "In other words, you're what I want."

At that moment, Sam realized some people *are* worth pursuing, at any cost. She pulled Ellen onto her lap and ran her thumb along the sculpted cheekbones. "I want to be your best friend, your playmate, your confidante…" she pressed her cheek against Ellen's shoulder, "and your lover."

"And you will be. I am insanely attracted to you, but I have to finish things with Lee first, so we need to take it slow until she moves out, okay?"

"You are *so* Catholic," Sam muttered.

"I'll make it up to you," Ellen promised, pressing closer, her hands setting Sam's skin on fire, "And it'll be worth the wait."

Sam nuzzled her neck. "You smell amazingly good."

"I taste even better," she whispered.

"Oh, God…I think I'm about to spontaneously combust."

Ellen brushed her lips along Sam's jaw. "Did I *whet* my baby's appetite?"

"My appetite," she squirmed, "and so much more."

Ellen laughed and held her face. "Samantha O'Shea Perry, kiss me."

Their mouths came together…slow and easy…warmth and heat. Sam felt as if she were taking a full breath for the first time, her body and heart responding with a yearning she'd never experienced before.

"I've wanted to do this since the first time I saw you blush," Ellen murmured, teeth gently biting her lip.

"Took you long enough."

"Are you going to complain or kiss me again?"

"Hey, I am the queen of multitasking."

Ellen put a finger to Sam's lips and then took her breath completely away.

They spent the rest of the afternoon comfortably entwined, savoring the heady rush of discovering something both exciting and comforting. A little after six o'clock, Ellen reluctantly stood up. "I should go."

"I'll walk you down. I have to go to the grocery store anyway." Sam closed all the sliding glass doors to the patio and grabbed her keys.

In the elevator Ellen said, "Do you know, I can't remember the last time I was in a grocery store."

"Clearly, I'm not the only one who needs to get out more," Sam said under her breath.

They walked out the front of the building, hand in hand. Ellen leaned against her car to take in the late summer sky. "It is really a spectacular day. I know I should probably go home, but is it awful that I really just don't want to?"

Sam thought a moment. "Have you ever had a date shake?"

"At Hadley's? No, I never have."

"Me, neither. I always thought it actually sounded kind of gross, but want to go try one anyway?"

"I would. Want to grab some sushi for dinner afterwards?"

"That'd be great. And over many bottles of sake I can tell you all my bingo stories…or you can dish the dirt on all your former co-stars. The choice is yours."

"I'll tell you everything you want to know, baby. Of course, it might take all night."

"Promise?"

Ellen flashed a dazzling smile that made Sam's heart do a backflip and tossed her the BMW keys. "Here, you drive."

As they neared the Whitewater turn off on Highway 111, the wind kicked up, blowing gusts of swirling sand across the road. Over to the left, under an outcropping of rocks, a half-buried, tattered envelope flapped in the wind revealing a worn DVD inside labeled *August.* Next to it an improbable desert flower shimmered brilliantly in the glow of the setting sun.

CPSIA information can be obtained at www.ICGtesting.com
Printed in the USA
LVOW07s1613170915

454593LV00008B/846/P